THE DEVIL'S GLOVE

To Charlene --
There's hope. There's always hope.

THE DEVIL'S GLOVE

Best wishes,

COUSIN VINNY

Cousin Vinny Agrello
cousinvinny10@yahoo.com

TATE PUBLISHING
AND ENTERPRISES, LLC

Published by Tate Publishing & Enterprises, LLC
127 E. Trade Center Terrace | Mustang, Oklahoma 73064 USA
1.888.361.9473 | www.tatepublishing.com

Tate Publishing is committed to excellence in the publishing industry. The company reflects the philosophy established by the founders, based on Psalm 68:11,
"The Lord gave the word and great was the company of those who published it."

Book design copyright © 2013 by Tate Publishing, LLC. All rights reserved.
Cover design by Rhezette Fiel
Interior design by Joana Quilantang

Published in the United States of America

ISBN: 978-1-62746-222-8
1. Fiction / Religious
2. Fiction / Romance / Suspense
13.07.22

"A person's soul cannot move on, until his body has been discovered; death must never be left to speculation."

—Folklore

"Be not forgetful to entertain strangers: for thereby some have entertained angels unawares."

—Hebrews13:2

THE HISTORY OF
MICHAEL AND BILLY

It was the most restless night he had ever spent. He pretended to sleep; although in reality, his mind was in overdrive as he tossed and turned repeatedly. All he could think about was his boy and the sequence of events that played out during that baseball game.

Something extraordinary had taken place the night before, and morose thoughts filled his consciousness. Something was definitely wrong. A primordial sense of doom overwhelmed his psyche. Frustrated, he glanced over at the nightstand where his alarm clock sat. It was 6:00 a.m.

This was much too early for him to start his day, considering the fact that the game wasn't starting until late in the afternoon, but this was not an ordinary day. Being the chief grounds keeper for Comiskey Park for many years now, he thought he needed to make a trip over there and try to figure out Billy's whereabouts. He couldn't find him after the game, and that was troubling him. He thought, *Where could he have gone without changing his clothes?*

As far as he could tell, he was still wearing his Chicago White Sox uniform. He thought, *Now, why would he do that?* There were just too many questions and just not enough answers. He was frustrated as he climbed out of bed, and he showed it by sneering at his reflection as it appeared in the mirror that was hanging over the dresser. The only thing he knew for sure was that he had to find Billy.

Billy Green was the son he never biologically fathered but who shared such an amazing spiritual affinity with him that all who knew them believed they were kin. Michael, for all intents and purposes, had practically raised the boy, who by the way was now almost thirty-two years old and a full-grown man. He was also the apple of Michael's eye, being a baseball player. If the truth is to be told, he was living, for the most part, Michael's dream. Michael always wanted to be a ballplayer but being ambisinister did not help him achieve this lofty goal.

Billy, on the other hand, did not have this problem. His coordination was just fine. He had three major problems though. First of all he was chronically inaccurate when it came to throwing runners out. Secondly, he threw the ball with his left hand, which is a monumental problem for a third basemen, because while throwing a runner out at first base, he always had his back turned to home plate. This second problem became larger as he moved closer and closer to the major leagues. It is very bad to have your back turned to runners who could very easily race home while you're throwing to first. Lastly, due to being left-handed and playing third base, most balls he had chances to field were hit to his left, which made him have to field almost every ground ball backhanded. Backhanding balls is much more difficult than fielding them with the forehand. These fielding problems were his undoing, and he just couldn't overcome them, especially with his throwing woes. Because of these problems, he had been knocking on the door of big league success for too many years to count and always falling just short. Michael marveled at the kid's fortitude and his perseverance. Michael had the good fortune to witness the boy's transformation into a major league prospect.

Throughout their many years together, the boy became rather adept at the game they both loved so much. Since Billy was old in baseball terms, time was no longer his ally, and this was the stress of his life. This stress was compounded by his poor performance in his first major league game last night. Just when everyone was convinced that he had overcome his throwing woes, he somehow regressed. His overall play, especially his defense, was abysmal; and everyone now knew that Billy was on his way back to the minor leagues. Most likely because of his age, he would never get another chance at that proverbial brass ring. For many years now, Michael feared how Billy would react if things did not go right for him. He was always afraid that the boy would go off the deep end and on this morning that fear circulated throughout his entire body. He knew the boy had to be crushed by the demotion, and he wanted so badly to comfort him during this painful period; but when he went to look for him after the game, he was nowhere to be found. He recalled how he had searched the stadium in vain the previous night, only to find the boy's street clothes. *Where had he gone in his uniform? What if he didn't leave the stadium?* These unanswered questions figuratively dropped his stomach down to his feet. And it was a sickening sight to see this proud old man crumpled down on the floor bawling his eyes out and praying that nothing had happened to his boy. He muttered to himself in anguish, "Why can't that boy realize that there is more to him to love than how well he plays the game?"

Michael pulled himself up off the floor and got dressed. Momentarily he was out the door, replaying in his mind all the events that took place the night before. As he drove his car toward Comiskey Park, he recalled his conversation with Billy before the game. The boy had seemed more or less at peace with himself. The anger and resentment that had surfaced during his last years in the minor leagues seemed to have disappeared. He became a team player once again. That phase he went through back in the minors of cheering against his own teammates was now just a memory, and as far as Michael could tell, the only player that he wished misfortune upon was Hector Rodriguez, the White Sox's

Cuban third basemen who stood as far as Billy was concerned between himself and stardom.

As he maneuvered his vehicle through city traffic, he recalled how radiant Billy looked when Rodriguez pulled up lame after stealing second base. This was the moment that Billy had waited his entire life for. It was the culmination of his dream. Tears flowed down his cheeks as he recalled how Billy had taken the field the night before and how he glowed when his name was announced over the public address system. Suddenly, Michael became aware of the tragedy that had been staged for the world to see. Billy Green, a kid who had never been quite good enough for the major leagues had his glaringly obvious deficiencies exposed on his opening night. This should have been a joyous occasion for the young man who had dedicated his entire life to the pursuit of this one opportunity. But Michael thought there was some kind of trickery taking place here. From Michael's perspective there was just no other explanation for it. He ruminated over the strange sequence of events that took place during that game and had one overwhelming thought about Billy's performance: As soon as he stepped into the limelight, he immediately played down to the minor league form he had always been known for. His vastly improved skills of late that had finally earned him his chance at making the big club seemed to have disappeared over-night. *Now how could that have possibly happened?*

This was a complete mystery to the people who followed his prolonged and prodigious rise as a ballplayer. Some would have written it off as a case of the opening night jitters; but Michael, a very religious man, was sure that it was something much more sinister. He believed in good and evil, and his religious upbringing convinced him that there was such a thing as a deceiver in this world. Satan was God's nemesis, and he saw plenty of examples of his handiwork. World War II was littered with them. The extermination camps, those horrible pictures he saw of the concentration camp victims, and the horrendous treatment of prisoners of war in general had convinced him that Satan had a very strong hold on this earth. After mulling it over he thought Satan had to be to blame for Billy's performance problems. Who else, he reasoned, *Was callous enough to rake Billy over the coals and humiliate him in front of all those people?* There was no way to change his mind on this issue. It was a moot point. Aware of how fragile the boy's ego had become in recent years, he could do nothing but pray that this devastating blow was not the catalyst that pushed him over the edge. Watching him commit not one but three errors on routine ground balls was all the evidence that he needed to conclude that Billy and the scouts, who brought him up to the White Sox, had been misled. The boy was obviously still not ready for the major leagues. In fact, until this year, Michael was convinced that the boy was destined to be a career minor leaguer but almost overnight the boy's skills started to improve. Defense was no longer a deficiency and suddenly there was interest in the boy as a major leaguer when there hadn't been any interest in years. In addition what was to be thought of those dreams he had? *What kind of dreams were they?* These were the predominant questions that filled his mind as he flashed back to the events of the past evening. As he reached the ballpark, a glimmer of hope came into his eyes as he thought for a second that Billy might have gone home to his parent's house. He reasoned that maybe he was so embarrassed by his performance during the game that he left immediately, avoiding any confrontations that might have occurred with his teammates in the showers or in the locker room, but as quickly as that thought came into his head, it was rejected. The reason being that he knew deep down inside that Billy's father would have been anything but consoling toward his son, especially after learning of the demotion. He knew that Billy didn't have a strong enough constitution to deal with the callousness of his birth father.

Michael cautiously entered the ballpark and observed nothing unusual. He pondered the thought of Billy leaving the park and getting drunk at a local tavern, but that didn't explain why he didn't change his clothes. Due to his poor performance during the game, he doubted seriously that he would go out in uniform and draw extra attention to himself. From all the years he had spent with him, he knew for sure that Billy wasn't a glutton for punishment and only a glutton for punishment would go out in game uniform after that performance. As everyone knows, Chicago fans have a long history of being very nasty to their fallen sports heroes. He knew Billy wouldn't subject himself to that.

Still feeling uneasy but needing to do something constructive with his time, he decided to take a trash-collecting walk around the field. In the process of performing this chore, he glanced up toward the stadium seats and discovered Billy. What he saw shocked the hell out of him. Hanging by the neck from the upper deck was Billy Green, dressed in his White Sox uniform, wearing his green shoes, and his unique green glove. Michael was in no way ready for this, and he grimaced in pain as his worst fear had become a reality. He stared up at him in disbelief and then let out the most tragic moan that the old ballpark had ever heard expelled. It was a dying groan, very primeval, the kind that was repeated too many times throughout the history of this world. It was the worst kind of agony, the kind of personal anguish that was never meant to be felt—as unnatural as a father outliving his son.

The overwhelming sadness of this occasion cannot be properly expressed here. Hanging by the neck from the upper deck of that stadium was the extinguished dreams of a new generation. A part of the old man died with the son whom he never biologically fathered but whose spirit was eternally joined with his. He became painfully aware that the rest of his days on this earth would be nothing more than an extended death sentence. For the rest of his life, he would never experience the joy of love again. Michael couldn't stop crying. The tears flowed down his face as if someone had left a faucet on.

He thought about those mean-spirited "fans" who heckled Billy the night before. Those fans got what they wanted although they would never know about it. He would see to that. They wanted to see the kid break, but he would take away any pleasures that they might have received by knowing that they had succeeded in pushing the kid over the edge. They would never know they broke him. He had one overwhelming impulsive thought and that was to conceal his body, so no one would ever laugh at Billy again. He couldn't bear with the shame of knowing that the son that he loved the most in the world had taken his own life, so he decided to take the body and bury it right on the stadium grounds. He knew deep in his heart that the boy would approve of his decision because he was now bitterly sure how much the boy was willing to sacrifice for the game he loved. So Michael decided to keep the boy in the stadium that he worked his entire life to play in. The only question in his mind was where to bury him. He needed a place where the body would never be discovered and then he thought of it, *There was such a place.* He gently cut down Billy's body and then struggled to carry it throughout the maze of seats, tunnels, and out on to the field. He knew of an old empty storage shed out past the fence-in left field and decided that this would be Billy's final resting place. It took some time to get there but eventually he did. His overworked muscles were so relieved when he finally set Billy's body down that he immediately collapsed on to the ground and gasped for air. He stared over at Billy's body and tried to brainwash himself into believing that he was just asleep but could not convince himself of this fantasy. He then wondered if he could survive the intense manual labor of digging a grave using only a pick and a shovel. After catching his breath, he decided to gather some supplies for this endeavor and traversed a short distance to another storage shed. He opened the shed where the extra field tarpaulin was stored and cut off a large piece. He thought, *Thank God for this extra field tarp because without it, Billy would have to be exposed to the elements and I couldn't bear with that.* He scanned through the many tools that were hanging from the various metal hooks that protruded from the wooden walls of the shed and finally located a roll of duct tape. He quickly grabbed the tape, shoving it into his pants pocket, and proceeded to drag the large piece of field tarpaulin over the dew-wet grass toward the old empty shed. When he arrived there, he noticed that he forgot to grab a shovel and raced back to the tarp shed to retrieve one. He grabbed a shovel that was leaning against the wall and carried it back over to where the body awaited.

Upon arrival, he rolled Billy's body, uniform and all, into the tarp. He took some extra time to wrap his prized green glove that was covered with all that unique artwork in some newspapers he found in the shed. The paper would help keep the glove from disintegrating in the ground. He went out of his way to make sure Billy and his possessions would stay dry for eternity. After it was wrapped, he placed the glove inside the tarp too. He didn't want bugs or animals to get to Billy's body, so he sealed him in tight with tape, covering up all the air holes. Before sealing the portion of the tarpaulin that would shroud Billy's face for eternity, he leaned over and gave him a kiss on the cheek and through his tears reminisced back to brighter days when the two of them first became acquainted.

It was the month of May in the city of Chicago, and the weather was unusually perfect for baseball. Comiskey Park was jammed to the rafters with folks who were dying to get a good look at Ruth, Gehrig, and the visiting Yankees from New York.

The year was 1931 and the city along with the rest of the nation was right in the midst of the Great Depression. The ballpark became a getaway for the fortunate who still had jobs. Although the White Sox were not playing particularly good baseball at the time, the people still gathered at the ballpark to escape from the very real problems of poverty and unemployment that they faced in their daily lives. Baseball was America's favorite game, and Ruth and Gehrig were two of its greatest heroes.

Outside the ballpark on any given game day numerous children played pick-up games in Armor Square Park. These children had big dreams and played their pick-up games with the same intensity as the major leaguers who played inside the big stadium.

One of these children was Billy Green. Billy loved the atmosphere that surrounded the ballpark on game days. There was electricity in the air that purged the world of all of its troubles and gave him the will to survive and fight through the worst of times. On that note, let me not forget to reiterate that these were the worst of times. When having a full stomach becomes the measuring stick as to whether or not a kid has had a good day is all the proof that's needed to ascertain that these were hard times indeed. Besides not having enough to eat, the biggest disappointment in this ten-year-old's life was the fact that he couldn't afford to buy a ticket to the ballgame, but he took solace in the belief that he would someday play in that big ballpark next door. As he stood in the batter's box staring up at the lanky twelve-year-old on the pitcher's mound, he thought about how exciting it would be to be all grown up and playing in that big ballpark in front of all those cheering people. Just the thought of this gave Billy the chills and a rush that energized his entire body. As the pitch came soaring in, Billy, powered by an incredible amount of adrenaline, swung the bat on a collision course with the incoming ball and hammered it. The ball looked like it got shot out of a howitzer as it flew in a very low line drive trajectory between the left and center fielders. In what seemed like an instant, he confidently stood smiling on second base.

By participating in many of these local pick-up games, Billy was acquiring the skills necessary to give him a chance to see his big league dreams come true. He and the other kids would play until the White Sox had finished their game inside Comiskey. As soon as the crowds started to head toward the exits, he and his friends would make their way toward the locker rooms. This was the only opportunity available for poor kids who wanted desperately to meet their baseball heroes. He, along with a lot of other kids, would wait sometimes for hours by the locker room doors to get autographs or at least a handshake from their favorite baseball stars.

On this particular day, Michael was taking the trash out from the visitor's locker room when he noticed a young boy impeding his progress.

"Mister, is Babe Ruth and Lou Gehrig still in there?" Billy asked, turning on his puppy dog eyes.

Old man Mike, who wasn't quite as old back then, told the boy that the Bambino and Columbia Lou were just about to leave for their hotel rooms. He added that he was surprised that anyone was still waiting around.

Billy replied, "I'd never give up on either the Babe or the Iron Horse," adding, "Mister, did anyone ever tell you that you're awfully lucky to have a job like this? To be honest, mister, I'd do your job for free."

"It's not quite as glamorous as you might think," Michael stated.

"Sure it is. It's a job. That's more than most people got. Do you think there's a possibility that I could come into that locker room? I mean, I'm only talking for a minute or two."

"What would you do if I let you in there?"

"You mean you're actually considering it?"

"Maybe. What's your name, boy?"

"Billy Green. What's yours?"

"I'm Michael. It's a pleasure to meet you, Billy Green."

"Mr. Mike, the pleasure will be all mine if you let me in that locker room."

"Well, let me go inside for a moment and see what I can do."

"Sure. But you're not going to forget about me, are you? You'll come back, won't you?"

"Yes. I'll be right back," Michael said as he disappeared inside the large metal door.

Billy thought it seemed like an eternity before Michael returned, but in reality, it was closer to ten minutes. Billy looked up at him with bated breath awaiting his reply. "Well?" Billy anxiously asked.

"They said it would be all right for you to come in for a short visit," Michael announced casually.

"Wow! I can't believe it! Wait until I tell my friends about this!" Billy exclaimed with excitement. He added, "I told those jerks to stick around, but they wanted to go home and eat. I would have starved for this. Come to think about it, I did starve for this. Michael, you are the best!"

Michael led the super charged Billy into the locker room, and the boy couldn't believe his eyes when he saw the Babe stretched out on a trainer's table while receiving a massage.

"You're Babe Ruth!" Billy screamed out excitedly.

"That's right, kid." The Babe chuckled.

"What's wrong? You hurt?"

"Kid, when you've been playing this game as long as I've been, you're bound to have an ache or pain or two," Ruth stated jovially.

"I'll bet. Did you get a home run today?"

"No. Just a couple of doubles. Didn't you see the game?"

"No, I missed it. If I can save a little money, I'll catch the next one," Billy said in embarrassment as he stared down at the laces of his shoes.

"Hey, will you look up at me, kid? There's no shame in being poor. Heck, I was poor myself at one time, and if I remember correctly, I was no bigger than you are."

"It's hard to believe that you were ever my size," Billy said as he followed the Babe's wishes and looked up at him; in fact, he looked him straight in the eyes.

"Well, believe it, kid. And here." The Babe motioned to a locker room attendant, grabbing his attention. "Joe, give this kid a couple of tickets to tomorrow's game on my account. You can make it, kid, can't you?"

"You better believe it, Mr. Ruth. I wouldn't miss it for the world," Billy stated in reverence. "Do you think I could get your autograph too?"

"Sure. How about better yet, I give you an autographed photo? It beats a signature. You know what I mean, kid?"

"Do I ever. You know, Mr. Ruth, when I grow up, I'm going to be just like you."

"You mean without the aches and pains, don't you, kid?"

"Aches and pains or not, I want to be just like you."

The Babe had a tear in his eye as he autographed the photo and handed it over to the boy. They shook hands and then Michael led Billy into an adjacent room, filled with lockers, and introduced him to the Iron Horse, Lou Gehrig. Gehrig was much more shy and reserved in comparison to the Babe. Gehrig shook the boy's hand and continued to dress.

"I can't believe I'm standing here in front of Lou Gehrig," Billy stated with wide eyes.

"What's your name, son?" Gehrig asked.

"Billy Green. Mister Gehrig, you don't mind if I tell you that you're the most incredible hitter I've ever read about. Nobody hits for power and average like you do."

"Billy, you mean you've never seen me play?"

"Not yet. But that's going to change 'cause Mr. Ruth gave me tickets to your game tomorrow."

"Well, that's great. That was mighty nice of Mr. Ruth. Congratulations to you. You're going to have fun. Billy, would you mind if I told you something?"

"No. I don't mind. Tell me anything you want," Billy asserted nervously.

"I wanted to tell you, Billy, that you shouldn't get so hung up on ballplayers. You know, we're only human. We put our pants on one leg at a time, just like you do. We're not special, Billy. We're lucky that we get to play a kid's game for a living and we're able to meet nice young men like you."

"Mr. Gehrig, you and Mr. Ruth are truly two of the kindest people that I've ever met, and I'd like to thank you for the time you've spent with me. I know neither of you had to do this for me, and this is something I'm going to remember for the rest of my life. Maybe someday, with a little luck, I'll get to be a ballplayer too, and I swear, I'll try to be just like you were to me today," Billy said solemnly and with a respect and maturity, far greater than his years.

"I hope you get that chance someday. You are a well-spoken and articulate young man. I'm sure your parents are very proud of you. You just keep hanging in there, okay?"

"I'll try. This was awfully exciting. Thanks again for everything," Billy said, smiling.

On that note, Gehrig autographed a photograph of him and gave it to Billy. Michael took Billy by the arm and led him outside again.

"Thank you so much, Mr. Mike. You really made my day," Billy confessed.

"No thanks are necessary, kiddo. I think you really impressed your heroes today, and I know that you impressed me."

Billy turned to walk away when Michael suddenly called out to him, "Hey, Billy, don't forget to come back and visit me sometime, okay?"

"You name the time. I'll be there. Do you like to play catch?"

"Sure do. But only inside the ballpark."

"You'll let me play where the White Sox play?" Billy asked in astonishment.

"Anytime except on game days," Michael said with a smile.

"You got yourself a catch partner then, Mr. Mike. How many days do you work here?"

"All the time. I'm the caretaker."

"Sounds great! I'll stop by and see you tomorrow before the game."

"That's right. You're going to be at the game tomorrow, aren't you?"

"You bet. Thanks to you." On that note, Billy started to race for home.

The sound of the boy's voice back then reverberated in the old man's mind, and for a moment, he could picture young Billy running for home that first day. Michael broke away from these pleasant memories and folded the plastic that shrouded Billy's face. With some tape, he sealed the body bag that he had created. He knew the job ahead of him was going to be a long and tedious one. He had never dug a grave before in his life, and it gave him plenty of time to reflect upon happier days gone by. The first thing he had to do was carefully remove segments of sod from the area where the boy was to be buried. He realized that this was the best strategy in order to avoid future detection. He figured that he would bury the boy and replace the sod over the surface of the grave, and no one would ever notice the upheaval. As he broke the earth with his shovel, his mind began to wander and suddenly he was reliving the past.

He got a mental picture of the ten-year-old Billy arriving at the stadium early in the morning, carrying his ball and glove. Michael invited him in, and they made their way onto the playing field together. The boy was mesmerized by the view of the stadium from field level. Michael noticed the hypnotic effect of the huge stadium on him. "Gives you a whole new perspective on things, doesn't it?"

"I've never seen anything quite like it. How many people can they fit in this stadium?" Billy asked in wonder.

"Forty-five thousand. That's a lot of fannies in the seats, isn't it, Billy?"

"You ain't kiddin'."

"So what position do you play?"

"Third base. You gotta bat? You want to hit me some grounders?"

"Do I gotta bat? Where the hell do you think we are, Billy? What kind of question is that? How many do you need?" Michael said facetiously.

"It's a dumb one, but then again, what are you waiting for?"

"Got me there, kiddo. I'll be right back. Don't you go away."

These memories brought more tears to Michael's old, tired eyes as he continued his dispiriting deed. Despite the tears, the memories continued to play back in his mind.

He recalled that the boy was a mighty good ballplayer for his age. On this particular day, he hit him many hard grounders, and he always made the play. On one of the ground balls, he made a diving stab and miraculously came up with it. He was also fascinated by his left-handed throwing style. His throws seemed to naturally curve, and they tailed away from whomever Billy was throwing too. Billy was just plain unique as far as Michael was concerned.

"I don't think I've seen major leaguers make plays any better than that, kiddo, and boy do I love to watch you throw. Left-handers are so much fun to watch," Michael complemented.

"It is kind of neat, huh? You know if I keep practicing, one of the major leaguers you'll be talking about someday will be me. Don't you think so?" Billy asked insecurely.

"You never know, my boy. But I certainly think you've got a better chance than the majority of them."

"My dad thinks my older brothers got more talent than I do but that's only 'cause he doesn't spend any time watching me play. But I'm going to show him. I'm going to show everybody someday."

"Well, even though I haven't seen your brothers play, I'm inclined to think that your father is very mistaken in his lack of respect toward your ability."

"You really think so? You wouldn't be just gassing up my head, would you?" Billy asked, looking for sincerity in Michael's eyes.

"Nope. I wouldn't patronize you, kid. I'm a straight shooter. You'll always get the truth from me, and I've been told on many occasions before that I've got a pretty good eye for talent."

Billy, sensing Michael's sincerity, ran over and gave him a big hug. The two walked side by side as Michael started to do his job of creating the baselines. Billy grasped his arm tightly as Michael pushed the lime machine down the base and foul lines. The lines the two created were perfectly straight.

All this digging was causing too much stress on the old man's back, and he halted momentarily. He was perspiring profusely when he checked his watch that now registered 8:00 a.m. He had a panicked look on his face as he momentarily feared discovery. He took a peek out of the storage shed and looked around the ballpark. It was completely empty as his lucid mind would've concluded; it was at this time that he knew that the anxiety of this predicament was starting to get the best of him. Nevertheless, he took a deep breath and made a sigh of relief as he stared out into the stillness of the empty stadium. His mind continued to wander, bringing him back to the days when he and Billy would talk for hours in the same stillness that surrounded him now.

He recalled how they used to sit around the empty ballpark in the early evening and discuss baseball trivia. Baseball was Billy's favorite subject, and he and Michael would debate for countless hours the particular merits of the game's heroes. As he began digging, again he tried to focus in on the details of these particular conversations they shared. Suddenly he was overjoyed by the fact that he could specifically recall the events of a day he spent with his beloved, Billy.

Michael recollected the days when he and the boy would sit together behind the White Sox dugout. This happened during the times when the team was out of town. Billy had a habit of throwing a baseball up in the air and catching it as he kept up his end of the conversation. A smile came to the old man's lips as he remembered this, and he started to hear the boy's words once again.

"Hey, Michael, do you think anybody will ever top the sixty home runs Ruth hit in 27?"

"Maybe. I mean, Hack hit 56 last year."

"Yeah. But he's slumping this year. Plus, I think last year was a fluke."

"Maybe so, my boy. Maybe so."

"Hey, Michael, why do you think there were so many more home runs hit during the twenties than before then?"

"From what I hear, they played with a dead ball back at the turn of the century. When they changed the ball to one that was livelier, the home run totals naturally went up."

"Well that makes sense."

"A lot of things about the game have changed, Billy. Did you know that in the old days if you hit the ball on the ground and it continued to roll past the rope at the end of the outfield, you could continue to run as far as you could go? There were no ground rule doubles."

"You mean there weren't any fences?" Billy asked in astonishment.

"There was no such thing, my boy. The game was in its infancy back then. It wasn't nearly as organized nor, may I add, as popular as it is today."

"Wow. Michael, you know everything about baseball, don't you? What do you think's wrong with the White Sox?"

"It's the management."

"Yeah, but I think it's the players too. Second to last, the last two years and the way things are going this year, it sure looks like dead last to me. The players are too used to losing. My dad says, 'Losing's contagious.' He says, 'It's a cancer that has to be removed before it spreads.' I never agree with him, but I do on this particular issue. I think they need some new personnel. I'll tell you what they really need, they need me if I could only, somehow, grow up faster."

"You don't want to grow up that fast, kiddo. Enjoy your youth while you've got it. Believe me, you'll have plenty of days to discover the not-so-enjoyable benefits of being old."

"You're old, but you're having a good time of it."

"Come on, Billy. Please don't bury me yet. Hell, I'm only forty."

"Speaking about that, my dad says it's strange that you're not married like everybody else," Billy said with a large grin on his face.

"Well, what am I supposed to say to that one? You tell your dad that I haven't met the right girl yet. And if he talks back, you tell him to find me a nice girl. Tell him, I'm open to all suggestions," Michael said in jest.

"Believe me, you wouldn't want any girl my father found for you. When he's away from Mom, you should see some of the barkers he stares at. What can I say? He has very bad taste."

"I kind of figured that. Especially after you told me about how he thinks that your brothers are more talented ballplayers than you are. I didn't tell you, but I went out and saw all three of your brother's play in the game the other day."

"You did?"

"Well, I figured if I saw them play, I'd have a better understanding of the situation you're in. Anyway, kiddo, you've got nothing to worry about. If your father really favors the athletes in your family, then you're going to be the apple of his eye, and as you would put it, 'that ain't no lie.'"

"Me, the apple of my father's eye, huh? That's a good one," Billy questioned dubiously. "Oh, by the way, Mike, my father said he would like to meet you. He has some 'reservations' about why you and I are such good friends," Billy mimed.

Michael exploded into laughter as he observed Billy's portrayal of the "concerned father." Billy broke into a chuckle himself when he noticed that his performance had amused his friend.

"Well, we don't want him to think that there's anything funny going on now, do we?" Billy said while displaying a limp wrist, in an attempt to be funny, poking fun of the effeminate mannerisms of some homosexuals.

"I hope he's not thinking anything like that," Michael said mortified.

"With him, you never know. I can just picture it now. We sit down to dinner, and he looks over at you and says, 'So, Michael, why the great interest in my son?'"

"And I reply flippantly, 'At least someone is showing him some interest.'"

"Then he gets up and knocks you on the floor like he does the rest of us when we give him some lip," Billy quickly interjected.

"All right. You've convinced me to try a different approach. I've got it. I tell him, 'Mr. Green, I have no children of my own and that paternal urge is starting to take over.'"

"And he snaps, 'If you want to be a daddy, go make your own baby.'"

"Probably. So what do I say to him?"

"You don't have to say anything to him. Just be polite. Hell, you've been more of a father to me in the two months we've known each other than he ever was. And if you ask me, you're twice the man he'll ever be."

"That's very nice of you to say. I'm pretty fond of you too, Billy."

The boy dropped the ball and scooted over to Michael, giving him a big hug. Michael squeezed the boy tightly. He suddenly broke out of his daydream and decided it was time to take a rest. The summer heat wave was making this job a monumental task.

The humidity alone made any kind of physical labor unbearable at this time of the year, not to mention the fact that the old man's back was beginning to feel the strain from all the shoveling. He knew that if he was going to help Billy save face, he had to work on. He figured that he probably had two more hours before the other park employees would arrive on the scene. So under that time constraint, he began to dig once again. As he lifted out of the grave many shovels full of dirt, he reflected back upon more adventures with Billy. He recalled the dinner table when Billy first brought him home. It was a large mahogany table and all six of Billy's brothers sat in assigned seats around it. They had squeezed in an extra chair for him so he could sit next to Billy. This was one of the few considerations that the family gave to either one of them. Mr. Green, who made his living as a plumber, sat at the head of the table while Mrs. Green waited on him hand and foot. The old man recalled how Mrs. Green seemed more like an indentured servant than a wife. She was not allowed to eat until her husband and sons had their fill. Mr. Green, a heavyset, rugged-looking man recited a prayer for the food they were about to receive. After he finished, all at the table were silent. No one spoke unless he was spoken to. Mrs. Green had adorned the table with her best china; she stood back away from the table obsequiously, like a waiter, waiting to accommodate the needs of anyone seated. The old man remembered how he pitied this woman who in posture and attitude resembled an old mule.

The most outstanding memory of Billy's real family was the lack of love between them all. Mr. Green's marriage was loveless and this air permeated throughout the household. He recalled that the event took place on a Sunday in the late afternoon. The family was having baked chicken. There was a pecking order as Mr. Green made his selections of the pieces of chicken he preferred first. Billy's three older brothers made their choices next. By the time Billy and Michael made their picks, only legs and wings remained. Billy and Michael both had legs. The three younger boys had mostly wings. When the meal was over, all that was left was a wing, some liver, and gizzards for Mrs. Green to dine on. Sadly, she dined alone.

At the end of the meal, Mr. Green started a conversation with Michael. He remarked that he had heard from his son that he was involved in baseball, and he wondered in what capacity. Michael started to relive the conversation in his mind.

"Yes. I've been involved in caretaking at Comiskey for almost ten years," Michael responded.

"So, you were around during the Black Sox scandal, huh?" Mr. Green asked.

"No, sir. That was a few years before my time with the club."

"Did you play ball?"

"I played a little, but I never really was very good at it."

"Well, Michael's the name, right?"

"Yes, sir."

"Well, Michael, my older boys are very talented ballplayers. They're all playing on the same team at the high school. I don't want to beat around the bush with you, what I'm trying to get at is, whether or not you've got any connections with the Sox, so maybe they'd send a scout out to come down and give 'em a look-see?"

"Regrettably, sir, I'm not involved in that end of the business."

"Well, Billy, this guy's no use to you. Why are you spending so much time with him?"

"Because I like him, Dad. What's wrong with you? Haven't you ever heard of friends before? Haven't you ever liked anyone because you liked them, and not for what they could do for you?"

"Watch your mouth, young man! I'll paddle your ass right on the spot. I don't care whether your friend is here or not! What's he going to do about it?" Mr. Green said menacingly as he looked over at Michael confrontationally. Michael did not take the bait and stayed out of the argument.

"Then paddle my ass! You're nothing but a colossal embarrassment to me! You know that?" Billy screamed as he ran away from the table.

Michael got up and raced after him, finally catching up to him on the front porch. Billy started to cry his eyes out on Michael's shoulder. Through his tears, Billy said barely audibly, "Oh, Michael, I'm so sorry that my father is such a jerk. Please still be my friend."

"I love you, kid. I'll always be your friend," Michael said comfortingly.

Those words from long ago echoed in his head again. That was the first time he had ever told the boy he loved him. He stopped his shoveling and looked over at the tarp that enclosed Billy's body and said, "And I still do love you. And I'll always love you. And I'll always be your friend."

The tears of loss started to flow down his face again. His irrational side told him to climb right into the body bag and die alongside his beloved son, but his rational side took over and told him to cover up the shame and the embarrassment of this suicide. He resigned himself to the belief that he was obligated to help save Billy's dignity and memory. Thoughts of Billy's dignity and pride during life filled his head. Suddenly he found himself observing one of Billy's high school baseball games. Michael was very proud of Billy's accomplishments while playing high school baseball, and he attended the games so religiously that many thought that he was the boy's father. The boy brought his game to a higher level when he knew Michael was in attendance. Even in little league, Michael was the only family that attended the games. Billy's dad was too busy watching his older boy's high school games to show any interest in his middle son; although, that trend changed when Billy finally started playing high school ball. In time, his father came to the realization that his older boys had come to the end of the road at least as far as baseball was concerned. Michael had called it correctly many years before when he told Billy that his brother's baseball talents were not extraordinary. Mr. Green was now leaving it up to Billy to make up for his brother's shortcomings. Although Billy was aware of his father's expectations, he felt no pressure during the games because he knew that he had the God-given talent to move on to the next level. Michael recalled the events that took place after Billy hit a late inning home run to win a game. He remembered how Billy always found a way to avoid his "fair weather" father's company when the games ended. Billy's rationale was based simply on the fact that his father never took any interest in him until all other family options were exhausted. So why should he now allow his father to bask in his glory when he had always been treated like an afterthought? Billy showed his loyalty to those who were loyal to him, and so he chose Michael before his father. He and Michael always found a way to meet up secretly after games to celebrate. He recalled how on this occasion they met up at a large picnic area next to the road and sat across from each other and discussed the game.

"Michael, what did I tell you would happen if you hung a curveball in front of me?"

"I do recall that you told me that you would 'dismiss it' from the ballpark."

"And what did I do?"

"You dismissed it all right, with extreme prejudice."

"That's right. I like that 'extreme prejudice' adjective. Can you picture me hitting that same pitch out in Comiskey?"

"Sure I could. But you can't make it to the major leagues and not be able to hit a ball like that out of the ballpark, Billy."

"Hey, Michael, don't rain on my parade, okay?"

"I'm just trying to keep you down-to-earth, kid."

"I'll tell you what I do know, Michael. I know that I have enough talent to play professional ball. What level? I'm really not sure. But I am sure of one thing. I won't get cut by any D-level team, like Maddensville, like my brothers did."

"You're right. Right now, you're good enough to play in the minors. If your game continues to improve, you could possibly even make it to the majors. But, Billy, believe me there's a lot more to life than baseball."

"There is?" Billy remarked in a snide manner.

"Yes, there is, Billy. You might want to dismiss it sometimes, but there's a lot more good in you than the fact that you can hit a baseball. Billy, I'd love you if you ended up being a garbage man. It's the person that counts, not what you do. You know, sometimes I think you want to prove something so that your old man will give you the love that you deserve, but what you don't understand is that if he doesn't love you now, he won't really love you then either. So if you want to be a pro ballplayer, do it for yourself, not for me or your father, but for you because you're the one who's going to have to live with it."

"See, I thought you told me a long time ago that you'd never lie to me. But you're doing it right now. You couldn't possibly love me as much if I was a garbage man."

"Guess you'll have to go and be a garbage man to find that out," Michael declared humorously.

Billy got up quickly and grabbed a couple of paper cups that were littering the picnic area. He deposited them into the refuse container. With a big smirk on his face, he then inquired, "Do you still love me?"

Michael saw Billy asking that half serious question from so long ago as vividly as if it had happened yesterday. The memory of the alive and fun-loving Billy brought him back to reality once again. "Why did you do it?" Michael muttered to himself. "I told you how much you meant to me. Why didn't you believe me? Why couldn't you have at least come and talked it over with me? We could have worked it out. Why? Why? I have to know why," he lamented. He became suddenly aware of his lack of emotional stability and tried his best to calm down and reason out the answers to those enigmatic questions. Unfortunately for him, there were no acceptable answers. What the boy did was uncalled for. These painful thoughts made him want to dwell on the past even more. He knew at least in the past there was life; he could only wish that the same held true for the future. He took off his shirt that was now totally drenched with perspiration and continued to dig. His thoughts brought him back to 1939, the year that Billy won all-city baseball honors. One evening, while the White Sox were out of town, he invited Billy to come out to the stadium with the prerequisite that he come dressed in his game uniform. He had a crystal clear picture of Billy in his head as he arrived at Comiskey that evening. All the lights were turned off in the stadium, and he had left the gate open for him. He watched intently as Billy, for the most part blindly, made his way on to the field.

"Michael! I'm here! Michael! I'm here! Hey, Mike! Why don't you turn on some lights?" Billy announced into the darkness.

Michael did not respond, instead, he kept a close eye on Billy's progress from the stadium control room. He noticed that Billy was wandering around aimlessly, so he finally decided to give him some instructions over the public address system.

"Billy, find your way to the diamond. In fact, go to the pitcher's mound. I will join you shortly," Michael's voice blared over the loud speakers.

Michael sat back and watched Billy's shadow arrive at the middle of the baseball diamond. He then turned on the new stadium field lights. Billy stared out at the mesmerizing lights that surrounded him and, for an instant, got a taste of the future of professional baseball. Billy looked around in awe at the illuminated stadium surrounded by the nighttime skies. Michael saw the joy on Billy's face as he proudly stood in game uniform on that infield grass. A few minutes later, he came down to join him on the field.

"It's amazing, huh, Billy?"

"You ain't kidding. This is the big time. I want to play on this field someday, Michael. Did you ever think that you would live to see night baseball? 1939 is going to be one hell of a year in the city of Chicago."

"Technology, my boy. That's what this is all about. But to answer your question, sure it's hard to believe. But you got to remember I was born into a world where there were no cars or planes or anything that your generation has taken for granted. So, Billy, what do you think of baseball in the future?"

"I think it's going to be absolutely great, Michael, and I'm going to play a big part in it."

"What are you talking about?"

"I'm talking about being signed by the White Sox. They gave me a minor league contract," Billy gloated.

"You're kidding me, right?"

"No joke. I'm supposed to report to some team called the Longview Cannibals. That's one of their C-class farm teams. They play in the East Texas League. I leave next week. Considering the enormous amount of money they're paying me, cannibalism might just turn out to be a viable option," Billy joked. "Seriously speaking though, can you believe it? I told you this was going to happen."

"Well, congratulations, Billy. I know this is what you wanted, and you worked mighty hard to get it. I'm very proud of you, kiddo," Michael said while fighting back his tears.

Billy saw Michael's eyes well, and that was all the catalyst needed to bring about his own emotions. As he fought back his tears, he pledged, "Even though I'm going to be far away. I'm going to come back and see you as often as I can. I'm going to miss you, Mr. Mike."

For the first time in his life, Michael truly started to feel like he was getting old. The boy he raised for the last eight years was now a man. He lectured, "I don't want you to worry about visiting me. You've got enough things to occupy your mind with other than worrying about finding time for me. I'm going to be just fine. I want you to go to Longview, wherever that is, and give it your all. Go down there and find out how much you really like the game. We're talking about your life, my man, so you go down there and decide if that's what you really want. I'll come down to see you as often as I can. I just know you're going to do really well, Billy. And if for some unknown reason you decide that it's not your cup of tea, well then, there are plenty of other things you can do with your life. So don't sweat it, kid. You hear me?"

Billy acknowledged Michael's thoughts, but his words were never given full credence. Michael realized that Billy was living a dream, and as long as there was clear sailing and cloudless skies, he would continue to climb that same mountain. Michael knew that the only thing that ever changed the course and direction of dreams was adversity, and he knew that Billy had not tasted the kind of adversity that he would be force-fed in the minor league baseball system. He knew that professional athletics had always been a precarious type of existence, especially for those athletes who lived on its fringes. He also knew that everybody in baseball's minor leagues was hanging on by threads for their very existence. The most prevalent fact in professional baseball is that if you don't cut it, you certainly will not be hanging around for long. The competition has always been fierce, and if you happen to fail, there's always somebody new who's anxious to take your place.

Michael also knew that it wasn't his business to discourage Billy from pursuing his dream. He only hoped that his words would carry some credence with him in the event that in the long run, circumstances didn't work out for him.

Michael reached into his jacket pocket and handed him a gift that the young man would treasure for the rest of his life. Billy's eyes lit up in disbelief as he gazed at the autographed baseball of the 1932 World Champion New York Yankees that now rested firmly in his palm. The memory of his haunting smile on that occasion brought Michael out of his delirium. He stopped shoveling dirt for a moment so he could compose himself, but his mind kept wandering back to how this tragedy could have taken place. Then he recalled the change the boy made when he finally, after nine long years, got called up to the Triple-A Hollywood Stars. From listening to the kid, you would have thought he had made it to the major leagues. He was over the moon because he was now on the doorstep of making all his dreams come true. Michael got a taste of Billy's delusions of grandeur when he went to Los Angeles, California to see the boy play.

He remembered visiting the boy in his little room that contained a wooden desk and a single bed. It was located in a dormitory type facility. Michael recalled having to walk down a long hallway to use the bathroom and while there he noticed a public shower area. It sure wasn't living high off the hog and was nothing to brag about, but that didn't stop Billy from creating his new facade. Maybe it was the movie stars who attended the games or the glitz and glamour of Hollywood itself, but he believed he was on his way to the major leagues and he was bound and determined to improve his image. He was going to stand out.

While Michael sat next to him on his bed, Billy informed him of all the new changes he was implementing. Billy proudly displayed his new green leather cleats and then opened his dresser drawer to reveal his new pride and joy. Wrapped in expensive tissue paper, he revealed his newly dolled up infielder's mitt.

"Look at this, Mike. I had an artist friend of mine design this for me. All the scenes were created through dyeing the leather. See the baseball diamond and the dugout. Look how intricate this work is. It's an absolute masterpiece. So what do you think?" Billy asked excitedly.

"You want my opinion?"

"Sure. Fire away."

"Well, the shoes are rather snazzy, but I would lose that glove. It's hideous," Michael stated with heartfelt honesty.

"No it's not. It's just different. My artist friend put in a lot of work creating that design and quite frankly it's an attention grabber," Billy professed defensively.

"I won't argue that point with you, but my question is: Do you really want that kind of attention? You didn't see Babe Ruth do that and you certainly didn't see Lou Gehrig ever wear anything gaudy," Michael edified.

"It was a different day and age. They were old school. I want to be from the new school, a trendsetter like the area I am living in now. I want to stand out. I don't want to get to the major leagues and just blend in."

"Well, if that's what you're trying for, you've succeeded but you're not at the 'show' yet. Don't you think you're getting the cart out in front of the horse, so to speak?" Michael asked as if he was puzzled by this new ostentatious presentation by his dear friend.

"This is just a pit stop before I get to the 'show,' Michael. It's a done deal. I didn't come this far to be mired down here," Billy said with fervor.

But unfortunately, mired was what he was, Michael thought as he stopped digging and stared sadly over at the make shift body bag. Billy had started his celebration prematurely because the curse of being a left-handed infielder earned him a demotion the very next season. It would cost him another four years playing for Double-A Memphis. He took a brief rest and realized that although it was going to be painful, for his sanity's sake, he was going to have to focus in on his observations of the boy in the recent past. Only these recent memories could possibly hold a clue as to why Billy committed suicide. He figured the best place to start was when he began playing really well in the minor leagues since that was so atypical of him.

He put his shovel down and stared in bewilderment at the grave he had been digging. To him, looking down into that hole was like looking into the abyss, and his mind wandered away once again. He recalled the phone call he received from that photo journalist Billy had befriended while playing for the Double-A Memphis Chickasaws. The photo journalist, whose name was Eisen, told him that Billy was acting very strangely and was totally not himself. The conversation started to replay in his mind.

"Why are you calling me and telling me about this?" Michael asked.

"Because Billy told me that you're his closest friend."

"That's right. So what seems to be the problem?"

"Well, I don't know if you know it or not, but Billy's always been a very popular player around here. And lately he just hasn't been so popular."

"That doesn't seem like much of a reason to panic. Did you ever think the boy might be just a bit discouraged? I mean, he's only been kicking around the minor leagues for close to fourteen years now."

"Believe me, I've considered that possibility. But there's something strange about him."

"What do you mean?"

"What I mean is that he's changed drastically. It's like he's two different people entirely. Don't get me wrong, he's still flamboyant, and I'm sure he always will be. The team should have left him in California. He was much more suited for the Hollywood "Twinks" than here. He still keeps that same persona with the green glove and the flashy shoes and everything, but lately, he's been just plain selfish and overbearing. He used to be everybody's friend around here but not anymore. What I'm trying to say nicely is that I can't stand him anymore, and I never thought I'd ever say that about him. It's like he's some kind of imposter. He looks the same, and that's where the similarity ends. He's no longer happy-go-lucky. He's like some kind of monster. It's almost like he's possessed. I think if you polled his teammates they would say the same thing about him. He's become an outcast down here."

"Well, all I can say, at least from what he's told me, is that things couldn't be going any better for him. He's really having a great season."

"That's true statistically speaking, but what I'm telling you is that his whole nature has changed. He went from being the rah-rah guy to the voice of doom and gloom in the dugout. Many of his teammates are accusing him of putting hexes on them. The kid is literally in a fight every other day."

"They're all probably just jealous of him. The kid's having a banner year and just might possibly, finally, get a call up and they're having a rough time with it. I mean, Billy has kept me informed of the stat sheet down there, and from the looks of it, he's the best player they've got. He's the reason they're soaring to the Southern Association title."

"Well, you can think what you want. I just wanted to talk to you in hope that you might possibly talk to him."

"Well, I'll talk to him. The kid's probably just going through a phase. I'm sure he doesn't mean any harm. It's just the kid's been through a lot."

"Listen, please do me a favor and don't tell him that I talked to you. We were real good friends before, and maybe if he snaps out of this, we'll be good friends again."

"You've got my word on it. Thanks for the call."

Michael thought for a moment that this behavior change in Billy was his way of reaching out for help. He couldn't bear to think that he had somehow ignored the telltale signs of imminent mental illness. He then remembered the startling conversation he had with him when they discussed the matter. He visualized himself with Billy at that roadside diner after watching Memphis lose to the Chattanooga Lookouts. Billy had an outstanding game that afternoon, but one player does not make a team. The rest of the team put forth a pathetic effort. Billy had eight chances at third base and did not make an error; he even made a barehanded play on a bunt down the third baseline, not an easy chore for a left-handed third basemen. He had to run past the ball and jerk his body around in an unorthodox manner to make that throw for the put out at first base. Making things even better for him, his hitting was exceptional; he had three hits in four times at bat, including a long home run over the center-field fence, which accounted for the only two Memphis runs.

"Michael, there's rumors going around the club house that I might be brought up to the 'show' soon."

"I certainly could understand that. You're hitting the damn tar out of the ball, kid. And you're throwing accuracy is uncanny. What's got into you lately?"

"I don't know. My fielding just improved. I'm finally staying down on the ball and my throws, like you said, couldn't be any more accurate. It's like my vision is totally improved. I swear I can read the laces on the grounders hit to me lately. It's pretty slick being Superman, you know? I love it! I'm finally on a hot streak. I hope this never ends. I'm really having fun with this, Michael," Billy gloated.

"I'm sure you are. Come on, Billy, level with me. What are you doing differently?"

"Nothing in particular."

"Nothing in particular, huh? I don't know about that. You raised your batting average over a hundred points in the last month and a half and at last you're fielding like a Gold Glover. You must be doing something differently."

"Let's just say my overall outlook has improved; it's no secret that I was mighty depressed in the beginning of the season, you know? I was really worried that I was going to be eating crow for the rest of my life. All that showy crap I've been pulling over the last six years just to get stuck down here was getting to be a little too disheartening, even for me. I was starting to feel like a dud firecracker—all fizzle and no pop. To be honest, I was losing hope. You know if you don't start showing some improvement, they start to hint to you that maybe you just don't have what it takes, and hell, I'm thirty-two years old this year."

"You don't have to remind me about that."

"Well, anyway, I was real down. I mean I had worked my whole life to get somewhere, and it didn't look like it was going to happen for me. I was ready to quit, Mike. I was thinking about different places in the world that I could maybe hide so I could feel comfortable looking people in the eye again. I had drawn so much attention to myself and I just couldn't live up to the image I created. I felt helpless. To be honest with you, I think I was having a nervous breakdown. I was crying myself to sleep every night, just praying that somehow this miracle I've been living would occur. I mean I was getting desperate. I started telling myself that I would give anything, and I do mean anything, in order to improve enough to get me to the 'show'. Well, anyway, one night I have this weird dream. It was the strangest dream I've ever had in my entire life. From the look on your face, I know this probably sounds pretty silly to you."

"No. I'm not making fun of you. So go on. So you had a dream that you were going to become this fantastic ballplayer who could live up to the image of your fancy glove and shoes, huh?"

"Well, not exactly. Like I said, it was weird. I found myself at this deserted major league ballpark, and I was at the plate, ready to bat but there was no pitcher on the mound. Like I said, it was strange. Anyway, to make it even weirder, you won't believe who I saw."

"Who'd you see, Billy?"

"I saw the Babe and Gehrig."

"That's some weird dream."

"But it gets better. They both tell me to stop groveling. So I tell them how badly I want to move up to the majors and then the Babe tells me that if I truly wanted to know whether I could make it or not, he could arrange a test for me. Isn't that crazy?"

"It sure is. I wish I had dreams like that. I've always had dreams of the stupid variety. You know, pigs flying and stuff like that. So what did you find out, kid?"

"Well, you know me. My curiosity always gets the best of me, and I was dying to find out what he proposed. So I told him to arrange it, and when I looked back at the pitcher's mound, you'll never believe who I saw there."

"Who?"

"Michael, I swear to God it was the Big Train, Walter Johnson, in the flesh, staring me down. I looked over at Gehrig, and he told me that if I could get a hit off of old Barney, then I could, without a doubt, make it to the major leagues. So I went up to bat and that son of a bitch struck me out in three pitches. Worse than that, I could hardly even see the damned ball it was going so fast. When the third pitch went by, I remembered thinking, 'What a depressing dream this one turned out to be.' I remember saying to Ruth, 'So that's it?' And he casually replied back that I had gotten my answer. But then I turned back to face the pitcher's mound again, you know to get another look at old Barney, just to find out that he wasn't there any longer. You know, I was kind of hoping for another chance. Next thing I know, there's this really distinguished-looking man in a dark suit on the mound. He tells me that my heroes just made a fool out of me and that he would give me a fourth strike to truly find out whether or not I could hit good enough to make it in the major leagues. Since, like I told you, I really wanted another turn at bat, I took him up on it. He told me that if I could get a hit off of him, that indubitably, that was his exact word, I was major league material. Let me tell you, he was talking my language. So I readied myself in the batter's box, and you'd never believe it, the fool hangs a curveball, waist high over the center of the plate. Needless to say, I smack that sucker right out of the ballpark. And the weird thing is that while I was admiring my home run, the stadium suddenly became filled to the gills with people, and they were all screaming my name. It was the best dream I ever had. So what do you think about that?"

"That's some dream. So you're telling me that ever since you had that dream that you've been on a tear?"

"Yeah. Basically."

"That's pretty unbelievable. So with all this great stuff happening to you, why then am I hearing all these horror stories about you being so unsportsmanlike with your teammates? I would think that you'd want them to share in your good fortune."

"Well, of course I'd like to be popular with them, but sometimes, sacrifices have to be made."

"What are you talking about, Billy?"

"Well, I know it's wrong, but I've been kind of wishing bad luck upon all of them lately," Billy whispered.

"Well, that's awfully mean. Why are you doing that? I don't get it. So you're openly praying that they play badly? Why, so you'll look better than them? And then you make sure they all know about it. What are you thinking about? No wonder they hate you. These are your teammates, Billy. They're your friends. You're supposed to be wishing them well. What in hell is getting into you? And you think that this is somehow improving your play?" Michael asked, completely baffled.

"Look, I don't need a lecture from you about sportsmanship!" Billy snapped. Adding, "I have my reasons. It's got something to do with karma. You've got to understand something about us ballplayers. We're superstitious. When we're in a groove, we don't change things. I made a deal, and I'm not going back on it!"

"What do you mean, you made a deal?"

"That's all I got to say. So drop it. I hear enough of that shit from them. I don't need to hear it from you too," Billy scolded.

The old man snapped out of his daydream and pondered the same question in his mind repeatedly. *"Made a deal with whom?"* He then stared into that half-dug grave and decided it was time to resume his digging. The grave was actually starting to look like one, except for the fact that it needed to be dug a lot deeper.

Michael looked down at his hands, which were by now very sore. He realized that he was starting to blister badly from all the shoveling he was doing. He also realized that in his situation he could not take pain into account. He had to continue digging regardless of the discomfort. He relied on his faith in Jesus Christ to continue this ordeal. He figured that if Jesus could suffer through crucifixion, then he could suffer through the blisters on his hands.

These thoughts of Jesus also gave him a greater awareness as to what might have actually occurred to Billy. He recalled a story that he had heard years before at his church about a lonely old man who had offered anything in order to have his dead wife return to him. The pastor told the congregation that the old man had gotten his wish from Satan himself and that the old man's body was found dead in his bed, next to the skeletal remains of his wife. The pastor's message was simple that day, be careful of what you ask for because you just might get it. The pastor declared that when you offer too much for something, you invite unwanted associations into your life. *Could Billy have invited the devil to intervene into his situation? Could that have been the deal he was talking about?* These unanswered questions were giving him fits as he dug on.

If the pitcher dressed in black in Billy's dream had been the devil in disguise, then Ruth and Gehrig must have been heavenly helpers, he reasoned. This train of thought was starting to make sense to him. He rationalized that after observing the attempt to defile one of his children, God would've sent help to counteract any Satanic influences. Unfortunately, for Billy, he must have leaned toward the evil side instead of the good. That would explain why he was so mean-spirited during his last year at Memphis. What didn't make sense is if he had really sold his soul to the devil, then why did he fail so miserably as a White Sock? This was the piece of the puzzle that didn't fit as far as Michael was concerned. He asked himself, *What variable in the equation had changed since the boy had made it to the majors?* He repeatedly pondered that thought throughout his labor and then the answer dawned on him. He recalled the discussion he had with him at Comiskey the day he arrived from Memphis.

Never had he seen Billy in better spirits than upon his arrival. The two had to put the celebration on hold though because the White Sox were in the middle of a home stand with the Indians.

After the game, in which the White Sox defeated the Indians, Billy and he went out for a late-night snack. They stopped at a diner and got a couple of burgers to go. The night was beautiful, and the two men devoured their burgers while taking a long walk around the city. Michael recalled in detail the conversation that took place that night.

"You know, it's almost like a dream. Just being here is really amazing to me. Do you realize how rare it is for a ballplayer to skip over Triple-A and go to the majors?" Billy asked as he reflected upon his unique situation.

"They had to do it, Billy. They had to strike while the iron was hot. If you were going to the majors, it had to be now. They didn't have time to do things orthodox with you anymore because it was getting too late in the game for you. I hate to emphasize the obvious, but you're awfully old to be making your Major League debut. I wish you could have solved these problems years ago. Well, anyway, enjoy it while you're here, my boy. And by the way, you earned it, kid. You worked hard, and you stuck with it. And you deserve to be here," Michael rationally explained but what he didn't realize was the pernicious effect these words had on Billy. Michael had brought to vivid realization all the dreads and fears that the boy had tried so hard to camouflage.

"It's just hard for me to believe sometimes. Last year I would have never believed that any of this was possible. I guess it just goes to show that dreams really do come true," Billy said, trying his best to bandage the wound that Michael exposed and continue his façade of self-assurance.

Michael humored him proclaiming, "It was a gift from God, my boy. That's what it had to be. How else could a miracle like this have occurred?" He added, "So what do think about the team, kid?"

"We've got some talent, that's for sure. As soon as they get me into the lineup, I think I can give the team a little boost. But let's face it, we'll go as far as the pitching will take us."

"So what do you think of your competition, Hector Rodriguez?"

"Do you want the truth, or do you want me to lie to you?"

"Honesty is always the best policy, Billy."

"Well, let's just say that I wish he would break his leg so that I can come in and take his place. Honest enough for you?"

"Yes. Do you feel that same way about all your teammates?"

"No. Not at all. In fact, tonight from the get-go, I was cheering for Billy Pierce to shut down those Indians. I mean, you've gotta cheer on your own team. How else are we going to make it to the Series?"

"Well, I'm glad to hear that you're back to your senses again."

"Yeah. I was only being like that in order to get here," Billy divulged unintentionally.

"What do you mean by that?"

"Oh, nothing. I don't know what I'm talking about half the time. My mind just isn't totally here yet. You know all this excitement is just a little too much for me. It's going to take a little time for me to adjust," Billy said deceitfully.

"I was only being like that in order to get here?" That statement of Billy's kept ringing in Michael's head. He thought, *A gift from God, I think not. I should have known better. So was that the deal? Was it the cheering against his teammates that enabled Billy to have the ability to rise to the major leagues in the first place, and if it was, then why didn't he continue to put his hex upon them? He couldn't have thought that it was just a temporary deal or could he? Was the*

boy that naive? Michael's biggest question was, *Why did he choose death? Why did he think that was the only way out?* These were the questions that haunted Michael until the day he died. As far as the grave was concerned, it was never discovered. The Billy Green disappearance was never solved and it, along with the Black Sox scandal, became just another part of the folklore that surrounded the old ballpark. The World Series would make its way back to Comiskey in 1959, but the Sox would lose in six, and with so much life and history taking place within the confines of the stadium, Billy would continue to lie undisturbed until 1991.

In 1991, the White Sox ownership had the old Comiskey Park demolished as the team moved into a brand-new ballpark.

THE UNCONFIDENT
EDDIE ROMANO

Eleven-year-old Eddie Romano was scared to death as he waited for his turn at bat. Secretly, he wished that Bret Jones, his teammate, who was currently at bat would make the last out to save him the embarrassment.

When it came to playing baseball, Eddie was, in a word, "unconfident." He never had any success before, so he assumed that he just didn't have any God-given talent. Although he felt worthless as a player, he still loved the game. He just didn't love being the center of attention, and he knew that's exactly what he would be if he got up to bat. So far, Eddie's secret wishes were not coming true as Bret was ahead in the count three balls to one strike. Eddie stared out toward the bleachers that were filled with every little leaguer's number one fan and at the moment Eddie's number one nightmare: parents. Seeing his folks in the stands gave him a sunken feeling in his stomach. Then suddenly he heard, "ball four" screamed out by the umpire, and he knew his worst fears had just materialized.

It was the bottom of the sixth and his team, the Astros, was behind 3 to 2 with runners on first and second base with two outs. As Eddie walked up to the plate, he heard shouts of encouragement coming from his coach, Mr. Mitchell. He heard the fans, his parents included, screaming out for him to do well. At this particular moment he wished he could have been anybody on the earth other than himself. He thought, *How can they really expect me to get a hit when all I've done all season long is strike out? Why should I even bother going to bat? This whole situation is absurd. I'm just going to embarrass myself. I don't want to do this.*

Looking very much like a death row inmate taking that final walk toward the electric chair, Eddie looked down at the plate and suddenly started to tremble. He immediately stepped back out of the batter's box. He did a quick about-face and ran back toward the dugout.

"I can't do this coach. Haven't you got anybody else?"

"Eddie, I've used up my bench. Just give it your best try. Okay, kid?" Mr. Mitchell pleaded.

Johnny Mitchell, the coach's son and the star of the team, intently eavesdropped on the conversation between his dad and Eddie. "What kind of shit is this, Romano? You better get your ass out there before I decide to tear you a new asshole! I swear to God, Romano, you're worthless! You know that? A coward like you doesn't even belong on this team!"

"Cool down, Johnny. I've got this situation under control," Mr. Mitchell informed his son, then added dejectedly, "Please, Eddie, just go out and do your best. Will you?"

The big, fat volunteer umpire waddled toward the dugout and asked Eddie in a sarcastic tone of voice, "Hey, kid, do you think we could possibly get this game going sometime this century?"

Eddie didn't respond to the umpire verbally; he just turned around and began a slow and mentally stressful walk up to the plate. He reluctantly entered the batter's box. He looked up into the bleachers and saw his parents screaming out encouragement to him. He prayed that the end would come mercifully. It did. The pitcher threw him three strikes, and he was called out. Eddie hung his head low as he made his way back to the dugout.

Johnny Mitchell looked at Eddie in absolute disgust as he watched him put his bat away in the bat bag. "Way to go, Romano! Thanks for that tremendous effort," he snapped angrily. Eddie looked like he was about to cry; and Johnny, noticing this, added with some compassion, "I'm sorry Eddie. Really, I am. Just please, get out of my sight. Okay? I'm just really pissed off with you right now." Johnny exasperatedly kicked over the Gatorade dispenser. The lid flew off and Gatorade and ice drenched the dugout.

Eddie's other teammates weren't quite as upset or callous, and they all made a concerted effort to come over and give him a compassionate pat on the back. He looked up momentarily and saw his father looking on. Eddie was surprised to see that his dad looked really sad. He had always thought that his father only had feelings for successful people.

"Eddie, forget about it, kid. It happens to the best of us. Tell you what. You and me are going to cheer up together at that baseball card show tomorrow," Mr. Romano said consolingly.

"Really, Dad? Wow! Ryne Sandberg's going to be there. You're the best dad in the whole world. I promise, I'll do better next time," Eddie said in much better spirits than before.

"I know you will, my boy."

EDDIE AND HIS DAD BOND

Eddie had never seen so many card tables. They weren't kidding when they said on the radio that there would be card tables galore. This was Eddie's first card and memorabilia show, and he clung to his father's arm as they fought the crowds to observe each fascinating exhibit.

It was billed as the Fifth Annual Windy City Sports, Collectibles, and Memorabilia Show and from Eddie's eleven-year-old perspective, it looked as if the whole city of Chicago was in attendance. He tugged hard on his father's arm when he caught a glimpse of Ryne Sandberg signing autographs behind a table in the corner of the auditorium. He was amazed that he could spot anyone through this endless maze of, from his perspective, trees that were walking along and obstructing his view.

"Dad! Ryne Sandberg!"

"What'd you say, Eddie?"

Eddie quickly pulled his six-foot father down to his level. "Dad, Ryne Sandberg's over there," Eddie said, pointing a finger in the direction of Mr. Sandberg.

"You want an autograph?"

"Yeah," Eddie said excitedly.

"What do you say?"

"Please!"

"That's better."

Mr. Romano debated with himself over whether Sandberg would charge for his autograph since nothing else in this ultra-commercialized gathering went for free.

The Romano duo fought their way through all the hustle and bustle and arrived at the Ryne Sandberg table. They then found a place in the long line and stood patiently.

"Eddie, what are you going to have him sign?"

"My baseball glove, Dad."

"Hey, wait a minute there. I just bought you that glove. Don't even think about putting that glove away, Eddie. I didn't buy that glove to have it sit on your shelf. Gloves are way too expensive these days to waste. You hear me?"

"Loud and clear," Eddie lamented.

"Good. You know when I was a kid they didn't have card shows like this one. But collecting baseball cards was a big thing in my neighborhood. I collected the entire 1970 series, but you'll never believe what I did."

"What did you do, Dad?"

"When I was just about your age, I traded Johnny Bench for some common player named Joe Keough. I was really hung up on the idea of completing my set at the time. If I only knew then what I know today, I would never have made that trade."

"Oh my god! You allowed yourself to get ripped off! Tell me that you're kidding. Tell me you didn't do that. Come on, Dad, you know you're pulling my leg, right?" Eddie chuckled.

"Unfortunately, I did do that. Don't look at me that way. You'll make a few mistakes before you're through too, kid."

"Maybe so, but nothing as big as that, Dad."

"You want to hear another big-assed mistake of mine?"

"Sure. I love to hear stories about my dad screwing up."

"Well, your grandfather for Christmas that year gave me a baseball card locker to store my cards in. And I had so many cards that they all didn't fit properly. Well, anyway, it was such a tight fit that I ended up bending them all up, trying to get them into that locker. Years later, I find out that I wrecked the card's value by blunting their edges and storing them like that."

"That's right. Cards lose their value when you bend their edges. Boy, Dad, you were a complete moron, weren't you?" Eddie emphasized the obvious while breaking out into a laughing fit.

"It's Mr. Moron to you, wise guy. Seriously though, like I said before, if only I knew."

"What a dunce. Glad I didn't grow up back then. The music was lame too." Eddie snickered.

"Someday your kids will be telling you the same thing."

"No way! José!" Eddie immediately started to fidget a bit while waiting in line. He alternated his weight distribution rhythmically from foot to foot. Eddie anxiously awaited further chitchat from his father and losing his patience initiated a line of conversation, "Dad, who do you think was better, Babe Ruth or Hank Aaron?"

"Well, Eddie, I got to see Hank play when I was a kid, and he was a real good ballplayer. I never got to see the Babe. He was quite a bit before my time. But from what I've heard, the Babe was a better hitter. Let's just put it this way, he got his 714 home runs in a couple thousand less at bats than Hank Aaron did."

"So Babe Ruth was the best," Eddie announced.

The line had moved ahead considerably, and the two were now waiting near the display cases. Eddie eagerly looked over the different baseball cards contained within the display. His eyes were firmly focused on a Babe Ruth card.

"Dad, look, they've got a Babe Ruth card in there. I wonder what it costs."

"Forget the cost, kid. You ain't getting the card. What? Do you think your old man is made of money?"

"No. I just want to know what it costs."

"Too much."

Eddie continued to look into the display case and focused in on a card that lay next to the Ruth card. "Dad, who's Lou Gehrig?"

"Well, Eddie, I can tell you a little bit about him, but again, he was way before my time. They have a movie about him called *The Lou Gehrig Story*. He was the captain of the New York Yankees, and he played alongside Babe Ruth. From what I hear, he was an amazing hitter. He hit a lot of home runs and had a real high batting average too. He played in more consecutive games than any other player in the history of the game and that's how he got his nickname, the Iron Horse. But his career was shortened because he got a terrible disease, Eddie, and he died at a young age."

"How old was he?"

"I think around forty."

"That's really sad, Dad. That's about your age. Hope nothing like that happens to you. I guess I'll have to watch that movie."

"It's a real tearjerker, kid. But I'll rent it for you, and don't worry about your old man. I'll be here to keep you on your toes for a long time."

"What about poor Shoeless Joe Jackson? That was mean what they did to him in that movie."

"That happened to him in real life, Eddie. That movie *Eight Men Out* was a depiction of what really happened to the 1919 Chicago White Sox."

"You mean they really threw him out even though he never threw a game?" Eddie asked in disbelief.

"Yes."

"But that's not fair. Do you think he plays baseball in heaven, like in *Field of Dreams*?"

"If I remember correctly, they were supposedly playing in Iowa. They just thought it was heaven."

"But do you think he's playing in heaven?" Eddie anxiously demanded an answer.

"Yes. I'm sure of it. "

"Good. Because that's only fair. Do you think we're ever going to get to the front of this line?"

"One of these years, my boy."

Mr. Romano gazed over at a display that contained a lot of cassette tapes. These were authentic recordings and interviews of players and events from major league baseball's past. The display sat on top of a glass chest that all had to pass on their way to Ryne Sandberg's table. "Hey, look what they got here, Eddie."

"What, Dad?"

"They've got original recordings of a couple of the ballplayers we were talking about."

"Who, Dad?"

"Well, they've got the Babe talking baseball, and look, that's Lou Gehrig's farewell speech from Yankee Stadium. How would you like to have those, Eddie?"

"Wow! Yeah. Please, Dad!"

"Your wish is my command," Mr. Romano said, trying his best to imitate the genie from Aladdin's lamp.

"Thanks, Dad, but do me a favor. Don't quit your day job, okay?" Eddie wisecracked.

Mr. Romano waved at the clerk and got his attention. "I figured as long as we're going to be waiting here in this line, we might as well do a little business."

"Just these two, sir?"

"Yup. How much longer do you think we've got?"

"The line seems to be moving pretty quickly now. A few minutes at the most," stated the clerk.

"Eddie, we'll be up there in no time." Mr. Romano yawned in boredom as he handed Eddie the cassettes.

"Thanks again, Dad. I can't wait to get home to listen to these."

"I've heard that Lou Gehrig recording before. It's quite a speech. He tells the crowd that he feels like he's the luckiest man on the planet even though he's very, very ill. Well, that's depressing. Let's get on to a more uplifting topic. Are we going to go see the White Sox play again this year?"

"You bet we are. Boy, didn't we have a lot of fun last year? That Jack McDowell is becoming some kind of pitcher, huh, Dad?"

"Yes indeed," Mr. Romano responded subconsciously while his thoughts were somewhere else. He wistfully added, "You know, Eddie, it's going to be strange going to that new ballpark this year. I had a lot of great times in that old one. A lot of memories are dying with that old ballpark."

"That's right. They're tearing the old ballpark down. I forgot all about that, Dad."

"Incredible. They're supposedly making it into a parking lot. I heard on the news that they began tearing it down earlier this week."

"Dad, do they wreck ballparks on Sundays?"

"No, I don't think so, my boy. Sunday is a day of rest except for those who like to wait in lines at baseball card shows," Mr. Romano answered facetiously.

"I'll bet you that there are a lot of great souvenirs to be found at that old ballpark."

"Probably. I mean, hell, they've been playing there for ages."

"Well, if they're not working today, I don't know why we can't go down there and hunt for some souvenirs?"

"I'll tell you why not. Construction sites are dangerous, Eddie."

"Live a little. Will you? There's still plenty of daylight left, and I'm sure we'll be careful. Never know what we might find, Dad."

"Eddie, that's out of the question. It's also against the law."

"I won't tell if you don't tell, Dad. Come on, Dad, this is a chance of a lifetime. I mean, Dad, how many times do they wreck famous ballparks?"

"Not often, Eddie, but…"

"Please, Dad. I promise I'll be real careful. It will be so much fun. We can go on our first adventure together. Please!" Eddie begged.

"Why do you have to do this to me? I knew I should never have brought that up. Damn it, Eddie, you're a pain in the ass, you know that?"

"But that's why you love me so much," Eddie said affectionately.

"Well, I'm not promising you anything except that we'll go down there and check it out. If it looks too dangerous, we're not going to go hunting around, understand, kid?"

"Yes, Dad. I knew you'd see it my way. That's why I tell all the kids in the neighborhood that I've got the coolest father ever," Eddie flattered.

"Don't be a smart-ass. Now go get your autograph and let's get out of here."

Eddie walked over and shook hands with Ryne Sandberg, and despite the fact that he was a Chicago Cub and Eddie an avid White Sox fan, he was elated to have him autograph his baseball glove. Mr. Romano was amazed to find out that there was no price tag involved for the transaction. Eddie turned back toward his father gleefully and said, "Let's go."

FINDING A SOUVENIR

The Romano's Toyota Corolla sedan pulled up alongside the curb near where Comiskey Park used to be. The old ballpark was no longer recognizable. Wrecking balls had literally pounded the infrastructure into the ground.

Both Romanos exited the car and stared in disbelief at what used to be a ballpark. What was left reminded Mr. Romano of pictures he had seen of Germany after World War II. All of what used to be was just a memory now. Surrounding the wrecking site were long sawhorse-like blockades that were put up by the police department to discourage trespassers. The area was covered with yellow plastic tape strips that warned trespassers of eminent danger.

"You really want to go through with this?" Mr. Romano asked.

"Come on, Dad, sometimes you've gotta break the rules."

"I suppose. But if it looks too hazardous, we're going back, understand?"

"Sure, Dad," Eddie said unconvinced.

"I can't believe I let you talk me into this. I feel like I'm the eleven year old. Who's the adult here anyway?"

"You are, Dad. Come on, it's going to be fun," coaxed Eddie.

On that note, the two climbed over the barriers and entered the forbidden zone. The two carefully navigated their way through the wreckage. The path that they walked along was shaded by the remnants of the once-proud stadium. Mr. Romano didn't understand it, but as he progressed, he felt that forgotten but once familiar childhood rush. He was actually breaking the rules, and he felt good about it. He reminisced back to his child-hood when he and his friends used to explore the sewers in his hometown. He recalled how he used to spend entire afternoons walking through drainage pipes in search of treasures, like dead animals or other such notable things of interest to young boys. He couldn't believe that he was actively participating alongside his son on one of these great adventures. He kept asking himself, "How old are you?" He shook his head in amazement when he pondered the thought of being the father of an eleven-year-old boy. How time had flown by was the predominant thought on his mind during this adventure.

The two continued farther into the wreckage when Eddie spotted a baseball wedged underneath a couple of wooden boards.

"Dad, look! It's a baseball. I told you that this trip would be worth it, didn't I?"

"You sure did, my boy," he said, totally amused by Eddie's childish antics.

Eddie grabbed the mostly white baseball and quickly rubbed the dirt off of it. "I wonder what year this ball's from."

"I don't know, Eddie. Despite popular opinion, even I don't have all the answers. Too me, all baseballs look pretty much the same."

The two then continued on with their exploration. Their path was impeded by an earth-moving machine. This piece of heavy equipment was left in the middle of the wreckage by the workers, who presumably would continue their excavation on Monday. As the Romano duo circumvented the earth mover, Eddie noticed that the earth mover's shovel had broken the ground. Eddie peered down into the hole the earth mover had created and something green caught his eye. This was something unusual.

"Dad, what the heck is that?" Eddie asked, pointing down into the hole at the green object.

"I don't know. Here, let me help you. You go down there and take a look."

"Dad, it's kind of deep."

"Well, I'm certainly not going down there. So if you want to find out for yourself, I'll give you a hand, other than that, let's keep on moving."

"Hold on! I'm going."

Mr. Romano made a loud sigh and then held both of Eddie's arms as he lowered him down into the hole. Eddie was relieved when his feet finally hit the ground.

"Dad, move! You're blocking my light."

Mr. Romano stepped away from the hole, and Eddie knelt down by the green object. As he touched it, he immediately recognized the leather texture. Instantaneously, he dug it out with his hands. He looked it over in amazement.

"Dad, it's some kind of fancy baseball glove. You should see it. It's really cool. It has all kinds of fancy artwork on it."

"Well, bring it up and let me take a look at it."

Mr. Romano reached his hand down in the hole and Eddie grasped on to it. Mr. Romano proceeded to pull Eddie up and out of the ditch.

"Let me take a look at that," Mr. Romano demanded as he took the green infielder's glove from Eddie. "Wow, Eddie, this glove's ancient. We're talking the forties here, maybe even earlier. And look at all the intricate artwork done on it. This had to be somebody's pride and joy. I wonder how it got buried like that. It must have been a practical joke that got played on somebody. You know this is an infielder's glove, Eddie? You have no idea how rare this glove is. It's for a southpaw like you. I don't know if you know it, but traditionally, most southpaws don't play the infield."

"I don't care what kind of glove it is, Dad. Just give it back," Eddie demanded.

"Well, that's a nice attitude, son. Here, take your glove." Mr. Romano threw the glove over toward Eddie, who caught it and held it tightly.

"I think it's time to get out of here Eddie," Mr. Romano notified as he was obviously annoyed with Eddie's bad attitude.

"I like this glove. It's a pro glove, and I'm going to use it from now on," Eddie announced, wrapping both his arms around it.

"It's your glove Eddie. Do what you want with it."

"That's right, Dad. At least we got that straight. It is my glove and from now on, nobody is touching it. You hear me?"

"Calm down, son. Nobody wants to touch your glove. Gee, what in hell has gotten into you, kid? We were having such a nice day, and now you've got to catch an attitude and go and spoil it all."

Eddie didn't respond but followed his father out of the wrecking site.

THE TRUE MEANING
OF HELL

He didn't know what day or year it was. He had no con-
cept of time. His only "friend," speaking in the loosest of
terms, stood in the shadows most of the time in a baseball
dugout. He was not allowed full access to that dugout either, and
it annoyed him that he could only go as far as the stairwell that led
there. He was utterly confused. He looked up at the perpetual overcast sky and it was a constant reminder of how dismal and dreary his
existence had become. He had nothing to do and all the time in the
world to think and obsess about it. There was nobody to talk to. He
was, for the most part, doing a life sentence in solitary confinement.

The ballpark that he now called home was one he was not
familiar with. He was sure that he never played at this place
before. He spent a lot of time examining and re-examining
his whereabouts, trying to figure out what city it belonged in.
It was nothing like Comiskey Park and that was the last place
he remembered being at. He really missed Michael and wanted
more than anything to dream about him and the good times they
shared, but when he slept he had a recurring nightmare. The only
dreams he seemed capable of having were ones that repeated the
events of the worst night of his life, and because of this he tried
not to sleep at all. Sometimes he was unable to accomplish this

seemingly monumental feat and he ended up reliving his only night in the Major Leagues. He heard the fans heckling him over and over again after each fielding error. He saw that jerk in the stands angrily telling him that he'd be better off dead. He ducked when those kids threw apples at him and verbally abused him, ranting about how their throwing accuracy was better than his. He remembered how his teammates refused to look at him, which made him feel even more like an outcast. Tears welled in the corner of his eyes as he sat by himself, shaking his head sadly and praying to God to make this nightmare go away.

The monotonous silence was suddenly broken as the Manager stepped out of the dugout and declared, "We're going to have company."

The sound of his voice jerked him back to reality, and with a blank stare he tried to comprehend the words the Manager had just uttered. He gathered himself and looked over at the distinguished looking man in black and replied in surprise, "Visitors?"

"No. Visitor. Some kid has your glove. I think he needs some coaching. I think you're the man for the job. We're going to give him the same deal I gave you, but let's see to it that he doesn't renege, okay? Don't let me down. This kid is your ticket home. Understand me?"

"Yeah, loud and clear. I'll do whatever is necessary to get back home. You promise I'll get there, right?"

"Oh yeah. You'll get there."

EDDIE'S ADDICTION

At home, the unique green painted baseball glove became the major topic of conversation as the Romano's gathered at the dining room table for their evening meal.

"Eddie, take that dirty glove off your mother's table," Mr. Romano ordered. Eddie took his glove off of the table as instructed and rested it upon his lap. It was evident that he was paying more attention to the glove than the dinner being held around him.

Mrs. Romano had spent hours cooking her son's favorite meal, spaghetti and meatballs. She had labored over the meat sauce, an old family recipe that always put a smile on Eddie's face. She found it quite odd that all her time and efforts seemed to have been wasted upon an unusually, uninterested eleven-year-old. She stared at him disconcertedly and tried her best to be "doctor mom."

"Eddie, are you feeling okay?"

"Yeah, Mom," Eddie responded apathetically as he picked at the meal in front of him.

"Eddie, is the sauce okay?" she asked with concern.

"Don't bother with him. He's been like this ever since he found that stupid glove," Mr. Romano explained, wearing a large frown of frustration.

"Didn't the two of you have a nice day together?" Mrs. Romano inquired in astonishment.

"The day went fine, Lucy. I don't know. Maybe the kid is going through a phase, but to be honest with you, I've never seen anything quite like it. He was an absolute delight—clever, witty, and totally charming until he found that ugly glove."

"Mom, can I be excused?" Eddie asked nonchalantly, making light of his dad's growing anxiety.

"But, Eddie, you hardly even touched your meal."

"I think I just lost my appetite."

"Listen Ed, if you're not going to eat after your mother slaved all day long to make you this good supper, then you better not even think about coming down here later on to munch out. I'll put a freaking padlock on that refrigerator. I'm not kidding you, kid. You're really starting to piss me off," Mr. Romano said exasperatedly.

"I'm not hungry. May I be excused?" Eddie asked flippantly.

"Go! Get out of here!" Mr. Romano snapped impatiently.

Eddie got up from the table and ran upstairs to his bedroom carrying his special glove and cassettes. Mr. Romano shook his head at his wife in disapproval and then continued to eat.

"He seems mighty attached to that baseball glove. Where did you find it?" Mrs. Romano queried.

"You'd never believe me if I told you," Mr. Romano announced calmly, feeling the weight of the world being lifted off his shoulders since Eddie was no longer in sight.

"Try me."

"You're probably not going to like this, but we went scavenging through the debris at the old Comiskey Park, and we found it there."

"Vince, are you crazy? Don't you know that demolition sites are dangerous?"

"Well, of course I know that. Look, the kid had his mind set on going, and you know how he is when he has his mind set on something, so I brought him. Shoot me."

"Well, at least you two are okay."

"Let's put it this way. I'm okay. I'm not too sure about the kid."

"He's probably just tired and cranky. I wouldn't worry too much about it. He's had a long day."

"Yeah. You're probably right."

"I'll say one thing though, that glove looks to be in pretty good shape. That's a nice find," Mrs. Romano marveled.

"It surprised the shit out of me. You know that's an old glove. It had to be in the ground for at least forty or fifty years. It's just amazing that it isn't deteriorated."

"They must have treated the leather with something special or maybe it wasn't in the ground as long as you think," Mrs. Romano hypothesized.

"Possibly, but the kid found it buried in a hole that was dug out by an earth-moving machine," Mr. Romano pointed out.

Mrs. Romano gave him a puzzled look. They both finished their evening meal in peace.

A LOOK INTO THE PAST

Eddie sat on his bed listening to the cassette tapes his father bought for him at the memorabilia show. He looked over at the posters of the major league ballplayers he had pinned to his bedroom walls. He kept making mental comparisons between his antique glove and the gloves his heroes wore. He didn't understand why he was so attracted to his new glove; he just knew he was. Ever since he found the glove it had a hold on him, the same kind of effect that a narcotic has on an addict. Not to say that Eddie knew anything about narcotics since he certainly didn't, but like a drug, the glove became a source of security for him.

He listened to the recording of Babe Ruth talking baseball for the third time. The more he listened to it, the more he found that he had a natural affinity toward baseball's greatest legend. He also enjoyed the calming effect that Ruth's earthy-type voice had on him. He got up off the bed and grabbed a copy of the *Baseball Encyclopedia* off his shelf. He handled the book with tender loving care since it was a gift from his father. He looked up Babe Ruth and examined his lifetime statistics.

He marveled at his 342 career batting average and the two seasons in which he hit 59 and 60 home runs. He stared over at the poster of Cecil Fielder on his wall and knew that he would never look at it in quite the same way again. To Eddie, Fielder's 51 home runs and 277 batting average in 1990 was a joke when compared to Ruth's 59 home runs and 378 batting average in 1921. He concluded that the baseball legends of the past were obviously of higher quality than the legends of the game today. He examined his new glove and smiled at it in adoration. Since finding it, he had never been so happy. His glove was from the past, and now after close examination of the facts, his heroes would be too.

The phone rang abruptly, disturbing the moment's peace and tranquility. Eddie picked up the receiver.

"Hello."

"Hi, Eddie."

"What do you want, Johnny?" Eddie asked in an unfriendly tone of voice.

"Well, excuse me. My father told me to call you and tell you that we're having practice the day after tomorrow. So are you going to be there?"

"Sure. What time?"

"Four thirty for you. He says that you and Billy Ray both need some extra batting practice. I concurred wholeheartedly," Johnny answered arrogantly.

"Yeah. Well, did he include you on the list too?"

"No. Now why would he do something like that? Everybody knows I'm the best hitter on the team," Johnny needled.

"Not for long."

"Oh yeah? Who do you propose is going to take away my title?" Johnny asked, stunned by Eddie's reply.

"Me."

"You?" Johnny chuckled. "What is this, an episode of *Candid Camera*? I got it. This is a goof call being recorded for one of those morning radio shows."

"Yeah. Think what you want but you'll see."

"You're serious, aren't you? What a joke. You know something, Eddie, when I first met you, I thought you were a nice kid. A lousy ballplayer but a nice kid, but do you know what I think now?" Johnny asked condescendingly.

"No. And quite frankly, I don't give a damn."

The next thing Johnny heard was the sound of a dial tone. Eddie stared down in amazement at the phone receiver he had just hung up. He marveled over his newly found courage. He didn't know why he had this feeling that he could actually do the things he was saying. He just knew that he felt that he could and that was making all the difference in the world to him.

He got off his bed and inserted that new cassette into his boom box. Lou Gehrig's famous farewell speech from Yankee Stadium blared out through the speakers. Remembering what his father had said about Gehrig made the speech very touching to him. It just didn't seem fair to him that this humble voice was extinguished at such an early age. Eddie started to say a prayer for poor Lou Gehrig and also prayed that he would never die from disease. He reasoned that death by disease was unnatural and therefore painful. Eddie knew firsthand that he didn't want anything to do with pain. He flashed back to when he was five years old and had to get his tonsils removed. He remembered in vivid detail that painful ordeal and how his parents had tricked him into going to the hospital. Before he allowed the doctors to anesthetize him, he was assured by his parents that this was standard procedure for an astronaut before taking a trip into space. Eddie recalled how he woke up with the worst sore throat of his life. He thought it was a really mean trick, and he felt that experience had made him an expert on pain. If Gehrig had suffered anything like that, Eddie surmised, he must have welcomed death. Eddie looked up Lou Gehrig's statistics in the *Baseball Encyclopedia* and was thoroughly impressed. He sat down and compared his statistics with Hank Aaron's and concluded that Gehrig was a Hank Aaron–type power hitter with a much higher batting average.

All this research was making him very tired. His eyes became very heavy, and his mind started to wander off toward destinations unknown. It was like watching a continuous movie marathon of different faces and voices with very little plot to the stories when suddenly Eddie found himself looking into a bedroom. Its furnishings were very old, reminding him of the background set for that television show *Leave it to Beaver*. This room contained an early model black-and-white television set that rested upon a beat-up old oak writing table. In this bedroom, an intelligible drama was taking place. This was definitely a baseball player's room. Posted on the walls were many newspaper clippings of accounts of games. The teams they referred to though were not recognizable. Resting upon a cheap dresser was Eddie's green baseball glove. A ballplayer, wearing a uniform, was lying in bed. He was restlessly tossing and turning. He kept repeating the same phrases over and over again as if he was trying to brainwash himself. He repeated monotonously, "I'm finally going to the majors, and I'd rather die than come back here."

Eddie observed and listened to the monotone speech of the ballplayer until finally another voice could be heard.

"Would you really rather die than go back to the minors?"

"You better believe it," the ballplayer responded, sounding almost like he was sleepwalking.

"I'm not so sure. I don't think you've got the guts to harm yourself," the voice goaded.

"You'd be surprised at the kind of guts you develop after fourteen years down here," the ballplayer whispered with his eyes completely closed.

"I'm not convinced. I don't think your heart is in it. I think you're used to this place. This has become your home. You've got a minor leaguer's mentality. You've really got no pride anymore."

"What in hell do you know? I'm telling you that I'll kill myself before I ever get sent back down here again. And I mean it.

Nobody is going to be able to talk me out of this," the ballplayer argued passionately.

"Do you swear it?" The voice laughed in complete ecstasy.

"Yes, I swear it. I'd even shake on it. Face it, if your word is no good, then you're no good," the ballplayer theorized.

"Those are words of wisdom, my boy. Those are truly words of wisdom. I'll probably live to regret this because it goes against my better judgment to trust you or anybody for that matter but I'm going to give you a chance. I'm going to bless this gaudy mitt of yours and give you what you've always wanted out of life, but if you renege on me and our agreement, you will spend all of eternity regretting the moment you did and that's not a threat my young disciple—that is a promise. And I will see to it that you will live up to your word and kill yourself if you try to cheat me and go back on your promise. Just remember your handshake signifies a binding contract with me. Now, it's time to shake on it!" the dark man said with exuberance.

The ballplayer stopped rambling about killing himself and fell back asleep, and soon after Eddie saw a very distinguished looking man in a dark suit appear at his bedside. The man in black leaned over the sleeping ballplayer and grasped on to his right hand, shaking it severely. He then forced the player's hand into the baseball glove that Eddie found. The ballplayer woke up suddenly, but the man in black was nowhere to be found. The ballplayer looked amazed as he stared down at his right hand and saw that he was wearing his dolled up glove.

"What a weird dream that one was. I could almost swear someone was shaking my hand. Wow. And how did my glove get on my hand? I swear it was on the desk when I went to bed. Something funny is going on around here, but you know something, I'm just too tired and too depressed to worry about it now. God, I really hate my life. You know sleep has become my only solace. That's why I need to get back to sleep. I really can't take much more of this," the ballplayer declared in frustration and self-pity.

Suddenly, Eddie jumped up. He must have dozed off. He thought, *Now that's a cool dream.* He got up, turned off the lights, and dropped his *Baseball Encyclopedia* on to the floor. He then closed his eyes again, hoping to resume that dream. Eddie never caught up with that first dream ever again. It shared the same destiny of most dreams, becoming lost in the thoughts of the waking mind, but other dreams would become prevalent and the details of those dreams would never be forgotten.

SLEEPING YOUR
LIFE AWAY

Eddie went to school but it seemed to all who knew him that he was just sleepwalking through it. He was going through the motions of being an ordinary middle school kid and that's all. He would sit in his classroom, literally stare out the window, and not take a single note. He had no interest in school anymore. As far as the world was concerned, they could clearly see that he had decided to become a drop out. His teachers stared curiously over at him, wondering what had gone wrong. His whole attitude had changed overnight and let me add, not for the better. He used to be a very good student. He was attentive and answered questions in class, but now he was unresponsive. He told them not to bother him and just sat there fiddling with his old, antique baseball glove.

Mrs. West, his English teacher, was so alarmed by this new behavior that she wrote down in her daily planner that a parent-teacher conference needed to be arranged immediately. She had asked Eddie for his essay and he had flippantly told her to "bug off." Eddie had never been disrespectful to his elders before.

Mercifully, as far as Eddie was concerned, the final bell rang and he and his classmates stampeded towards the awaiting school buses. Eddie quickly boarded his bus and sat impatiently waiting to get home. He never said a word to anyone. It was almost like he was being drawn into his own private fantasy world. It was a world of obsession. That glove literally was all that Eddie was concerned with anymore. He held it in a vise grip and never let it out of his sight.

As soon as he got home he raced up the stairs to his bedroom and shouted down to his mother that he needed to take a nap.

Mrs. Romano ran up the stairs after him and inquired, "Is there something wrong, Eddie?"

"No, mom. Everything's great. I just need to rest. It was a long day at school and I'm still worn out from that treasure hunt that Dad and I went on yesterday," Eddie asserted.

"I didn't get a chance to tell you, but I like your mitt. I felt like wringing your father's neck for bringing you to such a dangerous spot, but you certainly were rewarded. I don't think I've ever seen a glove like that one."

"It is really cool. I don't think I've ever liked anything as much as I like it. I wouldn't sell it, no matter what. It's so one of a kind, I can't believe it. I'm the luckiest kid in the world, Mom," Eddie declared as he jumped off his bed to give his mother a big hug. He added, "I'm so happy that you love it too."

"I never was lucky enough to find anything like that. I'm sure that was somebody's pride and joy. I'm sure they would be happy that a nice boy like you found it. I know if I lost something special I would want the finder to truly cherish it."

"I do, Mom. I do cherish it. Don't tell Dad, but it makes me dream," Eddie said while holding the glove proudly.

"Well, I don't want to disturb your dreams, so I won't wake you until supper's ready at six, okay?"

"Yeah, Mom. That would be fantastic. I'm starting to get sleepy right now. I can't wait to dream. I can hear my pillow calling for me. Goodnight, Mom. I love you."

"Goodnight, Eddie. Sweet dreams," Mrs. Romano whispered as she closed Eddie's bedroom door.

Eddie held his glove against his heart and quickly fell into a deep sleep. He began to dream and saw numerous human faces flash through his mind until he was staring up at the most beautiful, handsome face he had ever seen. *This must be a dream*, he thought, but suddenly this handsome young man spoke to him.

"Eddie, Eddie, wake up. You're here!" The handsome man in the old-fashioned Chicago White Sox uniform said.

"Where?" Eddie asked in confusion.

"You're with me."

"Who are you?" Eddie questioned in amazement.

"I'm your coach. I'm your dream coach."

"A dream coach?" Eddie asked in utter fascination.

"I've been waiting an awfully long time for you, Eddie. So you're the boy who found my glove. Let me take a look at it. Wow! It hasn't changed a bit since the last time I saw it," the dream coach remarked.

"It hasn't? Just tell me one thing. Please tell me that you don't want to take it back," Eddie worried aloud.

"No. It's yours to keep, Eddie. I'm here just to teach you how to use it. It's 'magic.'"

"I knew it," Eddie gloated. He then added, "So you're going to teach me how to control the magic. You're going to be my new best friend, aren't you?"

"That's right."

"Well, in that case, give me a hand up, will you?"

"Certainly," the dream coach replied, dragging Eddie to his feet.

Eddie looked around curiously at the abandoned stadium. The actual field was very well manicured, but the building itself was weathered with age. It looked like it must have been a palace at one time, but somebody forgot to maintain it.

"The field's nice, but the place is a dump. Do you live here?"

"Yes."

"Are you by yourself?"

"At the moment, but that won't always be the case."

"Where do you sleep?"

"I don't. Well, occasionally I do."

"That's not what I asked you. I asked you where you slept," Eddie queried.

"Oh, I sleep sometimes on the roof of the dugout and other times on the grass of the field. Don't you love the smell of freshly cut grass?"

"Yes. I do indeed. It must be depressing to live here. It seems awfully dreary. Where's the sun?"

"I don't know. I never see it. Look, let's not waste any more time with chit chat because I have a job to do. I'm supposed to teach you how to play baseball like a real pro. Would you like to learn?"

"There's nothing I would enjoy more than learning how to be a great ballplayer," Eddie stated affirmatively. He added, "I hope you realize, I'm going to be a real project."

"That's what I'm here for. That's why they pay me the big bucks," the dream coach vocally projected in a most sarcastic manner, as if he was on stage, hoping that someone important might just hear his gripe.

"I thought nobody's here with us."

"Believe me, nobody is. I guess that's what you call wishful thinking. Well, where do I begin? I guess we'll try to improve your hitting."

Eddie and the dream coach worked on lots of fundamentals of hitting and fielding until Mrs. Romano created a cacophony by banging loudly on the bedroom door. The startling noise shocked Eddie back to reality. Suddenly he was swept away from that field of play back to the familiar confines of his bedroom.

"Wow! What a trip," Eddie screamed out as he arrived back in his bed.

"Are you coming down for dinner?" Mrs. Romano urgently inquired. Then she obnoxiously added, "If you are, you better hurry before your food gets cold. Hello! Earth to Eddie! Did you hear me?" She asked while making more rude noises by slapping her hands together.

"Loud and clear. Give me a moment, will you?" Eddie begged as he gathered himself mentally to go and enjoy dinner with his family.

A NEWFOUND CONFIDENCE

E ddie and his teammates gathered together at the old high school practice field backstop. The field was a bit on the dilapidated side due to constant use over the years. It was a familiar landmark for the little leaguers. Many of them had seen their older brother's play and practice on this same field during days gone by.

Eddie hated the practice field because of the many rocks hidden within its sparse infield grass. They had a tendency to cause ground balls to bounce funny. On one occasion, the year before, he had a baseball take a bad hop off one of them and strike him in the forehead. He recalled the embarrassment of going to school with a big knot in his forehead.

Mr. Mitchell, the manager of the team and his son, Johnny, traversed their way toward the practice field. Johnny dragged the team's equipment bag behind him and stopped to slap hands with all his teammates except for Eddie, whom he made a point of sneering at. Upon arrival, Mr. Mitchell told both Eddie and Billy Ray to grab their bats and start taking some batting practice. He told the rest of the team to go out and play the field.

"Are you sure that's necessary, Dad? I mean, look who's batting. Those two are hopeless. They couldn't hit the ball if their lives depended on it." Johnny snickered.

"Why don't you shut up, Johnny? I can hit the ball better than you can," Eddie asserted after overhearing the insult.

"What a laugh. This is the same kid talking who struck out on our last turn at bat. What can I say? Yeah, man, you're a real clutch hitter!" Johnny screamed sarcastically.

Johnny scrutinized Eddie, while he was selecting a bat out of the equipment bag, and he paid special attention to the old green glove that he was carrying. "What's the matter, Eddie, can't afford to buy a new glove? Where'd you get that one from? Let me guess…the Goodwill Industries?" Johnny laughed boisterously.

"Keep on laughing, Johnny. This is a pro glove. And it happens to be magical. It's a lot better than anything you've got," Eddie boasted.

"Eddie, what are you doing with that glove? That glove is way too big for your hand. What happened to your other one?" Mr. Mitchell inquired.

"It's autographed by Ryne Sandberg, so I'm using this one instead, plus, this one's magical, Mr. Mitchell."

"I'm sure it's magical, Eddie, but it's too big for your hand," Mr. Mitchell said patronizingly.

"And it's a piece of junk to boot," added Johnny cruelly. "Magical? What a joke," he screamed and chuckled for all to hear.

"Tell you what, I'll use it today. If I don't play well with it, then I'll bring the other mitt next time," Eddie bargained.

"That's fair. Come on! Let's get started. Stevie, you're on the mound. Keith, get behind the plate. The rest of you spread out. Stevie, give them the best stuff you've got. They're never going to improve if you give them gofer balls to hit because that's not what they'll be seeing during the games."

"Gotcha, Coach," replied Stevie. The average-sized twelve-year-old pitcher started to warm up slowly, throwing the ball back and forth with Keith. With each toss, the velocity increased, and Eddie examined Stevie's pitching form with great interest.

Eddie knew in the back of his mind that Johnny was right when he claimed to be the best hitter on the team, but since finding his magic glove, he felt a great confidence boost. Previously, he had always approached the batter's box with a feeling of imminent doom, but today, he actually felt like he could get a hit. His father always told him that he looked scared while standing in the batter's box. It was true, he was always afraid of being hit by a wild, fast pitch, but today those fears for the most part subsided. Today he stepped into the batter's box fearlessly.

Mr. Mitchell immediately noticed a difference in Eddie's approach. He looked confident. He looked like he owned the dish. He was astonished to see Eddie crowding the plate. As he looked on, he took mental notes on how completely changed the boy's approach to hitting had become. All he could do was keep repeating, "Wow, Eddie, you're looking so much better."

Stevie noticed the difference too. Stevie recalled how his father told him explicitly that if a hitter ever tried to crowd the plate, he was to throw at him. Stevie sensed that Eddie was trying to take control of "his" turf, so he followed his father's instructions and reared back and threw a fastball at Eddie's head.

Eddie jumped back, just in the nick of time and fell on the seat of his pants. He got up, dusted himself off, and stood in the same exact position in the batter's box he occupied before.

"Watch the bean balls, Stevie," Mr. Mitchell warned and added, "Way to hang in there, Eddie."

Stevie reared back and threw another fastball; this time, it ended up a foot outside.

"Why don't you try throwing the ball over the plate?" Eddie asked in a surly tone of voice while pointing his finger at the plate.

Stevie was immediately enraged. He was the best pitcher on the team and one of the weakest hitters had just directed a derogatory remark at him. At that moment, the only thing on his mind was that Eddie Romano was not going to make him look foolish. He was going to put a quick end to this tough-guy routine.

"Come on, Stevie! You don't have to pitch to him carefully. He's a wiffer. He's always been a wiffer. Strike the bum out!" Johnny screamed out obnoxiously.

Stevie was taking too much time getting ready, so Eddie stepped out of the batter's box and walked over and picked up his magic glove. He gave it a quick kiss, set it down, and returned to the batter's box.

Stevie sneered over at Eddie and spit intimidatingly in his direction. Stevie wound up and pitched a letter high fastball over the middle of the plate, and Eddie hit it with the sweet spot of the aluminum bat barrel. The ball took off as if it was fired from a rocket launcher and soared over the left fielder's head.

Eddie stood and watched the flight of the ball in complete amazement. Never in his entire life had he hit a ball any harder. Superstitiously, he retreated back to his glove and kissed it again. He then marched back into the batter's box. "Stevie, pitch me another one just like that," Eddie said with a smile.

Stevie was not amused with Eddie's newfound confidence and proceeded to deliver another bean ball that failed to hit its mark. Eddie got up from the ground quickly and dusted himself off once again.

"You throw at me again, and I'm going to take this bat to your head. Understand, Stevie?" Eddie forewarned.

Stevie could see from the fire in Eddie's eyes that he meant business and that was the last time he ever attempted to throw at him. Stevie, now more than slightly intimidated, reared back and threw a fastball knee high over the center of the plate, and Eddie bent down and took a golf swing at it, driving the ball over the center fielder's head.

Eddie learned an important lesson that day and that is success builds confidence. This is not to say that every time Eddie stepped into the batter's box he was successful because that wasn't the case, but unlike previous outings, he went to the plate with the knowledge that he had the ability to be successful. His teammates instantly gained a new respect for his prowess with the bat. Most importantly during practices they would no longer play the outfield at a shallow depth when Eddie came to the plate.

After receiving much praise from Mr. Mitchell, Eddie took his green glove over to the shortstop area and prepared for fielding practice. He found very little opportunity to field while Billy Ray was at bat. Billy Ray looked like the same weak hitter he had always been. After watching him strike out five times in a row, Mr. Mitchell decided not to waste the team's practice time attempting to improve Billy Ray's hitting. Mr. Mitchell then told the team to fall into their respective positions and that he would hit them some grounders. Billy Ray and Eddie were both shortstops and alternated taking turns fielding the hard grounders that were smashed their way. Mr. Mitchell was amazed at how well Eddie fielded ground balls with that antique mitt that seemed way too big for his hand. His teammates were quite surprised too. Eddie was usually barely adequate as a fielder, but he didn't make an error. If the truth is to be told, he made a number of impressive diving stabs of well-hit line drives off the bat of Johnny. Johnny was so mad that Eddie had showed him up that he threw his bat down in disgust.

When the practice was over, Eddie's teammates came up to congratulate him on his improvement, but he walked away without acknowledging any of them. Billy Ray, who was always Eddie's best friend on the team, was surprised by his attitude. He shouted at him saying, "Eddie, they're just trying to be friendly. Eddie, did you hear me? Eddie, what's wrong with you?" Eddie pretended he was deaf and ignored Billy Ray and exited the practice field by himself.

"He thinks he's too good for us now. Today was just a fluke. You watch, tomorrow he'll play just as crummy as he always does. The only difference will be, that no one will feel sorry for him when he screws up, especially after today's display," Johnny announced bitterly to his teammates.

"He gets a few lucky hits, and he becomes all stuck up. What a clown," Stevie commented resentfully.

"C'mon, fellas, leave him alone. He's probably having problems at home. Just get off his case. He's improving and that helps the team. Believe me, that is a benefit to all of us. Okay?" Mr. Mitchell pleaded.

The team begrudgingly grunted an assent to their coach's demand and hurried away from the practice field.

LET'S MAKE A DEAL
OR A BATTLE
IS BREWING

Eddie came home from practice and without even say-ing hello went straight upstairs to his room. His mother, who was in the kitchen preparing the evening meal, saw only his shadow as he climbed the stairs. She found this behavior quite odd and climbed the stairs after him. She found him lying on his bed.

"You tired again, honey?"

"No. I just want to be left alone," Eddie stated in a totally self-absorbed state of mind.

"Practice didn't go well, huh?"

"No. It went great."

"Did the team like your new mitt?"

"Johnny made fun of it, but that was to be expected."

"Well I made you a nice dinner, fried chicken with mash pota-toes and corn."

"Sounds great, Mom, but I'm really not hungry."

Mrs. Romano looked over at the many baseball player posters hanging on the wall and said, "Eddie, if you don't eat, you'll never make it to the major leagues."

"You've got a point there, Mom. Give me a little time to myself, and I'll be down later."

"Good. Your father will be home a little bit late this evening, so maybe you two could eat together."

"That's a possibility."

"You sure you're all right, honey?" his mother asked, again sensing that something was wrong.

"Just fine, Mom," Eddie insisted.

Mrs. Romano looked at him suspiciously. She had some kind of intuition or a mother's sixth sense that trouble was brewing, but since Eddie wouldn't fess up to anything bothering him, she just shrugged it off and closed his bedroom door.

He got off his bed and pushed the play button on his cassette player and listened to Babe Ruth talking baseball again. He listened to the same tired recordings so many times it was hard to believe that they continued to interest him. It wasn't long before Eddie started to tire and soon he lay daydreaming on his bed, wearing his green glove. Before he knew it, he found himself back at that incredibly dreary major league ballpark, taking infield practice from the same young, handsome, ballplayer he had met the night before. In Eddie's eyes, the ballplayer was the only thing that wasn't dreary about this place. Somehow he seemed out of place. He just seemed to have way too much energy and life in him to be hanging out in such a drab and dismal place. His entire persona was vibrant and bright from his ancient White Sox uniform to his patent leather green baseball cleats. There was one thing for certain about this guy, he was an original. He reminded Eddie of an old-fashioned version of the football icon "Neon" Deion Sanders. He must have been the first prototype of the trend that would encompass sports in the years to come. He just seemed very ostentatious, and he caught the ball like a real showboat. Every time Eddie would throw him the ball back, after fielding it, the ballplayer would catch the ball as if he was a Harlem Globetrotter basketball player. He put on a show, catching the ball barehanded or behind his back, using a remarkably plain-looking baseball glove.

Realizing that Eddie was pretty much warmed up as far as "easy" fielding was concerned, he threw that plain-looking glove on the ground and picked up a bat. He decided that it was now time to truly test the boy's prowess with the glove. He tossed a ball into the air and smashed it with the bat toward Eddie, whom he had playing shortstop. The ball skipped underneath Eddie's glove uncontested. Eddie looked between his legs in amazement as it whizzed by.

"Damn, you hit that ball hard!" Eddie exclaimed.

"Eddie, you've got to get your entire body in front of the ball. That way if it takes a bad hop, you keep it in the infield. That could save your team a run someday. Believe me, I'm talking from personal experience now. I learned that lesson the hard way. I flubbed way too many of them in my day," said the ballplayer whose wisdom seemed to be far greater than his apparent years.

"I can't believe that you ever flubbed anything," Eddie said in astonishment.

"Kid, believe me, I made my mistakes." Before another word could be said along these lines, somebody dark and menacing walked out of the dugout. As he came into view, Eddie saw that he was a very distinguished-looking man wearing a dark suit. He just stood near the ballplayer as if to make his presence known.

"I guess you weren't lying, there are other people here," Eddie commented.

"I may not always speak the truth, but I never lie, Eddie. By the way, I have to tell you one more thing, and that is if you want to continue to improve your play, you're going to have to start wishing that your teammates do poorly," the ballplayer said under the silent duress of the ominous figure in black.

"Really? You mean I could lose the magic in the glove?" Eddie asked with concern.

"Yup. The magic only works if you wish that your teammates do poorly," the ballplayer said in an unconvincing tone of voice. "Just remember that. Now, let's get back to some more fielding tips. Now, Eddie, you've got to bend your knees and put your glove right down to the ground when fielding those grounders. This way the ball won't go underneath your glove, and if it takes a bad hop, you can make a quick adjustment. Here, try it on this one."

The handsome young ballplayer picked up a ball, tossed it in the air, and smashed a hard grounder toward Eddie who this time got his glove down and his body in front of the ball. Eddie made the play.

"Way to go, Eddie. You sure fielded that ball a lot better. You know something, kid, I think you've really got some talent there." The dark menacing figure again stuck his head out of the dugout and gave the ballplayer a dirty look.

"Who's your friend?" Eddie asked pointing toward the dugout.

"Let's just call him the Manager."

"Oh, he's your boss, huh?"

"Yeah. He keeps me on my toes."

"I can tell. You know this whole dream is weird. I swear I never saw you before last night and usually I don't dream about people that I've never laid eyes upon. But I really appreciate all the help you've been giving me. I had my best practice today, ever."

"Just remember the rules, kid. Make sure you do what I tell you to do, and you'll continue to improve."

"I believe you. You're a pretty good coach, you know? You probably would've made a great manager if you didn't end up here. How did you get here anyway? And for that matter, where are we?"

"I guess you could say we're in dream land," the coach said with a nervous laugh. He added, "And as far as how I got here is concerned, it's really too long of a story to tell."

"That's what I like about you, never a straight answer. You're like a nice Freddy Krueger, you know that?"

"I'm afraid you've lost me, kid. I'm not quite up to date with, what did you call him? Freddy Krueger? You'll have to tell me more about him sometime. But right now, we've got baseball to learn. Okay, now here's the situation: You've got a runner on second and one out and the ball's hit to you. What do you do?"

"I check the runner, and I throw to first."

"Absolutely. Why do you check the runner?"

"Because I don't want him to advance. I want to freeze him at second and get the out."

"You bet. You want to take some batting practice?"

"Sure. I did exactly what you told me to do today. I went to bat, real aggressive like, and I took control of the plate. I stood so close to the plate that the pitcher threw at me."

"I told you that was going to happen, didn't I?"

"You sure did, and believe me I got out of the way fast."

"Good boy. Now remember keep your head down and your eyes focused. Try to read the laces of the ball as they approach the plate. Don't forget to crouch. Remember, crouching shortens the strike zone. Make sure you sit. That means keeping all your weight on your back foot. That gives you leverage when you swing the bat. Only when you swing do you step out on to your front foot and shift that weight forward. That will give you increased power. And why do you get practically on top of the plate?"

"Because if you do, your bat can reach the outside corner. That way, you don't get struck out by any unhittable pitches."

"Absolutely correct. Kid, you've got a great memory. You must've done great in practice."

Eddie smiled and was overjoyed that he was receiving praise from his coach. He then stepped into the batter's box and crowded the plate while awaiting the pitch. Suddenly, the Manager came out of the dugout to observe. His presence so alarmed the coach that he aborted throwing the pitch. He suddenly stopped in the middle of his windup and asked Eddie, "In order for the glove to perform its magic, what must you do?"

"I've gotta wish my teammates bad luck, right?"

Before the ballplayer could respond, an old man with beautiful white hair walked out on to the field and approached the group. An ethereal light surrounded him. "My son, why do you preach falsehoods to the boy?" the old man asked in a divine tone of voice.

The ballplayer was speechless as he recognized this man from his past. Suddenly, he gathered himself together and said, "Michael, what are you doing here?"

The man in the dark suit rudely interrupted what was beginning to be a tearful reunion. "Get out of here, old man! This isn't your place. Go back to where you came from. We don't need you here."

"I see. The deceiver still has a hold on you my boy," Michael deduced.

"Leave, old man, or you will experience my wrath. And tell your boss that he is nothing compared to me. And tell him that I will make him pay if he keeps interfering with my business."

"Yes, I will leave but not because of your idle threats but because I cannot stand for very long the stench of your effluvium, but I will be back. I'm here to let you know that we intend to fight for this child," Michael forewarned.

Eddie suddenly awakened from this confusing dream to the ringing of the telephone. He picked up the receiver and groggily said, "Hello." The voice on the other end sounded oddly familiar.

"Hi, Eddie, I was told to give you a call."

"Who is this?"

"You know who it is."

"I know who it sounds like."

"It sounds like who it is."

"So you expect me to believe that it's Babe Ruth, right?"

"I expect you to believe the truth," the Babe stated.

"You're dead though."

"Yeah, I know."

"So where are you calling me from, heaven?"

"Good guess."

"Well, what do you want?"

"I've been told that you need some help with your hitting."

"This is just great," Eddie announced in disbelief. "Let's get real. You expect me to believe that Babe Ruth is calling me to be my personal hitting instructor?"

"Yeah, but that would be only telling half the truth, kid. You see my friend Lou Gehrig is going to give you some tips too," Ruth stated frankly.

"Sure. I'd love to hear Gehrig give me a few tips. Is he going to be calling me from heaven too?" Eddie asked sarcastically.

"Sure is. Would you like to talk to him, kid?"

"Yeah. Why not? Put him on the phone."

"Hi, Eddie. I really did feel like the luckiest man on the face of the earth that day at Yankee Stadium. And I feel very lucky that I've been chosen to help you with your hitting," Gehrig stated humbly.

"You both sound so authentic. But this just can't be. Somebody's pulling my leg," Eddie reasoned.

"This is no joke. Life is a miracle, son, and so is death. It's a whole new ball game. If you can believe in God, you can believe in us. I remember when I was alive I always tried to figure out why we existed. It didn't make any sense then. I remember taking the universal questions back as far as possible and asking myself, how could God just be? You know what I mean? If God created the world, then who created God? There was no answer then. And the only answer, I can tell you now is that God was always there. Illogical? Yes. Improbable? No way. Anyway, Eddie, we've been told to look out for you and to give you the best baseball hitting instruction that's ever been given at least in my humble opinion.

If you want it, we're prepared to give it to you. But unlike in your dreams, with us, you call the shots, kid," Gehrig articulated.

"Why all this interest in me?"

"Because you're in a very special situation."

"Can't you be any more specific than that?"

"I'm sorry, Eddie. I've said all that I can say. It's your destiny. We're only here to try to steer you in the right direction. But we're not allowed to influence your final decision. Only you can make those choices."

"You know, I can't get a straight answer out of any of you guys, but I think I'm getting it. This is like the Flintstones, right? You two are like my guardian angels. The voices that try to tell me to do good and my dreams are like the devil, trying to tell me to do bad."

"It sounds like these Flintstone's have a good handle on things, Eddie."

"I always knew it, Mr. Gehrig, life is like a cartoon. Now all I need is The Great Gazoo to help me sort out this mess."

"Whatever you say, Eddie," Gehrig responded in confusion. "Now, Eddie, fill me in on any hitting problems you have."

"Well, Mr. Gehrig, I've been getting good hitting instruction in my dreams lately, so what I probably need help on is like fine-tuning my swing, stuff like that. I'm playing a game on Saturday. Maybe you and the Babe could stop by and make sure my mechanics are in order."

"We'll do that Eddie. We won't be there physically, but we'll be watching, and we'll call you on the pay phone if you're doing anything wrong."

"Good. There's a pay phone right near the dugout."

"I'll tell you what you do. After every turn at bat, take a stroll over to the phone, pick up the receiver, and we'll be on the line, okay?"

"You've got yourself a deal. Until Saturday."

The phone line suddenly went back to a dial tone, and Eddie headed out of his room. Knowing he was late as usual, he raced down the stairs to get to the dining room for his evening meal.

Mrs. Romano heard her son's approach through the creaking of the wooden stairs. "Well, it's about time. Your father is here, and I just took the chicken out of the oven!" she screamed.

Eddie turned the corner and entered the kitchen. "Hi, Mom. Hi, Dad."

Mr. Romano looked up momentarily from his meal, spotted Eddie wearing his green glove, and quickly went back to devouring his chicken breast. With his mouth full, he asked, "Why do you have to bring your glove to the dinner table? Can't you leave it in your room?"

"What if somebody steals it?"

Mr. Romano finished swallowing and asked, "Who's going to steal it, Eddie? There's only you, me, and Mom. I'm certainly not going to steal it, and I can guarantee your mother has no interest in it."

His father's words stung and caused Eddie to cry. As Eddie ran from the kitchen, his dad got up from the table and chased after him, finally catching up to him at the stairs. "Eddie, what's wrong with you? Just forget what I said. Okay? If it means that much to you, then you just bring it to the dinner table. I'm sorry."

Eddie started to get his composure back again. His mother appeared near the stairs and commented, "See, Vince. This is just another example of what I've been talking to you about. I'm telling you, there's something wrong."

"Lucy, he's calm. Let's just drop it now. Okay?"

Mr. Romano comforted Eddie, holding him tightly in his arms. He then picked him up and carried him into the kitchen. He set Eddie down in his chair and the family continued to eat their meal. Eddie immediately began to devour his chicken breast.

"See Lucy, the boy still has his appetite. Good chicken, huh, Eddie?"

"Um. Real good."

"So your mother tells me that you like those recordings I got you. She tells me you play them all the time."

"They're great, Dad. Both Ruth and Gehrig are going to help me out with my hitting."

"Well, that's great, son," his father said patronizingly. "Speaking about batting, how'd practice go today?"

"It went great. I'm finally becoming a good hitter. And it's all because of my new glove."

"Well, Eddie, I'm sure it has something to do with you too."

"No. It's the glove, Dad. Guess what?"

"What, Eddie?"

"Mr. Ruth and Mr. Gehrig told me that they're going to watch my game from heaven on Saturday."

"What did they do? Call you up and tell you that?" Mr. Romano joked.

"Yeah, they called me just a little while ago. They're going to help me with my hitting."

"Great. I'm sure you'll improve a lot under their tutelage," Mr. Romano said, humoring his son.

"With all the good coaching I've been getting, I'm going to end up being the best ballplayer on my team."

"Didn't I tell you, Lucy, that I thought that Mr. Mitchell was a hell of a good coach?"

"You sure did, dear."

"Dad, I'm not talking about Mr. Mitchell. I'm talking about my dream coach. He's really nice, and he's given me all kinds of good tips to improve my game."

"Eddie, you're something else. You know that? You literally eat, sleep, and dream baseball, don't you?" Mr. Romano inquired in an amused tone of voice.

"I do, Dad. The way things are going, I'm going to be a major leaguer too."

"You sure will, and if you don't make it there well, then, maybe you should really think about becoming a writer since you've really got a great imagination, kiddo."

"Maybe you just spelled it out, Vince. Maybe the problem is his imagination. Maybe we have a future artist in our household," Lucy hoped, trying her best to put a bright spin on their current dilemma.

The chimes of the doorbell interrupted the conversation, and Mrs. Romano got up from the table and headed toward the front door. She opened it and found Billy Ray standing on her doorstep.

"Hi, Mrs. Romano. Is Eddie home?" Billy Ray inquired in good spirits.

"He sure is, Billy Ray. We're just finishing dinner. You wanna come in?"

"Sure. You guys ate late tonight, huh?"

"We did indeed."

Billy Ray followed Mrs. Romano into the kitchen. "Can I get you something to drink?"

"No thanks, Mrs. Romano. Hi, Eddie. Why'd you race off so fast after practice?"

"I got better things to do with my time than hang out with you fellas," Eddie snapped.

"Eddie, that's rude. Apologize to Billy Ray," Mr. Romano demanded.

"Sorry, Billy Ray," Eddie said flippantly.

"Eddie, what's wrong with you? I'm your friend. Why are you treating me like this?"

"He doesn't mean it, Billy Ray. Something's obviously troubling him."

"That's just your opinion, Mom," Eddie interjected as he continued to eat his meal, showing little interest in the conversation taking place around him.

"So how does the team look, Billy Ray?" Mr. Romano asked, trying to move on to a new subject.

"I guess we're getting better. The coach was certainly impressed with Eddie's play today. He's really improved a lot. Stevie said to me after practice that Eddie looked and acted like a completely different hitter. Everybody was happy for you, Eddie. We were all coming up to congratulate you and you just took off."

"I'm not interested in the team's good tidings, Billy Ray. They're all a bunch of two-faced hypocrites. They don't like me, and I don't like them. They don't wish me well, and I certainly don't wish them well."

"That's not true. That might apply to Johnny, but it doesn't apply to the rest of us. I mean, until you acted so stuck up today, you were awfully popular. I just don't understand you."

"Billy Ray, I don't care what you understand and what you don't understand. So do yourself a favor and mind your own business."

"I thought we were friends. I guess we're not anymore, huh?"

"Guess not. I don't need friends," Eddie said flippantly.

Billy Ray turned and raced out of the kitchen. Mr. Romano followed his exit. He caught up to Billy Ray by the front door.

"I'm sorry, Billy Ray. I don't know what in hell is wrong with him. He hasn't been himself for a couple days now. I'm sure he'll snap out of it," Mr. Romano stated with concern in his voice.

"I hope so. He's just totally different. He's like night and day. He's going to lose all his friends if he keeps up this attitude. Some people aren't quite as tolerant as I am. I'm used to moody people. You should see how my mother acts when she gets her rag."

"Billy Ray, you shouldn't be talking like that. Where do you boys get your education these days?"

"I got mine from my older brother, but some guys learn a lot just by reading the bathroom walls," Billy Ray said with a grin.

"Get out of here," Mr. Romano said playfully. "I'm going to have a long talk with him, so don't you worry." Billy Ray exited the house with his head hung quite a bit lower than it was when he first arrived.

THE BIG GAME
OR EDDIE'S
LEGEND BEGINS

Eddie couldn't wait for Saturday. His team was playing against the Southside Tigers, and he had practiced so well during the week that Mr. Mitchell inserted him into the starting lineup. This marked the first time that he had ever started for the Astros. He was assigned shortstop duties, and his hitting improved so much that Mr. Mitchell penciled him in for the fifth spot in the batting order.

Eddie was extremely overbearing all week long as he bragged about his newly acquired baseball prowess to his family and anyone else who would listen. He informed everyone that Babe Ruth and Lou Gehrig were both going to be giving him batting tips between each of his turns at bat. His seemingly unbelievable remarks became a major target of criticism by his teammates. He was the butt of many of their jokes in the dugout, but their criticisms seemed to have no effect upon him. Eddie was oblivious to all outside influences except those that he perceived would affect the magic of his glove.

The Romano family arrived early at the little league ballpark. Mrs. Romano parked her Jeep and began freshening her makeup in the truck mirror as Eddie and Mr. Romano exited. She wanted to look her best for the community social event disguised as a little league baseball game. Since her son did his best imitation of Muhammad Ali all week long, trumpeting that he was going to be the star of the game, she hoped for his sake that his predictions would come true. As she looked out toward the field at her husband and son playing catch, she recalled how she told Eddie that people would like him better if he didn't brag so much. She told him that he would be better served by letting others compliment him instead but realized that her words were wasted on deaf ears when he told her, "It ain't bragging if you can do it." There was a general feeling of alarm contained within her all through the week. She couldn't put her finger on it, but she knew that something unusual was occurring to her son. What had happened to the loving, considerate, and humble boy that she had raised? This was the question that ate at her during all her waking hours. She feared that he was having some kind of psychological breakdown. That would explain his make-believe phone conversations with his baseball heroes. As she climbed down from the Jeep, an overwhelming sense of dread came over her. It was like she was attending her son's public execution. Mrs. Jones, a board member of the PTA at the middle school, noticed her immediately and came rushing over to give her an insincere greeting.

Mrs. Jones wore a dress with flower prints and a large red flowery sun hat. "Well, look who it is. It's the star of the game's mother." She said facetiously as she snickered. "I'm sorry, Lucy, I had to throw that in. Bret's been telling me all week long how your son has laid claim to being the star of this game. I, myself, thought it was kind of amusing that an eleven year old, who last week was afraid to step up to the plate with the game on the line, could suddenly lay claim to such a notion but anyway you must have really overdone the confidence training in your family this week," she added condescendingly.

"Well, I'm glad that you find Eddie so amusing, Lori. But maybe it would be better for you to focus your attention upon your own boy. Why don't you tend to him and let me take care of mine," Mrs. Romano fumed.

Mrs. Jones raced off in a huff, going out of her way to make a scene shouting, "Some people just can't take a joke!"

Looking for her husband, Mrs. Romano approached the bleachers. She spotted him in the first row of seats, munching on a hot dog and washing it down with a can of soda. As she approached him, she could clearly hear the muffled whispers of some of the other parents in attendance. Pretending not to notice, she sat down next to him.

"Vince, we've got a problem. Eddie's been bragging to everyone."

Mr. Romano, a very proud father, gave his wife a dumb look in reply to her remark. "The boy is eleven years old. Are you forgetting that fact? Who's really going to hold him accountable for the things he says?"

"They are, Vince," Mrs. Romano stated, gesturing to the other parents in attendance.

"Screw 'em. Who cares what they think? Who are they anyway?"

"Vince, we have to live in this community."

"Look, Lucy, if they're going to make a big stink about the talk of an eleven-year-old boy, then they've got serious problems. If that's the case, maybe they belong back in middle school. Now, just drop it. I came here to enjoy my son's game. I think it's great that he's finally developing some self-confidence."

"I'm happy that he's getting some confidence too. But I don't want him to become the town braggart."

"Let's see how well the boy does before passing judgment. Believe me, nothing will shut these people up faster than success. If Eddie plays half as well as he says he's going to, you won't hear a single peep out of any of them. That I guarantee."

"So you think it's okay that we're raising the next Muhammad Ali?"

"Lucy, he's eleven years old. He's obviously going through a phase. I think you're jumping the gun just a bit." Mr. Romano grinned.

A great big round of applause interrupted their conversation as the Tigers took the field. The Tigers were in first place in the little league standings while Eddie's team, the Astros, were in dead last. Many of the parents of the Tiger players began shouting encouragement to them. Seated directly behind the Romanos was a short heavyset, thuggish-looking man of Italian descent with oily skin. He was dressed in a leisure suit and wore dark sunglasses. Besides his obnoxious mouth, his most salient idiosyncrasy according to the Romano's was his habit of constantly taking his handkerchief out of his pocket to wipe the sweat from his forehead. It seemed like he was performing that action every other minute.

"Come on, Rocco! Strike these bums out," screamed the man who turned out to be the father of the Tiger's pitcher. He was loud, crude, and lewd. He made sure his presence was known by all around him.

Mr. Romano glanced back and gave the man a dirty look. The pitcher's father immediately took notice and smiled arrogantly as he realized that he had accomplished his mission of annoying someone. It was as if being the center of attention was his main objective in life. The man relished the fact that he had grabbed the spotlight and someone was paying attention to him. He declared, "That's my boy out there. Best pitcher in the league. You're going to die when you see this kid's fastball. You watch. These Astros, when they go up to bat, they'll be shaking in their boots. Don't worry it won't be too unpleasant for them, they'll get used to it after a while. They all do. They'll just swing three times and go and sit their asses right back down where they belong, right on that bench, collecting splinters. Sometimes you're just outclassed, you know what I mean?"

"Boy, you can say that again." Mr. Romano chuckled, thinking that this obnoxious man had just made a Freudian slip. He added, "Mister, you see that's why they play the game. You're guaranteed nothing. My son plays for the Astros, and I want to make you a promise right here and now. You see he's such a good hitter, that he's going to blast one of your son's pitches right out of this ballpark."

"What do you think of that?" Mr. Romano smirked and challenged.

"You really think so, huh? You wouldn't mind risking a small wager on that?" prodded Rocco's father.

"Sure. How much do you want to lose?"

"How much you got?"

"I got a hundred bucks."

"Vince! This is a little league game. I don't think you should be betting on it," Mrs. Romano interrupted.

"Yeah, Vince. I don't wanna take your money but if you insist."

"Yeah. I insist. A hundred dollars says that my boy, Eddie, will hit a home run off your boy within three official turns at bat. If your son isn't pitching by his third official turn at bat, then all bets are off. Deal?"

"You're on, sucker!" Rocco's father exclaimed doing his best to make sure that everyone knew about their wager.

The first batter for the Astros came up to the plate, and Rocco's father became louder than usual, "Come on, Rocco! Turn on the gas, my boy! Strike that little runt out!"

Mrs. Romano thought to herself that this objectionable loudmouth was a godsend in disguise because at least temporarily the other parents were concentrating their ridicules upon him instead of upon Eddie. She was also very upset with her husband for making a bet with this rude creature. She thought that the wager just encouraged his abhorrent behavior.

It didn't take Rocco long to strikeout the leadoff hitter, Stevie Smith. Stevie walked back toward the dugout shaking his head in disbelief and announcing, "He's fast man. You blink and the ball's by you."

Mr. Mitchell yelled out to the next hitter, Davey Miles, "Choke up on that bat, Davey!"

Davey approached the plate with great confidence. He looked fearless as he inched closer and closer to the plate. He waited patiently, chewing a large wad of bubblegum. Rocco stepped off the pitcher's rubber and spit disdainfully in Davey's direction. Rocco picked at the rear end of his baseball pants, presumably to relieve the discomfort from his underwear crawling up the crack of his ass. After making the adjustment to his uniform, he quickly sniffed his fingers and then began rubbing up the baseball. Davey grew tired of waiting for him and stepped out of the batter's box momentarily. When Rocco stepped back on the pitcher's rubber, Davey took a deep breath and entered the batter's box once again. Davey immediately began inching his way closer and closer to the plate. Davey was almost on top of the plate when Rocco went into his windup. With a menacing smile on his face, Rocco delivered a high fastball that hit Davey right on the batting helmet. Davey hit the dirt, and his helmet flew off his head. He lay motionless, grasping his head with both hands as Mr. Mitchell raced out to attend to him. After a scary moment, Davey got up and dizzily proceeded down to first base. Rocco arrogantly kicked some dirt off the pitcher's mound toward home plate, then looked over toward his father in the bleachers and gave him the thumbs-up sign.

"Way to go, Rocco! That'll teach him for crowding the plate. Come on, Rocco! Bear down, son!" His father screamed joyously, enjoying every minute in the spotlight with orgasmic delight.

The vast majority of folks in attendance were corporate executives and their spouses. The rather sedate parents in attendance were absolutely shocked at the behavior of this working-class heathen among them. Whispering voices filled the bleachers and this time they weren't directed at Eddie or the Romanos.

"When's your boy coming up?" Rocco's father laughed.

"Keep on smiling, mister. At the rate your son is going, he'll be lucky if he doesn't get thrown out of the game," Mr. Romano predicted.

Eddie sat in the dugout studying Rocco's every move, completely unaware of all the dissension taking place out in the stands. Keith Strong was currently at bat, and Eddie noticed that Rocco had firmly established his control of the plate. By showing a "wild streak," he had intimidated Keith into standing too far back in the batter's box. Although Eddie noticed this, keeping with his bargain with his dream coach and the Manager, he kept his mouth shut. He didn't want to do anything to diminish the magic in his glove. Rocco proceeded to easily strike Keith out, throwing fastballs over the outside corner of the plate. Although Keith swung at these pitches, from where he stood in the batter's box, it was physically impossible for him to reach them. With two men out, Johnny Mitchell stepped into the batter's box self-assured. He was the team's best hitter, and his father spent many hours helping him with the finer points of the game. Unlike Keith, he stood close enough to the plate to be able to reach the outside corner with his bat. Eddie stepped into the on deck circle and observed. He wished his hardest for Johnny to make an out. It didn't take any prodding to make him feel that way either. Johnny was always rotten to him, and he prayed for a little bit of reverse magic to knock him off his high horse. Rocco delivered the first pitch high and inside for a count of ball one. The crowd began whooping it up for Johnny as he awaited the next pitch. Rocco looked toward the stands and sneered at the well-wishers. He then went back into his windup and delivered a fastball that jammed Johnny on the wrists of his bat. The ball floated weakly into the air, and Rocco made the catch. He gave Johnny the finger as he strutted off the mound. Eddie started to clap and Johnny saw him do it and in retaliation, angrily threw his batting helmet at him. Eddie mocked him by throwing his hat in Johnny's direction. The Astros took the field, and Eddie proudly waved his antique glove toward the bleachers. This brought about some additional whispers in the stands.

"Hey, you sure you can afford the hundred bucks? From the look of your kid's glove, I can see it could be better spent," chided Rocco's father. "What did you do? Give him, like, a third generation hand-me-down?"

"You know, you're starting to get on my nerves, fella. I don't mind a little good-natured ribbing but I think you're getting just a little bit out of hand. So do yourself a favor and put a lid on it, okay?" Mr. Romano stated angrily.

"Vince, just ignore this jerk. We're not going to have a fight here," Mrs. Romano pleaded.

"Who you callin' a jerk, lady? I've had better one night stands than you!"

That remark was the straw that broke the proverbial camel's back as Mr. Romano grabbed Rocco's father by the throat and some of the other "sedate" parents sitting behind him, grabbed him too. Rocco's father was caught completely off guard, and he struggled helplessly as he was pinned down between the seats of the row directly behind him.

"Let go of me!" Rocco's father demanded as he struggled to get free.

"Apologize to my wife!"

"Okay. I'm sorry. Now let me up!"

"Are you going to stop harassing me?" Mr. Romano screamed into his face.

"Yes. Just let go of me! Now!" Rocco's father ordered.

Mr. Romano let go of him and the others holding him followed suit. "Do you think you two could just kindly quiet down? This game is for the kids," pleaded a man who sat behind Rocco's father and who had helped subdue him.

"Go, Rocco! Go, Tigers!" Rocco's father immediately started cheering, trying his best to irritate.

Meanwhile on the field, the Tiger's got their leadoff hitter on base with a walk. Rocco came up to bat next and quickly lined a single into right field, putting runners on first and third. Stevie, the Astros pitcher, called for a conference on the mound to discuss strategy. While Stevie and Keith conferred about how to pitch to the next batter, Eddie joined the gathering.

"What do you want, Eddie?" Keith questioned.

"Keith, let's try a new play. I learned this one the other night. You know they're going to send the runner from first to second, figuring that you won't dare throw down because of the possibility of the double steal. So this is what you do. When the kid from first bolts toward second, you make a low throw toward the second base bag. I'll race in, intercept that throw and fire it back to you and you put the tag on the guy trying to steal home. What do you say?" Eddie asked anxiously.

"It sounds great, but we never practiced that play before, Eddie," Keith squabbled.

"Don't worry. All you have to do is throw a fastball toward second low enough for me to cut it off. Believe me. I've practiced the play."

"With who, Eddie?" Keith asked incredulously.

"Don't worry with who. Let's just do it, okay?"

"Look, if coach yells, I'm telling him that this was your idea."

The umpire approached the gathering. "You got to break it up, fellas. Let's get this game going. I've got to take the wife shopping later and boy does she love to shop."

The boys shrugged their shoulders in unison and then headed to their positions. Stevie anxiously stood on the mound, unsure of what they were about to attempt. As the Tiger player stepped into the batter's box, his manager signaled down to Rocco to leave on the first pitch. Stevie began his motion from the stretch position, checking both the runners on first and third. The runner on third looked awfully anxious for the ball to be pitched, obviously he was anxious to make his decision whether or not to bolt toward home. He knew that if the catcher contested the stealing of second base by throwing the ball down to the second basemen, he would immediately make a mad dash for the plate and gloriously steal home.

Stevie ignored the runner on third and threw a fastball for a strike right down the middle of the plate. As the ball hit the catcher's mitt, Keith saw Rocco hightailing it toward second base. He immediately threw down in the manner instructed. The Tiger manager, completely surprised by the contested steal, yelled at his boy on third base to run home. Before the words completely left his mouth, Eddie raced in, cutting off the throw and fired it back home. Keith took the throw from Eddie and tagged out the lead runner with plenty of time to spare. The crowd in the bleachers exploded with applause as the normally hapless Astros had pulled off the play of the game.

Mr. Mitchell couldn't believe his eyes when the umpire called the lead runner out at home. He had never seen a little league team pull that play off before. He was even more astonished that it was his little league team that pulled it off. He signaled for a time out and raced out to the mound.

"Who called that?" Mr. Mitchell asked in complete bewilderment.

"It was Eddie, Coach. He's to blame, not me," Keith said nervously, fearing that Mitchell was not happy with the call.

"Well, way to go, Eddie!" Mr. Mitchell said, patting him on the back. "Stevie my boy, this has got to be our day. So you settle down. With a little luck, we're going to win this one."

"No problem, Mr. Mitchell. All right, Eddie!" Stevie screamed in appreciation.

Stevie found some new confidence in his teammates and closed out the inning without a blemish. In the stands many of the early "whisperers" came over and congratulated the Romanos on their son's fine play. Mrs. Jones announced to the crowd, "Maybe I'm going to have to eat my words on this one." There was one other major change and that was Rocco's father actually quieted down for two thirds of an inning but that was not to last. The second inning began with Rocco on the mound facing Eddie. Eddie kissed his antique glove superstitiously and set it down on the dugout bench. He then made his way out toward the batter's box. Upon arrival, he planted himself in a perfect hitting position. His bat comfortably reached any spot on the plate. Rocco's first pitch was a high and tight fastball that was intended to push Eddie further off the plate. Unfortunately for Rocco, Eddie wasn't budging an inch from his initial position in the batter's box. Rocco's second pitch was a rising fastball that Eddie swung through for a one ball and one strike count.

"Way to go, Rocco! Strike that bum out! He's a wiffer!" Rocco's father exclaimed after the first strike. "I told you that your boy can't hit him. That hundred bucks is like money in the bank."

"I think he's still got two strikes to go. You don't see me worried, do you?" asked Mr. Romano calmly.

"You should be. Like P. T. Barnum once said, 'A fool and his money soon part.'" quoted Rocco's father.

Rocco went back into his windup and threw a slow change of speed pitch over the center of the plate that Eddie swung too early on, for strike two. Rocco began laughing on the mound and taunting Eddie.

"Way to go Rocco! That's my boy! He's a master pitcher that one. This bet's like taking candy from kids," Rocco's father bragged.

"Come on, Eddie! You can hit him! Watch for the fastball!" Mr. Romano screamed at the top of his lungs.

Rocco went back into his windup and delivered a fastball waist high over the outside corner of the plate. Eddie swung late but connected as the metal ping of the aluminum bat pierced the ears of the crowd.

The ball was driven on a line drive out into right field and directly into the glove of the Tiger's right fielder, who hardly had to make an adjustment. Eddie threw his bat down in disgust and looked toward his dugout with disbelieving eyes. Fire shot into those eyes when he realized that Johnny Mitchell was playing with his magic glove. Eddie instantly exploded with rage and raced toward Johnny with his fists clenched. In an instant, he was on top of him pummeling him into the dirt.

"Don't you ever touch my glove! I'll kill you! You hear me! Don't touch it!" Eddie screamed in anger as he struck Johnny Mitchell with a barrage of punches.

It took most of the Astros team to pull Eddie off Johnny who was by now bleeding profusely from the mouth. None of his teammates could believe how viciously he attacked their comrade. Eddie distanced himself from the team, threatening them all with bodily harm if they ever touched his glove. After witnessing this brutal display, none of them ever entertained that action again. Mr. Mitchell raced over and demanded an explanation from Eddie for his behavior.

"No one touches my glove. Understand me?" Eddie responded.

Mr. Mitchell just shook his head and walked away in disbelief. Eddie had, in an instant, lost all of his friends on the team. From then on, all his teammates moved away from him when he approached. No one would sit next to him in the dugout, and many secretly feared his explosive temper. His teammates came to the conclusion that it was better to stay far away from him then by chance touch his glove and become the next victim of his wrath.

Unaware of the events taking place within the Astros' dugout, Mr. Romano told Rocco's father that he was sure that his boy could drive one out on Rocco.

"The boy was just plain lucky. It just goes to show that if you're lucky enough to catch up to a great fastball, like Rocco's, you can drive it. But the fact remains, what was the net result? I'll tell you what it was, what language would you like to hear it in? How about zip, gotz, nada, nole, or my favorite, nothing. A lot of noise but just another out," Rocco's father explained.

Back in the dugout, the Astros were attending to Johnny Mitchell. Billy Ray had run down to the snack bar to get some ice to prevent any swelling. Johnny sat on the bench shaking his head in disbelief and mumbling, "What in hell was that for?"

His teammates were at a loss for words too. Meanwhile, Eddie left the dugout and headed over toward the pay phone. A young girl was on the line talking to a friend when he just rudely hung up the phone on her.

"What's your problem, kid?" The girl asked, shocked by his unmitigated gall.

"Your phone call's not important. So bug off," Eddie snapped.

"Who in hell died and left you in charge?" The girl asked angrily as she raced back to the bleachers.

Eddie brushed off her comment like a grain of salt and nonchalantly picked up the phone receiver, discovering Lou Gehrig on the line as promised.

"Eddie, you shouldn't treat people like that. Haven't you ever heard of the golden rule? You know, do unto others as you'd have them do unto you? How would you like it if she just came over and hung up the phone on you?"

"I wouldn't like it. I just lost my cool I guess. I was mad. Johnny Mitchell touched my magic glove," Eddie rationalized.

"For a magic glove, it certainly didn't help much. I mean you flew out to right. Where's the magic, Eddie?"

"Who knows? Him touching it might have screwed it up. Did you ever think of that? Anyway, there isn't any magic that is one hundred percent foolproof."

"Who told you that?"

"Never mind. Did you notice anything for me to improve upon?"

"Yeah, your attitude. You're really starting to grate upon me, kid. Let me turn you over to the Bambino, maybe he wants to deal with you," Gehrig criticized.

"Hey, kid, you've got to stop beating up on your teammates. You're not going to win any popularity contests like that. As far as your hitting is concerned though, it ain't half bad. I suggest since he's such a fast pitcher that you choke up considerably on that bat of yours. You've got a choice, you either choke up or you increase your bat speed. Your bat speed is going to take some time and effort to increase, so choking up will give you a temporary fix. Remember when you choke up, your bat won't reach as far across the plate as it did before. That means you're going to have to get closer to the plate. Also, I noticed that the pitcher gives away his changeup. When he comes directly over top, he's throwing a fastball. If you see him release three quarters over top, he's throwing a change. With that information, you should be able to swing early enough on his fastball to pull it to left field. Oh, kid, another thing. I'm not supposed to tell you this but your dad has got a bet going with the pitcher's father. So why don't you hit one out of the park for your old man. I mean, if it wasn't for him, you wouldn't be in this situation. Understand, kid?"

"Got you, Babe. Thanks a lot."

"Remember, kid, try to be nice."

"I'll try. Talk to you again after my next at bat." Eddie hung up the phone and wandered back to the dugout.

As he turned the corner to the dugout, Mr. Mitchell spotted him. "Where in hell have you been? Get the hell out there!" Mr. Mitchell ordered impatiently.

Eddie raced out on to the field as the Tiger's batter stepped up to the plate. The game continued to be deadlocked through the next three innings. In the fourth inning, the Astros had the top of their batting order up again. Up to this point, Rocco seemed practically unhittable.

"Listen, fellas, you've got to make this kid throw strikes. Right now, he thinks he can throw anything he wants and you'll swing at it. I can tell a few of you guys are scared to death, and if I can see that, then he sure as hell can too. He's not even throwing the ball over the plate anymore. He's struck a couple of you guys out last inning on pitches that nobody should've ever swung at. Now, we've been playing real well so far, and we're in this game. This game is winnable, fellas. Don't let this kid intimidate you. Get up there, even if you have to just rest the bat on your shoulders and make him pitch to you. Now go do it up, Davey," Mr. Mitchell prepped his team.

Davey stepped into the batter's box with the fear of god instilled in him. That bean ball he took in the first inning changed his entire persona as a hitter. He approached the plate totally intimidated and in fear for his life. Rocco picked up upon his tentativeness and knew immediately that he was too scared to pose a problem for him. Despite his coach's instructions, Davey swung at every pitch Rocco threw. They numbered three before the umpire called him out, and he went back to find a seat in the dugout. With one out, Keith stepped into the batter's box, and unlike Davey, he heeded Mr. Mitchell's advice. He rested the bat on his shoulder and waited for Rocco to throw a strike. Rocco walked him on six pitches. He swung at none of them. With Keith on first base, Johnny came up to the plate. He was still smarting from the beating he received from Eddie and was in an ornery mood as he awaited Rocco's first pitch. He was looking for some pay back, and he directed his anger at Rocco.

The first pitch came, and it was high and outside.

"Come on, Rocco! Find the plate, boy! Pitch to them! They can't hit you!" Rocco's father shouted encouragingly.

The crowd in the bleachers became strangely quiet, almost as if they sensed an impending rally by their much maligned Astros. Rocco spit out his bubblegum and threw it toward Johnny in an intimidating manner. Johnny shrugged it off and waited patiently in the batter's box. Rocco sneered at him as he pitched from the stretch position. He delivered a high fastball, ball two. Rocco kicked some dirt off the mound, removed his hat, and took a deep breath. He immediately started his approach and promptly delivered ball three, inside.

The Tiger's manager screamed at Rocco, "Pitch to him, son! Throw strikes! They can't hit you, Rock!"

Johnny, while waiting in the batter's box, blew Rocco a kiss. He knew that Rocco had to throw him a strike. He also knew that it was going to be a good one since he figured Rocco would assume that he was going to take it. Johnny had other plans in mind when Rocco started his approach and delivered a waist-high fastball over the center of the plate. Johnny began salivating as he drove that meatball into centerfield for the Astros first hit of the game. Keith decided to play it safe and halted at second.

With runners on first and second, Eddie stepped up to the plate.

"Park one, Eddie! He's rattled, Eddie! You've got him, my boy! Take him deep, Eddie!" Mr. Romano cheered boisterously.

The bleachers suddenly came to life as the parents stomped their feet and clapped their hands in a unison, synchronized manner. Omnipresent was the sound of "Boom! Boom! Boom! Boom! Boom! Boom! Boom! Boom! Boom!" That was all that could be heard, and it filled the air in a monotonous, repetitive, and rhythmic manner. A chant of "Eddie" could be distinctly heard from the crowd that was now firmly behind the underdog. Eddie planted himself almost on top of home plate and choked up on the bat handle just as the Babe suggested.

Rocco gave him an intimidating stare as he began his approach. He studied Rocco's release point and knew the fastball was coming. It soared toward his head, and he evaded it at the last second. He sneered back at Rocco as he arrogantly crowded home plate once again. Rocco angrily began his approach, and Eddie watched the three quarters overhead release, which amounted to a changeup, cross the plate for a strike. He sensed that a fast-ball was forthcoming, so he choked up on his bat even farther. The crowd began to cheer once again, but Eddie heard nothing as he completely focused in on the task at hand. Rocco began his approach and released the ball directly over top. Eddie knew immediately what was coming. He read the laces of the fastball as it approached the plate. He began his swing very early so that he could get the bat all the way around on it. Suddenly there was contact. Eddie's bat located the knee-high fastball on the thickest part of the aluminum barrel. Eddie's upward swing propelled the fastball rapidly over the left field fence and out of the ballpark. It was one of the longest home runs anyone had ever seen in a little league game.

The crowd erupted with applause as Eddie stared up into the air following the flight of his monumental home run. Simultaneously, Rocco threw his mitt down in disgust.

In the bleachers, Mr. Romano turned to Rocco's father with his hand extended. Rocco's father reluctantly reached into his pocket and put a crisp one hundred dollar bill in Mr. Romano's awaiting hand.

"Pleasure doing business with you, sucker." Mr. Romano snick-ered as he tucked the hundred dollar bill into his shirt pocket.

Mrs. Romano screamed out, "That's my boy! He did it, Vince! He really did it!"

Eddie danced around the base pads in a most obnoxious man-ner. He stepped on home plate and jumped for joy. His team-mates greeted him as he entered the dugout. They chanted simul-taneously, "But don't touch his glove!" He even found a bit of humor in their needling and let out a repressed chuckle.

"Fellas, that one was complements of the Babe," Eddie bragged.

Billy Ray, who had been sitting on the bench the entire game, said, "Hey, Eddie, tell the Babe to give me some hitting instruc-tions too."

Eddie ignored the friendly remark and sat alone at the end of the dugout. In the sixth inning, Eddie turned a double play to give the Astros their first victory over the Tigers 3 to 1.

SCHIZOPHRENIC?

Eddie's baseball success snowballed after the Tiger game. The regulars, who followed the team, were amazed at his progress. During the games there was much debate by Astro fans as to the reasons for Eddie suddenly blossoming into one of the top players in the league.

Eddie became the team's superstar and his quirkiness was often discussed in whispers.

The elder Romanos, who attended each and every game, were well aware of all the conjecture surrounding their son's successes. Many times they discussed the issue with him and were always given the same illogical answer, "I've improved so much because of the magic in the glove and because I'm getting great instructions from my dream coach, the Babe and Gehrig."

Mr. Romano, always wrote his son's answers off as the product of an overactive imagination, but Mrs. Romano took the matter a lot more seriously. She became genuinely concerned with her son's mental health. One evening after school she sat Eddie down at the kitchen table and questioned him repeatedly about the long phone conversations he had been engaging in. She insisted on knowing who he was really talking to. He kept insisting that he spoke for hours to Babe Ruth and Lou Gehrig. As you may have anticipated, his mother did not believe him. In fact his answers did nothing but infuriate her. She was bound and determined to prove him a liar. She decided that the only way to definitively prove her point was to monitor his phone conversations. She figured that if she caught him in a lie, he would have to start leveling with her. She was mistaken.

One evening she waited quietly in the hallway outside Eddie's bedroom and listened intently with her ear up against the door. For hours she waited, hoping to catch him on the phone conversing with one of his make-believe friends. At last, on this particular evening her patience paid off. She could clearly hear Eddie picking up the phone and discussing his game with some unknown person. She immediately raced over to her bedroom and picked up the receiver that earlier in the day; she ingeniously removed the mouthpiece from. Her interruption into the conversation was therefore supposedly unnoticed. She listened carefully for another voice, but the only one she heard was Eddie's. There was no one on the line. All she heard was a dial tone and Eddie speaking to persons unknown, "That figures. So she's on the line? Well, she doesn't believe that I really talk to you. Can she hear you?…No…Well, that makes sense, and it's probably for the better. I don't think she's cool enough to handle this situation."

Mrs. Romano hung up the phone and raced over and barged into Eddie's bedroom screaming, "You little bastard! You've been lying to me! I know that you're not talking to anyone! Damn it, Eddie! You better start telling me the truth!"

"I'm telling you the truth. You just can't hear them," Eddie countered.

"You insolent little brat, you're going to sit there and continue to lie to me even after I catch you in the act! Your father is going to hear about this one! You hear me? You need help! I think you're crazy. I'm going to start bringing you to the doctor."

"Why, Mom? I'm not sick."

"We'll see about that, Mr. Man," she fumed.

Mrs. Romano slammed his bedroom door closed and raced down the stairs. She could feel her blood pressure rising as she waited impatiently for her husband's arrival. She thought at last the truth was finally going to be known, and her son was finally going to start getting the psychological treatment he so desperately needed.

A Conspiracy
is Brewing

His mother's shenanigans were the least of Eddie's worries. He wasn't perturbed about seeing doctors and things like that because he had more serious issues to deal with. At school he had overheard some kids talking about how he was going to get what was coming to him. These kids were unaware or tight lipped about the details, but at least he now knew that something was being planned in retribution for the beating he gave Johnny Mitchell. From that moment on he was on "red alert." When he walked to and from class his head was on a figurative swivel, looking back to see if anyone dangerous approached.

Johnny Mitchell was a very popular kid and he wanted payback for what he considered a senseless and ruthless beating that he took at the hands of Eddie at that Astros game. He didn't know when this great event was going to take place yet, but he did know that he was definitely going to get even with Eddie Romano. His plan was to take away and burn the only thing that Eddie seemed unable to live without, his precious baseball glove. Johnny just needed to find the right moment to strike. He had tried to recruit some help in this endeavor, but there were no volunteers. His friends told him that Eddie was obviously emotionally disturbed and they didn't want to trigger someone like that. Everybody knew about the pounding Johnny took in the dugout and nobody wanted to be the next victim of the Linus-like "sicko." The whole middle school thought Eddie was just plain unstable, especially if it had anything to do with that baseball glove of his. Most kids thought Johnny was off his rocker when he spoke of getting even with Eddie, except for a new kid named Eric Best.

Eric Best had moved in from Indiana and had a lot of disciplinary problems at his old school. He was a straight up "greaser." His dad was an auto mechanic and he spent a lot of time working on engines alongside him. He mimicked everything about his dad, including smoking cigarettes. He always came to school with dirt underneath his nails and portrayed himself as a tough guy. He was eager to make a name for himself at his new school and reveled in the fact that the school's most popular kid had befriended him. It was plain to see that Eric Best was fast becoming Johnny Mitchell's new right hand man. They went everywhere together and kids joked about how they were conjoined at the hip. It was a strange pairing since the two of them were so different. Johnny was the school's best athlete and Eric was just trying to fit in and be popular. Eric was a slender but muscular kid who always wore a leather jacket. He modeled himself after Fonzie, a character from the popular television show, "*Happy Days.*"

Eddie knew that if trouble was coming at school, it would be coming from Eric. His instincts were absolutely correct with this supposition. One morning before first period, Eddie walked quietly down the hallway toward his home room when Eric stepped out in front of him, impeding his progress. Eric took a drag off his cigarette and blew the smoke in Eddie's face. Eddie clenched down hard, putting a death grip on his "magic glove" and stood nose to nose with Eric. Eric disdainfully flicked away his cigarette and told Eddie, "So you're the punk that everybody's afraid of around here. Well, you don't scare me."

"Look man, I don't have a problem with you. I don't even know you and to tell you the truth, I don't even want to know you. So why don't you do us both a favor and step out of my way," Eddie declared with no emotion.

Suddenly the hallway was filled with onlookers as they stopped to witness the confrontation. Johnny Mitchell was among them and he smirked as he observed the altercation that he had dreamed about. A few kids started chanting, "Fight, come on fight!"

Eric Best took a full step back, removed his black leather jacket, and threw it over into the awaiting arms of Johnny Mitchell, who gave him the thumbs up sign of approval. Eddie stood calmly, waiting for whatever was about to take place.

Eric startled those gathered by shouting, "Boo!" and without provocation proceeded to slap Eddie across the face. Eddie stood there motionless with a stoic look on his face. Eric proceeded to slap him again and received the exact same forbearing response. "Come on, defend yourself! You're taking away all the fun. I thought you were some kind of tough guy."

Eddie just stood there with one hand at his side and the other clenched like a vise on to his "magic glove." Johnny Mitchell walked over and whispered in Eric's ear, "Grab his glove."

Eric just smiled and stepped forward into Eddie's personal space, making a sudden move to wrest the glove away from Eddie. Eddie thoroughly expected this move and countered by springing like a cobra, applying a vice grip upon Eric's arms, locking them to his side. Then he systematically head butted Eric's face into a bloody pulp. There was blood everywhere as Eddie broke Eric's nose, using his forehead as a battering ram. Next Eddie opened up a huge gash over the, would-be bully's eyebrow. Lastly, he crashed his forehead into the "greaser's" head, causing an instant concussion. This entire onslaught took less than ten seconds to complete and the crowd stood there stunned with mouths agape. Eventually a couple kids grabbed Eddie and pulled him away from Eric, who immediately fell harmlessly to the floor, unconscious.

Eddie looked over at the horrified spectators and asked if anybody else had a problem with him. There was no reply as many quickly made their escapes.

Eddie's demolition of Eric Best was the fodder of the school for many weeks to come. Nobody had ever seen anyone fight like that before. The physical act of head butting someone's face into a bloody pulp was unheard of. To most of the onlookers it was the most shockingly brutal act they would ever witness. Eddie's animalistic fighting technique became legendary at that school. From that moment on, kids—for the most part—kept their distance and nobody else ever entertained the thought of provoking him. Unfortunately for Eddie, that was not to last.

A Security Blanket?

Three years had come and gone, and Eddie was still as addicted to his antique glove as the day he discovered it. No matter what the occasion, the glove never left his side. At school it went to and from class with him. At home, it went to bed with him. Classmates joked that it should have been surgically attached to him. His parents and teachers coped with this addiction by thinking of the glove as Eddie's security blanket.

For years now, Eddie was nicknamed "Linus" by his classmates, after the familiar "Charley Brown" character who carried his blanket everywhere he went. Eddie brushed off those derogatory comments like a grain of salt. He could care less about what anyone would say or think about him. He became, at least in regard to his personality, an impenetrable island.

The past three years his mother had brought him to a bevy of different psychiatrists in a desperate attempt to find out what had happened to the gregarious, fun-loving, warm, and humble son she had raised for the last fourteen years. Unfortunately for her sake, the psychiatrists were unable to find any serious traces of mental illness. They concluded that Eddie simply chose to be an introvert and a loner.

Dr. Riesenberg, a clinical psychiatrist, summed it up best when he said, "Eddie displays behavior that ranges all over the emotional spectrum, from his braggadocio during baseball season to his quiet times at home during the rest of the year. He has a tendency toward what we call tunnel vision. He focuses his concentration on one goal and aggressively attempts to achieve it."

As far as the addiction to his antique glove was concerned, the psychiatrists determined that it had a psychosomatic effect upon him. The doctors concluded that Eddie truly believed that the glove was responsible for the improvement of his game, and as long as he believed this, it would have an effect upon his performance. They analogized his belief in the magic of the glove with a hypochondriac's belief that a placebo was curing his illness.

Dr. Riesenberg stated, "It's the belief that counts with the psychosomatically inclined patient. The glove has become superstition with Eddie. The old adage, 'If it's not broken, then why fix it?' comes perfectly into play in his situation. He has become successful believing that the glove is magical and any attempt to alter this belief could only be detrimental to him." Concerning Eddie's, "make-believe phone conversations" with his baseball heroes, Dr. Riesenberg agreed with Mr. Romano that it was a product of an overactive imagination.

After spending a considerable amount of time and money on Eddie's behalf, the Romanos gave up on their efforts of trying to change him. From then on, Mrs. Romano ignored her son's baffling phone conversations with dial tones, and Mr. Romano tried his best to reestablish a now-strained relationship with his son.

TORMENTING LINUS

The school bell echoed throughout the hallways of the high school and the students stampeded out of their classrooms toward their lockers. It was time to go home, and everybody was in a rush. Eddie, now a freshman, carried his books and antique glove with him as he departed his algebra class. He then tried his best to navigate his way through the chaos and confusion taking place in the hallways. As he made his way toward his locker, he was bumped or shoved at least ten times by fleeing students on their way to the buses that waited outside.

As he arrived at his locker, he noticed Sandy Roberts putting away his books and conversing with a friend. Roberts was the star pitcher of the high school team, and he stood about six feet four inches tall. He was a big man on campus with the girls and his peers. He looked like a California golden boy with perfectly straight white teeth, an indoor tan, and scattered freckles that covered a very cute boyish face, but Eddie wasn't concerned with how he looked, only how he pitched. Eddie couldn't help but eavesdrop on his conversation.

"Congratulations, Sandy. I heard you broke the radar gun the other day," commented Sandy's friend.

"Wow. News travels fast around here, huh?"

"From the sounds of things, not quite as fast as your fastball."

"I know. I was kind of amazed myself. I finally got the gun to register ninety plus."

"You see. You're exactly the reason I quit playing baseball my freshmen year. I would have been scared to death to stand next to a plate where somebody's humming the ball past me at ninety miles per hour. No siree Bob, that's not for me."

"Let's hope all the players on the other teams are in the same frame of mind as you are," Sandy said with a smile.

Eddie put his books away and thought, *Holy shit. He throws the ball over ninety miles per hour.* The thought of facing a ninety-plus-mile-per-hour fastball just boggled his mind. He knew the thought would bother him for the rest of the day, so he forced it out of his head. He looked around and saw that the hallways had cleared considerably of the congestion that had been so apparent just a few minutes earlier. He closed his locker on those unnecessary schoolbooks of his and headed down toward the gymnasium. As he progressed, he slapped a baseball back and forth into the webbing of his antique glove. As he turned the corner leading to the gymnasium, he noticed a gathering of junior and senior varsity baseball players who were intently reading something posted on the wall. He joined the gathering but stood behind them, trying his best to look between the player's heads to figure out what they were reading.

Eddie was unable to see the posted memo, so he tugged on one of the upper classman's shirt sleeves to get his attention.

"What?" the upper classman asked in annoyance.

"What's it say?" Eddie inquisitively asked.

The upper classman stared down at Eddie, and a sadistic smile suddenly appeared upon his face. He then replied, "I do believe it says that all wimpy freshmen should have pink bellies!" The upper classman shouted his inflammatory words as loud as possible, making sure that all the other upper classmen could hear him.

The older boys quickly turned away from the memo to stare at Eddie with their mouths watering like a pack of hungry wolves.

Eddie could see it in their eyes, the older boys would enjoy nothing more than abusing a lowly freshman on this boring afternoon, and unfortunately for him, he quickly realized that he was that "lowly freshmen." Bobby Jones, the older brother of one of his former Astro teammates, stepped forward out of the pack.

"Hey, fellas, that's Linus!" Bobby Jones laughed sadistically. "He thinks he's a hotshot! My brother played ball with this little obnoxious jerk back in little league. He never goes anywhere without that Salvation Army glove of his." He added, "He's attached to it, the same way as Linus was to his blanket. Why don't we take it from him and see what happens?" Bobby Jones enticed.

The older boys laughed loudly at Bobby Jones's remarks. The upper classman, who Eddie made the mistake of interrupting, quickly grabbed away his prized mitt and held it in the air, way too high for him to reach.

"Hey, look what I got everybody! It's the Salvation Army mitt!" The upper classmen announced while laughing hysterically. He immediately used his free arm to fend off Eddie's relentless advances.

"It's mine! Give it back! I swear to God, you're going to be sorry if you don't give it back now! You hear me? Give it back!" Eddie screamed out in delirium.

The older boys laughed antagonistically at Eddie as they spread out in different areas of the hallway. The older boys then began to play keep-away with his magic glove. Eddie became progressively more hysterical as his attempts to recover the glove became increasingly more futile.

"Give it back! Give it back! You freaking jerks! Give it back!" Eddie sobbed in an incredibly high-pitched voice. The more he cried, the greater the pleasure the older boys experienced.

A high school administrator heard the commotion and turned the hallway corner to investigate. He saw Eddie on the floor sobbing incoherently as the older boys threw his mitt back and forth while evilly laughing at him.

"Break it up! What happened here?" the administrator inquired.

The older boys stopped tossing the mitt back and forth, and Bobby Jones put on a straight face and professed, "It was a joke, Mr. Kirchstein. Me and the guys took Linus's glove to break his balls. I just wanted to see his reaction." Bobby Jones took the mitt and threw it down on the hallway floor next to Eddie and burst out laughing with orgasmic delight. The other boys followed his lead.

"That was awfully cruel. You boys should be ashamed of yourselves for tormenting this child," stated the administrator sympathetically. "Are you all right? C'mon now, straighten up. It's okay. It's over now. Your glove is right there next to you."

Eddie stopped whining long enough to snatch up his magic glove. He then dried his eyes and got back on to his feet again. He didn't utter another sound. He just walked over to the memo posted on the wall and began to read it.

The memo read, "All boys who are interested in playing varsity baseball should report this Friday to the gymnasium at 2:00 p.m. for tryouts. Sincerely, Skip O'Neil (coach)."

"See you assholes on Friday," Eddie yelled at the older boys as he stormed away down the hallway.

The administrator gave Eddie an astonished look and shook his head in disbelief. The other boys just snickered at his remark and disbanded.

SECOND THOUGHTS

It was a long wait for the late school bus, but Eddie was used to it. Since his arrival in high school, he never rode the regular bus home. The late bus became a sort of safe haven for him, a retreat from the ridicule he experienced throughout the school day. Very few people rode the later buses, and because of this, he felt assured that any derogatory comments would be few and far between. Eddie learned to believe the old adage that "there is beauty in numbers." This belief was reinforced by the fact that many of his daily hecklers, when riding alone on the late bus, were far less brave with their comments, especially since their friends were not around to back them up.

From day one in high school, Eddie had received very shabby treatment indeed. His reputation from his middle school days had preceded him. Back then, he was big enough to fight his battles, but in high school, it was a totally different story. He was nowhere near big enough, nor strong enough, to tangle with the tall, muscular, and older boys that inhabited the high school. In Eddie's eyes, those were the only kind of boys that ever started trouble with him. At times he had feelings of deep regret for the way he treated others during his middle school days because now his pugnacious behavior was coming back to haunt him. To him, every mean deed he committed in the past seemed to be repaid threefold. The upper classmen seemed to focus in on him as their new public enemy number one.

Losing his patience, he stared out yonder to see whether he could spot the late bus making its approach, but it was nowhere in sight. His mind was in torment when he thought about the details of that game of keep-away. The thought of them taking his magic glove infuriated him to such an extreme degree it's hard to explain in words. He kept trying to understand why he had been victimized and thought, *Why couldn't they have just left me alone? I wasn't hurting them. All I wanted was to see that memo on the wall. Was that too much to ask?* He came to the conclusion that obviously it was since they were compelled to mess with him and his magic glove. It seemed like everyone was always trying to mess with him and his magic glove.

Thinking about his ordeal caused Eddie to lose his cool, and he stomped his foot on the pavement angrily. The loud stomp disturbed the tranquility of the moment and the few other late bus riders gathered looked over toward him curiously. He pretended not to notice their stares by focusing his attention upon a stain that had appeared on one of his sneakers.

To Eddie, the most nerve-racking upcoming event was the varsity baseball tryouts. He knew that he hadn't matured enough physically to be a star on the varsity team yet. He also questioned whether he could hit the kind of pitching that he would have to face as a varsity baseball player. Thoughts of Sandy Roberts and ninety-mile-per-hour fastballs filled his mind. He questioned whether he was physically able to compete at such an advanced level.

The late bus made its way up the school road toward the bus stop. It turned into the turnaround and came to a screeching halt. A small group of students gathered in a single file line next to the entrance to the bus, waiting for the door to swing open so they could board. The students that boarded with Eddie were composed of kids who stayed after school for extracurricular activities and ones who had been forced to serve out disciplinary detentions. Eddie enjoyed their company because for the most part they minded their own business.

Eddie climbed up the stairs and made his way to his usual semiprivate niche in the back of the bus. He sat down on the hard plastic seat and stared out the little adjustable window. His mind and thoughts wandered as he mulled over how he was going to deal with all the adversity that was being thrown at him. He pondered the question as to how he was going to play baseball alongside his tormentors. He thought reconciliation with his new high school teammates would not be out of the question. He recalled how well he used to get along with his little league teammates before he discovered the magic glove. Maybe he could dig deep down inside and find that part of his personality, the part that everyone used to love. If it was there before, he reasoned, then it must still be there. He concluded that some soul-searching was in order.

A Rebellion
in "Heaven"?

With soul-searching on his mind, Eddie went to sleep that night. For years now, sleep was number one with him because he felt it was the only time he got to spend among friends but unlike most boys his age these dream friends were not of the feminine persuasion. No, Eddie never dreamt about girls or future sexual conquests, instead he dreamed of his coach.

Eddie loved his dream coach more than anybody in the world. The young infielder filled his nights with the promise of a terrific future. The two established a bond that few will ever experience. Any problem in life that he came across could easily be discussed openly with his only trusted friend, the dream coach. Because of their relationship, every sleeping moment was eagerly anticipated. He often debated with himself whether there was anything in the world that he wouldn't do for his best friend, so far he couldn't think of anything. Routinely, he would find himself at the old deserted ballpark with his coach shortly after laying his head down on the pillow. This night was much different though, the anxiety of the incident at school and the upcoming tryouts made him much too restless to fall asleep and hence delaying his arrival.

Eventually Eddie passed out and found himself wandering down the baseline toward the young infielder, who was nervously biting his nails by the dugout. He was dressed, as he always was, in his old fashioned Chicago White Sox uniform with those unique green patent leather baseball cleats.

"Eddie, my boy! It's good to see you. You had me a little worried, kid. For a while there, I didn't think you were going to show," the dream coach said with what seemed to be the weight of the world lifted off his shoulders. He joyously ran up the baseline to greet his charge with a big hug.

"I would've been here a lot earlier, but I just couldn't fall asleep."

"Yeah. I know about restless nights, Eddie. When I used to play, I could hardly sleep a wink."

The man in black started to stir in the dugout, and the dream coach immediately became aware of his presence.

"Coach, tell me about when you used to play?"

The man in black stepped out of the dugout and stared evilly over at the two. The coach turned away from Eddie and, using his hands, made a gesture for the dark man to relax.

"Eddie, I'm not allowed to talk about my life, so please don't ask me about it. Let's just concentrate on yours instead. I've been told that you're having problems with some of the older boys at school. You have to do something about these problems, Eddie. If you don't, the Manager says you won't be allowed to come here and visit me anymore."

"That's exactly one of the reasons I couldn't sleep, Coach. It's not like it was back in middle school. I'm not big enough to beat up everybody who messes with my glove these days. In fact, I think a lot of my troubles have come about because the word got out about my middle school reputation. Now I find myself having to deal with the older brothers of all the kids I beat up back then, and believe me, they haven't been very kind about it," Eddie said dejectedly.

The dream coach picked up a baseball that was lying on the pitcher's mound and began throwing the ball up in the air and catching it while continuing his conversation with Eddie. Nervously, he said in a staged and rehearsed manner, "Eddie, I told you that sacrifices must be made in order to uphold the integrity of the glove. No one ever told you that making sacrifices was going to be easy. You don't get anything in this world for free. You know that, and I certainly do. So far, the sacrifices you've made have been small ones. Beating up the kids who touch your glove, wishing your teammates bad luck during ball games, these are insignificant sacrifices, and may I add, small prices to pay for the kind of talent and instructions you've received since you arrived here."

"You know sometimes I don't believe that you believe a word that you say. Look at you, you're busy concentrating on catching that ball instead of looking over at me. Is that because you don't want to look at me, or maybe it's because you're making light of my problems? Because to be honest with you, Coach, those have been very significant sacrifices. Those very sacrifices that you say are so insignificant are the ones that are causing me the most grief in school. Coach, nobody even likes me anymore. Everybody wants to mess with me. I've been singled out as a target for abuse," Eddie pleaded in exasperation.

The coach suddenly dropped the ball. "I understand, Eddie. Believe me, I understand," the coach divulged with heartfelt sympathy, displaying the fact that his sense of humanity was still intact.

The dark man ran toward the gathering and pulled the coach over to the side. Immediately, Eddie heard the thundering sounds of a tornado that totally drowned out his ability to pick up on their conversation. It boggled his mind that there was no wind. He could hear the tornado, but he could not feel or see it. What he did see was the Manager screaming at his coach, and he wished more than anything that he could suddenly become a lip reader. Unfortunately, this was a gift that Eddie never acquired.

"If you don't stop with that bleeding heart bullshit you're going to find yourself teaching baseball with the others, and believe me, you won't like it there. There won't be any grass or any cool breeze, you understand me? You better get it through that thick, lame brain of yours that your job is not to show compassion for the boy but to show him the way to me! I've invested a lot of time in this boy, and I will not take kindly to any reversals of fortune. The boy's inner drive for greatness is starting to weaken. It's obvious that we're losing our grip on him. He's starting to worry about what people think of him. Just the tone of his voice tells me that he's starting to second-guess my ploy, and we must get those thoughts extinguished immediately. We must scare him into conformity! We must put him on the Procrustean bed. You tell him that I want those boys that played keep-away with his glove severely beaten or he can forget all about any professional baseball aspirations. This way he'll have to prove his allegiance toward us. You teach him how to beat those boys up or your services here will no longer be necessary," the dark man raved and threatened. "Do you understand me?"

"Yes," the coach said sullenly with his head bowed.

"Good. Now, go get to it!"

The dark man walked slowly back toward the dugout, and the tornado sound instantly was relieved from Eddie's ears.

"What in hell was that all about? I saw him chewing you out something fierce, but I couldn't hear a damn thing. You know I'm starting to dislike that guy!"

"The Manager is angry, Eddie. He says he's going to take away the magic in the glove if you don't get even with those boys that terrorized you. The Manager says no one is to touch your glove but you."

"Easier said than done. Did you tell him how big the kids are now? Did you tell him that they have no reservations about ganging up on me?" Eddie stated these facts sounding completely overwhelmed by his new problem.

"Eddie, there's a way around them ganging up on you. The most important thing is mind-set. To beat a bully, you have to think like one. The one thing you have to remember about bullies is that they like to give, a whole hell of a lot, more than to receive. Bullies have a notorious reputation of being afraid to receive the medicine they dish out. Every bully I ever ran into hated to get hit. They didn't mind doing the hitting, but they usually chickened out when faced with some legitimate opposition and to a bully legitimate opposition is anyone who doesn't lie down and take it. They enjoy beating up on pacifists or people who are just too afraid to defend themselves. Now Eddie, I don't think that you fit into either one of those categories. So here are a few ideas to ponder, kid: Number one, since they're bigger than you are, you need to cut them down to your own size. Number two, you need to catch them individually so that you won't have to deal with them as a group, and lastly, you have to appear to be so crazy in their eyes that the thought of retaliation will never cross their minds."

"How am I going to do all that? Don't forget I want to play on the same team with these guys."

"Intimidation, Eddie, that's how the game is played. That's how the Mafia works. That's how bullies are successful. That's how the world works, Eddie. All the world's strongest leaders are friends with the Manager and have adopted his policy that it is better to be feared than loved. You can persuade those boys that it is in their best interest to shut their mouths. Intimidation, Eddie, it really works," the coach recited these thoughts like a bad actor who indicates his feelings. He just wasn't very convincing and anyone perceptive would know immediately that these thoughts were scripted and not his own. He added, "Don't fret, Eddie. Before you awaken, you shall know what to do."

Eddie stared over at him curiously, thinking that something was definitely wrong but kept it to himself and replied facetiously, "That's what I like about hanging out with you guys you never leave anything up to chance. Whenever I leave here, I always feel like I have an edge on everybody else."

"That edge you're talking about Eddie, that's exactly why I'm here," the coach stated with underlying emphasis while deliberately looking the boy straight in the eyes.

As soon as those words were uttered, the dark man, the Manager of this little fantasy world raced out of the dugout and confronted the coach. With fire in his eyes he shouted, "I detect a betrayal! What are you trying to say to the boy?"

The coach stood shaking nervously trying desperately to regain his composure. "There's no betrayal here, boss. I'm not a traitor to the team. What I meant by what I said was that I was here to give him the edge. I swear that's what I meant," the coach pleaded.

The Manager stared deeply into the coach's eyes and he knew that trouble was brewing on the horizon. He was slowly but surely beginning to despise him and the telltale signs of this were written all over his face, but due to the coach's unique relationship with the boy, there was not much he could do without jeopardizing the overall scheme of things. So for the time being he tried his best to ignore the rebellion and begrudgingly started the long trek back to the dugout. As a result, Eddie took mental note of this incident. Little did he know at the time but this memory, among others, would be of the utmost significance to him in his future attempts to unravel the enigma that had become his life.

"Talking about intimidating. Boy, he has a short fuse, huh? Glad I don't have to deal with no managers like him. Don't you feel like punching him right in the snot box, sometimes?" Eddie asked, showing his coach a clenched fist.

"Eddie, don't say those kinds of things here, please. You don't strike the Manager. Remember that, kid. Because no matter how good you are, he still calls the shots." The coach sighed while intently watching the dark man go back into the dugout.

"Okay. We won't talk about that overbearing pain in the ass anymore, we'll just talk baseball. Do you know I overheard Sandy Roberts talking today about how his fastball was clocked at over ninety miles per hour?"

"That's awfully fast for high school. I'll bet you're afraid that you can't stand in against pitching that fast," the coach asked with concern.

"Well, let's put it this way, I've never seen pitching even close to that speed. I mean this guy's got a major league fastball."

"Eddie, the secret to hitting that kind of fastball is increasing your bat speed. In the old days, guys used to think that the bigger and heavier the stick, the more power they got. But that simply isn't the case. It's bat speed, Eddie. The faster you can move a bat through the strike zone, the more power you'll have. So what I'm trying to say is to forget about that heavy bat that you've been using. You go grab one a few ounces lighter and practice swinging it as fast as you can."

Eddie walked over toward the dugout and did what he was instructed to do. The coach watched his practice swings intently. He focused in on trying to find holes in his swing or other such problems.

"How's that feel?"

"Good…You're right. You can swing this bat a lot faster than the one I was using, but are you sure about that increase in power you were talking about?"

"Absolutely. It's the speed, not the lumber, Eddie. With that bat, you can catch up to a ninety-mile-per-hour fastball. Remember when a ball is coming in at ninety miles per hour it doesn't take much to send it a distance, just making contact with a speeding bat will increase the velocity tremendously and get it to its destination very quickly. That's why you hear about major league home runs getting out of the ballpark so fast."

"You're incredible, Coach. You know everything when it comes to baseball, don't you?"

"You give me way too much credit, Eddie. There are a lot of ex-ballplayers who've forgotten more than I'll ever know."

"I guess you're referring to my phone friends, huh?" Eddie asked as he practiced his swing.

"Whatever you think, Eddie. Another thing, kid, you've got to keep your swing level no matter how fast you're swinging the bat. That's why you have to practice so much. Fundamentals in baseball are everything."

Eddie immediately began adjusting his quicker but so far uneven swing to a more level one as his coach suggested. While his coach looked on, he quietly practiced this new quick and level swing for about ten minutes until he felt confident that he was starting to master it.

"Your swing is starting to look a lot better Eddie."

"Thanks, Coach. Can you throw a ball ninety miles per hour?"

"Wish I could, but I never pitched except in batting practice. And they don't pitch ninety miles per hour in batting practice, kiddo. And even if I could throw that fast, I wouldn't stand in against me. There's something called control that's relevant here. And I'm sure at ninety miles per hour that's something I'd be without."

"Gotcha, Coach." Eddie chuckled. "So you're telling me that you're not another Nolan Ryan?"

The dream coach looked over at him and asked dumbfounded, "Who's Nolan Ryan, Eddie?"

"I think he came after you. Can I ask you a question?"

"Sure. I can't guarantee that I'll be able to give you the answer you're looking for, but you're certainly entitled to ask."

"Well, I've been meaning to ask you this for quite some time now, but I just never found the right moment. I don't want you to take offense or anything, I just wondered, I know it probably sounds pretty silly to you but…are you dead? Ruth and Gehrig are, so I just wondered if you were too."

The coach's smile instantly left his face, and his expression became one of deadly seriousness. He looked Eddie straight in the eyes before answering in a most alarmed and defensive manner, "No, Eddie. I can't be dead. I've got a hell of a lot to live for. You know I've got a lot of other talents besides playing baseball. How in the world could I be dead? I mean, look at me, I'm vibrant. I'm strong. I have my whole life to look forward to. No way, Eddie. The thought of me being dead is definitely a silly notion on your part and just not feasible. Don't you agree?"

"Well, certainly. That's what I thought, I mean you look awfully alive to me," Eddie said happily but taken aback by the question. He realized that he had struck a very sensitive nerve in his coach. He quickly added, "And believe me, I know you have a lot more talent than just the way you coach baseball. No offense was intended by the question. I'm sorry for asking it, it's just that you're not very up to date on things. You know, the White Sox don't wear that style uniform anymore?"

"They don't?"

"No. I don't think they've worn that style uniform in a long time. Did you play for them?"

"Eddie, what did I tell you?" the dream coach asked in frustration.

"You're not allowed to talk about your life. I'm sorry. I'm really not trying to be a pest. It's just that I want to know so much about you. I mean, I see you all the time, and I really don't know anything about you at all. I don't even know your name. Ah, what the heck? Maybe this is just a dream after all."

"Eddie, you make your own reality. I'm as real as you want me to be and as far as my name is concerned, I think Coach, will suffice."

Sadly, Eddie stared out and gazed around the empty ballpark thinking, *What is really reality?* He questioned. *This place seems so real. Maybe I'm in another dimension,* he reasoned. He recalled an episode of the television show, *The Twilight Zone,* where people living in the world had identical twins in an anti-world. He thought for a moment that maybe he had entered into one of those anti-worlds. Thinking the entire hypothesis through began to give him a tremendous headache. His final thoughts on the matter were that maybe his coach really is alive, like he said he is. Maybe he just mysteriously got transferred to another realm of existence. Heck, if he could get here, why couldn't his coach? He came to the conclusion that life is all about, "passages". He theorized that maybe we just travel from one realm to another. Maybe we never really die. Tears started to fall from his eyes as he made this epiphany.

His dream coach perceptively asked, "What's wrong?"

"Nothing. I think I might have figured out what life is all about. Thanks to you, I think I've discovered our true destinies."

The coach shook his head in wonder as he watched the tears flowing down the boy's face. The boy was so emotional and reminded him of how he used to be at that age. "Kid, you're too profound for me. I'm just a ballplayer. I'm not an atomic bomb scientist. I don't know anything about life's destinies other than the fact that in spirit I'll always be here with you," he said in an attempt to comfort him.

"Well, that, my friend, if you ask me is a pretty good destiny. And don't try to snow me on your lack of intelligence. I think you're a lot wiser than you let on. You know, I always want to be able to come here and see you."

As soon as those words were uttered, the dark man came out of the dugout and made his way across the baseball diamond to home plate. He stopped and stared over at Eddie. It was almost as if he could look right through him. This was the moment the Manager had been waiting for.

"If you truly mean what you say, then you better listen to what your coach wants done to those boys that played keep-away with your glove, Eddie, or you won't be coming down here anymore, that I can guarantee," the Manager said threateningly.

"Don't sweat it, boss. I told you that I'll give him the 'divine inspiration' he needs. Believe me, when he awakens, he will know what to do," interjected the coach, putting an affectation on the words "divine inspiration."

"He better," said the dark man. "Don't fail me, Eddie, because I'm deadly serious about your plight," the dark man threatened while sneering over at the coach. He looked like the poster child for "Frustrated Control Freaks Anonymous" as he angrily wandered back to the dugout.

"I don't like him. I've heard about guys like him before. They always feature them on *America's Most Wanted*. They call them control freaks."

"*America's Most Wanted*, huh?" the coach repeated curiously. "What is that, like a radio or television show? You'll have to excuse me, I guess I'm not up on current events. All I do know is that they're the boss here, Eddie."

"Yeah, I can see that…Coach, do you think you could arrange for me to face a pitcher, who could throw the ball to me at ninety miles per hour? I'd feel so much more confident at the tryouts if I got a chance to face that kind of heat beforehand."

"I think the best I can do Eddie is bring in a pitcher who can throw in the high eighties. Believe me, that's close enough. You've never faced anyone who could throw that hard before."

"Cool. Who do you have in mind?"

"Eddie Cicotte."

"Eddie Cicotte? You don't mean the Eddie Cicotte who helped throw the World Series?"

"Yeah. That's exactly the Eddie Cicotte I mean. When you're here, you only deal with the best. When do you want to face him?"

Eddie had a dumbfounded look on his face as he pondered the question. "Eddie Cicotte, huh? Well, even if you could get him here, he'd be way too good for me. I mean, this guy should have been a Hall of Famer. I don't think I'd stand a prayer at bat against him."

"You will, if we limit his pitching arsenal. We'll tell him to throw you nothing but fastballs. Believe me, he'll do what he's told."

"Well, under those circumstances, I'd give it a shot, but his pitching location would be way too much for me."

"I'll have him throw the ball right down the center of the plate. Would that make you happy, kiddo?"

"Yeah. I mean, tell him I'm only fifteen years old. Tell him that I'm just learning the game."

"Don't sweat it, kid, old Eddie is an expert at delivering meatballs for a price. Let me go talk to the Manager."

Eddie watched in amazement as his coach marched toward the dugout. "You're serious, aren't you?"

"Of course I'm serious. What do you think I'm doing? Taking this walk for my health?" his coach said, grinning.

As his words died out, the coach disappeared into the shadows of the dugout. Eddie continued to practice swinging the bat evenly and quickly. He concluded that everything was possible in this dream world. Momentarily, the coach wandered out of the dugout with an average-sized man following him. Eddie tried to listen to the two men converse as they made their way toward the pitcher's mound, but for some unknown reason, their voices were muffled. It was frustrating for Eddie because nothing ever seemed to work the same way in the dream world as it did in the real world. His number one peeve was the deafness he suffered whenever he perceived that something important was being said around him. He was infuriated as he stared over at his coach and that ballplayer conversing while hearing absolutely nothing.

"Thanks a lot for thinking of me. I've been waiting to pitch for a long time," said the average-sized man wearing the ancient White Sox uniform.

"Well, the kid needs to get in with a real fastball, and according to the Manager, yours is as good as we've got," the coach stated frankly.

"How about I make a deal with you? If I'm able to strike this kid out, let's say ten times in a row, then I earn my wings and get to leave this wretched place. How's that sound?"

"I'm afraid it doesn't work like that, Cicotte. You're here for good, buddy. This is just a small vacation for you. I mean, if you've got a problem with that, we could always send you back to where you came from and find somebody else."

"No! No, no, no, no! That won't be necessary. Come to think about it, this seems like a pretty nice place to pitch. No! No, no, no! I'm in no hurry to go back. You're the boss. You tell me what you want from me," Eddie Cicotte said distraughtly in a panicked tone of voice.

"We want you to throw the kid meatballs, but we're mainly interested in the overall speed of the pitch. We want you to throw as close to ninety mph as you can. We're only interested in velocity, understand, Eddie?"

"Got you. Fast meatballs you want. Fast meatballs you get. Just like the Reds got. I was really serving them up during that series. There were no junk balls being thrown during the first two games I pitched, that I guarantee you," Eddie Cicotte said proudly.

The coach shook his head in disbelief after listening to the diatribe of the Manager's personal "circus act." Eddie Cicotte made his way to the pitching rubber. A young man dressed as a ball boy ran out of the dugout carrying a catcher's mitt and handed it over to the coach. The coach put on the catcher's mitt and squatted down behind the plate to receive Eddie Cicotte's warm up tosses. Cicotte might not have thrown the ball ninety miles per hour, but he threw it fast enough to put a good stinging on the coach's hands. The coach knew that the ball was coming in fast enough to test little Eddie's courage and bat speed. After about ten warm up tosses, the coach instructed young Romano to step up to the plate, but he was too mesmerized by the presence of Eddie Cicotte to hear the instruction.

"My little man, step into the batter's box," the coach repeated.

Eddie broke out of his trance momentarily saying, "That's really Eddie Cicotte. Can you believe it? This is just incredible. It's like I've stepped back in time. I can't believe my eyes, Coach."

"Well, believe them," the coach said with levity, brushing off the boy's concerns as if they were unfounded. "Now, listen, Eddie, relax. Concentrate on the baseball. Focus in on the trajectory of the incoming ball. Remember, with a major league fastball, all your decisions have to be made quicker than before. If you hesitate for a moment, I guarantee you that the ball will be by you. The moment the ball leaves his hand, you have to know whether you're going to swing or not. If it looks like the ball's trajectory will make it a strike, then swing. You have to make this decision almost immediately, understand?"

"Got you, Coach."

The coach waved at Eddie Cicotte to get his attention. "Cicotte! Remember, meatballs only!" the coach ordered.

Cicotte began his windup and fired a fastball letter high toward the center of the plate. Eddie's eyes became dilated and filled with fear as the speeding ball approached. With the fear of God in those eyes, he dove away from the batter's box just as the pitch crossed the plate dead center.

"What are you doing, Eddie? That was a strike," the coach blared out.

Eddie got back on to his feet and dusted himself off. "I'm sorry. I was scared it was going to hit me."

"Eddie, you've got to be brave, my little man. That ball was straight as an arrow. It was nowhere near inside. What are you going to do when you have to face a curveball and it looks like it's going to hit you until the very last second when it breaks across the plate?"

"I don't know. Maybe I'm not cut out to be a major leaguer after all. I thought the magic of the glove was supposed to take care of all that."

"You have to believe in yourself and the magic, Eddie. Trying to become a major league ballplayer is no easy chore. It takes hard work and dedication, including the bravery to stand up to a real fastball. Now I know that you have that kind of bravery. It's the same kind of bravery that you need to give a beating to those bullies at your school. And if you've got that kind of bravery, then you can stand up to these fastballs, can't you?"

"You bet I can. It completely slipped my mind, that's really Eddie Cicotte on that mound. He's a real pro, and he's got good control. There's no way he's going to hit me," Eddie rationalized in an effort to convince himself.

"Now you're talking, kid. So just stand in there. All I want from you is to just stand in that batter's box and get used to having that fastball cruising by you. So just rest that bat on your shoulders for the time being and relax."

"No problem, Coach. Sometimes I feel a bit stupid. I mean, I shouldn't have been a dunderhead in the first place. I should've known that Cicotte is a pro and not some wild throwing high school pitcher. It's embarrassing that I bailed out the way I did."

"It's okay, Eddie. Everybody forgets where they are occasionally. Believe me, I try to do it all the time. We'll just chalk it up to a temporary mind lapse," the coach said with a nervous laugh and an underlying bitterness.

Eddie stepped into the batter's box and fidgeted until his feet were set. He then nervously rocked his bat back and forth in a rhythmic manner as he waited the ensuing pitch. He watched Cicotte fiddle with a rosin bag before stepping on the rubber. Although he tried his best to act nonchalant, the sight of Cicotte on the mound in the flesh was simply overwhelming to him. His mind's amazement that this incredible event was actually taking place stunned him physically to the point that he had to step out of the batter's box and feel the pain of his own pinch to realize that this was all too real. He had an overwhelming compulsion to speak about this amazing event.

"Coach, forgive me, but I really feel like I'm at bat against a ghost. I'm just having the hardest time believing that I'm actually up to bat against Eddie Cicotte. I don't know for sure, but Eddie Cicotte's got to be dead. If he's not, he's an awfully old man. I just can't fathom how he could look so young for being so ancient. There's some kind of trickery going on around here. If this is really true, then somebody's not telling me the whole story. Coach, where am I?"

The dream coach signaled to Cicotte to take a break before attempting to soothe Eddie's apprehensions.

"Eddie, we've got to talk, my boy," the dream coach stated affectionately, placing his arm around the boy's shoulders. "Eddie, this is a place where dreams come true. People who are sent here never age. In fact, we're all given a choice to be any age we wish. Obviously, Mr. Cicotte would do you no good if he was pitching to you at over one hundred years old. So Mr. Cicotte chose to be his playing age. Believe me, that is Eddie Cicotte out on that pitcher's rubber."

"So then, you lied to me after all. You are dead, aren't you?"

"Eddie, you're only as dead as you feel. I certainly don't feel dead, so obviously I'm not dead."

"Very funny. Go ahead. Continue to play these mind games with me, but I think I'm starting to get it now. This has got to be the afterworld, the place where people go after their dead. So there really is life after death, huh? Wow! That's incredible! The only thing that doesn't make any sense is, how come I'm here? I really haven't understood that from the start. I know I'm not dead, so I can't quite figure out why I've been given this great privilege. I'm probably the only living person in the world who definitely knows that there is life after death."

"That's probably true, my boy."

The dark man quickly exited the dugout after hearing too much of Eddie's conjecture. He raced toward the batter's box where Eddie and the coach stood conversing. "I think it's about time that we tell you the truth, Eddie," the Manager said, lying with a poker face. "As you've already guessed from your remarks, this is the afterworld, Eddie. In fact, I'm very proud to inform you that this is the heaven that you've read so much about, and best of all, we're all angels here, aren't we, Coach?"

"Yeah, Eddie, we're angels all right," the coach mumbled in disgust.

"I figured it had to be something like that. So, Eddie Cicotte out there is an angel too, huh?"

"Sure. Of course he is," agreed the dream coach condescendingly.

"And you coach, are you an angel too?"

"Yeah, Eddie, I'm a special angel. I'm in the same boat that you're in. I got here by accident, just like you did. But unlike you, I haven't figured out how to leave this place yet. The Manager says that prophesy foretells that I will be leaving this place someday."

"Why would you want to leave heaven?" Eddie asked in amazement.

"What a dumb question to ask me. I hate to reiterate the obvious, but I'm alive. I don't belong here yet. How would you like to be stuck here if you were alive?"

"I am alive, but I understand what you're driving at. So why can't you find your way out? You know? Like I do?"

"Don't you think I'd give my bottom dollar to find that door? You are so lucky. You go back and forth, and I'm stuck here. It's just not fair," the coach complained.

The Manager was busy eavesdropping like usual and couldn't wait to add his two cents.

"Quit complaining, what more could you possibly want? You're literally surrounded by angels. Like the boy says, you're in heaven. What more could possibly have been given to you?

And if you ask me, this whole situation you've been blessed with is much better than what you deserve," the Manager interjected.

"You two fight like cats and dogs, and if you're all angels like you say you are, then how come I never got the feeling that you guys and the Babe and Gehrig are on the same team?"

"Don't believe the hype, Eddie," the Manager announced abruptly. "Heaven isn't such a perfect place, and angels don't always agree. There's a dispute going on in heaven between differing factions of angels on how you, my little man, should live your life. Our competing faction believes that everything is either black or white. Now you know that isn't true, Eddie. You know full well that there are gray and other colors. Our faction of angels knows that too. We also know that behavior in general can't be so simplistically categorized. We realize that all these conflicting messages you've been receiving must be confusing to you and that's why we're offering you a choice. Of course, by following our way of doing things, you receive an incentive, a magic glove. Tell me, Eddie, wouldn't the kids at school give their right arms for a magic glove that would give them the ability to become professional baseball stars? Wouldn't they?" the Manager asked excitedly.

"Yeah. I guess they would," Eddie admitted but still overwhelmed by the Manager's revelation.

"But hell, we're not asking you to give up your right arm. We know you'll need that to play with. As far as I know, your coach is only asking you to bludgeon the bullies who took your glove, that's all. Now is that asking too much from you?" the Manager inquired animatedly but in a very rational and reasonable manner. He sounded like a slick car salesman, trying his best to sound sincere while trying to close a very bad deal.

"Guess not."

"And what have the other guys offered you? Hold off on answering that question for a moment. I'll tell you what they offered you, nothing. You have absolutely no incentive to see things their way. And who wants to be associated with a group of do-gooders like that anyway? Believe me, Eddie, stick with us, and you'll get everything you ever wanted out of life and a whole lot more. What can I say, kid? We're a lot hotter than the other guys," the Manager said with a grin.

"I'm glad that you're starting to see things from a clear perspective, Eddie," the dream coach interjected, adding, "The Manager knows what he's talking about. He's right when he tells you that things are not black and white. In fact, I've often looked at dark deeds as a snowball rolling downhill if you get my drift." The coach said, using subterfuge hopefully to enlighten Eddie.

"Why did you use that analogy? What are you trying to say to the boy?" the Manager asked suspiciously.

"It's a pun on words. Don't you get it? A snowball rolling downhill gets larger, meaning he gets the most with us," the coach immediately responded adding, "Think about it."

"That's what you meant with that analogy? I've got some advice for you, stick to coaching baseball because you certainly aren't a poet," the Manager said condescendingly, knowing full well that he was being lied to and secretly seething inside over the obvious disrespect he was receiving.

The coach secretly hoped that Eddie would pick up on the analogy of the snowball rolling downhill, but so far, his message had not been received at least not by Eddie, but the Light that sees all things focused intently on the drama taking place at that dreary ballpark. The coach's words did not fall upon deaf ears as far as the Light was concerned. The Light immediately dispatched one of his heavenly helpers to the front line of the war between good and evil. "The Light" felt that it was an appropriate time to attempt to persuade the dream coach to betray Satan and earn his way to the real heaven. Michael, the dream coach's best friend during life was sent to the ballpark to assist in what was perceived to be a blossoming defection. Michael appeared on the scene surrounded by an ethereal light. The dark man noticed his presence immediately. He tried his best to act nonchalant, but secretly, he was rapidly reaching his boiling point. "Not you again. Eddie, this is one of those misguided angels I was talking about."

"Yeah. I faintly remember seeing him before. You can tell that he and coach are good buddies," Eddie remarked as he watched his coach's eyes light up in happiness due to the reunion with his best friend.

"That's the problem with your coach, Eddie. He's not a team player. He has no loyalty toward the team. In fact, he never had any loyalty for any team he was on," the Manager stated in disgust, keeping a close eye on the coach.

"Don't you think you're being just a little hard on him?"

"Excuse me, Eddie," the Manager interrupted as he bolted after the coach, who seconds earlier had run out toward the approaching Michael. The dark man was too late to prevent the emotional embrace taking place between the two men that very much resembled that of a loving son and his father after a long absence.

"Michael, you don't belong here. As much as I would like you to stay, you just don't belong here," the coach said with tears in his eyes.

"Neither do you, my son. It breaks my heart to see you here. You're deserving of so much better than this," Michael said, holding the dream coach tightly.

"You're wrong. I made my bed. Now I've got to sleep in it. Don't you understand? There's nothing you can do for me. I'm totally at his mercy here. This was the price I had to pay for that drink of water I had with the White Sox. You know I'm still paying," Billy admitted sadly.

"You don't give the Light enough credit. The Light is merciful, my son. Redeem yourself," Michael whispered in Billy's ear.

"How? If I betray him, he'll deny me passage back to the earth. I just need to find out how the kid does it, then I can follow him back and finally make things right."

"You're lost. He's got you so confounded and confused. I wish I could say more but you're going to have to figure this one out on your own. When the time is right, you'll know what to do, my son. Say no more. He approaches," Michael announced, placing a hand over Billy's mouth.

The dark man approached the two, trying his best to over-hear the gist of their conversation, but Michael's whispers were inaudible to the eavesdropping devil. The dark man was enraged by this fact. He always resented the fact that real angels and heavenly spirits had the upper hand when it came to any of his schemes. He could always overhear the words of his followers and any mortal visitors to his empire but actual heavenly beings were a different phenomenon entirely. The dark man exploded into a temper tantrum, expressed by the summoning of another windless tornado that temporarily deafened little Eddie.

"I smell a rat! Billy, you have done it this time! I'm at the end of my patience with you. You're a traitor, and you're going to burn in the lake of fire!" Satan threatened menacingly.

"I can explain," Billy said distraughtly. "I temporarily lost my head. I allowed the love I used to feel for him to blind me. I'm really sorry."

"That's your problem, Billy. You think you're too smart for me. You think you can pull the wool over my eyes. First, you thought you were going to break your pact with me in life by hanging yourself, but you learned differently, didn't you, my boy?"

"What do you mean?" Billy asked in shock. "I didn't actually do that. You told me I didn't succeed. There's just no way. I couldn't have succeeded. You told me that you saved me! Damn you! Don't you dare go back on that now! I'm alive! Don't you even try to pull this crap on me!" Billy passionately interrupted.

"Well, excuse me. I'm the devil. I lied. That's what I do. I didn't think there was actually anybody foolish enough to believe me. I must admit that you are one of a kind," the Manager made light of Billy's dilemma and smirked as if he was telling a joke.

Billy didn't catch the punchline and begged, "Please, stop playing this game. I'm starting to believe you."

Satan completely ignored Billy's emotional trauma and continued his rants, "And now you try to break your pact with me in death by conspiring with this heavenly being. Burn me once, Billy, shame on you. Burn me twice and shame on me. You understand me?"

"Yes, I understand you! But please tell me the truth! You know I'm not dead! So please take it back and let's be friends," Billy begged and pleaded.

Billy's pleadings were wasted on deaf ears as Satan continued his ravings, "We don't allow love here, Billy! We allow lust here! We allow obscenity here! We allow perversity here! But in my kingdom, *love* is a four letter word if you get my drift," Satan said with emphasis, mimicking the coach's earlier analogy.

With no reinforcements coming from Satan to support his longtime belief that he was still alive, Billy screamed out for one final reprieve, "Please, take it back! Don't tell me I really hung myself!"

"Well, of course you hung yourself. Don't tell me you actually believed that you could go back? You're going nowhere, Billy! You're just lucky I haven't sent you to the lake before this," Satan revealed with orgasmic delight.

Satan wanted one more crippling blow delivered to his meddling disciple, and with all the cruelty he could muster, he planted the image of Billy Green, hanging by the neck at Comiskey Park that fateful morning. Billy received the mental picture and fell to his knees screaming, "Oh god! No!" Billy got a sunken feeling in his stomach as he suddenly became completely resigned to his fate. He had always thought that he was special; now he was sure that he had always been living a dream. Satan had lied to him from the start, and he wanted so much to believe that lie, that he totally disregarded his own common sense. Satan never saved him from his suicide attempt like he had been told. No, he wasn't going back to the earth; instead, he now knew he was doomed to hell forever.

"Now that you know where you stand, tell your godly friend your true feelings toward him. Tell him how you and all of my servants feel toward former loved ones. Tell him what you'd really like to do with him now! Tell him! Let him know what you expect from him if he ever sets foot in this place ever again! Come on, Billy, prove your allegiance to me or burn like the rest of them!" Satan shouted for all to hear.

"I lied, old man. I don't love you. I only lust you! When I look at you, I think impure thoughts. I'd very much like to have my way with you. Now leave before I take my pleasures out on you!" Billy forewarned as Satan spoke through him and for him.

"May God have mercy on your soul," prayed Michael as he turned his back on Billy and exited the stadium.

Billy was stunned by the words he uttered to his surrogate father. He realized that he had no control when the dark man was present. Everything about his present reality was one big parlor trick. Although he wanted to apologize for the things he had just said to Michael, he was unable since Satan had taken complete control of his voice. The reality of this completely broke his spirit, and he hung his head low in despair.

"Good riddance, old man! Don't come back any time soon! And remember to remind your boss that every dog has his day, and mine is still coming! You tell him it's written in the scriptures. I will one day rule the entire world and everyone on it. And believe me, it will be for a hell of a lot longer than that stupid book of his predicts," Satan announced proudly.

When Michael disappeared out of the stadium, so did the tornado roar that engulfed Eddie's ears. Eddie was totally confused like usual after being deafened. He watched the Manager and his coach walking together with arms around each other as if they were best friends. He thought the whole situation he just witnessed was nothing less than bizarre. None of it made any sense to him. At first he thought World War III was breaking out between the two of them and now he didn't know what to think. He concluded that maybe it's better not to question anything that ever happened in heaven because none of it made any sense in accordance with common belief. He wondered how the church acquired so much misinformation in its depictions of heaven as such a great, harmonious place. He had a good mind to go to his local church and tell them just how chaotic heaven really was, but he knew that no one would ever believe him anyway, so he decided not to bother.

The Manager and his coach finally arrived together near the batter's box. The funny thing about the whole scene from Eddie's perspective was how they both acted so nonchalant. By the looks of those two, you could never tell that a major upheaval had occurred between them just a couple of minutes earlier. Eddie also knew that the "feud" between the differing factions of "angels" was more like an out-and-out war. Heaven was proving to be anything but peaceful and harmonious. From what Eddie had observed, it was loaded with anger, deceit, and suspicion; but he was ready and willing to overlook all of its pitfalls in order to keep the magic instilled inside his antique baseball glove. It was the magic that he most desired. He was sure now that it was his magic glove that made him so special in the eyes of the "angels" and gave him all these unique opportunities. Finding that glove changed his life and made him privy to information and experiences that others had to die for in order to get. He thought, *No wonder the coach wants me to beat the tar out of those kids who took my glove. That glove is sacred, and without it, I would be nothing.* He was sure now that he had it all figured out.

"Coach, do you think we could get back to baseball? I really need some practice hitting that fastball and poor old Cicotte's been waiting patiently for quite some time now. We don't want to see his arm tighten up, now do we? Then again those human-type ailments probably don't exist up here, but then again, maybe they do since nothing else up here seems to make any sense," Eddie stated enigmatically.

"Sure, kid. Let's get you some practice," the coach said with cold, spiritless eyes and never touching upon Eddie's enigma. "Yeah, let's practice."

CHOOSING SIDES

The jolting sound of loud music tore Eddie away from his sleep. Startled, he slapped the doze button on the electronic radio alarm clock and tried his best to resume his "heavenly" dream, but just when he thought he was making headway, the musical cacophony resumed, and he resigned himself to awakening for the day.

Eddie staggered out of bed in a daze and somehow found his way to the bathroom. He refused to turn on the bathroom lights because he hated to shock his eyes with the brightness of the illumination. So instead he felt his way through the shadowy bathroom, and with his eyes half closed, he regulated the water flow from the showerhead. After making sure that the temperature was just right for him, he stripped himself out of his pajamas and hopped in the shower. The blast of soothing warm water did not awaken him at first, but slowly, he started to open his eyes. This was his daily routine. It became the only way he could deal with awakening. The truth of the matter was he dreaded every morning. He didn't like to awaken because his dream life seemed to be so much more fulfilling. He never imagined that his earthly existence could ever possibly live up to the promise of his dreams.

As the warm water jolted him back to reality, Eddie forgot all about any plans of reconciliation with his high school teammates like he had thought about the day before on the school bus.

Now, he realized there was another way to deal with his bullying teammates. He had awakened with "divine inspiration" just as his dream coach said he would. He was now a man with a plan and at least on this occasion he was getting the feeling that reality might for once be just as exciting as his dreams.

As the warm water from the shower head splashed upon his face, Eddie briefly thought about what the future had in store for Bobby Jones, the kid who was one of the main instigators of the tormenting game of keep-away that had been perpetrated upon him. The thought alone caused him to break into an evil laugh.

A Solid Plan

All through the school day, Eddie kept a close eye on Bobby Jones. He pretended that he was a private investigator, researching the habits and tendencies of a suspect. He figured the odds of his plan succeeding directly depended upon how well he knew Bobby's idiosyncrasies. For that reason, he decided to devote all of his spare time to learning the boy's habits. He knew that Bobby had a girlfriend that he spent most of his free time with. It was common knowledge that Dolores Pritchard and Bobby Jones were quite an item at the school, and Eddie figured that he would most likely have to make his move after one of their frequent dates. Catching Bobby alone was a problem though, from what he observed, so far, the boy didn't spend much time alone.

Eddie immediately ruled out the school as a possible ambush site because Bobby was real popular with his classmates, and he feared retaliation from them. He concluded that Bobby's home was an equally poor choice, his reasons being twofold: firstly, the houses in the neighborhood were way too close together, leaving open a major risk of someone hearing something and alerting the police, and secondly, Bobby came from a large family and there was just too much risk that his brothers and sisters would hear the ruckus and quickly come to his aid. He knew the only way this ambush would work was if there were no witnesses.

After school, Eddie decided to skip going home and instead take the late school bus to Bobby Jones's neighborhood. He knew exactly which late bus to take because years ago he used to visit Bobby's younger brother Brett back in the days before he found the glove. Brett played alongside Eddie on the Astros in little league.

Eddie exited the bus and walked down the street toward the Jones's residence. Across the street from the Jones's was a large public basketball court. To Eddie, this court was a godsend. From this locale he could observe everything that was taking place at the Jones's and, best of all, not arouse the least bit of suspicion because he was merely hanging out like everybody else. Another fortuitous circumstance was the fact that the court was equipped with lights, so players could play on any given night until 11:00 p.m. This would make it easy for him to spy during the nighttime hours without looking out of place or suspicious, a situation that definitely benefitted his little subterfuge. What he liked best about this locale was the large grassy hill behind the court where he could lie undetected after the courts were officially closed. From the grassy hill, he could observe anything taking place at the Jones's during the night. He could take notes as to when Bobby arrived home from his dates and determine if he followed any set routines. An established routine was exactly what he was looking for. If he could find that Bobby followed an established routine, he could easily set up an ambush and win the approval of his coach in "heaven."

Upon arrival at the basketball court, Eddie discovered a group of kids playing a pickup game. He quietly walked past them to sit down on some bleacher seats that over looked the Jones's residence. From now on it was a waiting game.

EDDIE ROMANO, PRIVATE INVESTIGATOR

Eddie was rapidly discovering what all private investigators already know, spying is for the most part boring and tedious work. He had never seen so much basketball being played in his life. For hours now, he had sat on the bleacher seats and watched pickup game after pickup game being played while awaiting Bobby's arrival. He had been invited to play in at least a dozen games but turned them all down because he was afraid that he might miss something important occurring at the Jones's. He was now firmly convinced of how imbecilic that premise was. From his perspective, nothing ever occurred out of the ordinary at the good "old" Jones's residence. He was beginning to wonder whether Bobby ever came home after school or just made it his life's work to be out plowing Dolores's field every night. Sex was never very high on Eddie's list of priorities, and he had a hard time understanding why Bobby seemed to hold it in such high esteem. He thought, *Sex had to be the only reason why a guy would want to hang out with a girl in the first place. What else could they possibly have in common?*

Eddie was extremely happy that he brought a warm coat along with him on this spying mission because for the last couple of hours it was getting pretty chilly. He hoped that his mother found the note he left for her, telling her that he had to stay out late. He knew that when he eventually arrived home, she would demand an explanation from him, but like usual, he would tell her nothing. She wasn't open-minded enough to understand the kind of sacrifices a kid had to make in order to become a pro baseball player on the sly. And if he told her what his coach had asked him to do, she would have never believed it anyway. *Some things were better left unsaid,* he thought.

He was getting very impatient and fidgety as he watched the last basketball player of the evening, carrying a ball to his car and driving away. At last he was alone, and he knew the court lights would automatically shut off in ten minutes at 11:00 p.m. He knew that this was the time he would have to make his way up the grassy hill in order to maintain his surveillance. He had found out from one of the pickup game players that the cops patrolled the court after the lights went out. So he knew that on the hill was the only place where he could remain without being detected or disturbed.

He grabbed his duffel bag and headed up the steep embankment. As he made his way up the hill, he felt his socks getting wet from the early dew on the grass. He thanked God that he remembered to bring a blanket with him. He thought, *At least now he could rest upon the blanket without getting too wet.* When he reached an elevation, sufficiently high to avoid detection from the police, he opened his duffel bag and spread out the blanket on top of the damp grass. He lay down upon the blanket and fidgeted until he found himself a comfortable position. As he lay there constantly changing positions every couple of minutes, he remembered why he hated camping so much.

Eddie knew it was 11:00 p.m. because the lights suddenly went out on the basketball court. It was completely dark, and he was completely bored. His mind was having flights of fancy, wandering off to exciting locales as he stared out yonder at the inactivity of the Jones's residence. He saw himself surrounded by adoring fans after hitting the game winning home run for the Chicago White Sox. He pictured himself signing autographs like the stars he emulated. He imagined himself doing razor blade commercials like many of his major league heroes. He visualized himself doing that Right Guard Sports Stick commercial, discussing how he rid himself of offensive odors and talking about how civilized he was. He dreamed about the expensive cars he would buy and the beautiful homes he would own. After fantasizing about the perks of living the life of a star baseball player, he decided that the price the coach wanted him to pay was really a mere pittance. So he had to bludgeon a few assholes and rest his ass on the hard ground for a few nights while spying on the Jones's, he realized that these sacrifices were minute when compared to what he would gain from this whole ordeal.

He came back to reality just long enough to see that all the lights had gone out at the Jones's, and Bobby still wasn't home. He then started thinking about what he was going to do when Bobby did arrive. What could he do? He already ruled this place out as an ambush site. These questions ruminated in his mind and were majorly bumming him out. He concluded that he would just make note of the time of Bobby's arrival and start the long, five-mile trek back home. The thought of all the time he had spent waiting for him without any payoff in sight brought his spirits to an all-time low. He learned something about himself. He realized just how much he hated to make sacrifices, no matter how small they were, and he discovered for the first time in his life that his father might have been right when he told him that he really was a rather spoiled and shiftless human being. In his eyes, any sacrifices he made were monumental in comparison to any other persons. He started to take a good look at himself, and he wasn't particularly happy with what he saw.

Suddenly, like a preordained event, he finally got to see what he was waiting for, and he forgot all about any horrid self-portraits that he had drawn of himself. Bobby Jones's black T-Top Camaro pulled up and parked in front of the house. It was 11:15 p.m. according to his watch as Bobby bolted out of his still running car and made his way into the house. He thought, *Why didn't he shut off the engine? Where the heck is he going at this time of night?* His questions were momentarily answered by the gist of a boisterous conversation taking place outside the house. Bobby reappeared, dressed in a sweat suit. As he jogged over to his car, his mother, wearing a nightgown, appeared at the door saying, "Are you really going to go run again tonight?" To which he heard Bobby reply, "Mom, this is the best time to run. I've got to be in shape for try-outs on Friday." His mother then stated that she thought he was crazy and told him to keep his voice down because it was loud enough to wake the dead.

Eddie thought, *How convenient. He likes to run at night. I bet you that he's heading up to the school track. Boy is he going to be in for a surprise.* His concluding thought was that all his patience had finally paid dividends. He was pretty sure now that he had found an ambush site. He watched Bobby peel off in his Camaro as the lights of the Jones's home went dead. He gathered his stuff and headed home.

GROUNDED

It was half past midnight before Eddie finally traipsed through the front door. Since it was a school night, he immediately was met with some resistance by his worried parents.

"Where were you, Mr. Man?" Mrs. Romano confronted him in the living room.

"I was out. Didn't you get my note? I left you one," Eddie replied.

"Of course we got your note," his father interjected. "But that doesn't explain why you're out to the wee hours of the morning on a school night. Where in hell have you been?"

"I was working on a school project."

"Nice try. We called the library. It closed at nine. Tell me something, Eddie, how come I can never get an honest answer from you anymore?" Mr. Romano asked sarcastically.

"Look, it's none of your business where I've been," Eddie lashed out in rebellion.

"It's not, huh? Well, let's just say I'm making it my business. And you, my boy, have just earned yourself an indefinite grounding. I don't like the surly tone of your voice, and best of all, I'm not going to put up with it."

Eddie hated the way his father always invaded his personal space when making a point. He always felt like telling his father how bad his breath got whenever he got mad but decided against it in the interest of his own well-being.

"Dad, say it. Don't spray it," Eddie smart-mouthed.

"I'll spray it anytime I freaking feel like it! And what are you going to do about it?" Mr. Romano challenged, poking his index finger forcefully into Eddie's chest.

Eddie was beginning to feel physically threatened as he watched his father's face become beet red with the veins bulging out of his forehead. He had seen his father in this condition many times before, and he knew that this was the extent to which his old man could be pushed without guaranteeing an escalation to violence. He knew in the best interest of his physical wellbeing it was time to back off.

"Eddie! Shut your mouth and go to your room before you give your father a coronary," Mrs. Romano ordered.

"I'm sorry, Dad. Calm down, will you? I left a note. I thought that was good enough. I mean, you can't say that I was totally inconsiderate."

Mr. Romano took a deep breath in order to calm himself. "You're fifteen years old, kid, please try to remember that. As long as you live under my roof, I want the truth from you. I won't be lied to, Eddie. Your mother and I have been mighty fair with you, and we deserve better than this. Now, I don't want you out this late again on a school night. So when you decide to tell me where you've been, your grounding will be lifted, until then, you're grounded until further notice."

"Dad, what about baseball? Tryouts are on Friday."

Mr. Romano scratched the top of his head before replying, "You can go to your tryouts and any other baseball practices because I know how important that is to you, but other than that, I want you home. Understand me?"

"Yes, Dad. I'm sorry I worried you and Mom."

"Go get some sleep. Think it over. I want the truth, Eddie."

Mr. Romano watched him as he picked up his duffel bag and carried it up the stairs toward his room. He looked over at Lucy with saddened eyes. She too was sad. They were losing the battle for their son, and the pain of that awareness had finally come to light.

LOOKING FORWARD

Unlike most mornings since discovering the glove, Eddie awakened with a sense of purpose. He sprung out of bed, totally energized to face the coming day. Everything seemed wonderful on this chilly March morning, and why wouldn't it be? Today was the day that he would get a chance to earn some brownie points in heaven. During this day, if things went as planned, he could insure that the magic in the glove would continue to exist. As long as the glove's magic stayed strong, he felt confident that he would succeed at the varsity baseball try-outs and make the team.

After spending another night practicing hitting fastballs in heaven, Eddie found the lost confidence in his baseball abilities that had been missing since his arrival in high school. He was no longer afraid of Sandy Roberts' fastballs because he had mastered Eddie Cicotte's. He had learned to hit the fastballs of a legend and a mere high school pitcher seemed like a joke in comparison, but he also knew that the edge he had been given over others was very precarious. He knew that the Manager expected results from him or his little excursions to heaven during the night would come to a screeching halt. He knew that he couldn't take a chance on that happening and losing out on all the fabulous coaching he had been receiving. Another concern of his was how attached he had become to his dream coach. By this juncture, he considered him the older brother he never had. He realized deep in his heart that he would be totally crushed by the loss of his coach. Just the thought of it made him sick to his stomach. With those fears very much in his thoughts, he got himself prepared for the school day.

ANTICIPATION

To Eddie, there was something about anticipation that was dreadfully painful. As he sat staring up at the clock while Mr. Meehan lectured on algebraic formulas, he thought that this day had to be the longest one on record.

Eddie peered around the classroom and saw a few others who also lacked interest. Some were doodling instead of taking notes. Peter Bush sat in the back of the room, running his fingers through his wavy dark hair and collecting a few strands that fell out. He watched, with devious delight, as the boy took each strand of hair and chewed the whitish end that was previously attached to his scalp. A sick smile came over Eddie's face as he witnessed this because he knew how his father complained all the time about how his hair was starting to thin. He entertained the thought of seeing Peter in the future, hopefully in a similar situation to his father's, with him knowing in the back of his mind that he spent his dull moments back in school pulling out his own hair, hair that he could very much use to fill in those voids that were now ubiquitous. Eddie took it one step further and started to visualize what Peter would look like bald as a billiard ball and he fantasized about seeing him on a commercial for "Hair Club for Men."

After observing Peter's antics for a while, Eddie got bored and began to look out the window toward freedom. He couldn't understand why anyone would need to know algebra. Didn't the teachers know that he was destined to be a professional athlete? What would school ever do for him? As far as math was concerned, he could always hire an accountant to handle his multi-million dollar contracts.

Just at the moment when he felt like making a major distraction in class, he was saved by the bell. Every kid's favorite bell rang loudly throughout the building signifying, in Eddie's estimation, *The end of another tedious, six-hour boredom session.*

He expelled an extremely loud and exaggerated yawn as he prepared to leave the classroom. Mr. Meehan took umbrage to the gesture and stepped in front of the doorway, blocking his exit. He just stood there silently giving Eddie a prolonged dirty look. Eddie didn't return the look but instead concentrated on watching the toe of his sneaker slowly tap against the tiled floor. Realizing his ploy wasn't working, Mr. Meehan gave ground, and Eddie pranced by continuing to pretend to not recognize the confrontation that had just occurred. He had better things to do than think about his stupid teacher's nonsensical actions.

As he fought his way through the chaos in the hallways, he tried his best to dream up some exciting way to kill off the next eight hours before ambush time. Unfortunately, he couldn't come up with anything. He figured that he would go home and at least give the illusion of serving out his grounding. This way his parents would be satisfied, and he could easily sneak out of his bedroom window when it was time for action. The only thing he dreaded was the waiting. He found out that he was unable to focus his attention upon anything but his impending plans. This tunnel vision was beneficial when it came to achieving goals, but it also caused time to move exceedingly slow, especially during the moments in between.

Eddie went to his locker and opened it. He grabbed a handful of books to bring home with him. For his folk's sake, he had to keep up the ruse of being locked up with nothing to do but study.

He ran down the hallway toward the exit where the buses awaited. Upon arrival outside, he stared out at the many buses parked. He had never taken the early bus before, and he was confused as to which one to take. Luckily, he saw a familiar face board the bus farthest to his left. Since the girl he recognized just happened to live in his neighborhood, he decided to take an educated guess. Just to make sure, he asked the driver if the bus stopped at Cedar Trail. He was pleased when informed that it did.

THE FINAL HOURS

As Eddie sat obsessing in his bedroom, counting down the minutes before departure time, he displayed some classic symptoms of a psychopath, like the excessive need for novel, thrilling, and exciting stimulation, which of course he was unable to obtain considering the intolerable waiting game he was presently engaged in. For the last seven hours, he had behaved with the single-mindedness of one of those flesh-eating zombies you see in the movies. He couldn't sleep. He couldn't eat. He couldn't get his mind off the ambush for a single moment. In fact, if the truth be known, for days he had spent almost every waking hour with that one thought on his mind. His only fears were that Bobby Jones might not show up or that he might have guessed wrong as to which track he ran at. These were the themes of recurring nightmares that gave him serious doubts as to whether he could persevere through another monotonous day like the one he had just suffered through. As the time neared, he started to think positively. With a little luck, a great opportunity would soon avail itself to him. Within hours, the annihilation might be complete and finally he could prove to the Manager that he was truly worthy of having a magic glove.

Eventually, Eddie took a peek out the bedroom door to see if everyone had retired for the evening. He noticed that his mother's door was closed. This was a telltale sign that she had gone to bed.

The only unanswered question left, he thought was, *Where was his father?* Eddie snuck down the stairs and headed toward the kitchen before finding him in the living room. He was passed out on the couch with the television blaring. He quietly walked over to the television and turned the volume down. He then grabbed a crocheted blanket that his mother had made by hand and, with tender loving care, spread it out over top his dad. He loved his daddy despite their problems. He took a deep breath and prayed that things would work out for him. He hoped that he would still have a future after all of this and then he gathered the courage to say to himself, "Let's do this."

As Eddie made his way back up the stairs, his heart grew cold in preparation for the events that lay ahead. He made sure he dressed warmly before embarking on this adventure. At 10:00 p.m., Eddie equipped with a duffel bag, containing a flashlight and of course his beloved magic glove, made his way out the second-story bedroom window and onto the large oak tree that lay adjacent to it. He shimmied down the tree and began the three-mile hike to the high school.

THE AMBUSH

The trip to the high school track took longer than expected. It was a breezy March night, and the winds he fought on his journey had made his cheeks rosy red. Eddie was surprised at how cold it actually was. He could tell how frigid it was by the mist that was created from his exhalations. He hoped that all this effort was not made in vain. He was beginning to doubt whether Bobby Jones would really brave the low temperatures and make his regular midnight jaunt. He discovered that he started to get cold as soon as he stopped moving. This fact alone made him feel less than optimistic in regard to his chances of completing this mission.

As he stared out at the deserted track, his thoughts examined Bobby Jones's motivations. He wondered what could possibly motivate one to run at this time of night. He could understand why someone would choose to run at night during the summertime. Summer nights were the best time to run because the temperatures were bearable. *Why would anybody choose to run during the nighttime of early spring?* That was a question that boggled his mind. The only answer he could come up with was that Bobby spent so much time during the day plowing Dolores's field, which left only the nighttime for keeping in shape.

He believed that he had come up with the correct solution to that enigma, so he turned his flashlight on to illuminate his watch. He saw that it was now 11:00 p.m. He could feel his heart beating faster as the moment of truth was growing near. The excitement of what was in store for dear old Bobby brought about the need to urinate, and he pulled his pants down and relieved himself. From that moment on, his every sense was on red alert. He knew that his adrenaline was flowing because he didn't seem to feel the cold as much anymore. He was now wide awake and alert for whatever crisis lay ahead. The only intangible needed now was for the prey to fall into the trap.

Eddie was astounded at how aware he had become. Every audible sound expelled by the natural surroundings was intently focused in on and decoded by his enhanced sense of hearing. He now had some idea as to what a soldier on watch must have felt like during the war. He knew the animal kingdom was always aware. Lack of awareness for them carried a guarantee of impending doom. He thought for a moment about how soft the world of humans had become. Humans spent most of their lives unaware of the dangers that surrounded them. *Bobby Jones was definitely unaware of the danger that would surround him if he came out to run tonight,* Eddie thought. To Eddie, it seemed like human beings were the only animal on the planet that didn't live by the rule of the jungle. *What happened to the rule of "kill or be killed"?* It baffled him that in the human world the fittest didn't always survive. He never could quite cope with the fact that some small wimpy guys were the most powerful men on the planet while some of the most muscular were on the unemployment line. He debated whether humans had developed their society in a total contradiction to Darwin's theories. "Might makes right" wasn't the key to things in the human world; intelligence seemed to hold the greatest value. These small wimpy guys had somehow parlayed intelligence into money and in the human world; money was the key. This conclusion was upsetting to him because he was an athlete. He felt that athletes were more deserving of power and social prestige than the bookworms that held that spot on the totem pole of life. He thought it unfortunate that the rest of the world didn't seem to feel the same way, but he still left out a trace of hope that the world would someday see its error and that the strongest physically would once again be king.

He suddenly realized that his thoughts were drifting off onto a tangent and taking his focus away from the task at hand. He needed to be completely aware of what was going on around him. He figured it was time to stop thinking and start preparing since Bobby Jones could arrive at any time now. The first issue at hand was to scour the wooded area alongside the track in search of a large tree branch. It didn't take him long to find one the length of an average-sized baseball bat. The branch he chose was an inch thick in diameter and had quite a few smaller limbs protruding from its sides. He made fast work of breaking off the smaller limbs and leaving himself with a thick irregular stick. This stick was to be the equalizer between himself and the larger boy. With this stick, Eddie could cut Bobby Jones down to his size.

He sure hoped his theory about the stick was right because minutes later the test dummy arrived. It was like it was predestined as Bobby Jones arrived right on schedule. The second that Eddie noticed Bobby's Camaro approaching the track parking area, he felt his blood pressure begin to rise. He was afraid. He actually believed he could hear his heart pounding; although, his ear was nowhere near his chest. He quickly hid underneath the bleacher seats and began holding his breath trying his best to alleviate that paranoid feeling of being discovered.

The track that surrounded the high school football field had bleachers on both sidelines. He was presently hiding underneath the bleachers that resided closest to the track parking area. After composing himself, he realized how fortunate he was to be hiding in this particular area of the bleachers. Although he had been caught by surprise, due to the fact that Bobby had actually arrived, through some stroke of luck he had found himself resting at the same spot that he had concluded, would be the best strategic location during preparations. It was only logical to be positioned there because Bobby would have to pass his hiding place in order to get back to his car. He, once again, had it all planned out. He figured that he would allow him to get his run in and then attack him when he was all tired out. Eddie had nothing left to do other than keep calm, watch, and wait.

Bobby walked toward the track shortly thereafter. He was dressed in a gray sweat suit. Eddie could see the color of his clothing due to the lights that illuminated the parking area. Alongside the track, the only light available was that of the full moon that hovered high in the sky. He hoped only the moon would be a witness to the upcoming events.

Eddie watched quietly as Bobby began to do some stretching exercises to loosen up his leg muscles before beginning the run. Bobby was physically a lot more developed than Eddie. One could easily tell that Bobby was an athlete. He had broad shoulders and a streamlined physique. As Eddie watched him warm up, he became more convinced that only the element of surprise would allow him to prevail over the older boy, especially if it came down to a fight. He was becoming insecure once again, and he reached into his duffel bag to feel the leather of his magic glove. Knowing his security glove was so near helped him regain his confidence as he watched Bobby Jones begin his run. Eddie quickly got cold again from standing still and waiting, but he didn't dare come out of hiding because he was too afraid of being discovered. He kept rehearsing his plan over and over again in his mind but was having a problem keeping it focused because of the cold. After thinking through the plan of attack, he came to one conclusion and that was how important it was for him to incapacitate Bobby on the first blow. If somehow he misfired on his initial swing, he knew he would be in for a world of hurt. He kept reminding himself that if he made one mistake, Bobby would most likely pulverize him and leave him for dead. He also knew that no one would blame Bobby for doing it, especially after learning of the ambush. Indubitably, he knew that he had to be very careful.

Eddie watched Bobby as he completed another lap of the quarter-mile track. He was running at an increasingly faster pace. The first lap he jogged for the most part but now he was running with long strides. As he looked on he hoped that Bobby would exert himself even more and increase his pace. He was thinking, *Go ahead, Bobby, knock yourself out*. Luckily for Eddie, "knock yourself out" was what Bobby intended to do. Bobby was attempting to keep a relaxed breathing while exerting himself at progressively higher levels. To Bobby, that was what conditioning was all about. He was an avid boxing fan, and he recalled in his mind how Al Bernstein, a boxing commentator for ESPN, always remarked how the tired fighters were breathing through their mouths instead of through their noses. Taking Bernstein's words into consideration, he tried his best to run fast and breathe only through his nose.

Eddie was getting fidgety as he continued to squat down to conceal himself behind the bleacher seats. He was cold and anxious as he watched Bobby pass by his bleachers and continue on for another lap. He noticed that his back was starting to feel uncomfortable due to the hunched over position he was in. He thought, *How many laps is this kid going to run?*

After passing the one-mile point, Bobby decided that since it was colder than usual, he would limit his run to just one more mile. As he progressed around the track, he started to think of himself as a racehorse. His dad was an avid horse racing buff, and the boy had been to the track a fair share of times. He thought, *It might be of interest if there was a human race track where folks could wager on people instead of animals*. But then he changed his mind and decided that human races would be even more crooked than horse races. In Bobby's humble opinion, thinking made the laps go by quicker and less monotonously. He liked to think because his thoughts kept him entertained.

Eddie was also thinking but, unlike Bobby, his thoughts were not reserved for entertainment's sake but for questioning whether or not the boy would ever tire out. Eddie was flabbergasted by the fact that Bobby still looked awfully fresh for a guy who just ran over a mile. Eddie was getting impatient because it didn't look like Bobby's run would ever conclude. This was the most painful part of the evening for him. His anxiety was starting to get the best of him aided, of course, by the elements. All of his adrenaline was flowing, and he felt like he was ready to explode, but he knew that he had to wait or take a huge chance of blowing the entire plan.

Bobby raced down the stretch to complete his seventh lap. Knowing that he had only one lap to go, he turned on the speed that made him such a successful runner at three hundred meters for the high school's indoor track team. He had run the three hundred meters in thirty-five seconds flat during a meet in December of the past year. He wasn't quite running at that pace because of the energy he expelled during all the previous laps, but he was running very fast. As he made his way down the back stretch, he started to feel a cramp coming on in his right rib cage, but since he only had a little ways left to go, he decided to continue to run full speed. The cramp didn't become really painful until he was three quarters of the way down the stretch, but by this time, he had only twenty yards to go; and he decided to ignore the pain and discomfort and finish his run strong.

As he finished, he slowed down immediately and bent over trying to catch his breath. He grabbed at his rib cage attempting to soothe the pain while continuing to fight for a good breath of air. He walked slowly down the track with his head hung low, completely unaware of the danger present. Eddie had come out from behind the bleachers and shadowed him as he progressed.

Although Bobby was still bent over with his eyes firmly focused on his feet, he thought he saw someone moving to his right. He immediately straightened up and looked toward the lurking stranger. The next thing he knew was that something had struck him with a lot of force in the mouth. He could feel the numbness in his gums and the distinct taste of blood as he swallowed. Without warning, he was struck again, this time across the side of his head. He felt dizzy from the blow, and the sweat from his brow burned his eyes and temporarily blinded him. Completely out of reflex reaction, he threw his arms up to cover his face when he felt an excruciatingly painful blow in his groin area. The force of it bent him over at the waist, and he feebly grabbed at his burning gonads. Instantaneously, he felt his teeth smash against each other from a blow to his lower jaw. It landed with devastating force, and he found himself falling face-first into the black asphalt of the track. He tried desperately to get his wits together so that he could muster some kind of defense, but he was unable. His head was in a total spin, and he couldn't breathe properly as the onslaught continued.

Eddie looked down upon the pitiful sight of the once mighty Bobby, all sprawled out in a heap in the middle of the track. He reared his leg back and kicked him squarely in the side of the head. "This is what you get when you mess with my glove, asshole!" The voice he heard shocked Bobby back to his senses. "Linus, is that you?"

The comment infuriated Eddie so much that he kicked him even harder, this time on the top of his head. "Don't call me Linus asshole unless you want more!"

Bobby felt like his head was swollen up like a balloon. Every single part of his body seemed sore. "Please, Linus! I'm sorry," he begged.

"You better believe you're sorry. And you're gonna be a lot sorrier by the time I get done with you!" Eddie said menacingly as he reached down and ripped out a hand full of the boy's hair.

Bobby screamed from the pain and for the first time began to cry. "Please don't hurt me anymore."

"What's my name, asshole?" Eddie asked while using his foot to drive Bobby's head into the pavement.

Bobby felt the warmness of his blood as it poured down his face. The last blow had caused a huge wound to open above his right eye. "Eddie, I'm bleeding bad, man! Please stop! You've made your point," Bobby screamed for mercy.

"I don't think I have!" Eddie shouted as he began a vicious kicking assault upon Bobby's exposed rib cage. He completely lost his head as he kicked the boy unmercifully.

Bobby lay there perfectly still, numb from the barrage. He resigned himself to the belief that he was going to die. He was sure now that Eddie was going to beat him to death. His lungs hurt badly, and he had a terrible time trying to catch a breath. "Kill me. If that's what you're going to do, then just do it," he whispered.

Eddie was satisfied. He was the control freak now. His actions meant life or death to the groveling bully that lay beneath his feet. "No. I'm not going to kill you. But if you breathe one word about how you got like this, I promise you, I'll be back to finish the job. And next time, I won't kick you in the balls, I'll cut them off. You understand me? No police. No family. No friends. If anyone finds out what really happened here tonight, it's your ass," Eddie said calmly in a sadistic tone of voice.

"Don't worry, I promise. I won't breathe a word about you to anyone. If anyone asks me, I'll tell them I got mugged," Bobby whispered in terror.

"You better not be lying to me because if you are, your family's next. Just remember, I know where you live, asshole," Eddie forewarned. "Hey, Bobby, guess you won't be touching my glove anytime soon, huh?"

Bobby was too weak to respond, so he closed his eyes and fell asleep. Sometime later, Bobby reawakened to a bright light aimed directly in his eyes. His body was cold and his mind was foggy as the light neared. "Please, Eddie! No more!" Bobby shouted out in delirium.

The policeman heard the shout and ran toward the obviously injured boy. "Are you all right over there?"

Bobby lifted his head up and, in a daze, looked in the direction of the voice behind the light.

The policeman's flashlight illuminated the blood cascading down the boy's face. He quickly turned around and ran back to his cruiser. He got on the radio and called in, "I've got a badly injured boy bleeding profusely at the high school track. You better get an ambulance."

FEELING GUILTY

E
ddie lay on top of his bed and stared at the ceiling. He
had tried to sleep but was so pumped up with adrenaline
that it became physically impossible for him to do so.
In all of his fifteen years of life, he had never been so restless.
Although the physical act was now over, the emotional trauma
remained. He just laid there shaking his head in disbelief that he
actually went through with it. There was a nervousness that circulated throughout his entire body that kept his senses on red alert.
He imagined, in his mind, how the police would soon come to
the front door to take him away to jail. Every common nighttime
sound was misconstrued as the police on their way to get him, but
astonishingly enough to Eddie, they never came.

Hours had passed by, making him even more flabbergasted by
the fact that he was still a free man.

The coach's plan actually succeeded; intimidation really
worked. *No wonder the Mafia was so successful*, he thought. As the
break of dawn approached, he became increasingly more confident that everything had worked as planned. He had a smug
look on his face when he concluded that his dream coach was
an absolute genius when it came to these types of situations. He
surmised that Bobby obviously was so intimidated that he was
afraid to squeal.

Suddenly a bell went off in his head and he thought, *What if I'm wrong?* Feelings of guilt overwhelmed him as a list of assorted scenarios went through his mind, *What if Bobby ended up dying because no one had discovered him yet? What if that was the reason why the police hadn't come for me?* He considered for a moment calling 911 but decided against it when he remembered that they trace every call they receive. He started to rationalize, with himself, that the beating he gave him was really not that bad. He tried to convince himself that Bobby wasn't badly hurt. The problem he faced was that he really wasn't sure, and he couldn't be sure unless he called someone. Most disturbing to him was the thought of Bobby still lying on that cold track, bleeding internally, with no help in sight. He was not mentally prepared to deal with the consequences of murdering someone, and for that reason alone, he felt compelled to act.

He got up off his bed and dressed himself warmly. He then snuck down the stairs and exited out the front door. It took him about eight minutes to hike down to the 7-Eleven at the end of his block. From there he called 911 from a pay phone outside the store. It was about 4:30 a.m. and still dark outside.

The 911 operator took the call and immediately knew that someone was trying to disguise their voice. The voice the operator heard was a muffled one saying, "You'll find an injured boy on the track at Palatine High School." Before the operator could get a word in, the line went dead. The operator immediately sent a squad car out to the 7-Eleven, but by the time it arrived, Eddie was well on his way home.

THE AFTERMATH

Hours later when Eddie arrived at school, he heard the chitchat about Bobby Jones being mugged at the school track. He took solace in the fact that the stories he overheard were a far cry from the truth. The gist of the stories being rumored were that a group of black teenagers from the inner city of Chicago had infiltrated their way into the fashionable northwestern suburban community. This group of hoodlums allegedly accosted Jones while he made his regular late-night jog. They attempted to steal his car and assaulted him so ferociously that he almost handed over his car keys but instead he decided to stand and fight. Despite being greatly outnumbered, his courageousness finally broke the spirit of his attackers, who gave up on the idea of stealing the car and made their escape instead.

During homeroom, the principal got on the intercom and told the frightened students that he was going to beef up security on campus. He told them not to fear these gangs of hoodlums but to report them immediately to the police when spotted. He commended Bobby's bravery and told them that Jones would be spending the next ten days in the hospital in order to recover from the splenectomy he underwent earlier in the day. He asked the students to take a moment of silence to pray for Bobby's speedy recovery and the equally fast apprehension of this "marauding group of terrorists."

Eddie found the story that Bobby concocted very amusing. He was not the least bit surprised that Jones had portrayed himself as such a courageous hero. He figured that Bobby had a reputation to uphold, and the truth would be considered rather demeaning. He also knew by now that Bobby was way too scared to tell the truth.

His plans could not have gone any smoother. He was happy that Bobby's injuries were not life threatening, and he felt good about the responsibility he showed in calling 911, but he also knew that Bobby Jones was not the only one who instigated the game of keep-away. He soon learned the name of the other culprit. Ray Mayberry was the kid, who he had asked to tell him what the memo on the hallway wall said. He was the kid who instigated the group of upper classmen to torment him by taking his magic glove in the first place. Eddie remembered him holding it so high over his head and pushing him off every time he'd try to reach it. He concluded that Ray Mayberry was going to pay for his foolishness. Last night he was a bundle of restless energy, unable to sleep at all but tonight that would all change. Tonight he would sleep like a baby and return to heaven triumphantly. He figured that his coach and the Manager would be pretty pleased with his inaugural performance. They wanted him to get even, and he certainly accomplished that. Having succeeded once, he was confident that he could give Ray Mayberry an encore performance and assure that the magic would forever remain in his glove.

As Eddie sat at his desk, while the attendance was being taken by the homeroom teacher, he stared out yonder toward the baseball field. A smile came to his lips as he thought about how in the last few days baseball had temporarily become a forgotten subject. Those had to be the only days since obtaining the glove that he wasn't thinking about the game directly. He snickered at the thought of himself becoming a well-rounded individual with diverse interests. He sure had diverse interest's all right, baseball and trashing people. He thought, *Nice combination.*

TORN

By the time Eddie arrived home after school, he was totally exhausted. It was now thirty hours since his last wink of sleep, and as he walked in the door, he just knew his bed was calling for him. Unfortunately, his mother was calling for him too.

"What do you want, Mom?" Eddie asked in a very weak voice that very much resembled the tone of someone sleepwalking. He was there physically but mentally he was far away.

His mother obviously did not pick up on this as she appeared in the front foyer and began to adlib a written list of demands, "Your father has some work for you to do. He says that he's sick and tired of the place looking so run-down. He also told me to make it clear to you that you live here too, so you had damn well better turn your hand over once in a while. He left me specific instructions to make sure you paint that fence out there."

Eddie was shocked back to reality by the verbal assault and let out an exasperated groan as he got the news. "Oh, you've gotta be kidding me, Mom. I'm so beat. I can hardly keep awake. Do I have to?"

"That's not your father's fault. You're being punished, and you've had plenty of time to sleep. Now is the time to work, Mr. Man."

"But, Mom, I didn't get a wink of sleep all night. I've been all worried about the baseball tryouts tomorrow, and I just haven't been able to sleep at all." Eddie sighed. "Can't I do it over the weekend?"

"I'm sure your father has other things planned for you to do this weekend. I don't understand you, Eddie. We never ask very much from you."

"I know, Mom, but I really feel like I'm going to pass out right on the spot. I promise I'll make it up to both of you."

"You know what your father's going to think, don't you? He's going to think that you never listen to a word I say."

"But that's not true, Mom. I swear to you, this is absolutely on the level. Just come here and take a look at my eyes if you don't believe me."

His mother stepped closer and peered into them. "You're right. Your eyes look like two burnt holes. Haven't you been getting enough sleep?"

Eddie was not amused by the question and replied, "Hold on for a second. Isn't that exactly what I've been telling you for the last five minutes? You know something, you're the one who doesn't listen. Look, I'm going up to bed. I've got a big day tomorrow. Tell Dad that I'll do his work later."

Before anymore words could be spoken, Eddie bolted up the stairs to his bedroom. Upon arrival, he quickly got undressed and buried himself underneath the covers. He was out like a light. Before he was even aware that he had fallen asleep, he found himself again at that dismal, old, deserted major league ballpark. As he walked down the first baseline toward home plate, he noticed his coach staring out toward the outfield in a daydream of some sort. He looked very sad and was totally unaware of his approach. This was very unusual behavior for him since he was normally alert and energized. Eddie just knew that something wasn't right with him. He had the kind of look on his face that you see on the lifers in state prison. It was a hopeless look, as if every dream of his had died, and what Eddie wasn't aware of at the time was that they had.

"Hi, Coach."

"Huh?" The abruptness of the young man's voice startled him. "Eddie. You scared me. What are you doing here?"

"Bad time, huh? I guess I fell asleep too early. Maybe I should try to wake up and come back another time."

"No. Don't worry about it. You're always welcome here with me. I hope you know that."

"Are you all right? You look like somebody died."

"I look that good, huh?" the coach said with a forced smile.

"Yeah, you look really sad. What's the matter?"

"Nothing. I was just daydreaming about what it would be like to go back," the coach said wistfully.

"You mean, back to the earth?"

"Yeah, back to the earth, back to playing baseball again. Back to life the way it used to be. You know something, Eddie, when I think back about it now, it really wasn't that bad," the coach said reminiscing.

"Hey. Cheer up, will you? You're sounding like you're never going back."

"Maybe I'm not," the coach said painfully.

"Well, of course you are. If you found your way here like I did, you can certainly find your way back. Remember, you're a special angel and special angels never die. Isn't that what you told me?" Eddie asked innocently.

The coach amusingly giggled over Eddie's naivety and then continued to play along with the charade that had become his existence. "Yeah, I did tell you that, didn't I?" Suddenly, the coach had a change of heart and was compelled to speak frankly. He sullenly articulated all the feelings his soul longed to say, "Hey, Eddie, I just want you to know something, kid, something I never told you before. You know, I think the world of you. You're going to be everything that I always wanted to be. I always want you to remember me and to know that no matter where I am, no matter how far away, I'll be with you every time you step on that infield grass. Believe me, I'll always be there with you. I'll see through your eyes, and I'll feel every pain and joy that you feel, and if you ever feel like you can't go on, you just reach deep down inside and feel my spirit inside you and try to take it just one step further for the both of us, kid. Because only when you push it to the limit do you realize just how wonderful life really is." The coach said these words while turning his head away from Eddie, trying his best to hide his tears.

"You're not going to die, are you, Coach?" Eddie asked in distress.

"No. Nothing's ever going to change for me. I'll always be here," the coach said with the anguish of someone coming to terms with the fact that they were truly condemned. Reality had set in, and it was a bitter pill for him to swallow.

"Well, I'm sure happy to hear that," Eddie replied, ignorant of the magnitude of the coach's words. "I wish you wouldn't get so down. It really bums me out to see you so depressed. Just remember I love you, Coach. And I hope you know that there's nothing, and I do mean nothing, that I wouldn't do for you."

"Yeah, I'm pretty well aware of that," the coach said bitterly.

Eddie sensed some animosity on the coach's face and asked innocently, "You're not mad at me, are you, Coach?"

"No. How could I be mad at you?"

"I mean, I did what you asked. Did you watch me? I put that kid right in the hospital. Your plan worked like a charm. He never stood a prayer."

"You must be proud of yourself, huh, kid?" the coach asked rather sarcastically, his tone not picked up upon by Eddie.

"You better believe it. Like I told you, there's nothing I wouldn't do for you."

"And, Eddie, you don't feel the least bit guilty?"

The Manager had been sitting in the dugout eavesdropping on the conversation. He felt like enough was said between the two and he hated to hear the word *guilt* mentioned so he decided that this was his cue to intervene. He stepped proudly out of the dugout and strutted like a peacock over to join the pair. "Why in the world would the boy feel guilty? All he did was protect his own interest. He did it for the glove. Right, Eddie?"

"Well, yeah. That and coach," Eddie replied.

"You're very loyal to your coach, aren't you, boy?"

"Well, yeah. Coach will always be number one with me."

"Well, I want you to know that you did a good job the other night, and I'm proud of you. There are a few things about the incident that need some improvement though. First of all, my little man, why did you go to all that effort to contact emergency services? I'll tell you one thing, if it had been my glove that he was messing around with, I would've left him there for dead. And secondly, I didn't appreciate all the apprehension on your part, and it truly confounded me how you could second-guess as to whether a plan of ours was going to work or not. Never doubt anything we come up with, Eddie."

"What do you mean by a 'plan of ours'? I thought that was my coach's plan?" Eddie asked suspiciously.

"Oops. Oh yeah. That's right. Your coach thought that one up, didn't he? My mistake. Sorry, kiddo. Little Freudian slip there," the Manager muttered sarcastically. "But now it's your turn on the hot seat my little man. So why did you do all those things, Eddie?"

"Quite honestly Mr. Manager, I didn't want him to die. What he did to me was not that bad, certainly not bad enough to die for."

"Oh boy! You're sounding soft, Eddie. You have a ways to go, my little man, before you become one of us. Coach, I think it's back to the drawing board with this one," the Manager flippantly announced in disgust.

"I'm sure he'll get it right one of these days," the coach announced apathetically.

"He better and, Eddie, I don't want to hear about you questioning whether or not our ideas will work again. Believe me, if it's thought up here in heaven, it's a guaranteed success."

Eddie suddenly acquired the look of a hurt child as he swallowed hard, trying to hold back his tears. "You guys aren't happy with me, are you? Damn it! Nothing I ever do is ever good enough. Not here or in the real world!"

"Listen, kid, you've still got one to go. I'm sure you can do better next time. Remember…the glove is the thing," the Manager said, revamping the old Shakespeare proverb.

"I'm going to make you two proud of me if it's the last thing I do!"

Suddenly, the phone rang, startling Eddie out of his dream and back to reality. Instantly, the dreariness and melancholy of the ballpark was replaced by the commonality of his bedroom as he picked up the receiver in a daze. "Hello," he mumbled almost inaudibly in a faraway voice.

"Eddie, wake up. What did you think? We forgot about you?" a familiar voice on the other end stated.

The familiarity of the voice immediately cleared the figurative cobwebs that had gathered inside his head due to being in such an exhaustive sleep. "Hey, Babe, how's it going?"

"Not so well, my man. I've heard some really bad reports about you."

"Oh, that figures. Nobody's pleased with me. Nothing is ever good enough with you guys."

"Please don't categorize me with those disgraces from your dreams," the Babe said revoltingly.

"Why not? They categorize themselves with you," Eddie fumed.

"Because you're talking apples and oranges, kid."

"You know it's all politics with you guys. You guys don't agree in heaven, so you spend all your time bashing each other. No matter what I do, I'll never please all of you! So why should I even bother trying?"

"Because you know right from wrong, that's why."

"What am I going to do? Get a lecture from you too?"

"No. That goes against the guidelines. You have to make your own choices. Your destiny is up to you. I've never once told you what to do, Eddie. I've never once threatened you or used duress upon you. Now, you think about it. Can those other guys say the same thing? Well? Can they?"

"No. But heck, they gave me a "magic glove" and a guarantee of future success. What have you given me?"

"So that's what it all boils down to? Right and wrong doesn't matter, just as long as you get something out of it. Well, for your information, I have given you a lot. I've given you my time. I've given you access to all the knowledge that I acquired throughout my lifetime. The things I've given you are priceless in comparison to that leather abomination that you call a magic glove."

"You know what irritates me the most about you guys? It's the fact that you've always tried to demean my glove. What you won't admit though is that the glove is exactly why you show all this special interest in me. If I didn't have that glove, you guys wouldn't give me the time of day. But you would never admit to that because, I'm sure, that goes against the guidelines too. All I know is having this glove has given me a window into worlds that no one is able to see into until they're dead. And that's pretty special to me. So don't try to make me think that this glove isn't magic," Eddie challenged as he tenderly stroked its leather.

"Someday, my boy, you will discover the error in your thinking, but by then, it may be too late. But until that day comes, I will be here for you. Lou and I will again this season help refine your game. I suggest that you take advantage of our help. The game is going to become more complex from now on, and it's going to take a lot of hard work to stay ahead of your peers, especially as the competition increases. But I have faith that you have the talent necessary to keep ahead in the game. Do you have any questions? I've been told that you're having tryouts tomorrow."

"That's right, Babe. Tomorrow's my big day. But I shouldn't have any problems with a high school tryout. I mean, I do agree with you as far as the competition is concerned and all. But I don't worry that much about the competition because I've been getting around on Eddie Cicotte's fastball lately and that my friend is no small accomplishment for a kid my age, wouldn't you agree?" Eddie asked arrogantly.

"That's no small accomplishment for a kid or, may I add, a man of any age if he's pitching up to snuff to you. You do know that Eddie was banned from baseball for throwing the World Series?"

"Yes. I'm well aware of that fact."

"Why don't you ask them why they don't have the Big Train pitch to you? You know, Walter Johnson? I mean, it would make more sense to me to have you face a real fastball pitcher if that's the element of the game that you're trying to work on. Ask them why they're having you face a junk baller instead of a real fastball artist?"

"What are you getting at this time?" Eddie asked in a surly tone of voice that showed his allegiances were leaning toward the other band of "angels."

"I don't know. I'd just love to hear their rationale. Just ask them for me," the Babe said, trying his best to sneak a monkey wrench into the devil's plans.

"All right, I'll ask them. So what are we going to do? Are we going to use the same system this year?"

"You tell me. Is there going to be a pay phone at the ballpark?"

"Oh. Let me think about that. Hey! Wait a minute. What are we going to do for the away games? I don't know if there's a pay phone at every ball field that we play at. Oh, that's just great. Now, what am I going to do?"

"What about your father's portable cellular phone?"

"Yeah. Good idea. How did you know about my father's portable phone?" Eddie asked in amazement.

"You'd be surprised at how much we know."

"Yeah, I believe that you all know a lot. The problem with you guys is that you're all too damned secretive."

"We have to follow the guidelines."

"You know someday when I die, I want to see these guidelines."

"If you keep your nose clean, I'm sure that could be arranged. Until then, you're just going to have to take my word for it."

Quickly changing the subject back to the original issue at hand, Eddie stated, "So that's what I'll do. I'll borrow my dad's cellular phone. I'll bring it with me to every game, and you can call me just like you did last year. You know, I'd sure like to see you sometime. Do you think that could ever be arranged?"

"Maybe, but only when the time is right."

"Oh, I get it, guidelines again?" Eddie jokingly asked a question that he knew the answer to.

"You said it. Not me."

"Whatever. Well, maybe someday is better than a definite no. So thanks again for the call, Babe. And try not to take too much offense to my snootiness. It's just that it gets awfully irritating to be lectured to all the time.

"Believe me, I understand. You're in quite a predicament but just try to do the right thing."

"See, there you go again."

The line suddenly went dead except for that old familiar dial tone. Eddie hung up the receiver and closed his eyes hoping to get a chance to think things through without any help from any outside influences. For the first time in ages, Eddie prayed that he could just sleep the night through without interruption.

TRYOUTS

After school, Eddie made his way down to the high school gymnasium where the varsity baseball tryouts were being held. Upon arrival, he stopped in the doorway and took a moment to ponder the adventure that lay ahead of him. He silently took in the overview of the gymnasium. The first thing that caught his eye was the wonderful baseball equipment that had been assembled.

In the middle of the gymnasium floor was a batting cage enclosed by netting so that all the balls hit would be contained within the temporary structure. Best of all was the fact that the pitching machine that it contained could be set manually to pitch up to ninety miles per hour.

The only time Eddie had ever seen this kind of equipment before was down at the local batting cage where you had to pay $5 to hit a bucket of balls. Although he had asked his father many times to go there, his visits had been limited due to the expense. He just marveled over the fact that the high school had one of its own, and this one could be used absolutely free.

Eddie was the only freshmen who dared tryout for the varsity team, and for this reason, he hesitated before entering the gymnasium. He just stood mesmerized in the doorway watching the older boys play pitch and catch and trying his best to muster up enough courage to enter the arena. The confidence he was lacking was not in his baseball abilities but in braving the negative reactions he was sure to get from the older boys. He also secretly feared retaliation for the Bobby Jones beating. Although he hadn't heard a word from anyone that he had been implicated, he still had a guilty conscience. He still wasn't sure that Bobby didn't tell the truth to at least someone on the team. He knew if that had occurred, a fight would surely ensue. After a few minutes of carefully scoping out the situation, allowing time for his butterflies of guilt to go away, he finally got the nerve to enter.

Eddie set his duffel bag down in the corner where all the other kids had set theirs. He opened his up for a moment and brought out his magic glove. His confidence increased immediately as he ran his fingers along its artistic design. As he stared down at it, the green grass that was depicted, surrounding the painted ball field, seemed to suddenly come to life. In Eddie's eyes it looked as if the grass was moving as if a divine wind was blowing it. He was overjoyed that his glove was as alive as he was.

While he stood in the corner of the gymnasium alone, in some kind of trance, the other kids began to notice him. Suddenly, they all stopped their games of pitch and catch and stared over at him in amazement. Not one of them said a word, but all of them were thinking the same thing and that was that Eddie Romano was a really strange kid. One overwhelming analogy filled their minds and that was that the "Salvation Army" mitt was to Eddie what a crucifix would be to a priest. They all became aware that the old antique mitt was more than a security blanket for him; it was obviously his Holy Grail.

Ray Mayberry wasn't the kind of kid that left well enough alone. He felt a seething inside his stomach as he watched Eddie's, pseudo-religious tribute to the secondhand glove. He hated anyone who was different. He had acquired a reputation around the school of being a badass, founded solely on the fact that he had once been arrested for beating up a "Moonie" at Chicago's, O'Hara Airport.

According to the police report, the "Moonie" had solicited him to buy a flower and was greeted with a punch in the nose. He later told the police that he didn't like the way the guy looked. He added that the guy must have been some kind of a faggot because he was wearing pajamas, and he had a stupid grin on his face. He always bragged to his friends about how that "silly looking shit wasn't smiling when I got done with him." For his efforts, his parents ended up paying a doctor's bill, along with a thousand-dollar fine to the city of Chicago.

Ray suddenly decided to take his "welcome wagon" over for a stroll to where Eddie was standing. Eddie was caught completely unaware of the approaching bully because he was still under the hypnotic spell of his magic glove. Upon Ray's arrival, the needling began. "What you looking at, Linus? Discovering it's time to buy a new glove?" he asked antagonistically.

Startled by Ray's remarks, Eddie jumped back. His conscious mind hadn't been aware of anyone approaching. After gathering himself, he responded courageously, "Hey, why don't you bug off, Ray?"

Ray bent down and brought his ugly, pimply face within an inch of Eddie's. Eddie was repulsed by his bad breath and tried his best to turn his head away from direct contact but to no avail. He held his breath as Ray stared coldly into his eyes remarking in a very low tone of voice,

"Such big words from such a small man. Why don't you make me?"

It was rapidly becoming the classic confrontation, David versus Goliath. All of the varsity baseball hopefuls sensed that a quick kill was eminent and gathered around encircling the two combatants. An angel must have been looking out for Eddie because within an instant the high school's baseball coach, Skip O'Neil, arrived on the scene. O'Neil was a short, stocky, muscular man in his mid-forties whose shape resembled a fire hydrant. He had a reputation around the school of being very personable and very fiery in disposition. He was a man who was feared as much as loved. He instantly noticed the gathering in the corner and shouted in his patented gruff voice, "What's going on, fellas?"

All the hopefuls knew that this was their cue to disperse as they quickly abandoned their "figuratively speaking," ringside seats and gathered around the coach. Ray Mayberry, upset, because of the loss of his audience, showed his displeasure by shoving Eddie real hard to the floor. Lucky for Eddie, his fall was broken by the many duffel bags that were piled in the corner. He remained on the seat of his pants while the others were now firmly entrenched around the coach. The coach noticed him still lying there and remarked casually, "Well, aren't you going to get up and join us?"

The other hopefuls laughed as Eddie picked himself up off the floor and joined the group. Eddie became seething mad as he watched Ray standing across from him, mocking him and blowing him kisses. Coach O'Neil picked up on this quickly and addressed the group.

"Well, I can see that trouble is brewing all ready. We're not even a team yet, cuts haven't even been made, and already we've got people down each other's throats. Now, Ray, I know you ain't a queer, so why don't you stop blowing the boy kisses? And whatever you're doing, that's aggravating Ray, why don't you cease and desist too? Now look, guys, if you're going to be a team, you've got to get along. Now that's not saying that you guys have to love each other because I know that's just not going to happen, at least not with some of you, fellas. I realize personalities clash, but all I'm asking from you fellas is to bury the hatchet, preferably not in anybody's head, at least not while you're members of this team. I don't care if you guys go out and kill each other during the off-season. I don't have to witness that. But as long as you're members of this team, I want some unity amongst you. Understand?"

Ray reluctantly announced his agreement to the stipulation because he didn't want to feel out of place with his teammates. Eddie didn't respond at all to the demand.

"Good. I'm glad that's settled. Now look, fellas, the first order of business here is to have a little screening-out process. As much as I'd like to have all of you guys on the team, it's just not going to happen. And believe me it's for your own benefit that a few of you guys will get cut. Think of it this way, if you get the ax, you wouldn't have gotten a chance to play anyway. Now obviously if you're here, you want to play. And if you get the ax, you'll probably have a good chance to play a lot on the J. V. squad. As a J. V. player you can improve your skills and try again next year. Now, from looking at you all, I can see we've got a good mixture of upper and lower classmen. Now most of you I've met before. Those that I'm not acquainted with, don't worry about it, we'll get to know each other soon enough. Now, are there any freshmen in attendance?"

The boys in the gathering started to chant, "Linus!" This really irritated Eddie to no end.

"Shut up! My name ain't Linus, assholes! My name's Eddie!"

"All right, guys, chill with Eddie, okay? You know, son, we have a freshmen team. I think it's pretty brave of you to be here, and I respect that, but you just might be better suited for the freshmen squad," O'Neil said compassionately.

"That's not fair. I haven't even tried out yet. You don't even know how good I am," Eddie said with a quiver in his voice and on the verge of tears.

"Boohoo! You little baby," Ray Mayberry antagonized.

"Shut up, Ray! The kid's got a point. This is a tryout, and he deserves as much of a chance as anyone else does," O'Neil conceded. "But I just want you to know something, Eddie, in all of my years here at Palatine we have never once had a freshman on the varsity team. I'm not saying that you can't be the exception to that rule, son, but I wouldn't get my hopes up if I were you."

"Coach, the only thing I want is an equal chance. I'll let my bat and glove, do my talking."

"He'll let his bat do his talking. Oh, please give me a break," Ray Mayberry mimicked sarcastically.

The rest of the team began laughing in unison, and Coach O'Neil wisecracked, "At least I know you fellas can do something together as a team."

Eddie wasn't appreciating the reception he was getting from them, and all their laughing made him so exasperated that he just snapped, "All right, fellas! You think I'm some kind of joke. You want me to quit. Well, I'll give you a chance to have me quit. You put Sandy Roberts out on that mound to pitch to me. If he strikes me out, I quit. If he can't, you guys get off my back. You hear?"

The hopefuls broke out into more chuckles at the thought of the boyish, undeveloped-looking fifteen-year-old facing the school's best pitcher.

"Hey c'mon, fellas! The kid issued a challenge. I think the least we can do is to honor it," Coach O'Neil announced.

Sandy Roberts stood among the hopefuls enjoying every minute of the challenge at hand. He loved the fact that his pitching was being used as the measure of excellence. He had worked long and hard on his pitching, and he felt like he was finally getting the credit he deserved. He was more than willing to pitch to the cocky freshman stating, "Coach, if you really want me to, I'll start warming up," Sandy anxiously offered.

"Good. Start throwing with Rick."

Sandy and Rick jogged away from the gathering and toward the far end of the gymnasium where another portable pitching enclosure was assembled. This net enclosure was minus the mechanical pitching machine. It contained a home plate and a portable pitching rubber. Sandy and Rick both entered the enclosure together, and shortly thereafter, Sandy began his pitching warm ups.

Everyone in attendance could hear the baseball making a loud thud as it collided with the thick protective leather of Rick's catcher's mitt. As Sandy's pitch count increased, so did the volume of the thud. He was really starting to groove his fastball, and many of the hopefuls left the gathering to marvel at the speed and velocity of his pitches. From the "oohhs" and "ahhs" vocalized by the hopefuls, one could tell that many of them had never seen such fast pitching before. Believe it or not, a couple of the hopefuls quickly gathered their belongings and exited after watching Sandy warm up. The kids that chose to leave realized that they were trying to bite off a bit more than they could chew, but there was no fear in Eddie. He nonchalantly made his way over toward the portable batting cage to view Sandy's little demonstration. From the look on his face, you could tell that he wasn't overly impressed.

"Okay, Eddie, you asked for a chance and now you're getting it. You sure you want to go through with this, son?" Coach O'Neil asked.

"Why not? Who is he? He's just a fast high school pitcher. Believe me, I've hit better," Eddie bragged.

Sandy overheard Eddie's remark, and it stuck in his gut. Eddie obviously had no respect for him, and he was bound and determined to earn some.

All the remaining hopefuls gathered around to observe the confrontation. Eddie selected a light thirty-four-inch bat from the bat rack. He immediately began practicing his swing. He liked the feel of it and decided to use it. After taking about fifteen swings, he set the bat down on the gym floor and went back to the rack and selected two more bats. He immediately grabbed the bat off the floor and started swinging all three simultaneously. Together, they were very heavy for him to swing, and their momentum knocked him off balance. The dream coach had told Eddie that swinging heavy bats was beneficial to increasing bat speed. The logic behind this school of thought was that once you had swung three heavy bats simultaneously, swinging one bat would be a breeze.

Eddie put two of the bats back on the rack and continued practicing his swing with the other. It now felt considerably lighter. He again practiced his swing and immediately noticed that he was quicker than before. He felt ready, and he took a deep breath as he entered the netted enclosure. He quickly made his way into the batter's box and stared out at the awaiting Sandy Roberts.

A hush filled the gym as all eyes were focused on Eddie as he bravely stepped forward to crowd the plate. Roberts was disgusted by the lack of respect that Eddie was showing him. He had never faced any hitter that crowded the plate the way Eddie did. Roberts decided to take charge right away and brush Eddie back off the plate with a high inside fastball.

Eddie choked up a bit on the bat and steadied himself for the ensuing pitch. As Roberts began his windup, Eddie's eyes were completely focused on reading the rotation of the oncoming ball. He noticed that there was no side to side spin as it made its way toward his head. At the last possible moment, he fell back on to the seat of his pants. He took a deep breath after realizing just how close the pitch came to hitting him. He became a slight bit infuriated as he got back on to his feet. He had never been thrown at by such a fast pitcher before. Eddie Cicotte never even came close to hitting him. Exasperated, he screamed out angrily, "You better cut the shit, asshole! Now put the ball over the dish, or I'm going to take this bat to your head. You hear me?" Eddie wasn't your typical bag of wind, so he did more than just threaten in fact he raced out toward the pitching rubber and feigned a swing that came dangerously close to Roberts' head. O'Neil quickly entered the netting, and made it clear to all involved that he wasn't going to put up with anymore of their shenanigans. O'Neil scolded, "Sandy, just pitch to him. And, Eddie, I don't want to see you threaten anyone with a bat ever again."

Thanks to O'Neil's ominous presence, the volatile situation quickly diffused, but Roberts was still a bit intimidated by Eddie's bat-swinging gesture. After all, everyone thought Eddie was crazy, but no one knew that he was becoming violent too. Roberts decided to play it safe and not tempt the devil. Eddie didn't know it at the time, but his intimidation tactic with the bat was about to pay great dividends for him.

Eddie had flustered Roberts' pitching philosophy. As he stood on the pitcher's rubber, he decided it wasn't worth the risk to pitch to him on the inside of the plate. He was afraid that if he let one get away from him and it ended up hitting him, the boy just might misconstrue it as being a deliberate attack, and he didn't have a doubt in his mind that Eddie was crazy enough to go after him with that bat.

The thought of being struck with a baseball bat gave him a chill down his spine, and he immediately eliminated the inside portion of the plate from his target area.

Eddie soon learned that the only part of the plate he had to be concerned with was the middle and the outside. This gave him a definite advantage in the duel.

Eddie stepped back into the batter's box and again crowded the plate. He relaxed as he awaited Sandy's next pitch. Sandy began his windup and delivered a ninety mph fastball, waist high, down the middle of the plate. Eddie let it go by, but it was definitely a strike. He momentarily stepped out of the batter's box to gather himself. Immediately, he was greeted by a good heckling from the hopefuls who were looking on.

Eddie started to mimic the obnoxious gestures of the hopefuls and concluded his point by giving them the finger. He then stepped back into the batter's box. He screamed out to Sandy, "Remember what I said, throw at me again, and I take the bat to your head," he said this for only one reason and that was to reinforce his message about inside pitching. He concluded that Roberts was too intimidated to throw inside. He justified his conclusion by the fact that the last pitch was thrown right down the center of the plate. He now expected that all the pitches would be thrown in similar locations. He was right.

The next pitch was again waist high and very fast, down the center of the plate, but this pitch never made it to the catcher's mitt. Eddie's swing had caught up with this fastball and rifled it at a low trajectory directly back at Roberts. The ball literally almost took his head off but settled with taking his hat off instead as it ripped into the netting. Roberts dove to the floor and began holding his chest. He couldn't recall a closer brush with disaster than the one he had just experienced or a time when his heart had beat so fast.

Eddie stood in the batter's box watching everyone's reaction toward his hit. He outwardly wasn't too excited; in fact, most witnesses would later say that "he was cool as the other side of the pillow." He came across to his new coach as just plain confident. He didn't showboat, like most would. No, he made it look like hitting ninety mph fastballs was an everyday occurrence for him. Coach O'Neil instantly knew that a freshman was going to make the Palatine High School varsity baseball team.

The group of hopefuls who moments before were heckling him, suddenly became strangely quiet. Even Ray Mayberry had nothing to say.

Eddie stepped back into the batter's box and taunted, "C'mon, Sandy. Pitch me another one."

Sandy who was busy retrieving his hat turned around suddenly and nervously replied, "Let's wait until we get outside. I don't think it's too safe inside this netting."

"I can't say I blame you, Sand. I wouldn't stand inside any narrow enclosure and pitch to me either," Eddie said with an evil grin on his face.

SELF-LOATHING

The excitement of the successful tryout fizzled out quickly thanks in large part to all the criticism he was receiving from the "angels" in "heaven." Although everything was working out as planned, Eddie could not overcome a feeling of quiet desperation. It was a feeling that was new to him but very abundant among humankind. It was the feeling of achieving a goal yet still not being satisfied with the success. He felt like he was losing control of his life. After his last "heavenly" visit, he started to feel like a pawn in a chess match. In his eyes, everyone was a king but him, and he was tired of being the one sacrificed. He needed to escape from these tormenting thoughts, and he decided that the best way to do this was to stay busy performing some brainless chore. So he decided to live up to his agreement with his dad and go out and paint the picket fence that surrounded the family home.

Eddie entered the garage that connected to the house through a door off the kitchen and scoured through the clutter to find a can of white paint and a halfway decent brush. His father didn't use the garage as a place to house his car but as a place to work. The garage for all intents and purposes was his father's combination tool shed and workshop. He pried off the top of the can of paint and began to stir it with a broken piece of doweling. After it was thoroughly mixed, he carried the can and the brush out toward the fence.

Eddie submerged the brush into the gallon container of paint. He brought it out and examined it, making sure it wasn't too saturated to be of use. His father had taught him to paint in this manner in order to avoid splattering, and he was anxious to do things right in order to alleviate some of the household tension that had been building up recently.

He was proud of himself because he had actually shown the initiative to begin this chore without any coaxing from his folks. He was proving that he was a man of his word. He had told his mother yesterday that he would paint the fence later and the later he was talking about was now.

Eddie applied the brush to the coarse surface of the picket fence that enclosed his front yard. Some bristles were getting caught in the creases and crevices of the wood. Seeing those bristles getting stuck in the wood's surface angered him greatly because they were making his paint job look shoddy. Frustrated, he threw his brush down on the sidewalk. Suddenly, all the nervousness and anxiety that had been building up inside him for days finally reached their boiling point in an effusive emotional display. The dam that was holding back his emotions broke instantly and a floodgate of tears spontaneously cascaded down his face. He was an emotional wreck.

In his eyes, nothing ever went right for him anymore. Although he had performed superbly during the baseball tryouts, he wasn't happy with himself. The pressures of trying to please everyone involved in his life was getting the best of him. He wanted so badly to please everyone, but he discovered that there was just no way of doing that. No matter what he did, somebody would be upset with him, and worst of all, he was developing a guilty conscience. Deep down inside, he knew the Babe was right. The Babe told him to try to do the right thing, and he knew too well that beating Bobby Jones the way he did was not the right thing.

He also knew exactly why he had acted the way he did after the deed had been done. Just the fact that he had called emergency services was in itself an admission of guilt. The Babe's conclusions were becoming painfully obvious to him, and he was growing exponentially more disgusted with himself by the minute, but he feared that if he didn't fulfill his obligations and carry out those evil deeds, his glove would lose its magic. Lastly, he concluded that without the glove's magic, he would have certainly struck out, earlier in the day, while facing Sandy Roberts. This dilemma was just too much for him to cope with, and tears filled his eyes as he desperately grasped for the answers to the perplexing questions of his life.

Suddenly, his thoughts drifted away from the self-pity mode and focused in on the changes he was noticing in his dream coach. He knew deep down inside that there was something wrong with him. In all the years that they had been acquainted, he never once saw his coach so down in the dumps. Now the keeper of all his secrets and his only trusted confidante was having his own problems. He made a habit of dumping all his problems on his coach but only one time had the coach opened up and revealed any of his problems. He started to feel even more ashamed as he realized just how self-centered he had become. He had never taken the time to reciprocate the friendship and love that had been showered upon him. He had known his coach for almost five years but never once inquired as to what made him truly happy. The million-dollar question was, "How could he love someone as much as he did his coach and not know everything about him?" He knew that some of the fault would lie with the coach for always being so secretive, but he also knew that some of it was his own doing. Until the other day, he didn't even know that the coach dreamed about returning to the earth and playing baseball again. He had just taken it for granted that all he wanted out of life was to cater to him and be his personal instructor and confidante. He couldn't believe how stupid he had been to have thought that the coach had no dreams of his own. Eddie wondered how his coach could be so fond of him when, in his eyes, he had proved himself to be nothing more than a self-centered, egotistical little bastard. The more he thought about his abhorrent behavior, the less he thought of himself and so began his self-loathing. He made himself a promise that from now on he was going to take a keener interest in his coach's problems, and he was going to find a way to repay him for all the kindness and support he had received.

Eddie knew that the coach was depressed because he feared that he would never be able to see the earth again. He decided to make it his own personal crusade to help him find his way home. He was able to come and go between both worlds as he pleased and he was now, bound and determined to help his coach find that doorway too. He made a promise to himself that from here on in, this was going to be his number one objective in life.

A Combustible Situation Arises

Before turning into his driveway, Mr. Romano noticed the abandoned can of paint that was left in front of the house. The sight of the abandoned paint can gave him mixed emotions as he got out of his Lincoln. First of all, he was happy to see some work getting done without him being the one who had to do it, but conversely, he wasn't happy with the fact that whoever began this chore just left everything for somebody else to clean up.

Mr. Romano, briefcase in tow, took a stroll down toward the picket fence. Upon arrival, he was alarmed to find that only one stroke of paint had been applied and the brush had been left on the sidewalk to dry. He suddenly became infuriated. He obsessed over the facts that no work had been done and a mess had been made. After a rough day at the office, this was all the catalyst needed to make him explode. He turned away from the mess and stormed toward the front door.

Eddie heard the front door slam shut as his father entered the house. He knew what his father was mad about, but he was so disheartened with life in general that he just didn't care. He heard his father screaming out to him, but refused to answer. He secretly hoped that if he ignored him long enough, somehow he would just go away. Unfortunately for him, things didn't work out like that.

The door of his bedroom was suddenly kicked open, and his father stared ominously over at him. He was beet red in the face, and as he screamed, he could clearly see his slightly yellowed teeth clenched together. His father, to him, looked like a madman; he imagined him as an ax-wielding maniac about to dismember his family. He decided for self-preservation's sake to sit still and pray to God that the storm would soon blow over.

"Nice freaking job, asshole! Can't you ever do anything right? How come you're not answerin' me? What are you, freaking deaf? Answer me, Eddie! I'm not going to put up with your foolishness anymore!" Mr. Romano screamed out angrily.

As Eddie quiescently watched the tirade play out in front of him, he decided that it was best to stay his course. He knew if he chose otherwise, his father would pounce on him and World War III would begin.

After his father got done blowing off steam, Eddie nervously asked for contrition, "I'm really sorry, Dad. I just can't seem to do anything right anymore. I really wanted to please you. That's why I started to paint the fence in the first place. But I can't even do that right. Everything I touch seems to turn to shit. The freaking bristles got stuck in the fence, and it really pissed me off."

"Why didn't you sand the fence first? Don't you know that you have to sand a surface before you begin to paint it? Where in hell is your mind lately? You're out in loony land half the time. What in hell is wrong with you?" his father asked with genuine concern.

"I don't know, Dad. I'm really confused. I've got way too much pressure on me."

"What pressures? You always talk about these pressures of yours, but I just don't see them. The only pressures I see are the ones that you put on yourself. I don't ask much of you, Eddie. Your mother never asks much of you. So what pressures are you talking about?"

"Dad, you'd never believe me if I told you."

"Sure I would. Try me."

"You're not going to like it."

"Don't give me that shit about the angels again, Eddie."

"But it's true!"

"It's sick. That's what it is!"

"But it's true! I mean it, Dad. I'm telling you, it's no joke. It's the God's honest truth," Eddie pleaded.

"Oh. Please, spare me. Why do you want to sell me this bill of goods so badly?"

"So you can understand what I'm going through," Eddie cried out desperately.

"But I don't want to hear about visits with angels and shit like that Eddie. I told you, you've let your imagination get the best of you."

"You see, talking to you is like talking to a brick wall. You'll never understand my life because you don't want to understand it. If you can't believe what I swear to you is the truth, then we've really got nothing to talk about," Eddie explained in frustration.

"Can you blame me? Would you believe it?" his father asked, looking Eddie dead in the eyes.

Eddie answered with hesitation, "Probably not, but believe it or not, I'm telling you the truth."

"Please, Eddie, don't tell anyone else about these visits with angels because they'll have you committed. If what you say is somehow really happening to you, you're just going to have to deal with it on your own. You've got to understand, nothing unusual has ever happened to me like that, so I have a hard time believing in the extraordinary. I want you to know that I'm not calling you a liar. It's just that I don't know how to deal with your problem. I've sent you to the best doctors, and they couldn't find anything wrong with you. So maybe there isn't anything wrong with you. But I just don't know how to help you," Mr. Romano stated passionately with the love of a concerned father.

"It's all right, Dad. I'll deal with it. But please, accept me for how I am. I know I behave strangely sometimes, but like you said to me a long time ago, 'I march to a different drum beat.' I think I do, Dad. Believe me, I never intended to be a bad son, and I do love you," Eddie said as his eyes began to well.

Mr. Romano let out a deep sigh before replying, "I know you do, my boy. Oh, Eddie, come here," Mr. Romano said with tear-filled eyes as he raced over to embrace his boy. "I'm too hard on you, kid. I'm sorry."

Eddie began to cry too and soon Mr. Romano's dress shirt was soaked with tears. Eddie straightened up just long enough to confide, "Dad, I just wanted you to know that I made the team."

"I knew you would. Believe me, Eddie, I have all the confidence in the world in you," Mr. Romano declared proudly.

"I just wish I did, Dad," Eddie said poignantly.

THE NOOSE TIGHTENS

After crying so much during the afternoon, Eddie became very tired. Emotionally he was an absolute wreck. A nervous breakdown was not far off. If he wasn't mentally ill before, he certainly was nearing it now. He was so depressed that all he wanted to do was sleep, and when he rested his head upon his pillow, it sure didn't take him long to pass out.

In what seemed like an instant, he was back at that dismal and dreary ballpark in "heaven." The sky there was perpetually overcast, which had the effect of compounding the melancholy mood he was chronically in. He hung his head low as he wandered around aimlessly along the outfield grass. Missing was the welcome wagon of days gone by. There were no smiles, nor anyone awaiting his arrival with bated breath. To put it mildly, there was simply an aura of doom and gloom and nothing more. He peered around the lifeless ballpark until he spotted his dream coach who was lying on top of the roof of the dugout, staring up at the dismal sky. His coach seemed to be in deep contemplation, so he decided it wasn't a good idea to disturb him. Instead, he sat down on the second base bag and began to let out all the hurt that was overwhelming his soul. His sobbing interrupted the silence of the ballpark just enough to catch the dream coach's attention.

Billy suddenly forgot all about his own ailing state of mind and motivated himself enough to get on to his feet, so he could get over to find out what was troubling his protégé. As he approached the boy, he immediately began to feel Eddie's inner pain. He couldn't understand why he was feeling human pain again, but he was. It was almost as if Eddie's pain had reached him through some kind of osmosis as if he and the boy were so emotionally interconnected that somehow they were becoming one. They had the same dreams, hopes, and aspirations. They had the same desires but only one of them would be able to live them. The other knew too well that he would have to experience his vicariously. Billy begrudgingly resigned himself to the fact that he was dead. He now knew that his fate was sealed, and he wanted most of all for Eddie to have a better destiny than his. With all this in mind, he took a seat on the clay next to him. He reached his arm out and pulled him close. The young man's tears began flowing down Billy's old White Sox uniform. This emotional purging brought about tears of his own; although for Eddie's sake, he tried his best to keep them under control. He silently said a prayer for Eddie. Mentally, he asked God to give him the strength to save the boy. His prayers to God were kept absolutely secret. He was at the wrong place and surrounded by the wrong elements to pray for God's intervention outwardly; consequently, he never uttered a word. Mentally though, he bargained with God, letting him know that he would suffer the tortures and indignities of hell forever if only his friend's soul could be spared.

After a long and deafening silence in which Billy repeatedly told himself that he couldn't bear with any more tragedy, he got up the nerve to inquire about the boy's troubles.

"What's wrong with you, kid?" the coach asked glumly.

Eddie let out another deluge of tears on his dream coach's shoulder. Although he had promised himself that he wouldn't burden his coach with anymore of his problems, he really couldn't help himself. His world was slowly but surely coming apart at the seams and his coach was the only one who he really trusted.

"Coach, I just can't take the pressure anymore." Eddie sobbed.

"Calm down, Eddie. You're a bundle of nerves right now. Just relax and take a deep breath. Now take your time and try to explain to me. What's troubling you?"

Eddie gathered himself and explained, "Coach, everybody I know is giving me all this conflicting advice on how to run my life. I feel like I'm losing my own identity. I really don't know who I am anymore. I just want to make everybody happy with me, but that seems to be impossible. It's impossible for me to do the right thing if I want to keep the magic in the glove. Can't you see that the things I've been doing are wrong? I wasn't brought up like that. I was taught to turn the other cheek, instead of being just plain vindictive, and let's face it, that's what I've become."

"Eddie, this is one situation I can't help you with. I really wish I could but I can't. I don't make the rules here, and I certainly can't change them. Just remember this, kid, there's a price to be paid for anything you get in this world. Sometimes the price is worth it and sometimes it's not."

"And you, Coach, is this the price that you had to pay for the things you did during your life?"

"You mean being here?"

"Yeah. That's exactly what I mean."

"Yeah. I guess you could say that. I made my own bed, and now I've got to lie in it."

"I understand. Let me ask you something, is this where I'm going to end up too, Coach?"

"No. You won't end up here," Billy responded hesitantly, taken aback by the boy's question.

The Manager, who had been eavesdropping on the conversation quickly stepped out of the dugout and trekked out toward second base interjecting, "Why won't he?"

"Because he doesn't seem to want to live up to his end of the bargain. He's not living up to the terms of the agreement that you set forth in order to keep the magic in the glove," the coach said nervously, explaining away his double intender and hoping the Manager would not realize that he was having a change of heart. Billy had decided that he would no longer cooperate with the dark man. He would do his best to undermine all future evil plans, regardless of the consequences and personal harm he might suffer on account of it.

"Well, I guess you won't be coming here any longer then, Eddie, and I guess that's the end of your baseball career. You'll never get to see your face on a baseball card. There won't be any razor blade commercials in your future. You can forget about any multimillion-dollar contracts. There won't be any bathing beauties, two on each arm. No television interviews on ESPN. Guess you can forget about any broadcasting career after you're playing days are over with and someday when you're nothing but a two-bit hustler lying in the gutter somewhere, thinking back about the days gone by. You can point out this defining moment as the time you started to descend. And why? Just because you started to feel a little bit guilty about bludgeoning a couple moronic bullies from your school. Yeah, that makes good sense to me. Yeah, I'd give up on fame and fortune just to save a couple of punks from getting what's coming to them," the Manager fumed sarcastically.

"It's all or nothing with you, isn't it?" Eddie asked.

"You can't have it both ways, kid. I mean, after all that you've been guaranteed, you're still considering giving it all up? I have to admit that your way of thinking completely mystifies me," the Manager said while shaking his head in total disbelief. "I hope you realize that if you break our agreement you won't be able to come and see your coach anymore?" the Manager coerced.

"Is that really true, Coach?" Eddie asked bewildered.

"Yeah, I'm sure it is, Eddie," the coach said despondently.

"That's not fair. I love Coach. He's my best friend. Why would you take him from me?" Eddie asked with tears welling in his eyes.

"Because special angels only belong with special people, and if you renege on our agreement, you are far from special," the Manager said condescendingly.

"You know something, if you ask me, you're more like the devil than an angel. And if this really is 'heaven,' then it's not such a great place. No wonder the coach wants to leave. I can't believe how cruel you are," Eddie said weeping.

"Believe it. It comes with the territory, my boy. So what will it be? Are you going to live up to your end of the bargain and still be able to see your coach and continue to receive all the wonderful benefits that you've been given, or are you going to be a Goody Two-shoes and leave it all behind? The choice is all yours, my boy."

"Some choice. Guess I have no choice, huh?"

"Such enlightened words. I'm glad that you're finally starting to see things my way. Believe me, you'll be happy that you made the choice to stay with our band of angels," the Manager stated confidently.

"I'll stay with you, but believe me, it wasn't by choice."

"Regardless, good to have you back on board. Now, I'll leave you two alone. Teach him some baseball, Coach. And, Eddie, do a good job on Ray. Remember, I'll be watching," the Manager laughed as he retreated into the dugout.

"He's the devil, isn't he?" Eddie asked his coach.

Billy, with his head hung low, made no reply as he walked away in shame.

POSSESSED

C old, that along with callous, became the nature of Eddie Romano since his last spirit-crushing visit to "heaven." As he kept moving in place, he was thinking how awfully cold it was to be practicing baseball. The weather was definitely more suited for long johns and football, but he and his teammates bravely endured it. Since this was the first outdoor practice of the season, things weren't exactly running smoothly yet.

Coach O'Neil was trying his best to organize his charges into platoons by position, but many did not fit into any one particular mold. Lucky for Eddie, he didn't have that problem. There was only one spot in the infield where he played and that was shortstop. He had made up his mind that he was going to show his teammates that his abilities did not end at the plate but that he was an excellent fielder too.

Despite the cold, he was extremely energized for this practice. He had spent many long hours in preparation for this, and to him this was the moment of truth. This was his chance to really show them what he was capable of. Almost every sleeping hour had been focused toward this very moment, and nothing and no one was going to spoil it for him. So it should come as no surprise that he was just a little bit unnerved as he watched Ray Mayberry hobble across the practice field to where the team was gathered.

At first glance, the Palatine High School team didn't recognize Ray as he approached. There was something different about him, but it only became apparent as he got closer. It was his face. At first glance, the players thought that he had covered it with black sun glare protector but as he neared they could clearly see that it had a purplish tint. As he finally arrived at the gathering, they noticed that it was covered with black-and-blue bruises. No one on the team had ever seen anyone's face so black and blue before. No one could even recall seeing a professional boxer, who looked as bruised, swollen, and battered as Ray did.

Upon arrival, he stared over at Eddie for a moment and then fearfully looked away. Among those gathered, Eddie's eyes were the only pair that were stone cold, showing no sympathy for the badly disfigured boy. Eddie strategically moved across into his field of view, continually giving him the evil eye. He maintained this menacing posture to guarantee that his presence would not be forgotten. He then quietly stood still and took in every word that the boy uttered.

"What in hell happened to you, Ray?" Coach O'Neil asked in shock.

Ray fixed his eyes momentarily upon Eddie's before replying, "Coach, I had an accident."

"I guess so. What kind of accident?"

"I wiped out on my bike and hit a tree," Ray responded loudly, making sure that Eddie could hear every word, loud and clear.

"When do you think you'll be ready to play again?"

"Probably soon; I've just got to wait for a little of this swelling to go down around my eyes."

"Well, this is really something. I hope this is not a sign of things to come. Two of my best players from last season get injured before the season even starts," Coach O'Neil announced loudly. "Ray, you heard that Bobby's probably not going to be able to rejoin us until late in the season? Those punks really did a number on him. He ought to thank his lucky stars that he's still alive."

"Believe me, Coach, I understand about thanking my lucky stars. I'm lucky I didn't fracture my skull," Ray stated in disbelief.

"What did you do? Hit it face first?"

"Yeah, you could surely say that."

"Boohoo, you little baby!" Eddie antagonized, mimicking the exact words that Ray used on him, a few days earlier at the gym.

"Put a lid on it, Romano!" Coach O'Neil snapped. "Well, you better get home and rest. You come back whenever you feel up to it."

"Thanks, Coach. I just wanted you to know that I wasn't out skipping practice. I just wanted to show you that I had a legitimate excuse."

"Obviously, maybe you need to think about taking up a new hobby. Bike riding seems to be pretty dangerous for you. I'm just kidding with you, Ray. Anyway, we'll see you when you're up to it," Coach O'Neil quipped as he turned away to resume his duties. "All right, fellas! Let's get started with a little batting practice. I want you guys to hit in alphabetical order!"

The players whose last names came at the middle and the end of the alphabet grabbed their gloves and raced out toward the field. A lot of chitchat could be heard between players as they tried to sort out where there last name fit in the batting order.

Sandy Roberts turned toward Ray as he hobbled away. "Hey, Ray! Did that Moonie you beat up at O'Hara look as bad as you do right now?"

"Hardly," Ray said dejectedly as he walked away with his head hung low.

"That's what I figured. Hope you feel better." Sandy immediately turned away and raced out to join his teammates in the field. As he made his way past shortstop, he stopped momentarily as he heard his name being called.

"Hey, Sandy! See Ray's face? That's what someone's face looks like after being bitch slapped with a baseball bat. Keep that in mind next time you think about throwing at me, okay?" Eddie said menacingly with a large smirk on his face.

Sandy didn't bother to reply. He just looked at Eddie's evil smirk, and a large chill went down his spine. From then on, Sandy Roberts kept his distance from Eddie Romano.

CREATING A MEDIA DARLING

During his first few varsity baseball games, Eddie learned firsthand that there wasn't a lot of glamour attached to high school baseball. Generously speaking, attendance at the games was sparse. He and his teammates would spend long hours perfecting their game just to find out that most people in town paid little or no attention to them. It was a hard pill for him to swallow when he learned that a local little league team was drawing greater crowds than his team did.

For his sanity's sake, he needed to do something to change that trend. Although on the surface he showed no signs of it, he had an overwhelming need to be liked by the community. He figured that he deserved a reward for the many friendships he sacrificed in order for the magic glove to retain its powers. Although he was alienated by his teammates, he knew that his raw ability alone could win him many adoring fans in town if he could only find a way to get them to come out and see him play. So he made it his personal crusade to get fans into those bleacher seats that surrounded Palatine field.

Eddie went out of his way to become a media darling. His entire persona was focused on being the most outrageous and skilled ballplayer in the metropolitan area. He got his mother to make a facsimile of the 1952 Chicago White Sox uniform, which just happened to be the same style uniform that his dream coach always wore in "heaven." He figured that he would make quite a spectacle by using his antique glove and wearing his ancient uniform. His assumptions couldn't have been anymore correct.

Almost immediately the newspaper reporters became interested in covering the talented and flamboyant infielder from Palatine. Coach O'Neil at first was not too keen on allowing his freshmen sensation to break all the team dress codes but conceded after noticing a major rise in attendance. O'Neil also liked the fact that he too was getting some publicity. Eddie's unique creation had O'Neil convinced that everything in life was marketing. This belief was reinforced by the fact that Sandy Roberts, a bonafide pro prospect, never received half of the media attention that Eddie Romano did. Needless to say, Sandy also became a direct beneficiary of the Eddie Romano media blitz. But indubitably, it was the Eddie Romano show at Palatine High School. During games he would point to which field he was going to single to. He started doing this after learning that the Babe did the same thing during a game in the 1932 World Series. The only difference being that the Babe pointed to the fence that he was going to hit it over. That was the only ingredient that was missing in Eddie's game. He hadn't the physical strength yet to become a home run hitter, but the media didn't seem to care. They fed upon his little quirks, like his cellular phone conversations from the dugout to his angelic batting instructors, Babe Ruth and Lou Gehrig. Although the reporters thought it to be a tongue-and-cheek joke, he swore that he really spoke to them.

He had created an entire persona that made people think of the past. The public's love of nostalgia was what he fed upon. His uniform and glove were antiques from the past and created the illusion that he belonged there. Many reporters concluded that his talk of the Babe and Gehrig being his batting instructors conveniently fit the nostalgic image he was trying to create, and they all played along with his antics.

Most importantly though, it was not all show with Eddie Romano. He was the most prolific hitter on his team and ranked in the top five in the greater Chicago metropolitan area. His fielding also earned him high praise. The reporters that interviewed him secretly couldn't wait to see how he would mature as a ballplayer. They were convinced that he was something special and believed from day one that he had a great shot at developing into a pro prospect, but for now, he was thought of as just a cute, oddball kid who happened to play baseball well. Some reporters were comparing his antics to those of Mark Fidrych, a former American League Rookie of the Year pitcher, who played for the Detroit Tigers in the mid-seventies. Fidrych, whose nickname was the Bird was best known for his odd behavior of replacing divots by hand before delivering each pitch and talking to the baseball.

One *Chicago Tribune* reporter said it best when he wrote that, "Eddie was rapidly becoming a high school baseball phenomenon." He compared him to what Michael Jackson had become to music during his childhood days with the Jackson Five, someone with great potential. The only question that remained in Eddie's case was whether his potential would boom or bust.

CELEBRITY IS
A DOUBLE-EDGED
SWORD

Three years had come and gone since that magical, inaugural baseball season for Eddie Romano, and he had answered every question about his potential in the affirmative. His stock as a ballplayer had unquestionably boomed. Entering his senior year, he had surpassed every batting record ever held at Palatine High. His name had become synonymous with baseball throughout the metropolitan area. Pro scouts were in attendance at all of his games, and he was basking in all the limelight he was receiving.

Everything was going according to plan. The newspapers were constantly doing features on him and his exploits on the baseball diamond. This season, he was targeted by many sporting publications to break the state of Illinois's high school home run record.

Eddie was no longer a frail fifteen-year-old kid with little pop in his bat. He had grown up to be a muscular, strapping six-footer. Since his sophomore year at Palatine, he had been hitting home runs in droves. His power, along with his flamboyant personality, made him the darling of the city's sports writers.

Unfortunately for Eddie, the sword cuts both ways. The *Chicago Tribune* and other newspapers were starting to print negative stories about him too. These stories came from sources that chose to remain anonymous. In one of the stories, the Tribune reported that former teammates of his claimed that he was a voodoo conjurer who put hexes upon them. One former teammate embellished the story saying, "Eddie actually stuck needles into little voodoo dolls depicting his teammates." Johnny Mitchell, a former little league teammate, openly said, "Eddie had the worst sportsmanship that I've ever had the misfortune to witness." He furthermore claimed that Eddie used to cheer against his own teammates during ball games. He added, "His behavior since obtaining that green antique glove has been nothing short of bizarre."

To say the very least, Eddie was very unhappy with this personal "smear" campaign. These allegations had tarnished what should have been the best year of his life. He didn't give a damn how much his teammates hated him; he'd given up on the idea of trying to win them over a long time ago. The affections of the general public were what he was truly concerned about. By smearing him in the press, these former teammates had severely hurt his public image, unforgiveable deeds in his eyes. He was learning a hard lesson that all media darlings are forced to memorize and that is: it's always open season on them. There is nothing the press delights in more than building someone up until they get an opportunity to tear them down. Public opinion has always been as capricious as the wind and skeletons in your closet are just the catalysts you don't need if you're going to live your life in the public eye.

With that premise in mind, he feared the growing possibility that his former teammates Bobby Jones and Ray Mayberry would now find all this public controversy an ideal forum to step into the limelight and reveal their dirty little secrets about him. Eddie couldn't think of any better way for those two to gain some semblance of revenge other than doing just that. He feared that their stories about how he had beaten them up would forever put a scarlet letter on his forehead and permanently destroy his public image. He didn't want to be America's next Tonya Harding. Unfortunately for him, the beatings of Bobby Jones and Ray Mayberry could very well turn out to be the year's "Nancy Kerrigan" story. This cancer had to be removed as quickly as humanly possible. Eddie was really starting to panic.

Mr. Romano reassured Eddie that from a public relations standpoint, all publicity was good publicity. His father told him that the time to worry is when they're not talking about you. He understood where his father was coming from but was less than convinced that this rash of negative publicity could be of any help to him. He concluded that what he really needed to do was to discuss this new twist of events with his dream coach. His dream coach was the only one who knew the truth and would understand the full magnitude of the kind of allegations that might be levied upon him any day now. He realized his dream coach might have a plan to alleviate this potentially scandalous situation.

PROBLEMS BEGINNING
TO COMPOUND

Restlessness had always been a recurring problem for Eddie since finding his magic glove. Whenever he had a problem, he would spend every waking hour obsessing over it, but worse than that, he would spend every resting hour bedeviled too. He was thoroughly bewitched by his troubles of late and his sleep cycle suffered commensurately. So one can easily imagine how much it was suffering from this recent public smear campaign. Usually after suffering through numerous restless hours, he would eventually pass out from complete exhaustion. On this particular night/morning, that's exactly what happened.

As soon as he reached a deep sleep, he found himself back at that dreary and deserted major league ballpark in "heaven." He curiously looked over toward the dugout to see if anyone was awaiting his arrival but, as usual of late, no one was. He then scoped around the infield and discovered his dream coach back in the doldrums again. He always knew when his coach was down in the dumps because he completely tuned out to everyone and everything around him. On this occasion he discovered him lying on the pitcher's mound, staring up at the overcast sky, seemingly oblivious to everything happening around him. This was not typical behavior of his dream coach, who for the last three years by force of will alone had lifted himself away from the depression that he had been suffering since being so rudely informed of his death. Of course, Eddie was kept completely in the dark when it came to the details behind his coach's depression. He simply thought it was a case of his coach giving up hope of finding that portal back to the earth. Although at times he debated with himself whether he had ever received the real story about his coach's predicament. Regardless, he couldn't remember seeing his coach in such a bad state of mind.

Eddie approached the pitcher's mound where his coach remained motionless in some sort of trance. He seemed completely unaware of his progression until suddenly he turned his head toward him and forewarned, "Beware! Someone is going to steal your glove."

"Is that a fact?" Eddie asked jokingly.

"I wouldn't be laughing if I were you. I'm dead serious, Eddie. Your glove will be stolen."

"How do you know?" Eddie asked with alarm reflected in his voice.

"Don't worry about how I know. I just know," the dream coach said urgently.

"Well, how's that going to happen? I've got that glove with me all the time. I never let it out of my sight for a second. I sleep with it. I eat with it. I even go to the bathroom with it. It would be impossible for anybody to steal it from me."

"You're wrong, my boy. It will be stolen."

"Well, that's just great. Now I've got something else to worry about," Eddie expressed bitterly.

"What other problems do you have, my boy?"

"I take it you haven't seen the newspapers lately," Eddie revealed.

"That, my boy, is a fair assumption."

"Well, for your information, the papers have started to print a bunch of negative stories about me. Supposedly, ex-teammates of mine have come forward saying that I'm the next nicest person to Attila the Hun."

"That bad, huh?"

"Believe me, it gets worse. I've been accused of being a freaking witch doctor, a voodoo conjurer who casts spells on his teammates. They even went so far as to say that I practice voodoo on my friends." Eddie chuckled sarcastically. "That's a good one, huh? What friends is more like it? The next thing you know, they'll be accusing me of being an ax murderer," Eddie said in disgust. He added, "Coach, I want the public to like me. What's the use of trying to be a superstar if everyone hates you? Can you give me an answer to that one?"

Eddie's last question really struck a nerve with the coach. He had experienced that same kind of thing during his lifetime. It was that same kind of situation that compelled him to take his own life. He too wanted to be loved. When he made it to the big leagues, he wanted to cheer on his teammates and be a real team player. He wanted to be popular again. He had enough of being the nay-saying superstar, prima donna who everybody hated, like during his last year at Memphis. Unfortunately, he had learned the hard way that you can't renege on your deal with the devil, especially if it's in his hands to provide you with the ability to play the caliber baseball that's needed to keep you in the major leagues. So obviously he followed a self-destructive compulsion and took his own life. He never quite understood that suicidal impulse though. He never really thought of suicide before, but he did remember standing on that stool that night at Comiskey with that rope around his neck. It just didn't make any sense to him, but it was too late to worry about that now. He obviously killed himself and now was stuck with these evil people for eternity. It just wasn't fair, and he had made up his mind that it wasn't going to happen again, especially not to anybody he loved. With all these thoughts running through his mind, Billy carefully thought out how he was going to respond to this question.

"You know, Eddie, I've thought about that question for a long time now. And I don't know if there really is an answer to it. All I do know is that people are always striving to have more than what they started with. People in general, commonly make the mistake of thinking that more is better. We all want to be superstars because we think that somehow their lives are more gratifying than ours, but that's not necessarily the case, my boy. I used to think that being a celebrity would somehow make my life more complete. You know, make me happier and give me a chance at getting the better girl, that kind of thing. You know? But I learned that the most important thing you should have in your life is love and friendship. Because believe me, Eddie, celebrity is a fleeting thing, but friends and loved one's last forever. So I guess what I'm trying to say is that it's not that important for those people to love you because they really don't know you in the first place. And anyone who doesn't know someone can't really love them. So I wouldn't worry about them."

"I'm not talking about them loving me, Coach. I just don't want them hating me," Eddie emphasized. "I mean, once a few of them start to talk, next thing you know everyone's talking and a few of them could seriously mess up my reputation. I've got to do something to stop them, Coach. Haven't you got any ideas at all?" Eddie asked desperately.

"Eddie, it's my ideas that put you in this predicament in the first place," Billy said while turning his head away in shame.

"It's not your fault, Coach. I had to do those things in order to keep the magic in the glove. Face it, if it wasn't for the powers of that glove, I wouldn't be in the position I'm in anyway. Remember, before I found that glove, I was a total zero when it came to baseball. The more I think about it, my whole life's been a scam."

"That's not true, Eddie," Billy said hesitantly, fighting off the urge to say more.

"It is too. Who are you trying to fool? Me? You can't fool me, Coach. You can't bullshit, a bullshitter. You're just trying to be nice and don't get me wrong, I do appreciate it."

"Well, then appreciate the advice I'm about to give you. I'll probably get into trouble with the Manager for telling you this because as we both know he only appreciates extreme measures, but in this case, I feel a little honey will attract more ants than vinegar. What I'm trying to say is that you should have a talk with both Bobby and Ray. I think that you should tell them that you're very sorry for what you did to them and that you want to make it up to them. Now, I'm sure the Manager will appreciate the next thing that I'm about to tell you and that is to offer them a bribe. Tell them that you'll make sure that their silence is well rewarded after you get drafted by the pros. Believe me, if I know anything about human nature, they'll take the money," Billy said while rolling his eyes and engraving his face with what seemed like a permanent ear to ear grin.

"You know something, Coach, I really like the way your mind is thinking these days. I have to admit though I'm pretty surprised to hear a pacifistic idea from either you or the Manager. I just didn't think you guys had it in you. Who would of "thunk" it? Maybe you're starting to mellow in your old age," Eddie said trying to be amusing with his affectation on proper English.

"More like, I'm starting to wisen up, my boy," Billy said proudly.

"You know, Coach, I feel a hundred percent better about myself now that I've had this little talk with you," Eddie declared joyously.

"Well, it's always a pleasure to be of service to you. Any problems with baseball lately?"

"Not really. I'm using the Babe and Gehrig again this season, you know, to help fine-tune my swing? I really think this could be my best year ever."

"Well, that's what I like to hear. Now, Eddie, whatever you do, don't forget to keep a close eye on that glove of yours. I hate to beat a point into the ground, but I just don't want anything to happen that could prevent you from being able to come and visit me. You have no idea what it means to me to have a friend like you," Billy spoke poignantly, trying his best to keep Eddie from seeing the tears that were welling in his eyes.

"I love you, Coach. You're my best friend, and I won't let anything interfere with that. Believe me when I tell you, I won't let that glove out of my sight."

"Good. So we'll see each other again? Soon, okay?"

"Sure," Eddie said as he turned to walk away. Suddenly, a foreboding feeling told him that this could be the last good-bye so he stopped dead in his tracks and turned around to face Billy adding, "Hey, Coach! Do you want to have a catch?"

"Now when have I ever been able to refuse an offer like that one?"

"I was hoping you'd say that," Eddie said elated to be doing anything together with his coach.

Eddie and Billy put some distance between each other and started to toss the ball gently back and forth. They were practically mirror images of each other, and the symmetry between them was truly a thing of beauty. Billy looked over at Eddie in awe, realizing the monumental price he had paid for that one irrational moment in life. No one will ever know how badly he wished he could have taken it back. He snapped out of his melancholy mood and smiled brightly over at his friend. He prayed silently that these moments would last forever.

THE LIGHT

Michael sat patiently on a gold chair, surrounded by many great men who lived throughout the ages on the earth. This gathering included souls from many other colonies throughout the universe. The view from his seat was absolutely breathtaking. This monumental structure was built by the greatest architects ever assembled. It was a huge gathering hall that was made of marble and rested upon a mountain that towered over a tranquil sea. This was the home of the creator known as the Light. This was a place that existed before and after life. Needless to say, it was so far away from the earth that it was beyond human comprehension.

Michael, Billy Green's surrogate father during life, had always kept a close eye on him. He felt so helpless in this current situation. His mind was always on Billy's plight instead of the loftier goals that the Light had set for him. He was bound and determined to approach the Light with his problem. He had made up his mind that when this gathering disbanded, he would do the unprecedented. He would ask for a private counsel with the creator. He sat restlessly among these heavenly beings.

The Light was glowing brightly upon the disciples gathered. The Light was everywhere and nowhere at the same time. The Light knew everything about all of its creations. At this particular moment, the Light was contemplating how to handle a tragedy of monumental proportions. A civilization, living on a planet in the star system Alpha Centauri was about to breach universal law. The Light had to make a decision on this matter. Should it intervene? This civilization that discovered how to split the atom was about to use its awesome power to destroy itself.

All the angels and heavenly beings were gathered to hear the Light speak about this horrific situation. All were fearful of the consequences. Violations of universal law were unheard of. None of those gathered had a clue what the Light was going to do about this. The gathered did not dare look into the intense light that surrounded the creator. They knew that blindness or worse would occur if they looked directly at the Light. It was an honor for them just to be invited to this gathering, so there was an air of excitement and apprehension among them as they awaited the speech. They bantered back and forth about the thrilling missions they had been assigned to until the Light spoke. The deafening silence was so intense that you could hear a pin drop as the soothing voice of the Light explained the consequences of this fated nuclear attack. The Light said, "There's a rhyme and a reason why the universe is the way it is. It's for this reason that civilizations have been kept isolated. I could not allow this type of poison to be spread throughout the universe and taint all the good I've created. This is exactly why there are such great distances between my different gardens of life. When I created the big bang, as our human brothers call it, I supplied the universe with all the elements of life. I created great big nuclear generators, in the form of stars, and scattered them all throughout the universe so that all my creations would have warmth. Now one of my creations has found a way to cause its own extinction. And so it shall be. All my creations were given free will, and this is the consequence. The only saving grace is that this poison will only affect this particular civilization. None of my creations other than the ones involved will ever know about this and therefore freewill will continue to exist throughout all my gardens. You are now excused."

Most of the angels and the heavenly spirits made a rapid exit as they were anxious to continue the tasks that they were assigned. Michael sat quiescently in meditation, gathering the courage to speak. He stood there facing the "Light" but not looking into it. The few remaining stared over at Michael, mesmerized by his courage or audacity. Impulsively he blurted out, "It's said that you take an interest in the lives and plights of all your creations."

"I know why you're here, Michael, and yes, we do have a problem," the Light said.

The Light pensively watched the disturbing events taking place at the abandoned ballpark, situated on the frontline of the never-ending battle between good and evil. Although eons away from that dreadful place the Light saw all. At that moment, Satan was busy giving Billy Green another terrible tongue-lashing for showing too much sensitivity toward Eddie's ordeal. He was outraged by the fact that Billy was disclosing too many details about his former life. He also didn't like the fact that Billy was suggesting methods of persuasion other than violence.

Satan made it clear to Billy that the only reason he wasn't swimming in the Lake of Fire was because he was so revered by the boy. He stated in no uncertain terms that he was going to get what was coming to him just as soon as Eddie Romano committed the ultimate sin.

After witnessing Satan's thorough castigation of Billy, the Light told Michael that it felt that Billy had some impressive redeeming qualities. It further declared that it was enjoying Billy's noble and valiant effort in attempting to undermine the satanic influences that surrounded him. It concluded that any soul that was loved as tremendously as Billy's couldn't be all that bad. The Light then judiciously considered a pardon, even intimating that it could possibly have made a mistake in its condemnation of Billy. According to the Light, the jury was still out when it came to Billy, and his actions from now on would determine his fate. The Light knew that Michael was eager to assist in this matter but wanted to make sure that there would be no breach of the heavenly guidelines. These were the guidelines that the Light had set for all angels and heavenly residents to abide by.

Michael humbly pleaded his case to the Light, "I want to help the boy, Eddie Romano, discover the location of Billy Green's body. I have heard that a soul cannot ascend to heaven unless its physical death has been discovered. As far as I know, the world still does not know that Billy Green is actually dead, and that's my fault. I found him hanging from the upper deck. I cut him down and secretly buried his body underneath an old tool shed at the ballpark. I tried in life to hide his shame. I wanted people to think that he just disappeared. I didn't want them to know the truth and now he will be forever in torment unless I do something about it. I cannot go on carrying this heavy burden. Dear God, please give me a chance to correct my mistake." As he finished pleading, Michael got down off his chair and prayed solemnly on his knees.

There was a hush among the remaining heavenly beings as many did not realize that Billy's body still remained undiscovered and many sympathized with Michael's plight. All felt guilt about mistakes they had made during their lives. They hoped the Light would show compassion in solving this predicament.

The Light understood completely the implications that surrounded this revelation. The Light could issue no pardon on Billy's behalf without the living world knowing the shame that surrounded his death. The Light also worried about setting a dangerous precedent here. It did not want people to think that suicide was a viable alternative or that it would help expedite their entrance into the kingdom of heaven. After carefully considering the issues at hand, the Light acquiesced to Michael's intentions. It proclaimed that as long as Michael did not directly interfere with any of its living children, it would be all right for him to give them the inspiration to make their own discoveries. The gist of all this was that Michael was not allowed to tell any living being where the body was located. He would only be allowed to heighten their curiosity.

Michael was only aware of one living soul that might still have some curiosity toward Billy Green. He decided to go and pay him a visit in a dream.

From
Disillusionment to
Inspiration

L ou Eisen sat reclined in his big easy chair, puffing on a big fat cigar in his living room. He was taking it easy these days. Since taking a permanent leave of absence from his sports editing duties at the *Chicago Tribune*, he had started to live the life of a hermit. His wife had left him many years before and his children had grown up and moved away, so he now had plenty of time to reflect upon days gone by. Retirement had turned out to be just the ticket that he needed after so many years of hustle and bustle.

Lou, a man, who formerly was obsessed with sports, completely disassociated himself with the sporting life. He never spent any time at ball games anymore and instead directed his energies toward studying a wide variety of subjects. His goal was to become well-rounded for the first time in his seventy-eight years of life.

Lately Lou spent a lot of time meditating. He knew that the grim reaper was not far down the block, and he was extremely curious about what might lie ahead for him. Every night, before going to bed, he prayed that he would discover that life was not just another dead end street.

What was most annoying to Lou was the fear that he might have spent his entire life acquiring wisdom for nothing. The thought of standing on the threshold of understanding what life was all about just to die without an afterlife was too painful for him to bear with. He really didn't like entertaining these kinds of thoughts, but since no one ever proved them wrong, he begrudgingly accepted them as a possibility.

On this particularly lazy Sunday afternoon, Lou busied himself skimming through the big thick edition of the *Chicago Tribune* that lay at the foot of his easy chair. After glancing at the headlines of the national section, he turned to the comics to get a chuckle or two. Next, he decided to help thin the paper out by depositing all the junk advertising in the waste paper basket that rested at the side of his chair.

He was at an age where he had seen enough of junk mail and bulk advertisements. Life seemed to be one constant sales pitch, and he frankly was tired of it. He was sick of all the advertisements that cluttered the paper. He believed that part of the reason that newspapers were dying around the country was that there wasn't any news in them anymore. As far as he was concerned, most newspapers were just one giant advertisement.

Even more sickening to him was the state of the television media. It was his belief that the networks sold out any semblance of decency in pursuit of the all-mighty dollar. He was fed up with seeing sex lines being advertised everywhere on late-night television. Although he liked looking at pretty girls as much as anyone, he didn't like how suggestive everything had become. He was tired of seeing those scantily clad young girls on his television asking fellas to call their 900 numbers at twenty-five dollars a pop. He didn't want to see douche commercials or Madonna trying to goad two homosexuals into making out with each other. He had enough of it all and in that respect was looking forward to death. The world the way it was now was completely alien to anything he had been taught or for that matter anything he believed in.

It wouldn't be stretching the truth too far to say that his spirit had been broken. There was only so much filth that a man like Lou could deal with before reaching his saturation point and that was the major reason why he had become such a recluse in the first place. Lou was experiencing a renaissance of his soul. He was trying his best to spend the rest of his days on the straight and narrow. He didn't want to take any detours and risk missing the pearly gates if there was such a thing. His entire life was different now. He was no longer obsessed with sports and gambling, two of the major reasons his wife left him so many years ago. Looking back upon it now, he really couldn't fault her for leaving. He had lost many a mortgage payment to sports bookies during his younger days and she deserved better than that. Since experiencing the tedium of retirement, he had many times felt that compulsive urge to gamble once again but so far he had fought it off. That urge was probably the main reason that he ignored the sports section altogether.

He had spent fifty years of his life mastering knowledge of every sport imaginable but at the moment wouldn't be able to tell a friend who was leading the divisional races in professional baseball.

Lou Eisen, the former sports junkie, had now gone almost three years without reading about sports but that was before last night's dream. It was so rare for him to remember them. He had always hated the fact that he would forget them upon awakening but last night's was different; he could remember almost every detail. A heavenly messenger had asked him to borrow his body and pleaded with him to start showing some interest in sports again. It was the strangest dream he had ever experienced. Everything about it seemed so real. The only problem for Lou was that he forgot the outcome. One thing he didn't forget was the pact he made with that messenger about showing some interest in sports again. So subliminally that was very much on his mind as he reached down to pick up the local section of the newspaper. For reasons unbeknownst to him, his eyes became fixated upon a photograph that headlined the sports section. He immediately forgot all about the local section and brought the sports page closer to his field of view. He reached over and grabbed his reading glasses off the end table and suddenly his eyes were able to focus in on the colored photograph.

Lou couldn't believe what he was looking at. There on the cover of his sports section was a picture of a kid dressed up like Billy Green. Lou immediately figured that the paper was doing a story about the age-old disappearance. After reading the fine print, he was alarmed to find out that the story wasn't about Billy Green at all. The story was about a high school standout named Eddie Romano.

Lou was fascinated by the color photograph of Eddie Romano wearing the green antique glove. Lou was sure that he had seen that same glove before. He wondered why Eddie Romano was trick or treating as Billy Green.

Lou had known Billy Green very well. They had been friends when Billy was in the minor leagues. He had always wondered what had happened to him. After working his butt off in the minor leagues for many years and finally earning a spot on the White Sox roster, he had mysteriously disappeared. Lou had been one of the few local sports writers to annually do a story on the age-old disappearance. He had always felt obligated to keep the story fresh in the public's mind since he and the missing ballplayer had been such good friends.

Billy Green's disappearance had always been an enigma to Lou. Although he had resigned himself long ago to the belief that Billy was most certainly dead, there still was no evidence to verify that. Just seeing someone dressed up as Billy brought him back to happier times. He was a young reporter back then, just starting out with an entire lifetime ahead of him. Memories of the flamboyant young infielder brought tears to the old man's eyes. Lou straightened himself out and examined the photograph once again. He got up off the chair and walked over to his cluttered desk, turning on a lamp to illuminate things. He opened up the bottom drawer and scoured through the memorabilia of a lifetime before uncovering the photograph he was looking for. It was a photograph of Billy Green he had taken when he was a photo journalist covering the Double-A Memphis squad back in1952. He redirected his attention away from the smiling face of his old friend and zeroed in on the glove he was wearing. He scrutinized while juxtaposing the photographs, comparing the glove in his photograph with the glove that Eddie Romano was wearing in the newspaper photo. The similarity was uncanny.

Lou wondered how and why Eddie Romano would make such a perfect replica of Billy Green's glove. It just didn't make any sense to him. It wasn't like Green was any big star. He wondered why Eddie would go through all the trouble of having that glove duplicated in such fine detail and why a kid playing baseball in 1998 would want to wear such an out-of-date glove. He came up with two plausible explanations. The first was that Eddie was one of those weird individuals with no identity of his own, so he patterns himself after an idol. He discarded that idea as nonsense because Green was no Ty Cobb or some kind of folk hero or celebrity. That left him with the second alternative, which was the most mind-boggling of them all, and that being that the glove was actually Billy Green's. And if that was the case, then Eddie Romano was holding the only tangible piece of physical evidence as to Billy Green's whereabouts that he'd ever heard about.

Lou Eisen suddenly felt that it was his duty to solve this mystery. He decided that he would soon make a trip to Palatine High School and meet with Eddie Romano.

Suddenly he felt a fire in his belly again. He finally felt passionate about something. His excitement was overwhelming. Lou had finally found something interesting to do, and it was beautiful.

EDDIE'S WORST NIGHTMARE COMES TRUE

O n his way out the door at the Jones's residence, Eddie took a quick glance at the public basketball court across the street. He thought about how much things had changed since that chilly March evening during his freshmen year. That night was really the first time he ever made a real sacrifice for the magic of the glove. Since showing his loyalty toward the glove and what it stood for, it had not let him down. He could only hope that in the future the glove's magic would continue to give him the edge in his never-ending quest for greatness.

So far his coach's plan seemed to be the solution to his current dilemma. Things had gone better than expected for him at Bobby's house. Bobby nervously accepted his apology with no questions asked. Three years after the fact, Bobby was still as intimidated by his presence as when they first met up on that high school track. He was made perfectly aware of this because he kept swearing to him up and down that he hadn't breathed a word about the incident to anyone. He had a lot of trouble calming the frightened young man down to explain to him that was not the reason for his visit. When he learned that he was there to pay him some hush money, Bobby was absolutely ecstatic.

As Eddie climbed into his car, he concluded that no bribe was necessary. Bobby would have kept his mouth shut regardless, but he would pay the money anyway because he was a man of his word. Earlier in the day Eddie learned that Ray Mayberry would play no role in the negative stories that were being printed about him. Ray and his family had moved to Texas, so he decided that he could deal with that situation later.

As he began driving home, he felt a tremendous sense of relief. He had finally gotten all the distracting monkeys off his back and now he could focus all his energies toward baseball once again. It was crucial for him to stay focused now because so many pro scouts were keeping him under a watchful eye. This would be his make-or-break season. His accomplishments playing baseball would directly affect how much bonus money he would receive for signing a pro contract. He knew that he was not the only ballplayer that the pros were interested in, and all the progress he had made during the last seven years of his life would be flushed down that proverbial toilet if he went into a slump now. Largely due to how well things had gone during the day, he felt certain that no slump was in the cards. All the obstacles in his way had been removed, and it sure looked like there was nothing but clear sailing ahead.

As he arrived in his neighborhood, he was in great spirits, the best in a long time. As he pulled into his driveway, it dawned upon him that he had promised his mother that he would bring her home a gallon of milk. The errand had completely slipped his mind until then. Finally having a clear head and a million times less stress on his shoulders, he decided to prove to his family that he had gotten his act together. He knew that they expected him to be forgetful. He was sure that the first words that he would hear out of his mother's mouth would be, "You forgot the milk, didn't you?" Today he was going to prove them wrong. He was going to turn over a new leaf and become a responsible member of his household.

With that intent, he pulled back out of his driveway and headed down the block to the 7-Eleven on the corner. He was there in no time. As he pulled his car into the brightly lit but empty store parking lot, he looked out toward the horizon and noticed that dusk had arrived. He thought about all the sunsets he had never taken the time to notice. These thoughts put a slight damper on this particularly bright day. As he exited his vehicle, he vowed to himself that from now on he would make an effort to be more observant and try to smell the roses for a change. For that reason, he took a quick glance toward the side of the building and noticed a gloomy shade, cast down from the large oak trees that separated his street from the usually busy convenience store.

As Eddie entered the brightly lit 7-Eleven store, he busied himself with tossing his magic glove into the air and catching it. He went directly to the dairy case and started examining the differing expiration dates that appeared on the milk containers. He was not going to make the same mistake he had made a couple of weeks ago. On that ill-fated occasion he had run a similar errand for his mother and brought back milk that soured too quickly. His mother never lived it down, and he was bound and determined to buy his mother milk that would stay fresh for the longest period of time. After making his selection, he carried the gallon milk container along with his glove up to the checkout counter. There he patiently waited for the clerk to come out of the back room to check him out. As he stood there idly, taking in a panoramic view of the store, the clerk finally arrived. He was a rather large black man with long corn-braided hair. Eddie thought that he looked too slovenly to be working in such a clean, antiseptic environment. He thought that this clerk appeared to be out of place but chalked it up to minority-hiring practices. In broken English, the clerk asked him how much the milk went for and he nonchalantly replied, "I think it's $2.89."

Eddie then set his glove down on the counter and pulled out his wallet. The clerk immediately stared down at the uniquely decorated glove. It was almost as if the glove had put a hypnotic spell upon him. Eddie noticed the clerk's peculiar fascination with his magic glove as he fumbled through his wallet seeking a $5 bill. He broke the ice by declaring, "I can see you like my glove, pretty cool, huh?"

The clerk said nothing as he continued to stare at it under some kind of spell. Eddie nervously handed over the bill, and the clerk pulled a gun out and pointed it in his direction screaming, "Just put da damn wallet on de counter cracker!"

Eddie froze in fear and quickly tried to translate what he assumed the man had demanded in his broken English. He did exactly what he thought the man had asked for. The man forced him at gunpoint to follow him behind the counter into the back room. Upon arrival, he saw the old woman, who normally manned the cash register bound, gagged and blindfolded, lying in the corner.

Eddie began to cry uncontrollably. "Please don't kill me! Oh, God, no! This can't be happening."

"Shut dat ho in yo face! Now hode still. Ize gots ta tie ya down. Ya hear me, cracker?"

Eddie now heard him too well. He started thinking that this just might be the end of the road and that he might be visiting Ruth and Gehrig a lot sooner than he originally planned. He just sobbed and shook his head in disbelief while the man tied him up. He prayed that the man wouldn't blindfold him like he had the old woman. If he was going to die, he wanted to see it coming so that he could prepare for it. His thoughts drifted to his dream coach. He regretted the fact that due to his current circumstances he might never get a chance to say good-bye. He hoped that he would be able to catch up with him again someday after becoming a permanent resident of "heaven." Suddenly, the man stuffed a gag into his mouth, and he was having trouble breathing. He began to hyperventilate as a blindfold was placed over his eyes. At this moment, he truly understood the helplessness that a condemned man must feel when they blindfold his eyes during hangings and electrocutions. He too was totally helpless, and he began to pray silently for one last chance. He promised that he would give anything to just have one more chance at life. He closed his eyes tightly and tried to drown out the outside world. He wondered how long it was going to hurt when the end finally came and that bullet exploded into his brain. The stress was too much for him, and he suddenly passed out.

He awoke to noise and confusion. He pinched his bound hands together to feel the pain of life. When he felt the pain, he knew that somehow he had been spared. He was still disoriented when he heard what he assumed to be a police scanner in the proximity.

"They're over here!" the police officer shouted to his comrades as he turned on the storage room light, revealing Eddie and the clerk. Eddie could only see a little bit of brightness through his blindfold, but he was now sure that he had been rescued. He started to wiggle around like crazy, and the policeman quickly untied him. As soon as his arms were unbound, he gave the policeman a great big hug and then started to cry uncontrollably. The policeman told him to go out into the store and wait. Eddie didn't budge an inch. He had soiled his pants during the ordeal and was too embarrassed to leave the storage room. The policeman immediately understood why he didn't follow instructions. He saw the feces stain on the rear of the young man's pants and he took off his long blue winter jacket and gave it to him to cover himself with. Eddie then proceeded out into the store like he was instructed until it dawned on him that his glove wasn't with him. During the confusion and terror of the assault, he had lost all track of its whereabouts. Now that things were relatively back to normal, he immediately started to panic. His eyes dashed wildly all around the store in a frantic effort to locate it. Unfortunately for Eddie, no matter where he looked, his glove was nowhere to be found.

"My glove! Where's my glove?" Eddie asked hysterically to no one in particular.

The initial officer's partner quickly came over to him in an attempt to calm him down. It quickly became apparent that there was no way to settle down the anxious young man other than return his glove.

"My glove! Where's my glove? We've got to find my glove," Eddie shouted, refusing to relax until his glove was back in his possession again.

"Relax. We'll find your glove. Believe me, I'll do everything in my power to find it for you," the officer's partner said in a patronizing manner. "You know, I think it might be best for you to take a little trip to the hospital. You've been through quite an ordeal here, and it might be better for you to go there and get a good night's sleep. Then you'll be well rested to sort things out in the morning."

"I'm not going anywhere until I find my glove! Where is it? You know where it is! Give it to me!" Eddie screamed crazily.

"What glove? Why don't you describe it for me so that I can look for it," the officer's partner said, trying his best to find a way to alleviate the young man's ever-growing unrest.

"You know exactly what glove I'm talking about. You probably stole it. Where are you hiding it? Probably out there in your cruiser, huh?" Eddie accused.

"Sir, I don't have the faintest idea what you're talking about."

"You do too! My baseball glove! Where'd you put it?" Eddie asked in dements.

"Sir, I didn't see any baseball glove. I don't understand what the problem is. If it's just a baseball mitt, go out and buy a new one," the officer's partner said, rapidly losing his patience.

"Oh, that's very funny. You can't buy a glove like mine. It's priceless. It's a bona fide, one of a kind, antique. Now where is it?" Eddie asked with insanity in his eyes.

Eddie watched the officer turn away from him and whisper something to one of the arriving ambulance technicians. The next thing he knew, he was being forcibly restrained by the ambulance crew. They strapped him on to a stretcher and put him in the back of the ambulance. Within minutes, he was whisked away to the hospital. The nightmare had begun.

DESPONDENT IN THE HOSPITAL

Eddie felt like he had been sleeping for days when he finally forced his eyes open. He had a pounding headache, and he was extremely disoriented. Before his eyes even had a chance to focus, they were greeted by the concerned eyes of his parents. He had no clue as to where he was until he looked beyond his mother's caring smile and took in the bland white walls that were omnipresent.

"The hospital" he mumbled and whispered in an almost inaudible tone. "How long have I been here?"

"What, honey?" his mother asked.

Eddie looked over at the tray that rested to the side of his bed and noticed a pitcher of water. He arose and poured himself a cup. He had the worst cottonmouth of his life. He quickly guzzled down the water and drank another cup for good measure. He then settled himself back down on his pillow and cleared his throat before repeating the question, "I said, how long have I been here?"

"This is your third day. Oh, Eddie, you just don't know how relieved we are to see that you're okay. When the police called us the other night, we were scared to death," his mother said with tears running down her face.

"I've been sleeping for three days? Oh, my God. I'll never find it now," Eddie moaned.

"Forget about that dumb baseball glove, will you? You should just thank your lucky stars that you're still with us," his father snapped.

"Oh man, I wish I was dead." Eddie groaned.

"How can you say that? You've got a lot of nerve, you know that? Your mother and I have been waiting here patiently for days. Never was there a boy that was more loved than you. And that's the thanks we get. You just go out of your way to say things to break our hearts. Well, thanks a lot, Eddie," his father chided.

"I'm sorry, Dad. It's just that everything is ruined now. I lost the only thing that made me special. Without that glove, I'm nothing. No pro teams will look at me now. You don't understand, I'm not the same player without that glove."

"It's all in your mind, my boy. Just like those doctors said years ago, it's psychosomatic. I've watched you play over the years, and I can say without reservations and without a doubt, you've got the tools to go as far as you want in that game. You just don't believe in yourself."

"You don't have the foggiest idea of what you're talking about, Dad. It's not psychosomatic. I've been telling you that for years. That glove was truly magic, and it's gone and now I've got to live with the consequences."

"Well, Mr. Man, I don't want to hear another word about that glove. It may be gone but you're here and that's what matters. It's easier to replace a glove than a son. So don't you ever say that you wish that you were dead to me again. That is unacceptable, Eddie. You're alive and well, and that's all that matters to your father and me," his mother said with fervor.

Eddie was too upset to respond. His mind was hard at work trying to figure out a way to locate his glove. The more he thought about it, the more it seemed like trying to find a needle in a haystack. All this thinking was making his tension headache worse.

He was in such a state of total depression that all he wanted to do was sleep. He tried his best to relax, closing his eyes in hope that the throbbing would somehow subside, but it was futile.

Just as he was beginning to calm down a bit, his father informed him that he would be going home later in the day. He told him that the doctors had determined that there was nothing wrong with him. Eddie didn't believe that diagnosis.

EDDIE CHOOSES
TO LIVE WITHOUT THE
GLOVE

For days on end, Eddie vegetated inside his house. Although he would sleep for long periods of time, his visits to heaven ceased entirely. He would constantly take naps throughout the day in the hope of receiving just one more visit with his dream coach, but it was not to be. He felt slighted by all his associates in the afterworld. He resented the way they ignored him since losing possession of the glove. He developed a large chip on his shoulder. His thoughts were filled with self-pity. His confidence was now just a fleeting memory from the distant past. He was seriously contemplating suicide.

For days he sat in his room and debated over which method of suicide would be the least painful. He thought about hanging himself but decided against it after watching a television program that said it could be very painful. The program stated that if the knot was not put to the side of the neck correctly, the victim would end up slowly choking to death. After hearing that, he totally ruled out that idea. He also feared that he didn't have the guts to harm himself, but he wasn't sure he could live with the very real possibility of never feeling special ever again. He longed for the days when his sleep periods were the most rewarding moments of his life. It suddenly dawned on him that he had no friends except the ones he had made in "heaven." He had allowed his entire existence to revolve around those special, otherworldly friends, and now that he was unable to make contact with them, he realized he had no friends at all. He had sacrificed everything for the love of that glove, and now with it gone, he had nothing.

His parents didn't know how to cope with him anymore. His father completely ignored him, referring to him disgustedly as that "zombie boarder." His mother thought it was time to seriously consider committing him.

The worst fate imaginable had become Eddie's reality. The Palatine High baseball team was giving up hope of his return; the professional baseball scouts that were once so high on him were losing interest rapidly and the likelihood of him finding his magic glove was slim to none.

With all these factors weighing heavily on his mind, he decided to stop pitying himself for the time being and take one last shot at getting that proverbial brass ring.

His mother almost fell off her chair in the kitchen when she saw him coming down the stairs dressed for school. It was the first time in over two weeks that he had actually gotten showered and dressed. She didn't say a word to him. She was afraid that he might change his mind. No matter how unusual this event was, it gave her hope that he might actually be coming back to his senses. She watched intently as he poured himself a bowl of frosted flakes and sat down next to her to eat. There was a protracted silence before he decided to speak.

"Mom, I'm going to school today."

His mother carefully thought out how she would respond. After an unusually long hesitation, she said, "Well, I think it's good that you're going to school. I'm sure they miss you."

"That's not why I'm going. I'm going because I'm wasting my life hanging around here."

"Well, that makes good sense to me."

"I've got to try to play without the glove. Maybe Dad's right, maybe it is all psychosomatic."

"I guess you'll never know unless you try."

"You're right. Look, Mom, I've got to go," Eddie said as he got up from the table and placed his empty bowl in the sink.

His getting up from the table stimulated a thought that had been lingering in his mother's mind for quite some time now. "Eddie, a man's been coming around here pretty regularly looking for you."

"Yeah? What kind of man?"

"An old man."

"What is he, a reporter? I'm not speaking to any reporters."

"Your father and I told him that, but he still insisted on speaking to you."

"Well, if he comes around again, you tell him for me to bug off," Eddie emphasized.

"I will. Now you hurry off to school."

Mrs. Romano was overwhelmed with hope as she watched him exit the house.

EDDIE HAS A MELTDOWN

After a solid week of tutors and catching up on his studies, Eddie was finally getting his grade point average high enough to be allowed to play baseball once again. He had never applied himself more to his studies than he had this past week. All the time away from school had put him in a deep hole, scholastically speaking, and he needed to do a lot of climbing if he wanted to get back to the surface again. But no matter how hard he tried to focus on his schoolbooks, the loss of his magic glove was all he could think of and a source of constant torment. He tried to deceive himself into believing that it was still in his possession but it was all for not. He secretly feared that all the time he spent studying would just end up being a colossal waste of time and effort. *What if they let him play ball and he wasn't capable of performing like before? What would he do then?* These questions were always on his mind.

Eventually his hard work paid dividends, and he was permitted to continue playing on the Palatine High baseball team, but it was obvious to all around him that something about him had changed. He just didn't have that same smug confidence in his baseball playing abilities as he did before losing the glove. As the kids put it, *"He had lost his swagger."*

Coach O'Neil immediately picked up on it during practice sessions. Although there was no doubt that he was still a talented ballplayer, it was apparent that he had lost his *"edge."* It's been said that what sets a champion above his challengers is his absolute belief in his greatness. He never doubts for a moment that he is the best. He believes in himself wholeheartedly. No set of obstacles will deter his belief. This is exactly the confidence that Eddie was lacking as he stepped off the team bus.

The entire Palatine High baseball team marched into the gymnasium entrance at Hersey High School. Since Hersey was one of Palatine's greatest rivals, you never knew what to expect. The people at Hersey were known for their psychological warfare of current opponents but even they had outdone themselves this time. Coach O'Neil and his charges were ushered to the visitor's locker room by an obviously gay member of Hersey High's janitorial staff. The custodial engineer seemed obsessed with Eddie and kept staring back at him with his perfectly plucked eyebrows and his immaculately made up eyes. He kept tossing his long thick freshly hennaed hair back and forth and giving all the boys on the team a come-hither look. He also put on an affectation of a female walk, throwing his hips from side to side and delicately pointing in the direction of the locker room. When he arrived there, he smiled sweetly, swung open the door, and said in an affected female voice, "Well there you go, boys. Have a good game and don't forget to come see me later."

The boys from Palatine were shocked by this entire welcoming. Never had they seen anything quite like it by any of the other schools they played. Worst of all, the openly gay janitor had led them into Hersey High School's girl's locker room. It was freshly painted pink, an obvious attempt by Hersey High School to try and psyche out the visiting Pirates of Palatine.

There was some grumbling by the Palatine team as they entered the effeminate-colored locker room. Eddie didn't need the paint job in order to be psyched out. In fact, he felt so little confidence in his abilities on this day that he deliberately left his replica of the ancient White Sox uniform at home. He was absolutely terrified of being in the spotlight. He rightfully figured that wearing that uniform would just focus unwanted attention. He wanted to be inconspicuous, like a fly on the wall, at least until he proved to himself that he could still play the game. All these behavioral changes were telltale signs that things were still not right with him psychologically.

While his teammates took up lockers and began preparing for the game, Eddie sat on the hard plastic bench in a daze. His teammates that occupied lockers next to his thought he was just mentally psyching himself up for the game until he suddenly unleashed a deluge of tears. He was having a complete nervous breakdown right there in front of them all. His teammates were stunned and shook their heads in disbelief as they witnessed "Chicago High School Baseball's, Mr. All Everything" sobbing like a beaten child.

Coach O'Neil was immediately informed that there was a problem with Eddie. As soon as he arrived on the scene, he was sure he knew what the problem was. He had seen this before in his own home. His eldest daughter had a similar breakdown between semesters her first year in college. In his daughter's case, the problem derived from her overwhelming desire to excel in school. During her high school days she had been a straight A student, but she found the going considerably tougher at the Ivy League school she was attending. He recalled vividly all the expensive therapy sessions his daughter had to go through in order to get her sanity back. He was hoping for his team's sake that Eddie could gather his wits together enough to play effectively. Since his original breakdown, the team had gone into a slump and lost six straight.

O'Neil sat down on the bench next to Eddie and placed his thick rugged arm around him. The team inconspicuously looked on from afar. In total amazement, they witnessed their ultramasculine, hard-nosed coach showing honest, genuine sensitivity toward Eddie.

Eddie responded immediately to his coach's embrace. His effusive emotional display concluded as quickly as it had begun. Just the fact that someone was reaching out to him gave him a sense of hope. Maybe things weren't as bad as he originally thought. He longed for the compassion he was receiving. This was the element that had been missing in his life since losing touch with the afterworld. He spontaneously buried his head deep into his coach's chest and wept quietly. O'Neil did his best to hold his own composure as he squeezed Eddie even more tightly.

O'Neil brushed his fingers through the boy's hair and reassured him that everything would be all right.

Eddie dried his eyes on O'Neil's sweatshirt, looked up at him and tacitly thanked him for caring. The sensory deprivation that he had been experiencing was over for the moment. He now knew that there was a living person other than his parents who cared for him.

"I'm sorry that I made such a scene, Coach," Eddie said while fighting to hold back his tears.

"You, my boy, are an emotional wreck, but I want you to know that I really do care for you. I'm going to do everything in my power to help lift you out of these doldrums. I know deep down inside that you're a fine young man, and I might not have told you this before but I've considered it an honor to have been your coach for the last four years. I think sometimes you've thought that I've just taken you for granted. You've always been such an important part of this team that maybe I've made you feel that way but it's not true, Eddie. Over the last four years, I've seen you grow as a ballplayer and as a human being. You've always come through for this team when we've needed you, and you can rest assured that this team will come through for you in your hour of need."

"I sure appreciate those kind words, Coach," Eddie said as he dried his eyes while bowing his head.

"You see that, fellas? He's not a freaking witch doctor like those damn newspapers would have you believe. He's just a kid, trying to do his best like the rest of you. He needs your support. I hope you'll give it to him."

There was a new sense of togetherness and unity among the team after O'Neil's speech. Eddie received many affectionate pats on the back from his teammates on his way to visit the uniform manager. The more emotional support he received from his teammates, the taller he stood as he walked by. By the time he caught up with the uniform manager, his head had gone from hanging low to being completely upright.

"I need a uniform. I left mine at home," Eddie whispered.

"No problem. That's why we bring extra uniforms. What number would you like?" The uniform manager asked.

"It doesn't matter. I'm not trying to impress anyone except maybe myself."

"That's the best person in the world to impress," the freshmen uniform manager said with a smile of sincerity.

Eddie grabbed a uniform and trekked back to his locker. Within moments, he was dressed and ready for the game. He reached into his sports equipment bag and pulled out the brand-new infielder's glove that his father had bought for him. He examined it and thought it looked so odd on his hand. Looking at it made his depression instantly recur. In order to alleviate this problem, he quickly put the glove back into his bag. He figured the less he saw of it, the better he would feel.

The team gathered around Coach O'Neil for their pregame pep talk and then headed out of their pink-colored locker room toward the field. Every player on the team was incredibly happy to be out of that locker room, so Hersey High's psychological ploy really worked.

Eddie deliberately kept a low profile as he and his teammates made their way on to the field. He tried his best to stay hidden among them. He glanced toward his team's dugout and noticed a familiar group of reporters hanging out there. So far they hadn't noticed him, but he knew that was to be short-lived. As soon as O'Neil announced the fielding warm ups, the so-called "cat" was out of the bag. It was kind of hard to miss him since all the reporters had to do was look between third and second base. There at shortstop you could always find him.

Before Eddie could field a single ground ball, the reporters literally engulfed him. They were so trite and insincere with their greetings that Eddie felt like throwing up on them. These were the same folks responsible in furthering the damaging rumors about him. Their propagations were a constant source of misery for him. They were figuratively a thorn in his side and the last people in the world he wanted to see at this particular moment. According to Eddie, these were mean-spirited people who seemed to bask in other people's agony. The thing that disturbed him the most was their eagerness to watch him fail. In his eyes, they resembled a group of vultures circling a wounded animal and patiently waiting for it to die. He looked around anxiously for an escape but none was to be found.

"Glad to see you back on the field again, Eddie. There's been a lot of anticipation about your return. What's this, an image change? What happened to your uniform?" asked Bob Howard, a television sports reporter, who had fashion issues himself as he stood in front of Eddie dressed in a pink suit.

"I forgot it," Eddie answered curtly.

"That's obvious, and your glove?"

"Well, I guess, Bob, if I forgot my uniform, I must have forgotten my glove too," Eddie asserted sarcastically.

Rene Remington, a local sports radio reporter, known for her gaudy dress barged into the conversation, "Ed-dee, it's been rumored that you've—how should I say it—had some sort of breakdown since the robbery?"

"Who told you that?"

"You know us, Ed-dee. We have our sources."

"Well, why don't you go and interview them? Why do you bother me? Because you know, if you piss me off, I'll be forced to pull out one of my voodoo dolls Rene and stick a pin in you," Eddie said, animating the pin sticking act for all to see.

Rene faked a laugh and quipped, "Ed-dee, you've got such a good sense of humor. Isn't he just a barrel of laughs?" Rene mockingly asked her colleagues.

"Just a bundle of laughs," Bob Howard remarked sarcastically.

"Look, do any of you have anything important to ask me? Because if you don't, I would really like to get back to warming up for this game," Eddie stated, rapidly losing his patience.

"Well, Eddie, I've got something to ask you. How are you coping with having to use that new glove?" Steve Smith, a reporter for the *Chicago Tribune* asked.

Eddie looked down at the pristine, brand-new glove he was wearing and disgustedly said, "I don't want to talk about it. Okay?"

"It must be tough having to face the world without your security blanket, huh, Linus?" Smith teased.

"Why don't you go to hell? Now get the hell out of my face," Eddie blasted adding, "Coach, could you please ask these reporters to leave the field so I can warm up?"

"Hey! You're going to have to leave the kid alone. Talk to him after the game," Coach O'Neil ordered.

The three reporters scurried off the field, looking like a group of frightened dogs with their tales between their legs. All of them openly wishing doom and gloom upon Eddie who they felt had just rained upon their parade.

As Eddie went through his pregame warm ups without further incident, he thought about the high price he was paying for fame. He determined that you could never become anybody without having the press thoroughly scrutinize your every move. It became painfully obvious to him why professional athletes were paid so much money because once they sign on that dotted line their lives became public record. Privacy for them, from that moment on, was nothing but a fleeting memory.

After warm ups, Eddie sat in the dugout staring out into the blue cloudless sky. So many thoughts filled his head. He wondered if he would ever see his dream coach again. He recalled how the dream coach had forewarned him about the consequences of losing possession of the glove. He now realized just how devastating the consequences really were. Now both he and his coach were permanently separated by space and time. He wondered if his dream coach was as depressed as he was. He wondered if his dream coach missed him too. These were the haunting questions that monopolized his every thought. He imagined him, peering in on him from "heaven." He thought about what a great disappointment he must be to him. They were best friends and now they were nothing. Soon his dream coach would only be a fond memory. He tried his best to paint a mind picture of his coach's smiling face during that last game of catch. For the first time in his life, he realized that he was truly alone. He had no crutches to fall back on anymore. There were no Ruth and Gehrig to bail him out of pressure situations. Today, when he stepped up to the plate, he could only rely on himself.

The thought of standing alone scared the hell out of him. He recalled how frightened he used to be when it was his turn at bat in little league back in the days before he found the glove. His present predicament was just like déjà vu. *He would have to make his own luck from here on in, and what if he failed? Wouldn't the world just enjoy that?* he thought. He knew those reporters certainly would.

With all of these varied thoughts on his mind, it should come as no surprise that he lacked focus. His head was just not in the game. There were too many things worrying him, too many outside influences affecting him. So when it came time to prove to him and the world that he was still a ballplayer who could be counted on in the clutch, he came up short.

Clutch time arrived during the top of the eighth inning. Behind 5-0, the bottom of his team's batting order had scratched and clawed their way back for two runs. With one out and the bases loaded, Eddie stepped up to the plate.

He could hear the cheers of the Palatine boosters in the air as he practiced his swing. After all he was the school's baseball hero, the one player who never failed in a crucial situation. Yes indeed, when the game was on the line, he was the man they counted on.

Hersey High's manager was well aware of Eddie's spectacular credentials. If there had been any unoccupied base to put him on, he would've issued him an intentional walk without a second thought but the bases were loaded and all he could do was pray.

He was unaware that the kid standing in the batter's box was not "mentally" the player who set all those records. This was a tentative Eddie Romano, an unsure Eddie Romano.

As he awaited the pitcher's windup, his mind lacked the singularity of focus it needed for him to succeed in this most crucial situation. He thought about the two fly ball outs he had made earlier in the game. He was thinking about how badly he wanted to come through for his team in their moment of need just like he had in the past. In fact he wanted to succeed so badly that he was "pressing" as the old-timers called it. All the lessons about hitting that he had learned he seemed to have suddenly forgotten. He wasn't loose; he gripped the bat so tightly that he lost his fluidity and lastly he thought about the absence of his magic glove. There was just too much thinking going on and not enough reacting, combinations that spell disaster when you're batting in a pressure spot.

He wanted to be the hero. Just making contact and getting a base hit was not good enough for him; he wanted a home run. With one powerful swing of the bat, he wanted to silence his critics and prove to himself that his game was back regardless of whether he had a magic glove.

So instead of trying to make solid contact with the pitch, he tried to overpower it. He swung with all his might. If strength of swing alone produced home runs, his ball would have ended up somewhere in downtown Chicago, but instead, it ended up speeding into the awaiting glove of Hersey High's shortstop. It was a routine double play ball. The shortstop made a quick flip to the second baseman who then promptly relayed it over to first, and before you could say snap, crackle, and pop, the inning was over.

Eddie threw his batting helmet down in disgust and made the long trek back to the dugout. He then had a temper tantrum like few had ever witnessed before. He started breaking bats over his knee and throwing them out on to the field. His teammates tried their best to restrain him but to no avail. After breaking numerous bats, he stormed away.

His teammates didn't bother to chase after him. He was way too far gone for any of them to communicate with, so they just let him go.

CLOSING THE DEAL

"**D**esperate times call for desperate measures." This was the prevailing thought that Eddie obsessed over during his long hike home. He just didn't have it in him to cope with failure, in any shape or form, and in his eyes that was all that existed on the horizon. No matter how hard he looked, he couldn't perceive any light at the end of the dark tunnel that had recently become his life. He became thoroughly convinced that without his magic glove, he was nothing more than a mediocre ballplayer. His performance in the game against Hersey had cemented that idea in his brain. The only question that remained was what was he going to do about it or, better yet, what could he do about it?

He felt like cursing the world and everyone who lived upon it. As far as he was concerned, the "angels" had played a dirty trick upon him. It was unfair to dangle all that glory underneath his nose and then take it away at the last minute. As far as he was concerned, this whole matter was beneath contempt. He wanted revenge. He would do anything for revenge. He was willing to pay any price in order to show up those "angels" that deserted him during his time of need. Their actions had proven to him that they were no better than those reporters that he despised so much. He had reserved a space in his dog house for all of them. All he wanted was just a chance to show Ruth and Gehrig that he really could play up to major league standards despite their shunning. He could almost understand the betrayal by the reporters, allegedly that was part of their job requirement, but the ostracism by Ruth and Gehrig was in his eyes totally uncalled for. *What was their excuse?* He knew that losing the glove had prevented him access to visiting his coach and the afterworld, but he couldn't understand why it would stop Ruth and Gehrig from contacting him. He was seething over the fact that Ruth and Gehrig, who had always contacted him before, were now mysteriously missing in action. They never once mentioned that their contacts had anything to do with him possessing the glove. *So why then wouldn't they be able to contact him now?* he thought. He considered their abandonment a personal affront. They were just traitors as far as he was concerned.

While sitting on his bed, he pondered a variety of revenge scenarios but only came up with ones that would end up hurting him in the long run. But then, the most evil thought suddenly came to him. Since he knew there was a heaven, he surmised there must be a hell too. He couldn't think of anything that would infuriate those "angels" more than him becoming a turncoat. They had betrayed him, and he was bound and determined to return the favor. He thought about the Manager and how badly he treated both he and his dream coach. He figured Satan couldn't be much worse than that. From what he had observed, there wasn't much difference between the "heaven" he used to visit nightly and the hell he heard stories about in church and on television. Halfheartedly, he decided to invite Satan into his life. He wasn't even sure that there was a Satan, so he tried this on a lark. He remembered a scene in a movie called *Somewhere in Time*. In that movie, the lead character attempted self-hypnosis by stating the same circumstances over and over again until he convinced himself that he was living on a particular date in the past and somehow he ended up there. Eddie was willing to give anything a try since he was so desperate, and he was running out of ideas to change that situation. Eddie started his rebellion by praying for Satan to intervene into his situation. He shut off all the lights and prayed aloud. As the monotony of his prayers lulled him to sleep, the last thought on his conscious mind asked for Satan's help.

It seemed like a miracle when he found himself back at that old abandoned ballpark. He couldn't believe he was actually there. He had resigned himself to the belief that he would never find his way back again. He made his way gingerly down the first baseline toward where his dream coach and the Manager patiently awaited.

"Don't be so cautious, Eddie. You're here. You won't fall back," the Manager said with an exaggerated smile.

"I can't believe that I made it here. How'd I get here without my glove?" Eddie asked completely baffled, forgetting what he had done just before falling asleep.

"It doesn't matter how you got here. It only matters that you did," the Manager stated, looking very much like the cat that swallowed the canary.

Billy looked over at Eddie with disheartened eyes. Although he loved him very much, he was not happy to see him at this moment but that didn't deter the boy's love for him. He immediately jumped into his coach's arms. Billy couldn't recall a time when he was squeezed so hard.

"Oh, Coach, I missed you so much," Eddie said with tears in his eyes. "Please don't ever leave me again."

"How sentimental, how touching?" the Manager said while rolling his eyes sarcastically. The Manager then let out a loud yawn.

"Why did you come back, Eddie?" Billy asked disappointedly.

"Co-a-ch, why would you ask a question like that?" Satan inquired in a condescending yet protracted manner. "The answer is as clear as the nose on your face. The boy loves yooou."

"I do, Coach. I was going crazy without you. Everybody deserted me. I had no friends. Life really totally sucked. I couldn't even play ball anymore."

Billy mulled over the thought, *Well, my boy, it might have sucked without me, but you have no idea how bad it's going to suck with me back in it again.* Like usual, he was totally unable to speak his mind, but of course, the Manager had no such problems getting his point across.

"Eddie, you were awfully lucky to find your way back to us."

"Boy, you can say that again."

"I don't know if you know it, Eddie, but you finding your way here carried about the same probability as being struck by lightning. Do you know how rare that is?"

"Not really, but I know it doesn't happen often."

The Manager let out a little chuckle and continued, "Well, Eddie, if it doesn't happen often, what's the likelihood of it happening again?"

"Next to impossible."

"That's a fair estimation, my boy. You do realize that this might be your last trip here, don't you?"

"Yeah, I guess so," Eddie said dejectedly.

"This is breaking my heart but the good thing is, that it doesn't have to be that way, Eddie," the Manager said slyly.

"No?"

"No."

"Well, what can I do about it?"

"Well, you know the glove is the key?"

"Yeah. But I wouldn't have the first clue where to look for it," Eddie conceded in discouragement.

"You've really given up hope, haven't you?" the Manager snickered.

"I don't understand why you're laughing. I don't find it the least bit funny," Eddie stated in shock as he ruminated over the Manager's levity, especially considering the dilemma he was in.

"Neither do I, my boy, neither do I."

"Then why are you snickering?"

"Because I know something that you don't," the Manager stated smugly.

"I bet I can guess. You know where my glove is, don't you?"

"Maybe."

"Well, look, I'm sick of your games. You either do or you don't," Eddie blurted out angrily.

"Coach, I think it's about time you ask him that million dollar question, don't you?" Satan queried.

Billy hung his head low and hesitated momentarily before speaking, "Eddie, do you think you'd be willing to make the ultimate sacrifice in order to get your glove back?" He asked this without ever looking back up again. He was so ashamed of himself that he just continued staring down at his green patent leather baseball cleats.

"Coach, what is the ultimate sacrifice?"

"The ultimate sacrifice is committing the sin of murder for profit, Eddie, and that's what has to be done in order for you to retrieve your glove with all its powers intact," Billy explained in a manner that would make one believe that these words were not his own and that he didn't believe a word of them. He then added with sincerity and conviction that, "It signifies once and for all the end of your innocence, my boy."

"Look, Coach, I can't remember being innocent. That was something I lost such a long time ago. So I guess it really doesn't make a hell of a lot of difference what I do. Who would I have to kill?" Eddie asked in a calm, cool, and collective manner.

"Just the fella who stole your glove."

"That son of a bitch? I hate to say it, but I'll kill him with pleasure," Eddie said boisterously with ice-cold eyes and adding, "In fact, that dude deserves whatever he gets. That son of a bitch literally scared the crap out of me, not to mention the fact that he ruined my life. I think the least I could do is return the favor."

"But, Eddie, the fact remains, scaring the crap out of you isn't killing you. Don't get me wrong, what he did was unforgivable, granted, but he still didn't harm you," Billy argued persuasively.

"Coach, you're confusing me. One minute you tell me that I have to kill the dude in order to get my glove back with all its powers intact and then next you give me a lecture about why I shouldn't kill him. I mean, make up your mind, will you?"

"My point exactly, Eddie, please spare us your nonsense, Coach. Eddie doesn't want to hear your self-righteous horse shit. Eddie wants his glove back, so he can come and visit you whenever he pleases. All he wants is what everybody wants. I mean, who doesn't want a meal ticket to a wonderful life? So why don't you just put a lid on it?" Satan interjected, rapidly reaching the end of his patience with the rebellious Billy.

"That's right, Coach. I'll do whatever is necessary to preserve our relationship," Eddie announced.

Although he knew that Eddie's intentions were somewhat honorable, Billy still felt totally ashamed after hearing his reply. Eddie had become a product of his environment. He had been exposed for years to ruthless people and now he too was ruthless. His soul had been corrupted, and he knew that he had played an intricate role in the corruption. He was suddenly overcome by guilt as he realized that Eddie's fate was now sealed alongside his own. As hard as he had tried to rebel against Satan, he had failed. He knew that it was just a matter of time before his services would no longer be needed at the ballpark. Pretty soon he would have to take up residency in the Lake of Fire just like the rest of the condemned. He knew that as soon as Eddie committed this murder, his days at the ballpark would be finished forever. Once that event took place, he would no longer be needed as the bait in order to entice the young man into escalating his evil deeds. Once that event took place, Eddie would forever be one of Satan's subjects, and he knew deep in his heart that the dark man couldn't wait to get rid of him and his meddling ways.

So while Billy was down in the dumps, Satan was ready to break out the champagne. He had succeeded in destroying another soul. But for reasons unbeknownst to him at the time, he suddenly felt a desperate urge to reinforce the message of murder in this young man's mind.

"Eddie, this better not be a trick. You better keep your word because if you don't, I swear to you the magic will cease. Don't think for a moment that retrieving that glove alone will give you special powers. Believe me, unless you carry out the deed, the glove itself will be useless to you. Do you understand me? I'm talking about the end of the magic unless you do the deed."

"There's no need to browbeat me, Mr. Manager. I'm reading you loud and clear. I said I'd kill the son of a bitch and I will. Did I stutter?"

"No. You didn't stutter. I just wanted to make sure you knew how serious this little deed of yours was to us. You're a very good boy, and I'm proud of you," the Manager said smiling while giving Eddie a pat on the back.

"You guys just tell me where my glove is, and I'll ice the son of a bitch who has it," Eddie boasted proudly.

Eddie's murderous words echoed throughout the ballpark for all to hear. Suddenly he was greeted by hundreds of condemned ballplayers who raced out of the dugout.

They were dressed in team uniforms that spanned the spectrum and were representative of almost every baseball team that ever existed.

Eddie was overwhelmed by the presence of all these ballplayers that he never knew existed. In all the years he had been coming there, he had never seen hide or hair of any of them with the exception of Eddie Cicotte. The welcome he was receiving from these ballplayers was as warm as if he had just hit a walk off homer, to win the World Series. He was confounded by the sense of unity and camaraderie he was receiving from all these "angels" from baseball's past. He couldn't comprehend what he had done, that was so exceptional to warrant this deluge of well wishing? He felt like an insider for the first time in many years. He was surrounded by a group that made him feel like he belonged.

Eddie Cicotte danced his way over to him, merrily shaking his hand. "Congratulations, kid. I'm glad to hear that we're going to be seeing a lot of you from now on," Cicotte said excitedly.

"Thanks, Eddie. Can you believe all this?" Young Romano said with his mouth agape. "I mean, all this celebration just for me?"

"It's not just for you, Eddie. It's for the Manager too. The Manager really likes to whoop it up whenever he closes a deal. You were quite a conquest for him," Eddie Cicotte said gleefully.

"Oh. So this is like an initiation celebration?"

"Yes indeed. You're a member of the team now, and I for one am loving it!"

"Okay. I get it! Well, I want you to know, I really appreciated all the help you gave me," Eddie declared joyously as he gave Cicotte an obligatory hug.

"Ah, that was nothing! I enjoyed the vacation! Just like I'm enjoying it now," Cicotte exclaimed as he excitedly jumped away from Eddie and slapped hands with another ballplayer in a high five gesture.

Cicotte exited shortly thereafter, and Eddie became increasingly aghast with all the new friends that seemed so anxious to meet him. During this chaotic scene, he had lost track of his dream coach's whereabouts. He excused himself from his flocking well-wishers long enough to search the crowd for his coach. He wasn't about to forget the man who made all this possible. He looked long and hard through the crowd to no avail until his eyes picked up upon a solitary ballplayer walking alone. He was far out in the distance of center field. He was the only ballplayer who showed no interest in the celebration taking place. His back was turned on the festivities, and his distance apart from the others was increasing every second. Eddie immediately knew who that ballplayer was. He was faced with a choice. He too could turn away from his new friends and become an outsider once again, or he could stay and be one of the gang. In his mind, there was no decision to be made. He knew where his loyalties lie; he quickly turned his back on the party and raced after his coach. As soon as he turned his back on the group, he could clearly hear many scornful remarks that were aimed in his direction. Like all groups that share a common interest, these ballplayers were quick to denigrate him for bucking their system.

As he got closer, he saw that his dream coach's head was hung very low. His posture and appearance resembled that of a condemned man, taking his final walk.

"Coach! Wait up! What's wrong?" Eddie screamed at the top of his lungs, but Billy ignored him and kept on walking.

Suddenly he heard his name being called by a familiar voice coming from far out in right field. "Leave him alone, Eddie. He needs to make his own peace."

"Who is it?" Eddie screamed out.

"You know who it is. Do you still wish to see me sometime?" The familiar voice asked.

The voice aroused his curiosity, and he immediately changed his course and headed toward it in right field.

"If you still wish to see me, it can be arranged now," the familiar voice in the distance stated.

Eddie started to move more briskly in the direction of the familiar voice. Anxiously he began jogging toward the right field corner of the ballpark, near where the warning track began. Upon arrival there, he noticed a familiar face looking over at him from a field level seat, closest to the flag pole in right field.

"The time is right, Eddie Romano," announced the familiar voice.

"I can't believe it's you," Eddie stated as his eyes took in the likeness of George Herman Ruth, affectionately known as "The Babe."

"You asked to see me, so here I am."

"Where were you when I needed you today?"

"That's just it, you didn't need me."

"I sure as hell did. I made a damn fool of myself," Eddie said resentfully.

"You still didn't need me."

"How in hell do you know what I need?"

"There's nothing wrong with you, nothing that a little bit of confidence couldn't cure," the Babe said sincerely. "I'm here to give you a chance to get that confidence, Eddie."

"What do you mean?"

"What's your biggest fear, Eddie?"

"You know, not having what it takes."

"Would you like to find out whether or not, you have what it takes, Eddie?"

"Sure. Wouldn't everybody?"

"I'm not talking about everybody. I'm talking about you."

"What do you want me to do? Take a test or something?"

"Yes, but not your ordinary test, Eddie. Do you remember when you spent all your time trying to master fast pitching?"

"Yeah. How could I forget?"

"And you bragged to me about hitting Eddie Cicotte's pitching?"

"Yeah."

"Remember I asked you then to ask them why they didn't have a real fastball artist pitching to you? Well, did you ever ask them?"

"No. I forgot."

"You forgot. Well, I didn't forget, and he's waiting to pitch to you, Eddie. That is, if you've got the guts," the Babe challenged.

"Who's waiting to pitch to me?"

"Walter Johnson's waiting. You know, the "Big Train." The real McCoy, Eddie. A real Hall of Famer. A man who couldn't be bought. An individual with so much pride that he wouldn't throw a meatball under any circumstances. We told him about you, Eddie. He wants to face you. He wants a challenge. The question is, are you up for it?"

"He's real fast, isn't he?"

"He's as fast as they get, Eddie."

"And if I hit him? What then?"

"It's self-explanatory, Eddie. You'd be a shoo-in for the major leagues."

"And if I fail?"

"Then you haven't quite got it, kid."

"I see. Do I have to decide now?"

"It's a one-time offer, Eddie. Some people would call it the chance of a lifetime. It's here and now, and it's not negotiable."

"Well, in that case, I don't see that I have much choice, so let's do it."

"Okay, kid. Now close your eyes tightly because we're going for a ride."

Eddie closed his eyes as instructed and felt an airy feeling. It was almost as if his body was floating through the sky to destinations unknown. Within an instant, he felt solid ground underneath his feet. "You can open your eyes now, Eddie," the Babe announced.

Eddie opened his eyes and found himself in the most beautifully manicured ballpark he had ever laid eyes upon. This ballpark was totally opposite of the other one. The sky was not dismal and dreary but illuminated by a celestial light. Everything about this place was warm and bright. If one was to call the other ballpark "night" then this place would certainly be referred to as "day." It just seemed to be full of life in comparison to the other place. Following his new leaf on life, he took a moment to acquaint himself with his new environment. He felt a sense of awe right through to his soul as he gazed out at the beauty that surrounded him.

"This has to be the most beautiful place I think I've ever seen. This is more like a palace than a ballpark. Do people actually play here?" Eddie asked in amazement.

"I play here, Eddie," the Babe stated proudly.

"And so do I."

Eddie looked over at the dugout that looked to him like it was made out of solid gold and noticed another familiar face. "Oh, my God, it's Lou Gehrig in the flesh! Nobody would ever believe this," Eddie said, shaking his head in disbelief.

"Nobody has to but you. You know the truth," Gehrig declared.

Eddie continued to gaze around the park and was overwhelmed by the splendor that surrounded him. It took a minute or two before he calmed down enough to comment, "It's really funny, heaven, just like the earth, has its own affluent areas. The other place must be a low-rent district, huh?"

"Whatever you say, Eddie," Gehrig replied laughing. Ruth also was unable to maintain his composure after hearing Eddie's colorful observation. "Are you ready for your test?" Gehrig asked politely.

"You guys are awfully anxious to see me fail, aren't you?"

"Quite to the contrary, my boy," the Babe responded.

"Yeah, sure. I'm a big joke around here. That's why you're making this a once-in-a-lifetime offer. The least you could've done was allow me to get my magic glove back before making me take this test. It looks to me like you're deliberately stacking the deck against me."

"I'm sorry that you feel that way." The Babe sighed.

"I'm sure you're real sorry," Eddie snapped. "It's just my life we're talking about here. Why couldn't you have waited until I got my glove back? What? Is one day asking too much?"

"Why don't you just forget about that glove? Can't you just try, just once, to do it on your own? Can't you just take what you've learned from us and apply it?" Gehrig asked disappointedly.

"I tried that during the game today, and look what it got me, I hit into a double play."

"What do you think? You're Superman? You think you're never going to make an out? I don't care who you are or how good you are, you're still only human, and humans make mistakes. Nobody's infallible until they get here, and I'm not speaking about visits either, Eddie. I'm speaking about someone who's here on a permanent basis," the Babe lectured.

"Well, then why should I even bother going to bat? He's from up here and that means he's infallible. So how am I supposed to hit him then?"

"Because we've taken that little quandary into account, and we've put human limitations on him. He won't pitch any better than he did during his career," Gehrig interjected.

"Boy, Lou, you cut me a lot of slack there, huh? I mean, he only won over four hundred games during his career."

"Eddie, you know the deal. You either accept it or we take you back."

"Well, I guess you guys get to watch me strike out to the legendary Walter Johnson," Eddie said glumly.

"You see, that's your problem. It's mental, Eddie. When you straighten your head out, your bat will come along too. Just pretend that you still have that stupid glove. Remember how it made you feel when you went up to bat? Well, try that same approach now, you might surprise yourself," Gehrig lectured.

"Do what he says, Eddie. Go up to bat with a clear head. Remember, you're going to have that glove back real soon. Pretend it's here a day early, that's all," the Babe reinforced.

Eddie had nothing else to say, so he trekked his way over to the bat barrel and began rummaging through it. He quickly located an extremely light thirty-four-inch bat. He chose this bat because he needed all the bat speed he could possibly muster to get around on "Old Barney." Just for the hell of it, he decided to try and think in the manner instructed by Ruth and Gehrig. He tried to hypnotize himself into believing that he still possessed the magic glove. He completely convinced himself that this was the case. After five solid minutes of warm up swings, a smile came over his face. The confidence of the magic glove was with him once again. He strutted over toward the plate.

"I want some batting practice before I face the quote and quote real McCoy as you guys call him."

"No problem. I'll get you a batting practice pitcher," the Babe said as he wandered over to the dugout. Momentarily, a pitcher exited the dugout and jogged out to the pitcher's mound. The batting practice pitcher started to warm up with Gehrig slowly. While this was going on, Eddie carefully studied "Old Barney" who was now deep into his warm ups over in the bullpen. He was truly amazed at how fast Walter Johnson really pitched, but since he convinced himself that he had his magic glove, he didn't fear him.

"All right, Eddie. We're ready for you," Gehrig announced.

Eddie stepped into the batter's box and gave Gehrig a funny look when he saw that he was down in a catcher's crouch behind the plate. "Whatcha doing there, Lou?"

"I'm catching for you," Gehrig shyly replied.

"We don't need you to catch for me as long as he puts them somewhere near the plate," Eddie said with a confident smile.

Gehrig quickly abandoned his position behind the plate and gave Ruth a quick wink of the eye. The Babe returned Gehrig's gesture by giving him the thumbs-up sign.

Batting practice began and Eddie consistently hit the ball all over the field. His bat control greatly impressed his "angelic" batting instructors. They both could clearly see that he had mastered their lessons.

He quickly tired of hitting the meatballs that the batting practice pitcher was throwing to him and decided it was time for the challenge of his lifetime.

"Bring on Old Barney," Eddie demanded.

The tall, lanky right-hander made his way out to the pitcher's mound. His catcher lined up behind the plate, and Eddie gave him no cocky request to abandon his post like he did before. No, he knew full well that "Old Barney" was very capable of throwing them by him. He stepped out of the batter's box and observed

Johnson's last warm up throws. A look of awe came across his face as he marveled over the velocity of the incoming pitches. He assumed that they were going every bit as fast as Nolan Ryan's did during his heyday. He quickly got himself out of the marveling mode. He knew that too much marveling would put him in a definite disadvantage psychologically. This was a frame of mind that he could not afford to be in if he was to have any chance of success. He had to look upon Walter Johnson as just another fast pitcher. He stepped into the batter's box believing in his own ability.

His adrenaline was flowing as he awaited the first pitch. He was completely focused, and all of his faculties were at an increased state of readiness. He heard and saw nothing other than that tall right-hander on the pitcher's mound. As Walter Johnson started his motion, Eddie prepared himself.

The pitch was on its way. Eddie made a split-second decision and swung through a tremendous fastball that made a loud thud as it hit the catcher's mitt. He looked back at the catcher and made an exaggerated gesture, lifting his eyebrows and rolling his eyes in awe.

Eddie had lost the battle but winning the war was still a possibility. He stepped out of the batter's box and took a deep breath. He then took a second deep breath for good measure. Again, he felt relaxed as he stepped up to the plate. In his mind, he was running through the different pitching scenarios he might be facing. He figured that Johnson would most likely waste one, trying to get him to swing at a bad pitch. He concluded that most likely he would see some kind of breaking ball that would end up outside of the strike zone. There was one thing Eddie had learned from all his coaches and that was that every at bat was a game of dice for the hitter. A hitter could only really be prepared for one pitch at a time. That isn't saying that a good hitter couldn't make strong contact on a pitch he wasn't expecting, but it would be a lot less likely.

Eddie readied himself in the batter's box thoroughly expecting to take Johnson's next pitch. Within seconds, Johnson was back into his windup and released a slow curveball. He read the rotation of the laces and held off his swing as the curve ended up a foot outside the strike zone. The count was now one ball and one strike.

Eddie again stepped out of the batter's box and took a deep breath to calm down. Again his mind raced through the different pitching possibilities. He had a hunch that Johnson wasn't going to let him get ahead in the count. He figured that he wouldn't waste a pitch in this situation and then it dawned on him. He had an epiphany or a so-called "eureka" moment. He recalled how the Babe told him that Johnson was looking for a challenge. A little psychoanalysis was necessary in this situation. Eddie surmised that if Johnson was really interested in a challenge, he would throw him his best pitch. He would challenge him with that blazing fastball and not take any chances of getting behind in the count. He hypothesized that he would put it over the "dish." If his assumptions were correct, then the only question that remained was what part of the plate would he throw to? On this point, Eddie decided to make "his own" luck. He knew that if he crowded the plate, Johnson would most likely throw toward the inside corner to jam him. He decided to implement a very special plan of attack.

Eddie stepped back into the batter's box and positioned his body practically on top of the inside corner of the plate. Johnson sneered at him for this apparent lack of respect. He watched Johnson begin his long, deliberate windup, and as he did this, he made a last-second body adjustment. He quickly stepped backward and replanted himself a good fifteen inches farther from the inside corner of the plate. Johnson had no time to make any adjustments to his pitch that was now blazing its way toward the inside corner of the plate. Eddie swung his bat evenly at the low inside fastball. The pitch came right into his wheel house. He turned on it and hit it with the "sweet spot" of the bat. He felt a slight sting in his hands as contact was made. There was a loud crack, and Johnson immediately turned to look over his shoulder at the powerfully hit ball. It was a line drive shot that was pulled deep into left field. Eddie looked up momentarily and marveled at the ball that was now clearing the fence. He jumped for joy as he started his home run trot. As he passed second base, he looked toward the dugout and was astonished to see his high school teammates whooping it up and cheering him on. As he arrived at the plate, all his teammates ran out and embraced him. They were actually celebrating with him. In his entire life, he had never felt as loved as he did when he stepped on home plate. He was ecstatic. This is how he always wanted it to be. This was what baseball was all about. This was exactly the kind of camaraderie between teammates that he had always dreamed about but never could seem to find since living up to the requirements of keeping a magic glove.

He momentarily stopped embracing his well-wishing teammates and turned around to look at Ruth and Gehrig. The ballpark suddenly got totally quiet. The deafening silence shocked him into turning around once more and when he did this he discovered that his teammates had all disappeared. The ballpark was deserted.

Eddie looked over at Ruth and asked, "Am I really that good?"

"You answered your own question, didn't you?"

"Could it really be like that?"

"Sure it could. It's all up to you," the Babe answered compassionately.

"Hey, Eddie, I knew you had it in you, kid," Gehrig said with a grin.

Within an instant, it was all gone. All that remained was the memory.

A RACE AGAINST TIME

Eddie was totally confused as he awakened finding himself back in the familiar surroundings of his bedroom. He didn't know who he could trust anymore. Both factions of "angels" had argued their cases magnificently. To him, it seemed like a no-lose situation either way, but after closer examination, he quickly wavered on that matter. *There was a winner*, he thought. There had to be a winner; and the more he thought about it, the more convinced he became that it had to be the Manager. He was haunted by the Manager's words declaring, "That the chance of him finding his way back to 'heaven' without the glove was about the same as getting struck by lightning twice." Without that glove, he would not be able to visit his dream coach any longer. He thought that Ruth and Gehrig's test was legitimate and maybe he could make it to the major leagues without the glove but what about his dream coach? He couldn't imagine living an entire lifetime without his most trusted companion. He decided that there was only one thing that was absolutely certain in his life and that was for him to do whatever was humanly possible to retrieve that glove. That was the only way he could guarantee his continued relationship with his beloved coach.

Apparently, that decision was made a lot easier by the fact that he now knew where his glove was located. For the second time in his life, Eddie awakened with a "divine inspiration." The only thing that was left for him to do now was to go to the location, perform "the deed" he promised the Manager, and recover his magic glove. He figured if he accomplished this mission, he would hedge his bet so to speak. From then on, he could rest assured that he would make it to the major leagues and, most importantly, be able to see his dream coach whenever he wanted. To him, this seemed to be the only option available that would completely fulfill his needs.

An anxiety attack suddenly overcame him. He felt an overwhelming compulsion to act immediately. He couldn't afford to wait. The worst scenarios imaginable were ruminating through his thought process. *What if the thief moved his glove to a new location? What if the thief woke up early too with the intent to sell his glove to someone? What would he do if the glove was already sold? How would he ever locate his glove again if that happened, and without his glove, how would he ever make it back to "heaven"?* These thoughts bedeviled him and created an abnormal sense of urgency. He concluded that he was in a race against time. He popped out of bed and quickly threw on the first clothes he could find. There was no time for him to brush his teeth, comb his hair, or to get cleaned up in anyway. All that would have to wait until after he recovered his glove.

Mrs. Romano was in the kitchen preparing the Saturday morning breakfast when she heard the sound of feet rapidly coming down the stairs. "Eddie, is that you?"

"Look, Mom. I've got no time to talk," Eddie shouted out as he made his way toward the front door.

"Eddie, I just wanted to tell you that man was here again this morning," Mrs. Romano declared as she did her best to cut him off in the foyer.

"Good, Mom. Good for him. I've got to go," Eddie blurted out as he urgently made his way toward the front door.

As he arrived there, he grabbed his car keys that were hanging on the wall and the baseball bat that was propped up in the corner. He figured that it would be the perfect instrument for doing "the deed."

Mrs. Romano continued her pursuit of him, catching a glimpse of the outside of her home and the daylight as she helplessly observed him exit the front door. "Eddie! Where are you going?"

She never received a response to her question unless her answer was the front door almost slamming her in the face.

EDDIE MEETS
LOU EISEN

E ddie, carrying his bat, raced out toward the street where his car was parked. Upon arrival there, he played a game of hit and miss with the two similar keys that occupied his key chain. One of the keys unlocked his trunk, the other the driver's side door, the problem being that he always confused the two. While he tried to sort things out, he was approached by an old man who would have been considered stylishly dressed if only he was living in the early 1980s. The short and stocky man wore a very dapper gray fedora that covered the fact that he had lost most of his hair. He tapped Eddie on the shoulder to get his attention.

"Excuse me, are you Eddie Romano?" the old man asked as he loosened his really thick tie.

"Who wants to know?" Eddie snapped rudely.

"The name's Eisen. Lou Eisen. You're a tough guy to get a hold of."

"That's right. And now is not the time," Eddie said curtly as he opened the driver's side door.

"Where are you going in such a hurry this morning?" Eisen asked while unbuttoning his collar.

"That's for me to know and you to find out. So please excuse me, sir," Eddie said abruptly as he climbed into his Subaru.

"Young man! I've expelled a considerable amount of energy trying to track you down, could you at least answer one question for me?" Eisen demanded.

"Look, I've got no time for reporters. So could you please let go of my door?"

"Not until you tell me how you got a hold of Billy Green's glove," Eisen declared stubbornly.

"I don't know what in hell you're talking about. Who's Billy Green?"

"Don't play dumb with me. You know who Billy Green is. You model your entire life upon him."

"I don't have the foggiest idea what you're talking about. Could you just please let go of my door? I'm late. I've got some place to go," Eddie said exasperatedly.

Eisen pulled the *Chicago Tribune* newspaper clipping out of his suit pocket and placed it in front of Eddie's face. "Now, like I was saying before, where did you get that glove?"

Eddie stared at his picture in the clipping for a moment before responding, "Look, mister, I don't have that glove anymore. And I don't want to talk about it right now."

"Listen, Eddie, I'm seventy-eight years old. My days are way too precious to be wasted on a rude punk like you. Now, I'm not going to let go of this door until you tell me how you got a hold of Billy Green's glove," Eisen threatened as he removed his polyester suit coat.

"Who in hell is this Billy Green character?" Eddie shouted as he stormed out of his car.

"Who are you trying to fool, young man? As you are well aware of, Billy Green was the White sox third basemen who disappeared some forty years ago during his first stint in the major leagues. He was a friend of mine, and unless you designed that glove yourself, I'm pretty sure that glove belonged to him," Eisen said as he unbuttoned the cuffs of his dress shirt.

Eddie heard the old man's words, but he wasn't allowing them to register yet. He made up his mind that he was going to let him babble for a while and then be on his way. Eisen quickly picked up on this, noticing Eddie's blank return stare and asked, "Son, are you listening to me or am I speaking for my health?"

"Look, mister, I didn't design the glove. I found it a few years back, but I still don't understand what you're driving at," Eddie stated, showing a little bit more respect toward his elder this time.

"In order for you to understand what I'm driving at, you'd have to know the story of Billy Green. Outside of the Black Sox scandal, the Billy Green disappearance was a huge story here in Chicago. Billy Green was a perennial minor league ballplayer who made a cameo appearance with the White Sox—"

"You know I'd really love to hear your "Black Dahlia" story another time, but I've really gotta go," Eddie interrupted, making light of a serious matter.

"Just give me a second, okay?" Eisen snapped as he had reached the end of his patience.

"Fine, but do you think you could like cut to the chase? You know, cut out all the insignificant details and like get to the point," Eddie said in frustration, trying his best to be a wise guy.

"The point is, when Billy Green disappeared, so did his glove, his uniform, and his green baseball cleats—"

"Did you say 'green baseball cleats'?"

"Yes, I did. He disappeared after a White Sox game back in 1952. When they started searching for him, they found his street clothes still in his locker. Nobody could remember ever seeing him leave the stadium, and since it was assumed that he was still in his uniform, you might think he would've been pretty hard to miss now, wouldn't you?"

At last, Eisen captivated Eddie's full attention and the details he was revealing about Billy Green started to sink in with the boy. It was like a floodgate opened inside his head, allowing all of Eisen's previous words to finally assimilate. The mention of the green patent leather baseball shoes was the catalyst that brought about this chain reaction in his mind. He had always secretly thought that his dream coach's shoes were quite unusual. He never knew anyone else who wore green cleats, but he was now realizing that there were more similarities than just the green shoes. He was getting a clear mental picture of this Billy Green character and the only face he could assign to it was that of his dream coach. He knew that his dream coach wore an ancient White Sox uniform and that he desperately wanted to return to the Earth. He thought, *Could it be coincidental that his dream coach was a special "angel" lost in heaven while Billy Green was a special ballplayer lost on the earth?* Eddie was now truly curious.

"Mister, you don't happen to have a picture of this Billy Green, do you?"

"Yes, I do." Eisen reached into his suit coat pocket again and this time displayed the photo he had taken of Billy when he played for the AA Memphis squad.

Eddie couldn't believe his eyes. Staring him in the face was a photograph of his dream coach, wearing a minor league uniform. Eisen immediately picked up upon his astonishment.

"What is it?" Eisen asked eagerly.

"That's my friend."

"Then you know where Billy Green is? Do you realize that people have been looking for him for almost fifty years now? What happened to him? What is he a homeless bum or something? Where'd you find him on Skid Row?" Eisen asked in amazement.

"No. Nothing like that," Eddie quickly replied. Seeing the photograph of his dream coach reinforced the urgency of his desire to complete his "heavenly mission." "Look, Mr. Eisen, I've really got to get out of here. Could we talk another time? I really want to talk to you but you really caught me at a bad time. I've got some place to go, and I've gotta go now."

"But, Eddie, you didn't answer my question yet," Eisen reminded.

"Another time, okay? Believe me, I want to talk with you some more but just not now," Eddie said in an agitated state.

"Fine, I'll go with you then," Eisen announced, his curiosity piqued.

"That's not possible," Eddie said forcefully.

"I don't understand all this secrecy. Why can't you just tell me what I need to know, so I can be on my way?" Eisen lashed out in frustration. "Why do you have to waste my time?"

"Can't you get it through your thick skull, that I have things to do, and I don't have any time to talk right now? Why do you have to be so pushy?" Eddie exploded on the verge of hopping into his car and peeling away.

"I'm an ex-reporter, remember?" Eisen quipped in an attempt to alleviate some of the tension in the air.

"Well, that figures. Listen, Lou, this is one scoop you're not going to get today," Eddie emphasized.

"I don't understand."

"It's not your business to understand!" Eddie shouted as his patience came to an abrupt halt.

"It sure the hell is," Eisen snapped. "Do you have any idea how many hours I've spent hashing and rehashing the details of his disappearance? Do you have any idea how many stories I wrote about this, and now I'm staring at the one person who holds the key to the lock of this mystery and he's trying to give me the brush off. Well guess what buster? You're not going anywhere without me!"

"What is it with you? You can't take no for an answer?" Eddie asked, astonished at the old man's stubbornness.

"That's right."

"That's what you think," Eddie protested as he shoved Eisen away from his car.

The old man lost his balance and fell to the pavement. He got his wits back together just in time to see Eddie's car speeding off down the road.

As Eddie sped away, he thought that he had finally gotten the old man out of his hair. What he didn't know was that all he had accomplished was to increase the old man's resolve.

DIVINE INTERFERENCE

Eddie meditated during the thirty-minute ride across town, trying his best to psyche himself up into doing "the deed." All his conscious thoughts were directed toward finding the courage and intestinal fortitude to commit this murder. He knew deep down inside that murdering someone was going to be a lot different than just beating them up. He discovered that he was filled with self-doubt. He wasn't sure he had the stomach for it. The entire idea of snuffing out someone's life tormented him. He feared the repercussions of committing such an act. It took him the entire ride to decide that he was actually going to go through with this. During this ride, he discovered that saying something and doing something are two diametrically opposed positions.

With all these murderous thoughts on his mind, it should come as no surprise that he lost track of the things that were happening around him. He was totally oblivious of the fact that Eisen had followed him and was hot on his trail. Lou had to do some reckless driving, but he was able to catch up with Eddie. Eisen felt a little bit queasy as the reality of the dangerous neighborhoods they were traveling through finally sank in, but he had invested way too much time and effort to give up now. This was now a personal matter, as far as he was concerned. He didn't care what dangers he might have to face because he had lived his life.

Lou knew he could only die once and if it happened now, he was prepared for it. He thought about the alternatives of making this quest. Everybody else his age was in their rocker watching reruns on the television while he was out solving an ageless mystery. Any of his friends would have gladly embarked upon this noble cause if the alternative was sitting at home waiting to die. He always considered himself to be a brave man and he reminisced about the days he spent training to be an amateur boxer, although that was a long time ago. As he continued his drive, he began to have some reservations. At one long traffic light, Eisen locked all his doors, fearing for his life because of all the dirty looks he was receiving from the street people who congregated there. A little farther down the road, there was not a white face to be seen anywhere. Eisen wondered why Eddie was traveling in such dangerous parts of town. That wonder quickly became shock when he witnessed Eddie pulling up alongside the curb of an urban housing project.

Eisen wasn't the only person who was starting to get butterflies because of the change of scenery. Eddie was a bit unnerved himself as he shut off his engine in front of 144 Grove Street. The reason for his nervousness was the fact that he was now totally aware that he was out of his element. He gazed out his side window and took in the dilapidated concrete children's play area that surrounded the project building. Everywhere he looked he saw black. Every face he peered upon seemed to stare back at him with dark, angry eyes. He felt like a stranger here in every way. He couldn't comprehend just how much until he was suddenly approached by a tall, thin black man, who was garbed in a jogging suit, wearing dark sunglasses, and sporting many thick gold chains around his neck. The man tapped on his side window. Eddie rolled down his window slowly with his body filled with fears and reservations.

"Yo, what chew need bee? Ize gotz some jammies," the ignorant drug dealer touted.

"No thanks, man. I'm just here to visit a friend," Eddie replied nervously.

"Yo, you've gots niggas here? What chew thinkin', man? Ya'll is mad stupid," the ignorant drug dealer ranted with surprise written all over his face.

"Yeah, man. Maybe another time, okay?" Eddie stated in an attempt to ease what he thought might turn out to be a volatile situation.

The crack dealer turned and walked back toward one of the concrete benches, shaking his head in disbelief. He couldn't believe that Eddie wasn't there to buy his drugs.

Momentarily, Eddie exited his Subaru, carrying his baseball bat at his side. Immediately, Eisen started chasing after him.

"Hey! Eddie! Wait up! What in hell are you doing here?" Eisen shouted.

Eddie couldn't believe his ears as he turned around to find Eisen in hot pursuit.

"You've got to be kidding me! Damn it, Lou! Go home!" Eddie screamed out in disgust.

"I told you that you weren't going to give me the brush off," Eisen announced proudly as he finally started catching up to Eddie.

Eddie stopped dead in his tracks for a moment to allow the old man to catch up. "This is dangerous, Lou. Why don't you go home? Haven't you got an episode of *Wheel of Fortune* that you're missing?" Eddie asked sarcastically in a whisper, trying his best not to attract attention, but no matter how low of a profile he attempted to keep, his efforts were in vain. Just the fact that the two white men were visiting this part of town was in itself a spectacle.

"No shit Sherlock, of course it's dangerous and I didn't know that among your many talents that you were a comedian too. I thought you were just a ballplayer, but to be frank with you, I don't watch that show. Now here's a better question: what in hell are you doing here?" Eisen asked in a whisper.

"Why can't you just bug off? Can't you get the hint that you're not wanted here? You know you're really starting to piss me off," Eddie quietly volleyed.

"I told you, I'm not leaving you alone until you tell me where you found the glove," Eisen said firmly.

"Look Lou, I told you that I didn't have time to tell you about that right now. So if you've followed me for that, you're going to be going away disappointed."

"That's all right. You don't have to tell me right now. I'm just going to stick with you until you do." Eisen snickered.

Eddie was rapidly losing his patience with Eisen's antics. The old man was becoming a gigantic thorn in his side, and he had exhausted his supply of ideas on how to deal with him. He decided that at least for the time being it was in his best interest to just play along.

"Okay. Well, why don't you wait out here until I'm through with what I have to do?" Eddie suggested manipulatively.

Eisen glanced across the street to observe a basketball game that was being played on a court that had no nets. The group of punks, who were playing there, suddenly stopped and gave him hateful stares.

"No siree Bob. I'd feel a lot safer with you than out here by myself."

"Whatever," Eddie conceded in disappointment, shrugging his shoulders an exhaling loudly.

The two men proceeded to walk together toward the entrance of the building, trying their best to ignore all the stares that were directed at them. As Eddie progressed slowly, he continued to take occasional glances over his shoulder. He tried to make it look like he was a tough guy by walking aggressively. He heard that people who walked with a sense of purpose were less likely to get mugged. He knew that the elderly were the most likely targets for muggings and because of this he kept Mr. Eisen close by his side.

Although he found Eisen to be a gigantic pain in the ass, he couldn't help but admire the old man's courage and never-say-die attitude. As much as he would have liked to have denied it, he found something very lovable about this old man and he hovered over him in a very protective manner. He did this all the way to the building's entrance. It seemed like an eternity before they reached it. As they entered the housing project building, the first thing they noticed was the overwhelming scent of human urine.

The place stunk like an unkempt men's room. Eddie had never been in a place as filthy. Eddie and Lou made a beeline toward the elevator. He quickly pushed the up button and the two men did their best not to gag while impatiently waiting for the elevator to arrive. After two or three minutes of fighting for fresh air, a young black mother and her two small daughters entered the lobby and informed them that the elevators hadn't worked in months. She directed them toward the stairway and immediately they began their hike.

"I can't believe people live here. It's like living in the toilet," Eisen said as he began climbing the stairs. "Eddie, what are we doing here?"

"If you must know, I'm getting my glove back."

"What's it doing here?"

"It was stolen by a guy who lives here."

"Oh. I can't say I'm surprised," Eisen wisecracked.

"Neither am I."

The stairway was covered with graffiti and smelled even worse than the lobby. Eddie and Lou both tried to hold their breath for extended periods of time as they marched together up many flights of concrete stairs. Along the way they couldn't help but notice that the stairwells were littered with little plastic crack vials and hypodermic needles. At last they reached the tenth floor and gingerly walked down the drab hallway to apartment number nine. It was the farthest apartment on the left-hand side. Eddie was very nervous at this juncture. He stepped back away from the door and tried to gather his thoughts. He tried his best to dream up a successful plan of action. He needed some kind of ploy to gain entrance to the apartment. He had to make sure that the man inside didn't scream for help. He knew if the man was able to get help, he and Lou were history. He could just tell from the atmosphere alone that the people in this building were not particularly fond of white people. He was also sure that these people stuck together, and he had no doubts that they would immediately come to the rescue of one of their brothers, especially if he was really in distress.

These were frightening thoughts for Eddie. He knew that he was a long way from home, and if he screwed this up there would be no one to protect them. He heard that there were project buildings too dangerous for even the police to protect, and he concluded that this probably was one of them. As he stood in the doorway thinking, a plan suddenly dawned upon him. He knew that the man inside apartment number 9 would most likely recognize him. So he decided to work another angle. He was now very glad that Lou Eisen had crashed his party. He decided to use Lou as a decoy in order to obtain entry into the premises. He figured that if an old white man like Eisen pretended that he was lost and knocked on this man's door, the *"dirtbag"* inside wouldn't be able to resist the temptation to rip him off. This was exactly the distraction needed to gain access to the scoundrel's apartment. While the thief was focusing his attention upon ripping off the old man, Eddie could easily gain entrance to the residence. With any luck, the home invasion would be uncontested, and Eddie could finish his assignment. After mentally double checking all his conclusions, he filled Lou in on most of the details and soon the plan was ready for action.

Eddie checked his watch that now registered 10:30 a.m. as Eisen began knocking on the door to apartment number 9. There was no answer at first, so Eisen knocked harder, which of course equated to louder, until a man's voice could be heard from inside.

"Who iz it?" The man inside asked groggily, obviously disturbed from his slumber.

"Do you think you could help me? I'm looking for the Ramirez residence," Eisen shouted in an elderly sounding but articulate manner.

"Hode on dare," said the man inside.

Almost instantly, the large black man with the corn-braided hair appeared at the door. He looked like he just crawled out of bed. He was barefooted, bare chested, and wearing a dingy pair of gray sweat pants. He stared at the elderly Eisen, and a smile came to his big full lips.

"Hi. I'm sorry for waking you, but I'm looking for the Ramirez residence, and I'm having the damndest time trying to find it," Lou Eisen said with down home charm while feigning senility.

"Ramirez? Oh yeah. Come on in. I take u dare," the black man said with a sly look on his face.

Eisen slowly entered the man's residence, making a point of leaving the door open ajar behind him. Momentarily, the man pulled out a switchblade knife from a pocket of a leather jacket that was hanging off a hook on the wall. He quickly flashed its gleaming blade toward Eisen. "Gimme da damn wallet, you old cracker!" the black man demanded.

Eisen quickly acquiesced to the demand, and the black man started rummaging through every compartment looking for money. While he was doing this, Eddie quickly barged into the apartment and pushed Eisen out of the way. The man immediately dropped the wallet and held his switchblade in an underhanded fashion. One could tell that the man had experience in fighting with knives.

"Stay back!" the black man shouted at Eddie.

Using his baseball bat as a prod, Eddie backed the black man up until his ratty couch prevented any further retreat. He could see the fear in his dark brown eyes as his retreat came to a sudden halt. Like a cornered animal, the black man lunged forward with his knife. Eddie stepped back, evading the attack, and then delivered a solid blow to the man's left quadriceps. The force of the impact immobilized the man, and he almost instantly fell to the floor. The man, who dropped his knife upon impact of the bat, was now grimacing in pain. Eddie took another swing at him for good measure, this time striking him on the left shoulder. The man screamed out in agony as he lay helplessly on the floor.

"Paybacks are a bitch, aren't they?" Eddie announced, taunting his fallen foe.

The black man suddenly got very quiet. He stopped his whining and stared up at Eddie. His posture resembled a slave after getting beaten by his master.

"Where's my glove, asshole?"

"It's on da table."

Eddie instructed Eisen to go grab the glove off the table. Eisen quickly picked it up and marveled over it.

"Eddie, this really is Billy Green's glove. Where in hell did you find it?"

"Don't worry about that now. We'll talk about that later. Look, Lou, I think it's time for you to leave. I can handle this by myself now. I certainly appreciated your help but there's some things I've gotta do in private."

"What kind of things, Eddie?"

"Please, Lou. Don't ask me any more questions."

Eisen picked up his wallet and took a step back toward the door. He stared over at the black man who was silent and trembling in fear.

"Eddie, you're not going to hurt this man, are you?"

Eddie was taken aback by the question and replied, "Maybe, but believe me, Lou, he asked for it."

"Turn the other cheek, Eddie. Let that rage go."

"Please, Lou, will you leave? You're making this a lot harder for me," Eddie pleaded.

"No. I won't let you throw your life away," Lou said adamantly.

"Look, if you're not going to leave, could you at least close your eyes or turn your head or do something?"

Billy doesn't want you to do this," Eisen proclaimed.

"How in hell do you know what he wants?" Eddie asked as he lifted his baseball bat over his head preparing to deliver a fatal blow to the man's head. The black man lifted his right arm in a feeble attempt to shield his face. Eddie stared coldly down at him and announced, "He who lives by the sword, must now die by it."

Eddie felt the adrenaline swell in his muscles, and they were just about to explode when suddenly he heard Billy's voice, repeating a statement that was so familiar to his ears, "But, Eddie, the fact remains scaring the crap out of you isn't killing you. Don't get me wrong, what he did was unforgivable, granted, but he still didn't harm you. Remember it signifies once and for all the end of your innocence, my boy."

The sound of Billy's voice caused a chill to run down Eddie's spine as he looked over toward where the voice emanated from. To his complete amazement, it was Lou Eisen, who was speaking Billy's words while standing perfectly still in some sort of trance.

Eddie knew that something unusual had just taken place. The first thought that entered his mind was that Billy and the Manager had changed their minds about the murder at the last possible moment and used Lou Eisen as their messenger. Frustrated, he immediately threw down his bat. What was most frustrating at this moment was that the reprieve was given after he had spent so much time psyching himself up into doing the "deed." This last second stay of execution convinced him that he did not have the constitution to go through this emotional roller coaster ever again. He concluded that he was not going to commit a murder today or any other day for that matter. He knew now that Eisen was there for a reason. He didn't just blindly show up at his doorstep. There was some greater purpose being served here. Suddenly he felt a tremendous sense of relief as if a giant burden had been lifted off his shoulders. He then remembered why he came there in the first place and wanted to lash out one last time at the man responsible for stealing his glove and making the last few weeks of his life so bleak and miserable. Evilly, he stared down at the severely injured black man and warned him, "I guess this is your lucky day. I suggest you shut your mouth or I'll come back and finish this job. You understand the words coming out of my mouth, you ignorant bastard?" Eddie asked in a very animated manner, pointing his finger toward his lips.

The black man nodded his head affirmatively. Unexpectedly, Eddie picked up his bat and feigned a swing in the scoundrel's direction. Eddie laughed boisterously and made it obvious that he was getting a big charge out of scaring the crap out of the man who had done the same to him at the 7-11. He then turned to Lou announcing, "Come on Lou. Let's get out of here. You've got a lot to tell me, don't you?"

"I guess I do. Remind me not to get on your bad side, you're a sadistic son of a bitch, you know that?" Lou announced under a nervous laugh.

"You mean the extra scare? It couldn't happen to a nicer guy. Remember he was robbing you too," Eddie said in glee with what looked like a permanent smile on his face.

"After what just happened, I almost forgot about that," Eisen said still baffled and amazed by the fact that his body had been momentarily possessed. He suddenly felt compelled to speak out about it, "Eddie, I've got to tell you about this dream I had."

"Later, Lou," Eddie stated as he and Lou exited the premises calmly, doing their best to not arouse suspicion. There was no doubt that an alliance was forming.

UNRAVELING
THE MYSTERY

After leaving the housing project, the two men met up with each other at a roadside diner in a better section of town. The men sat across from each other at a window booth and drank coffee. Both were baffled by the strange behavior that each had exhibited since becoming acquainted earlier that morning. Both had stories to tell but neither was overly inclined to share what they knew. Eisen originally wanted to tell about his dream, but the long ride to the diner seemed to have dampened his enthusiasm. Perhaps the reason they were both so reluctant to speak out was that they felt that their individual stories were too bizarre to be believable. They were both afraid of what the other would think of them if they revealed what was really on their minds, and for those reasons, they both sat silently. Eisen stared down into his coffee cup while Eddie was mesmerized by his newly recovered magic baseball glove.

After a while, the waitress noticed the strange behavior of her patrons in booth number six. She was intrigued by their catatonic indifference toward each other and the world around them and decided to attempt to find out what was the matter with them.

"Excuse me," the waitress interrupted the silence, "is everything all right here? Can I get you fellas something else?"

Eisen broke out of his daydream just long enough to reply, "No. Everything's okay. Thanks."

"All right. I was just checking. Call me if you boys need anything," she said while giving them a wry smile.

Eisen glanced over at Eddie and commented, "But the fact of the matter is that things aren't all right and obviously this is apparent to everybody around us. So why don't you tell me what's going on?"

"You first, Lou."

Eisen displayed a nervous giggle and answered, "No, you first."

"You're the one who was so anxious to tell me about your dream. So tell me about it," Eddie demanded.

"All right, but you've got to promise me that you're not going to laugh."

"Only if you promise first."

"Okay, it's agreed. No one is to laugh," Eisen vowed. "Quite frankly, I don't understand any of this, kid. I wake up remembering a dream about some angel who wants to borrow my body, and the next thing I know, I'm chasing after you, going to great lengths to solve a disappearance that was all but forgotten forty some years ago. Now, what's going on here, Eddie? First of all, why in hell would you risk your life, not to mention mine, in order to recover that glove? And secondly, why would you risk having them put you in jail and throwing away the key for the likes of that degenerate?"

"You'd never believe me if I told you, Lou."

"After what happened to me at that housing project, you might be surprised at what I might believe."

"All right. If the truth is to be known, this isn't any ordinary baseball glove, Lou. It's a magic glove. It unlocks the door to 'heaven,' and without this glove, I wouldn't be able to visit Billy anymore," Eddie said animatedly waving the magic glove in Eisen's face. "I told you that this would be too bizarre for you to believe."

"I'm not laughing though, but it sure does sound insane. And if it wasn't for the fact that I feel like I'm losing my marbles too, I wouldn't give a word you say a bit of credence, but what you're saying makes just about as much sense as what happened to me in that apartment this morning."

"You're wrong. That made perfect sense. You were the messenger."

"Messenger? May I ask, for whom?"

"Well, for Billy Green."

"And what was the message, Eddie?"

"Obviously, to spare the black man his life."

"I don't understand? Why'd you want to kill him in the first place?"

"Well, because I was told to," Eddie said exasperatedly.

"By whom, Eddie?"

"Well, Billy Green told me that."

"No. I don't believe that. The Billy Green I knew would've never told you to do anything like that. He would've found that most reprehensible."

"Maybe he still does. But that doesn't change the fact that a rule is a rule."

"Who's rule, Eddie?"

"It's the rule of the gray angels. I was forewarned that if I didn't kill that black man who stole my glove, I could be one hundred percent sure that my glove would lose its magic. It was made perfectly clear to me that if I didn't do what I was told to do, my glove would become run-of-the-mill from that moment on and that means I wouldn't be able to visit Billy anymore."

"Who told you that, Eddie?"

"The Manager."

"This is getting pretty confusing, Eddie. Who's the Manager?"

"He's Billy's boss and the leader of the gray angels."

"If you don't mind me asking, what are gray angels?"

"It's kind of hard to explain. You see, there are angels that believe that all deeds can be classified as either black or white. You know, good or evil? And then there are angels that realize that things aren't always black and white, they see the gray areas that are not so easy to distinguish. The Manager despises the black and white band of angels, calling them closed minded. You see, Lou, you can't believe the hype about heaven. The churches got it all wrong. From my personal experiences there, I can tell you that heaven is not the peaceful and serene place it's made out to be. The truth is it's filled with anger, mistrust, and deceit."

"What you're describing sounds more like hell to me."

"You know that idea popped in my head on more than one occasion but a beautiful person like Billy wouldn't end up in hell. Now would he?"

"You never know." Eisen sighed. "You might be wrong, Eddie. I mean, think rationally for a second, what kind of angels would insist on murder as the only solution to the theft of a baseball glove? I cringe when I think about what other solutions they've probably recommended to you in the past."

"Well, I can tell you one thing, they never told me to murder anyone before."

"Well, that's good to hear, Eddie, but somehow they just don't sound like angels to me."

"So what are you trying to say? That Billy's the devil?" Eddie asked, taking offense to the inference.

"No. Billy Green definitely wasn't the devil."

"Tell me about him, Lou."

"He was one of a kind, Eddie. He was a really special person. He had charm and charisma. When it came to baseball, he was a lot like you according to some of the things I've read."

"Read where?"

"Well, of course in the Tribune and some other newspapers."

"What did you do? Investigate me?"

"You've got to remember, I'm an ex-reporter, Eddie. I went into the newspaper morgues to see what I could find out about you before I even embarked upon this voyage. From what they say, you're a real showboat, and for your information, so was he."

"You know I kind of figured he was a character. Those green patent leather shoes of his are pretty neat. Did he play as sharp as he dressed?"

"I really don't want to tarnish your hero, Eddie, but if I am to be perfectly honest with you, I'd have to say that he was more show than go as you kids put it," Eisen said solemnly. "I will say one thing in his defense and that is there never was a player who wanted it more than he did. He dedicated his whole life to baseball. If his talent had only been half as big as his heart, he would've made it too. But Billy had no such luck, Eddie. You obviously know he was a left-handed infielder. You know that's a curse, don't you? How many big leaguers do you know who are left-handed throwers and play the infield other than pitch or play first base?

Eddie quickly took offense since he was left-hander and interjected, "Well, I hate to be the one to clue you in, Lou, but Don Mattingly played a full season for the Yankees at third base."

"That didn't last long though. He ended up being a first baseman, Eddie. That's also an exception to the rule. But getting back to Billy, he suffered the same problems that all left-handed third basemen suffer. And you know the problem. When you throw the ball to first base, your back is to the play. Isn't it, Eddie? I don't want to burst your bubble, but that's a big problem especially if you want to make it to the major leagues. It was a contributing factor in him ending up being a career minor leaguer until he had that one magical break-out season. He was thirty-two years old, and everything just seemed to change for him overnight. Balls he could've never fielded before, he remarkably made plays on. His throws were accurate, and his bat suddenly caught fire. Despite being left-handed, the big club took a chance on him. I think his success came on so quickly it even surprised him, but while all these good things were happening, his personal life started falling apart. His reputation of being a spark plug to his teammates went by the boards, and he was accused by many of them of being a doomsayer—"

"He was?"

"Yes indeed. He sure was."

"That's pretty funny. I guess I've got more in common with him than I thought. No wonder he knew all the right answers when I came to him with that problem."

"Like I said before, you two are a lot alike. And while we're on that topic, where did you find his glove, Eddie?"

"You would never believe me if I told you, Lou."

"After what you've told me so far, I'll believe almost anything."

"I found it while souvenir hunting with my father at the old Comiskey Park."

"When?"

"You know, back when they were wrecking the ballpark? So they could build the new one."

"That's very interesting. You know, that was the last place that anyone ever saw him alive."

"Well, you don't have to worry about that, Lou. He's alive. He's a special angel and special angels never die. Come to think about it, I'd bet even money that he was the special angel in your dream."

"No. It wasn't him."

"Well, of course it was him! You repeated verbatim exactly what he said to me."

"Eddie, it wasn't Billy in my dream. I would have recognized Billy. It was some old man. I swear I never laid eyes upon him before."

"But you spoke Billy's words. It had to be Billy, speaking through you, when you were in that trance at the project building?"

"Maybe then, but definitely not in the dream."

Things were not adding up correctly in Eddie's mind. Why would there be two different messengers? Eddie suddenly started to worry that he had been tricked into sparing the black man his life. He had broken his pact with the Manager and now he wasn't even sure who had sent the message. He was extremely fearful that he had blown his last opportunity to insure the magic of his glove and his window into "heaven."

Eisen immediately started to notice Eddie's increased anxiety commenting, "What's wrong, Eddie? You look like you lost your best friend. "

"Can't you see? I've blown it! If it wasn't Billy who took control of your body, then obviously I was tricked. Oh my god! Now it looks like I might never see him again," Eddie said with tears welling in his eyes.

"Don't cry, Eddie. I just don't know for sure who took over my body, but everything's going to work out just fine. I think we've been brought here together for a reason."

"You don't understand, Lou, he'll die without me. He's miserable. He's been miserable for a long time now. He and the Manager don't get along. The Manager is like one of those control freaks you see on *America's Most Wanted*. I swear to God he hates Billy. He keeps using our relationship to blackmail me into doing anything he wants. I've got this terrible feeling that he would hurt him if it wasn't for me. So now can you understand why it's so urgent for me to get back to 'heaven'? Now do you see how I've wrecked everything?"

"Don't give up hope, my boy. Maybe that's the reason we're here together, Eddie, to save Billy. That's got to be the reason why that angel asked to borrow my body. Maybe God wants Billy. Did you ever think of that? Maybe he too knows that Billy doesn't belong in hell. I mean, I hate to burst your bubble kid, but from what you've told me, there just is no other explanation. That manager you're talking about has got to be the devil incarnate, and you, my young friend, have obviously been spending many a season under his tutelage."

Eddie pondered Lou's words for a moment before conceding, "I hate to say it but that exact thought has popped into my head more than once. That surely would explain a lot of things, Lou. There's no doubt about that. That would explain why he's always so blue and why he acts like all of his dreams have died. It would explain his response to me after I told him that I always felt like I had an edge over everyone after visiting with him and the Manager. You know what he told me?"

"What did he say, Eddie?"

"He told me, 'That edge you're talking about is exactly why I'm here.' That's what he said, his exact words. You know I always knew that I got everything on the sly and now it's obvious that I was right. I never had any talent when it came to baseball, it was always just magic. Smoke and mirrors, the story of my life," Eddie stated dejectedly.

"I'm sure that you've got plenty of talent, kid," Eisen said comfortingly.

"He always made me feel that way, but it was all just a lie. He never even told me about the problems I was sure to encounter as a left-handed shortstop. I figured since Mattingly played third, I wouldn't have a problem."

"Maybe you won't. Maybe he wanted to spare you, the voice of doom and gloom story. He obviously didn't want to burst your bubble. Now I don't want to hear anymore self-pity from you. I thought we were here for Billy's sake?"

"Yeah. We're here for Billy. You want to hear something strange, Lou? I always thought that Billy wanted to live through me. It was almost like that was all that was left for him. He's lost, you know?"

"Yes. I know."

"I mean, not just here but wherever he is. He used to tell me that he was just like me except for the fact that he couldn't find the doorway back home. I've often wanted to help him find that doorway, Lou," Eddie confided.

"Maybe you will my boy, maybe you will," Eisen said sympathetically.

"He used to tell me that all he wanted was a chance to return to the earth so he could play baseball again. He even told me it was prophesied that he would find his way back home someday. I really believe he lives for that prophesy."

"Maybe we can make it come true for him."

"Believe me, Lou, there's nothing in the world that I would want more for him than that."

"Well then, I think it's about time for us to get out of here. We've got a disappearance to solve."

INTRODUCTION
TO ANDROLINA'S

It was business as usual at Androlina's Pizza Restaurant. The Saturday afternoon game day crowd shuffled in for a quick slice and a drink before entering the turnstiles at the US Cellular Field, a.k.a. the "new" Comiskey Park. The White Sox fans knew what a gouging they were going to take if they bought a slice inside the big new ballpark and made a point of visiting their new buddy, Antonio, the pizza man, who made them feel welcome and charged them a fair price.

Antonio was so proud of himself and his friend Ernie for saving the money to buy this tourist trap that rested on the warning track, near the center field wall of the old Comiskey Park. If you were a nostalgia buff, then it was the place for you. It was the perfect place to brag to your friends about visiting, especially if you were from out of town. For that reason, business was always booming, not to mention the fact that the regular baseball season was in progress.

His best friend's grounds keeping service had mowed many a lawn and trimmed many a bush in order to come up with the funds necessary to make Ernie a full partner. This was a dream come true for both of these childhood friends. Ernie would constantly wink at his dear friend when the place got swamped and that usually occurred on game days. Of course, Antonio never got a chance to witness the love and admiration of his lifetime friend's gestures because he was too busy concentrating on putting on a good show for the restaurant's customers. No one knew how to toss a pizza pie with the flair of Antonio. He flipped them in the air like Frisbees and caught them amazingly behind his back. The customers were mystified during the performance and Ernie kept doing his favorite thing in life, ringing up sale after sale on that cash register of theirs.

Due to a lull in the action, Ernie took a moment to reflect on just how lucky he and Antonio had been to acquire this spot, located directly on the grounds of the old, torn down, Comiskey Park. Antonio may have been the showman, who kept the customers entertained, but Ernie had a knack for decor and nostalgia. As you walked in the restaurant's door, the first thing you saw was a fight poster from June 22, 1937, promoting the world heavyweight championship fight between James J. Braddock, also known as the Cinderella Man and top contender Joe Louis. Louis ended Braddock's reign over the heavyweights by knocking him out cold in the eighth round that night, and where do you think that happened? The answer of course was on the grounds of the Old Comiskey Park. The exact spot might just be where the customers traipsed over when they entered Androlina's Pizza Restaurant. There was another fight poster touting Floyd Patterson versus Sonny Liston, a fight that took place on September 26, 1962. Sonny Liston won his heavyweight crown that night by knocking Patterson out and where did that fight take place? Well, of course, under your feet at Androlina's Pizza Restaurant. Ernie had a movie poster from *Eight Men Out* hanging proudly on the wall. It was a movie about the Black Sox Scandal of 1919 that also occurred on the historic grounds of Androlina's Pizza. Eight men had been banned from major league baseball for life because they took some part in the throwing of the World Series to the

Cincinnati Reds. Eddie Cicotte and Shoeless Joe Jackson were the most prominent of the banished.

It boggled Ernie's mind to think of all the sports history that had taken place right here underneath his feet. As you can imagine, the rent was exorbitant, but the profits during the baseball season more than made up for it. He and Antonio had been doing so well that they expanded and remodeled the rear of the building to include a lavish playroom for their children. It was any teenage boy's dream room, large and spacious, with all kinds of cool baseball simulation gadgets. Their sons spent almost all their non-school hours watching the big screen television or playing interactive video games in the cozy lounge area complete with couches and an EZ Boy reclining chair or experiencing the real life thrill of a completely enclosed fielding area that included a machine that bounced ground balls over an artificial turf surface to the awaiting kids. Practicing your fielding in this completely netted structure was thrilling to any boy with baseball dreams. This special commodious room was the envy of all who did not have such things in their homes and businesses and was a source of pride for the young men whose fathers had made this dream possible. To say the least, it was every kid's favorite place to hang out if they were lucky enough to be invited to spend time there. The biggest perk though, according to Ernie and Antonio, was it kept the kids close by and out of trouble.

ALERTING THE
AUTHORITIES

E ddie and Lou sat on a large wooden bench at the police precinct. They stared over at a slutty-looking young woman wearing tawdry clothes. She had a busted lip and a black eye. Eddie surmised that she must have had a pimp or a jealous boyfriend who obviously gave her a beating. Any way you want to slice it, he thought she was common white trash. He examined her as if she was an insect under a microscope in a futile attempt to figure out why she lived the lifestyle she chose. He continued to glare at her in disgust, concluding that her cheap blue eye shadow made it perfectly obvious that this little "lady" was for sale. Eddie thought that the question of the day was, *Who would pay for such damaged merchandise?* Eddie took one last look at this pathetic runaway and proceeded to shake his head in disbelief.

Lou was less concerned with the whore and more disturbed about how long it was taking the detective to come out and see them. He looked at his cheap Timex watch and calculated that forty minutes had already passed since the two of them had arrived. Lou was debating whether he would live long enough for the event to take place.

Fate was kind as a few minutes later a slender, shapely, middle-aged brunette in a tight-fitting police uniform walked out in front of the wooden benches and inquired, "Is there a Mr. Eisen here?"

Eddie quickly jabbed Lou Eisen with his elbow, awakening the napping senior citizen.

Eisen startled, awakened immediately, but was so disoriented that he helplessly looked over at Eddie.

Eddie motioned toward the police woman and Lou soberly asked her, "You looking for me?"

"Are you Mr. Eisen?" she replied.

"That's me, missy, and have I got a story to tell you."

"It says here that you've got some information on a missing person case. So why don't you follow me? We'll go talk upstairs in private," she asserted.

"This kid is with me and he's got some information too," Eisen declared, pointing his finger at Eddie.

"All right. Bring him along too. Let's make this a family affair," she wisecracked.

Eddie and Lou stood up and followed her. Eddie immediately took notice of her athletic rear end and the handcuffs that hung off her belt that adorned the area above her right butt cheek. He also took note of the semi-automatic holstered on her right hip. As they walked together in a single file up a flight of stairs, she turned around and introduced herself as Detective Dominguez. Lou immediately responded, "My first name's Lou, and this is my little buddy, Eddie Romano."

Reaching the top of the stairs, she quickly glanced back again and said, "Hi." She opened the iron door, and all entered her office.

Eddie's first impression was that this place was anything but welcoming and comfortable. It was lifeless, painted a drab gray, and had a foreboding air to it. Dominguez's desk was gray-painted metal with some kind of black inlay that surrounded its perimeter. It had some kind of desk monitor that was obviously attached to a computer and a rolodex. Dominguez had the only cushioned chair, and she quickly plopped her bottom into it. She motioned for Eddie and Lou to sit down in the solid wooden chairs that faced her direction. Eddie and Lou did as instructed and stared at the walls that were covered with pictures of the wanted with brief descriptions of the vile acts they were accused of. Eddie thought that he was damn lucky that his picture wasn't posted on this wall. It suddenly dawned on him how serious the consequences of his prior actions could have been. He imagined what it must be like for a suspect to be brought in here for inter- rogation. He was sure that the metal door that just closed behind them would not open without Detective Dominguez's assistance. Eddie surmised that a lot of the suspects would go directly from these hard wooden chairs that he and Lou were sitting on into the individual cold iron cells he noticed in an adjoining room behind Dominguez.

Dominguez stared over at the two men before locking eyes with Eddie. Her eyes were deep, dark brown, rather cold, and Eddie thought that she was looking right through him. Eddie, feeling very uncomfortable, quickly broke free from the eye lock and continued to focus his attention upon the wanted posters. Dominguez sensing Eddie's uneasiness changed her point of view, staring down Lou Eisen instead and then suddenly blurted out, "So what can I do for you, fellas?"

Eisen took a moment to gather his thoughts before replying, "Everything I'm about to tell you might sound crazy but believe me it's not. The missing person we're here about disappeared way back in 1952. He was a ballplayer who had a minor stint in the major leagues. He played for the White Sox. His name was Billy Green."

Dominguez stopped taking notes, scratched her scalp, and ran her fingers through her extremely short, manlike hairdo retort- ing, "Never heard of him."

"Well, this was quite a few years before your time so I wouldn't have expected you to," Eisen added nonchalantly.

"So we're talking here about a forty-some-year-old disappearance and a very cold case file. So, um, what have you got for me?" Dominguez inquired uninterestedly, focusing her attention apparently on a blister that had showed up on the palm of her hand.

"This kid discovered Billy Green's baseball glove about eight years ago," Eisen asserted.

"Wow! That's an old glove," Dominguez surmised as she looked up and stared over at Eddie's uniquely decorated glove. "Can I see it?" she asked.

Eddie hesitated before passing his "security blanket" over to the detective who immediately picked up on this.

"I can see that you're very attached to it. It really is very unique. So you two have got yourselves a souvenir. What are you doing here? You should be out playing catch," Dominguez wisecracked as she quickly glanced down at her wristwatch feigning like she had some other place to go.

Eddie quickly tiring of Dominguez's flippant attitude interjected, "You see, Lou. I knew this was going to be a complete waste of our time. She doesn't give a rat's ass about Billy or anything we've got to say." In utter dismay, Eddie bowed his head and began to pray silently.

"Save your pious crap for someone else, okay? I'm not the one," she announced, pointing a finger at Eddie. "You act like you have some personal connection here. Why don't you get a grip? Anybody can tell that you're not old enough to be a concerned party in this matter," Dominguez venomously added.

"Who in hell do you think you are? Telling me I'm not a concerned party? You need to hear the facts before you start judging people, lady," Eddie exploded. He then bowed his head in shame, realizing he was guilty of the same thing. He judged people too without knowing the facts as he flashed back to the beaten girl with the blue eye shadow that he had examined a few minutes prior.

Eisen quickly interjected with fervor and lucidly explained, "Listen, ma'am, I'm a former sports writer for the *Chicago Tribune* and I wrote many a story throughout the years about this disappearance. It was puzzling how this young prospect suddenly disappeared without a trace on his first night playing in the major leagues. No one ever saw the kid leave the stadium, and his street clothes were found in his locker. Therefore, he was still in his White Sox uniform, pretty conspicuous, you know what I mean? Don't you think somebody just might have seen him if he had left? And the kicker is, that the baseball glove the kid found was always with Billy. He never went anywhere without that glove. Considering the fact that the glove is totally unique as anyone can clearly see with the distinctive green-dyed leather and those unique artistic drawings all over it, I am one hundred percent sure that Eddie's glove is authentic, which means he's holding the only tangible piece of evidence as to Billy Green's whereabouts that I've ever heard about."

Her curiosity finally piqued, Dominguez asked, "So, Eddie, where'd you find the glove?"

"Under an earth-moving machine in the wreckage of the old Comiskey Park. It was almost completely buried," Eddie declared.

Dominguez shook her head in amazement, reflecting upon the foolishness of this treasure hunting mission and asked the obvious, "So what were you doing at a wrecking site? Do you have any idea how dangerous that was? Don't tell me, I know, you were out looking for souvenirs. You're unbelievable, you know that?" Dominguez scolded.

"I was eleven years old at the time, and I conned my father into breaking the law. Big deal," Eddie retaliated.

"I get this feeling that you make a habit of it. You seem pretty shady to me," Dominguez chided.

"So what's that mean? You're not going to help us now?" Eddie deduced disappointedly.

"Unfortunately, I can't make those decisions. My job is to find answers, and if I do nothing, it is a dereliction of duty. I want to keep my job. So I'll look into it. There's just one thing that bothers me. Why are you two fellas so interested in solving this disappearance?" she incriminated, staring directly over at Eisen.

Eisen immediately picked up on Dominguez's suspicions and denounced them categorically, "Look, missy, if you think I had anything to do with Billy Green's disappearance you are sadly mistaken. I was a friend of his, and when I found out that Eddie had found his glove and realized the significance of that fact, I decided to do all I could to help my friend. I believe he would have done the same thing for me if put in a similar situation, and quite frankly, I resent your intimations."

"Look, I'm just doing my job. Maybe this is all harmless fun. Maybe you really are a friend of this Billy Green, but until I know for sure, everyone is a suspect, except maybe you," Dominguez rationalized as she pointed over at Eddie, staring him down with a discerning eye. Eddie fidgeted in his seat uncomfortably and refused to give any credence to Detective Dominguez's assertion that she didn't believe that he had anything to do with all of this.

"So where do we go from here?" Eisen asked, breaking the tension-filled silence.

"I think we need more than that glove to warrant digging up that parking lot. I could go in front of a judge, but I don't think I'd get what you guys are looking for. This case is just too old and finding that glove is just not enough. I'll get laughed at. I'm not putting myself through that. If you guys come up with more, or if you'd like to confess to something, then you give me a call. I will reiterate, I haven't ruled anything out yet. Oh, by the way, here's my card," Dominguez announced as she handed Eisen her business card.

"Detective, you are barking up the wrong tree, but you'll find that out soon enough. Thanks for your time," Eisen stated adamantly.

"That's it? What a colossal waste of time," Eddie blurted out in frustration. "See, Lou, I knew before we even got here that they weren't going to help us. We're on our own again. It's enough to make you sick," Eddie whined.

Disgustedly, Eddie jumped up and tried to turn the doorknob that wouldn't budge. Suddenly, there was some kind of unlocking noise as Dominguez pushed the door release.

Eddie was now able to turn the door handle, and he exited quickly. Eisen looked back at Dominguez and forewarned, "This won't be the last time you'll see us."

As the door closed, Eisen could hear her mutter sarcastically, "I couldn't be that lucky, could I?"

BILLY'S CRY FOR HELP

E rnie and Antonio's boys thought it was the ultimate
    hangout, spot and they were on top of the world whenever
    they got a chance to be there and today was the pinnacle
of that experience. It was game day at the New Comiskey Park,
and the boys were "chilling" in their playroom that was located in
the far rear of the restaurant. The big screen television was tuned
to the White Sox afternoon game versus the Cleveland Indians
and the surround sound made them all feel like they were inside
the ballpark. Ernie's sons, Craig and Steve, laid claim to the black
leather couch and the EZ Boy black leather recliner. Craig—a
seventeen year old, chubby, freckle-faced kid—was in his favorite
reclined position with his eyes intently focused on the happen-
ings occurring at the ballpark across the street. He was stuffing
pepperoni pizza in his mouth and slurping down an ice cold Coke
while his brother Steve was sprawled lengthwise on the couch,
monopolizing the majority of its space. Steve was fifteen and had
the belly of a gal who was about seven months pregnant. He
was busy sucking down a really thick, extra-large chocolate milk-
shake. These boys were the epitome of "couch potatoes." Exercise
was not their forte, and they were not the least bit ashamed of it.

On the other hand, Antonio's son was a major physical fitness
and sports enthusiast. Mario was an athlete and his muscularly
defined, seventeen-year-old physique made everyone look his way.

He dreamed of playing for that team across the street. He was six feet tall, very limber, and quick. He spent an inordinate amount of time fielding ground balls shot out of that pitching machine. All one had to do was change the machine setting and instead of attempting to hit one hundred mile per hour fastballs, they could easily attempt to field those balls that were now directed to bounce off the artificial turf surface. The machine could be set at various speeds and time intervals so whoever was fielding would have enough time to get back on to their feet and reset themselves before attempting to make a play on the next ground ball. Since balls shot from the machine could reach 110 miles per hour, the equipment was considered dangerous, and Antonio made sure the fielding area was completely enclosed with a strong netted material. He didn't want Ernie's boys to be accidentally injured by a misplaced or a misfired ball. Of course, if you were inside the netted area, you were on your own and you better be on guard. In the interest of safety, Antonio had a large sign posted over the door of the netted area. It read, "To Whom It May Concern: Please stay alert when entering this enclosure! Baseball's travelling at high speeds will be coming your way! Enter at your own risk!" On that same door an additional sign was posted stating, "Do not enter without a baseball glove and stay alert!" These signs, for the most part, were posted for Mario's friends who seemed to fit into the dumb-jock stereotype. Antonio and Ernie did not want lawsuits, and since they were doing considerably well in business, they were targets for that kind of thing.

At the present time, Mario was in the "hitting and fielding room" and had the machine set for ground balls to be fired at various speeds with a forty-second interval between each firing. After fielding an easy ground ball, Mario had plenty of time to allow his devious mind to wander. A recurring thought was to shorten the delay mechanism when his friends entered the enclosure. He got a big chuckle out of this fantasy. He imagined one of his friends diving for a ground ball and just getting back to his feet as the next ball was fired at him. It was a preposterous idea, but the thought of one of his pals in complete terror having to dive to avoid being hit by the next ground ball fired from the machine really amused him. Since concentration and focus were of the utmost importance while being enclosed in this dangerous area, Mario decided to take a break and shut down the machine.

He allowed his eyes to wander around the now motionless area. He took a moment to think about how commodious the space was and reflected upon how fortunate he was to have such a place to practice. He then recollected how thrilled his friends were when he first invited them over to practice and share in his good fortune. There could be no doubt as to why he was so popular with his classmates. The word got out about his base-ball practice facility, and from then on, everybody who was cool from his school wanted to be his friend and get a chance to hang out at the most extraordinary spot around. The room became his badge of honor, and he built his identity around it. Mario sud-denly became melancholy as he pondered the thought of his dad and Ernie's plans to rent his special room out for birthday and little league parties. It bothered him that his father and Ernie were actually considering taking away his exclusive privilege but was pleased that so far it hadn't happened. He decided that it was time to exit the enclosure and spend some time with the other boys and watch the game. As he made his way toward the exit, he was startled by a baseball mysteriously rolling toward him. He watched it enigmatically as it came very close to hitting him and, in confusion, peripherally glanced over at the switch to the fielding machine that was in the "off" position. He leaned over and picked up the slow roller, tossing the ball back toward the machine. He shrugged his shoulders in acknowledgement of the odd occurrence before doing an about-face. He quickly put his hand on the door handle to exit when suddenly a ball hit him right between the shoulder blades. Alarmed, he did a quick 180 degree turn and stared over at the inert machine and asked nervously, "Who's there?"

There was no response to his inquiry. Mario looked around circumspectly and exclaimed, "Come on! Who's messing around with me?"

Mario's question went unanswered except this time another baseball rolled out toward him from the right side of the fielding machine. There was something different about this ball. As it stopped rolling, a good five feet in front of Mario, he noticed what he thought was an autograph upon it. Stunned and fearful of the unknown, he picked up the ball and read its message. It was not an autograph. He stared at it in disbelief as his mind came to terms with the words written on it, "Help me!" Mario felt like his stomach had fallen down to his feet. He was petrified. All he wanted to do was to get out of there as fast as humanly possible. Speaking out to no one perceptible, he said, "I can't help you. I've gotta go," and he quickly turned around to exit. A chill ran down his spine as he grasped the door handle and suddenly a sixth sense warned him of danger in close proximity.

Without warning, he was hit again by another baseball. This time it felt like he was hit by a pitch in a real game. The ball hit him right between the shoulder blades and it stung. He did another about-face and picked up the ball. There was another message. This time it read, "Please Help Me! You Don't Understand! I Really Need Your Help!" Some kind of movement caught Mario's eye, and he looked over to the right side of the ground ball machine and saw someone. He really wasn't sure what he was looking at except it resembled a baseball player. The most eerie thing was the specter's archaic uniform and his supplicant hand gestures. A feeling of complete consternation overwhelmed him as this ballplayer from another era inched closer toward him, waving his arms desperately and signaling for help. Mario froze in trepidation as the specter in the old White Sox uniform entered his personal space. Mario was afraid to look at him, so he stared down toward his feet and noticed the intruder's patent leather green cleats and then felt his cold touch upon his arm. Mario finally looked up at the ghost who wore a tormented expression on his face. Petrified, with tears cascading down his cheeks, he begged, "Please, you're scaring me, can't you just leave me alone? I can't help you!"

Mario turned away from the entity and stormed out of the "hitting and fielding room" in what seemed like world record time. He sprinted past Ernie's boys, startling them from their intent focus on the televised baseball game. Craig looked astonishingly over at his brother Steve and commented, "Man, must have been something he ate!" Both boys stopped eating and drinking immediately as they worriedly reflected upon their chances of getting the same food poisoning that they surmised had overwhelmed their friend.

Momentarily they heard baseballs being thrown against the door in the "fielding room." Solicitously, they both peered over toward the disturbance. Craig strained to get up and on to his feet and glibly quipped, "Don't fret, my pet. I'll handle this. Mario must have left that machine on."

Craig took a stroll to the enclosed area. He cautiously opened the door and gazed over at the machine. To his surprise, it was not operating, but something wasn't right with this picture. He immediately got a foreboding feeling as he let go of the door. That feeling was intensified when the spring in the door hinge made it slam and created a startling, loud cacophony that caused Craig to jump. As Craig turned to look back at where the door had slammed behind him, he noticed through his peripheral vision a baseball rolling toward him. He stared in astonishment at the approaching ball and then looked up to see the specter of the ballplayer approaching. Petrified, he stood quiescently and then began to tremble uncontrollably as the ghost closed in on him. The specter's pantomime seemed to be begging for Craig's help as it reached out to grab his hand. Craig, disturbed and fearful of the supernatural, prevented the touch and instantly turned and ran for his life. Craig bolted by Steve without saying a word. Steve, still on the couch and doing his best to focus on the game, looked up momentarily to witness his brother running by and remarked to himself unnervingly, "Must have been something they ate. Damn! Hope I don't get it."

Beginning the
Search

Lou Eisen found solace in the fact that he had slept the night through as he drove his big Cadillac over to the Romano residence. All the excitement of the previous day was too much for the nerves of the seventy-eight-year-old to endure. He silently thanked God for giving Eddie and him the wisdom to delay their search for a day. He had awakened with the stamina and vigor to attempt to accomplish this seemingly impossible task of locating Billy Green's remains. He was convinced that his longtime friend was now dead, and at least according to Eddie, his soul was in some kind of torment. This was the most personal crusade he had ever embarked upon. It was truly a holy mission and his first completely selfless act. If there really was a way to earn a ticket to heaven this crusade would best represent his most humanitarian moment. He was truly proud of himself for attempting this and believed in his heart that if he was successful this would be his crowning achievement.

He pulled up in front of the Romano residence and checked his Timex to make sure he was on time, which of course he was. Being prompt was a virtue he learned as a newspaper man. Eddie told him he would be ready at 11:00 a.m., and he patiently waited for the teen to make his escape from the Romano home.

You sure couldn't miss him when Eddie exited the front door of his residence dressed in his replica of Billy Green's 1952 Chicago White Sox uniform. Lou thought, *Talk about an attention grabber, the kid truly stands out like a sore thumb.* As Eddie got in the Cadillac, Lou commented, "What are we doing? Going trick or treating?"

"Very funny, Lou," Eddie volleyed. "I can't help it. I like dressing like this. I feel closer to Billy when I do," Eddie explained.

"Well, they say imitation is the most sincere form of flattery," Lou pontificated.

"Lou, you're a regular platitudinarian. Very original," Eddie wisecracked. "But seriously speaking, do you think we'll find him?"

"Platitudinarian, huh? Now that's a fifty-dollar word if I ever heard one. I didn't think the schools these days taught you much more than "See Spot run. Run, run, run." But obviously, I stand corrected. But to be serious as you put it, I don't know. I hope so," Lou said, shaking his head and pondering the momentous task they were about to begin. "I guess we need to start at the old ballpark. You know this could turn out to be impossible. They built over it. I think it's all a parking lot now, then again, there might be a few stores. This could be a complete waste of our time kid," Lou surmised.

"Well, we can't quit now. I owe it to Billy, and I think you do too. I'm sure he would have done the same for both of us. So let's go, Lou," Eddie demanded.

Lou started the car and revved the motor. He maneuvered the Cadillac away from the curb and merged into traffic. Their quest had begun.

Ernie and Antonio's Dilemma

At Androlina's Pizza, Ernie and Antonio had a serious problem on their hands. None of the kids wanted anything to do with spending any more time in that play area. In fact, if the truth is to be known, they didn't want to step foot on the premises.

As far as Antonio was concerned, the party was over in that expensive renovation of theirs. The kids swore there was a ghost inhabiting their playroom. All the reasoning and rational thinking he could muster fell upon deaf ears as the boys refused to set foot in the place. Antonio was enraged by the thought of this other worldly ballplayer camping out in "his" playroom. All he could think about was all the money that he and Ernie had spent going down that figurative drain. Both he and Ernie gave up on the idea of renting the space out for parties. What if this ballplayer showed up and terrified the kids? If word got out that they had a ghost in their back room, it would probably hurt business, and the rent was way too exorbitant to risk that happening. They could not afford any type of down turn, especially as far as business was concerned. If he had stayed up all night long dreaming up the worst possible scenarios, he couldn't have come up with one much worse than this.

Ernie, on the other hand, did not believe in ghosts or the supernatural and figured that there had to be some plausible explanation for the events taking place back there. Maybe somebody wanted to frighten the kids and their ploy was to sneak in and masquerade as a ghost. Ernie, as a child, had seen too many episodes of *Scooby-Doo* with similar plot twists, so he didn't believe that he actually had a ghost in his back room. With that in mind, he confidently marched into the back room to make sure that all the back doors were secured and locked. He wanted to make sure that there was absolutely no outside access to his party room. He figured that if someone was pulling a practical joke on them, he was going to make damn sure that it wasn't going to happen again. After taking a thorough tour of the "playroom," he got on the phone and called his son, Craig, who was at home at the time making himself a snack.

"Craig, I think you guys are just gullible. Somebody obviously pulled a practical joke on us. Why don't you come down to the store and I'll show you how I know, and we can talk about this."

Craig stopped eating just long enough to declare, "Dad, I sympathize with your dilemma, but Mario and I don't care how you're trying to sugarcoat this issue. We're not hanging out there anymore. Why don't you try to run your crap on Mario and see if he'll budge but I wouldn't get my hopes up if I were you."

Ernie argued, "What if I go to sleep back there? Will that prove to you that it's safe? Not for nothing but I just toured the whole room, and I didn't see anyone or anything unusual."

Craig stated tersely, "You can sleep anywhere you want, Dad, but I'm not going to hang out there again and that's that."

Ernie exasperatedly exclaimed, "It's not what you think it is! That's just not possible. There has to be another explanation."

"Yeah. Well, I saw what I saw, and I wasn't hallucinating! I wasn't high or on drugs or drunk! That thing tried touching me. Who knows? It could have been the Grim Reaper. If it had touched me, I might be dead right now, and don't forget Mario saw it too. So what are you trying to say, Dad? That Mario and I had the same delusion? You know, I really resent that, Dad," Craig notified indignantly. To emphasize his point of view, Craig slammed the phone down, abruptly ending their conversation.

After hearing Ernie's shouting, Antonio ran into the playroom and alarmingly asked, "What's going on? What's wrong?"

Ernie shook his head in dismay and announced, "We've really got a problem."

"What? Did you see it?" Antonio asked anxiously.

"No. I didn't see anything, but the kid's aren't going to come to work anymore or at least until we solve this problem," Ernie admitted dejectedly. He added, "And you know what that means, don't you? It means I don't get a single day off. It means that I'm stuck doing the deliveries. This is just a clever ploy for Mario to shirk his duties. You just wait until I get a hold of the person that's pulling this prank. I swear to God, Antonio, it ain't going to be pretty."

"It just goes to show there's no rest for the wicked," Antonio wisecracked.

"Keep talking, wise guy, and you'll be doing the deliveries," Ernie declared venomously.

A MENTALLY
TAXING DRIVE

Lou Eisen and Eddie Romano were now on their way to the site of the Old Comiskey Park. It took forty-five minutes to get there from Palatine, so the two men had plenty of time to contemplate the onerous task that awaited them. Lou steered his big Cadillac off route 53 south and merged on to interstate 90 eastbound for the thirty-mile trek to the stadium. Lou whispered a prayer, thanking God that the Sox were out of town. He knew that this quest would be next to impossible to accomplish under game day circumstances. By choosing to do this on a Sunday instead of during the regular work week, they avoided a mob scene, which was a good omen as far as Lou was concerned. He prayed that maybe the stars would align properly and a favorable outcome might result for the two of them. He tacitly nodded his head, hoping that God just might agree to give him a break, just this one time. Senescence was breaking him down spiritually, and he thought that this might be the only way to rebuild his tenuous faith.

Eddie's mind wandered as he commiserated over Billy's plight. He remembered the last time he saw him and recalled how completely disillusioned he looked as he made that lonely walk out into center field. Looking back on this whole ordeal, he realized that Billy was always castigated by the Manager, and it seemed like he just finally gave up. That celebration with all those well-wishing ballplayers was too much for Billy's spirit to bear. Reflecting back on that incident, he now realized that something had died in Billy that day. He remembered how the Babe said to leave Billy alone and to let him make his peace. He now knew that he had to find him and assuage the emotional pain that now seemed to so thoroughly engulf his hero's soul. Billy had taught him everything, and he felt deep in his heart that he would have been a complete failure without him. He was tormented by the thought of how he had let this situation get out of his control. He thought he had it all figured out until Lou got involved. He looked over at Lou and gave him an unnoticed disdainful look and then continued in contemplation. A sense of urgency overwhelmed him as he pondered the thought of Billy being in hell. All the pieces of the puzzle were coming together now. He remembered the time he commented to Billy about the Manager being the devil. Billy never gave him an answer to that observation. Maybe he couldn't answer him. Maybe he was being coerced too, but regardless of the conditions involved, he knew that he would be willing to march into hell to help his best friend. The problem being, *How would he get there?* He was so frustrated because he had no answer to that question. As far as he was concerned, he had been duped into breaking his bargain with the Manager. By not killing that scoundrel, he blew his only sure bet of finding his way back to Billy. He was so annoyed that he wanted to rip his hair out. He put his hands over his face and, with a feeling of complete demoralization and impending doom, shook his head back and forth methodically like a resident of a psychiatric ward.

Lou took a glance toward Eddie and told him that he better get it together. Lou needed the boy on point if they were to have any chance of completing this supernatural mission. He didn't need any more complications, and he was tired of driving. He just wanted the trip to end. He glanced again at Eddie, trying his best to console him, "Hey, cheer up. Will you?"

Eddie began to sob uncontrollably as if his best friend in the world had been taken from him. The tears just flowed constantly as the realization sank in that his friend Billy might be gone forever.

Eisen, witnessing this effusive display of emotions realized that Eddie was on the verge of a nervous breakdown. He implored, "Come on, kid. Don't fall apart on me now. Please, suck it up for me and for Billy!" Somehow, Eddie retained control of his emotions and sat taciturn for the remainder of the trip. That forty-five-minute excursion was the most emotionally draining event of either of their lives, and it took a miracle for Lou to stay focused enough on the road to keep them out of an accident.

LOU AND EDDIE DEVISE A PLAN

L ou Eisen maneuvered his Cadillac off South Wentworth
Avenue and took a right-hand turn on to West Thirty-
Fifth Street. He looked over at what remained of the Old
Comiskey Park. It was nothing but a large parking lot. Lou had
been to this sacred sight on many occasions during his younger
years. He thought about how much things had changed in his
lifetime. He took a quick glance over at the New Comiskey Park
but felt like something was missing there. There was something to
be said about going to a stadium where generations of your family had frequented. Lou reminisced about a game or two he spent
there with his father. The thought of him and his dad together so
long ago brought a welling of tears to his eyes. He realized everything about this mission, including the players involved, were
so close to him that it couldn't help but touch a nerve in his soul.
His friend Billy Green was buried somewhere on these grounds
without even a marker to pray at. Totally disillusioned with that
reality, he looked around in confusion trying his best to figure
out where McCuddy's used to be. It was the famous tavern where
Babe Ruth once slammed a few drinks down between games during a doubleheader. The thought of this landmark gone forever
gave Lou a terrible sense of longing. He noticed that where the

big scoreboard, the bull pens, and the bleachers used to be, there was some kind of strip mall. Everything about this place was too modern for his liking, and it stole away the nostalgia of the once hallowed grounds. He parked the big Cadillac in a space that may have rested above the old pitcher's mound. He and Eddie exited the vehicle and stared in dismay at the pathetic concrete tribute, literally poured into a corner of the parking lot that represented home plate at the old Comiskey Park. The two men wandered toward the monument, a marble plaque on the sidewalk next to the "new" Comiskey Park that read, "Comiskey Park, 1910–1990, Home Plate." It was in the shape of a home plate surrounded on both sides by the outline of the batter's boxes. Somebody had painted the foul lines as they ran diagonally from each side of home plate. Eddie and Lou were careful not to walk on the marble home plate and both secretly wondered if Billy Green was really buried underneath this monument. Lou tried his best to believe that this was Billy Green's monument, something like the Tomb of the Unknown Soldier at Arlington National Cemetery in Washington, DC. He tried to get solace from this belief but was unable to because the whole premise didn't make any sense to him. It was just too illogical of a place for him to be buried. He thought, *"Underneath home plate"? How could that have possibly been pulled off without detection? Why can't it be easy to find this body?* These questions were driving Lou mad. Lou looked over at Eddie, wearing that replica of the 1952 Chicago White Sox uniform and curiously asked him, "Do you feel anything here?" Lou really knew very little about Eddie at the time and was hoping that he was some kind of clairvoyant.

Eddie shook his head in a negative manner before commenting, "So this is all that remains of that ballpark that my father and I trespassed upon eight years ago? How are we going to find him here?" Eddie asked in disgust.

"Somebody obviously has plans for us and plans for Billy, or they wouldn't have put us together," Lou surmised and added,

"This partnership of ours did not happen by accident, my boy. Maybe we truly are predestined. I'm starting to believe that it's our destiny to solve this mystery and free Billy from whatever or whoever is tormenting his soul. This is our quest, and our lives will be unfulfilled if we quit now," Lou deduced.

"What if he's buried underneath this parking lot. Nobody's going to dig it up for us," Eddie rationalized and bitterly announced.

"Can't you see? We were meant to succeed. I believe that the man upstairs has a plan for us. I don't believe that he would've gone to all this trouble if he didn't know that we would have a high probability of success. My intuition tells me that we should forget all about this parking lot, remember this is where the field was. There's just no way somebody buried Billy's body underneath the field. They would've never gotten away with it. Somebody would have noticed that the field had been dug up. So he's not buried underneath this parking lot, my boy. He's got to be buried somewhere underneath a stadium structure. He's some place where no one would have noticed if the ground had been broken. Maybe underneath the bleachers? Maybe underneath that big scoreboard they had? That crazy one that exploded and shot off the fireworks. No, come to think about it, that wasn't there in 1952, but the big scoreboard was. Maybe he's underneath one of the utility sheds? Look, it has to be underneath an enclosed structure other than that, it would have been discovered. I think we need to start over there," Lou concluded, pointing a finger out toward the strip mall, some four hundred feet away. "Well, what do you think?" Lou inquired.

"I don't know," Eddie agonized. "That could have been where I found the glove. It's as good a guess as any. So why don't we split up? You start inquiring at the stores that begin down the left field line, and I'll do some detective work, beginning with the stores located down the right field line. We'll meet up in the middle, okay?"

THE MOST DANGEROUS
JOB IN CHICAGO?

Ernie wearily entered Androlina's, carrying a bunch of empty, red-colored pizza warming bags. He was out of breath, obviously not used to doing door-to-door pizza deliveries. He set the pizza warming bags down on a table close to the service counter and declared, "Antonio! No more deliveries to Mrs. Muhammad. Her kids are complete animals. They started throwing pebbles at me from the third story window. The bigger ones hurt. I felt like I needed a hard hat for protection against flying objects. I can't believe Mario puts up with this job and doesn't bitch about it. These people are messed up. When I finally got to the door, do you think she gave me a tip? Hell no! She paid me in change. I was surprised it wasn't pennies. This job is really for the birds. I hate to say it, but we really need to pay the kids more," Ernie vented.

Antonio was busy applying cheese to a couple of dough pies that so far contained only a ladle full of pizza sauce. He stopped for a moment and replied, "I told you that delivering in this city was not only hard work but dangerous work. I wish we didn't have to send the kids out at all but wish in one hand and shit in the other. You know what I mean?"

"Do I," Ernie responded. He added, "I've been doing some thinking about our problem in the back room. We could install security cameras so that we could monitor the situation from up front. It might be a good investment since we would need to know what's going on back there if we were to rent the room out for parties. Maybe the kid's would feel safer if we had twenty-four-hour taped surveillance of that area. A guy came into the store the other day and was pitching that, but I told him I wasn't interested. Maybe I've changed my mind. I think I put his card on the bulletin board."

"What kind of money are we talking?" Antonio asked curiously as he put the raw pizza pies into the oven.

"I don't know, but we got to do something. I can't be doing this delivery crap. The only other thing I could come up with was to have some sort of priest bless the back room, and quite frankly, I think that's a complete waste of our time and effort. There is no such thing as ghosts and spirits. If there was, my dad would have come back to tell me about it. He loved me that much, you know?" Ernie reflected sadly, recalling his father's passing.

"Yeah. I know, Earn. I loved him too. So I guess we'll try the security cameras. My god that room is rapidly becoming a money pit," Antonio epiphanized.

Antonio's words rung true as both men looked into the others eyes sullenly. There was no doubt that there was a tacit agreement in regard to that matter.

LOU LEARNS THE TAXI BUSINESS

Lou Eisen began his arduous task at the Taxi and Limousine Company office situated where the third baseline and the home run wall probably met at the old ballpark. It was a very small store front, out of which they dispatched taxicabs and limousines. Lou was embarrassed to enter the place and ask the questions he needed to ask. In complete chagrin, the old man walked up to the counter and rang the bell that was placed there to call for service. The busy telephone operators and the dispatcher glanced up at him and continued talking to their customers through the hand's free calling devices that all had wrapped around their heads. Lou felt like he was being ignored, so he rang the bell again, this time a lot harder and therefore louder. A sixty-plus-year-old, haggard-looking woman glanced up at him wearing a gigantic frown on her face. She had obvious false teeth, wore nerdy-looking thick-lensed bifocals, and was just too busy to be bothered with the mundane. Lou was repulsed by the persona of this woman. And because she ignored him for so long, he had way too much time to really inspect her body. After a thorough check, from head to toe, he saw more tattoos than the painted lady at the circus sideshow. He was reassured by the visual evidence that walked in front of him as to why he never chose to desecrate his body. The tattoos were old, faded, and covered wrinkled skin. He scrutinized her every move as she marched back and forth while continuing to ignore him and constantly complaining to her coworkers. He made a supposition about her character and concluded that she had a secret self-loathing, hated the world and life in general. She was just about as jaded as a human being could possibly be. He listened intently as she put on a tirade complaining that she was the only one who did her job and that there would be no supplies in that office if not for her meticulous attention to detail. After finishing her rant, she looked over again at Lou uninterestedly and asked in the most inhospitable manner, "Is there something *I* can do for you?" She overemphasized, stressing the "I."

Taken completely off guard by her "greeting," Lou asked nervously, "Has there been anything unusual happening here?"

With an inscrutable look on her face and an attitude of imposition, she sarcastically responded, "Unusual? In what way? 'Cause to tell you the truth, there's a lot of unusual shit that goes on around here. Last week for instance, two teenagers took a forty-dollar ride and bolted on the cabbie but maybe that's not juicy enough for you. Seriously, do you need a ride somewhere?"

"No, ma'am. I don't need a ride. I just wondered if anything out of the ordinary was taking place on these premises," Lou inquired authoritatively.

"What? Are you a cop? Jeez, do you guys ever retire? No. We don't sell drugs here, mister. You really need to be on your way," she declared. She then looked over at someone hidden in a back room and shouted, "Julio! You better get out here! I think there's trouble!"

Julio, an extra-large, obese Spanish man, who's most salient feature was the drool that chronically dripped out of his mouth, charged like a water buffalo toward the counter and menacingly demanded, "Is there a problem? Because if there's not, you really need to leave."

Eisen took one look at the giant's big, thick fist, and that fat finger pointing angrily in his direction and decided he had overstayed his welcome. Intimidated, he exited without incident. He hoped that his welcome at the other stores on his course would be a lot less stressful. He took a handkerchief out of his pocket and wiped dry his brow that was now sweating profusely. He wasn't sure he could handle anymore friction and volatility like he had experienced at that cab stand. He walked away, shaking his head in disbelief, trying his best to understand how people could be that hostile and still stay in business.

EDDIE MEETS ERNIE
THE HARD WAY

With a nebulous plan in mind, Eddie Romano pranced up and down rows of video arcade machines. The ambiance of the place was beginning to grate upon him. He stopped and pondered as to what to do next. How in the world was he going to locate Billy at a place like this? This current dilemma simply overwhelmed him and boggled his mind. He looked around for a moment and observed a pimply faced teenager who had mastered one of the shooting games. The kid kept pointing the plastic gun replica at targets on the video screen. The game was programmed to pick up on the infrared signals dispatched from the gun replica. The kid kept shooting and according to the monitor reloading as the game progressed from one scene to the next. This kid was completely fixated with this artificial world that had been created by some clever computer programmer. Eddie thought that this whole amusement center was just one great big waste of time, money, and effort. *Didn't these people know the score? Didn't their parent's warn them of the consequences of playing these games chronically?* This was just another addiction and a very unhealthy one. Eddie specifically remembered his father telling him that hemorrhoids came from sitting too long in one position and from lack of exercise. He had that thought in mind as he gazed over at another kid who was comfortably resting his bottom in a plastic simulated race car seat. The kid was literally camped out there. He had a burger, fries, and a malted resting on the seat next to him. He was a hemorrhoid waiting to happen. He recalled his father's words, "You know, Eddie, those hemorrhoids bleed, they itch, and they hurt. My suggestion to you is don't sit too long." He remembered looking them up online just to see what his dad was talking about. They were gross. They were some kind of protruding, keloid-looking vein that stuck out of someone's anus. He smirked as he imagined that fat kid playing that car racing game with some wormy-looking vein dangling out of his ass. Suddenly, he realized that he wasn't there to forecast future victims of the dreaded hemorrhoid but to do some detective work. He told himself to get it together and stop losing track of the issue at hand. He was here for Billy, not for his own personal amusement. He decided to approach a kid, his own age, who was working at the arcade, making change and selling tokens to the patrons. He snuck up behind him and tapped him on the shoulder. The employee spun around and gave Eddie a wry smile, and joked, "Hey! Aren't you in the wrong place? US Cellular Field is across the street."

Eddie was not amused by the remark and sarcastically let out a loud, exaggerated laugh, then quipped, "Yeah, I get it. You're making fun of my uniform."

The attendant, fearing that his remark might have been misconstrued to be thought of as impolite, quickly apologized stating, "Please don't take offense. I'm just kidding with you. Where'd you get that old thing anyway?"

"I had it made. A friend of mine wears one just like it," Eddie stated frankly.

Baffled, the attendant inquired, "So, uh…What can I do for you?"

"Anything out of the ordinary occurring here? You know like, recently?" Eddie asked timidly.

"Out of the ordinary? In what way?" The attendant asked with a puzzled look upon his face.

"I don't know. Anything odd? Anybody see anything that might be construed as ghostly?" Eddie articulated in chagrin.

"No man. No ghosts here. Except maybe a simulation game, but on second thought, I don't think so," the attendant replied adding, "Do you need tokens?"

"No. So, uh…There have been no reports of paranormal activity, huh?" Eddie asked, finally getting to the point.

"No. Not here, man. You're about as paranormal as we get. No offense. I'm just pulling your leg again. You see, I can't afford to offend anybody and lose my job. You know what I mean, Jelly Bean?" The attendant laughed nervously as he was obviously amused by his own wit.

"Thanks anyway and no offense was taken," Eddie remarked and thought, *But trust me, some offense was taken.* Totally humiliated, he made a rapid march toward the door to the street. He realized at that moment that this whole search he was embarking upon could end up being pretty embarrassing. He thought about the indignities he was willing to suffer on Billy's behalf as he finally reached the door.

Back outside again, Eddie decided to try his luck at Baskin-Robbin's, which was the next store on his route. He walked into the ice cream store that was kept at about the same temperature as your average household refrigerator and he promptly began to shiver a bit. To warm up, he paced back and forth peering down into the different freezer chests on display and checking out all the new flavors of ice cream and frozen yogurt there.

He was greeted just about as warmly as he had been at the arcade, especially after asking questions about ghosts and paranormal activity. He experienced a common theme and that was fear and trepidation in the eyes of all he questioned. To add insult to injury, the store manager there gave him an extended dumbfounded look. He was beginning to feel very silly and started to believe that this whole expedition was doomed and mired in futility.

Eddie made his way from one storefront to the next, receiving little encouragement from the people he interrogated. He was starting to understand how difficult Detective Dominguez's job was. People for the most part did not cooperate and were not forthcoming. Most everybody he questioned wanted to know his underlying motives. People did not want to get involved and for the most part minded their own business. He had no luck at the Cinnabon Store or at Starbucks Coffee. He got laughed out of the kosher deli before running into communication problems at the Chinese restaurant. Lastly, he found out that the lady at the fresh fish store was only concerned with sales. She had no time to talk and did her best to ignore his questions while focusing in on taking her customer's orders.

Wearily and timidly, he made his way to the front door of Androlina's Pizza. He hesitantly stepped back away from the door and peered in the window, watching Antonio practicing his pizza dough stretching routine. He wondered what obstacles he was going to encounter here. That question was quickly and abruptly answered. Without warning, someone had snuck up behind him and grabbed him by the neck, slamming him into the pavement. It was a good, old-fashioned, "horse collar" tackle as they call it in the National Football League. Ernie, arriving back from his deliveries, had noticed Eddie "loitering" out in front of the restaurant dressed just like their "ghost" and decided to take the matter into his own hands. Ernie's idea of justice was swift. He rashly decided to be judge, jury, and executioner and pounced upon the unsuspecting Eddie. After slamming the back of his head into the pavement, Ernie proceeded to put poor Eddie into a choke hold. Eddie was caught completely off guard and stared helplessly back into the enraged eyes of what he perceived to be a madman going completely berserk. Eddie's eyes were literally bulging out of their sockets, and he was just moments away from passing out when Lou Eisen wearily approached the melee. It took a moment for Lou to realize what he was witnessing and to come to terms with who the victim was. Suddenly, Lou put two and two together and rushed to the rescue of his friend. Without uttering a word, Lou Eisen promptly kicked Ernie squarely in the side of his head. The solidly delivered blow created a reflex reaction in Ernie, inducing him to release the choke hold. Ernie promptly jumped back to his feet in an attempt to engage Lou in fisticuffs.

"I wouldn't do that, son, if I were you. There are laws that protect us senior citizens. You strike me and it's a felony," Eisen forewarned.

Ernie snapped back to his senses and summarily broke off his attack after his adrenaline had dissipated. Bewildered, he stared over at Eisen in shock and reached up to feel his head, where a stream of blood was now cascading down from.

Antonio, who caught a glimpse of the altercation, raced quickly out the front door to assist his best friend. Without a word, he took off his apron and used it to stop the blood flow. "Are you okay, Ernie?" Antonio asked with concern.

"This guy kicked me," Ernie replied, wincing in pain.

"You got kicked because you were choking my friend," Lou stated adamantly.

"What's going on here? Who started this? This can't be going on around here," Antonio announced.

Lou Eisen ignored Antonio's questions and quickly attended to his friend. Lou got down on one knee and gave Eddie a tremendous hug. "You okay, Eddie?"

"What the heck happened? I'm getting ready to enter this pizza joint and this dude for no reason body slams me! Damn! My freaking head hurts really bad, man!" Eddie declared as he too winced and probed the back of his head, feeling the large contusion there. "Am I bleeding, Lou?"

"I don't think so, Eddie. All I know is that I saw this animal choking the life out of you," Lou attested to indignantly.

"Yeah. What's that all about?" Eddie asked in shock and disbelief.

"You know what it's all about! You lying little bastard, you're the one who's been scaring my kids! What's your problem?" Ernie accused.

"I haven't got the faintest clue about what you're talking about, man! I don't know your kids! Believe me I don't want to know them either! You're freaking crazy!" Eddie volleyed.

"Sure, buddy! You've been hiding out in our back room pretending you're some kind of ghost! You're just full of shit, that's what you are. Antonio, this is the freaking asshole who's been traumatizing our kids," Ernie charged.

Lou Eisen immediately interjected, "What are you talking about? Did I hear you say something about a ghost?" Eisen looked down at Eddie in total amazement.

"Look, you're not fooling me. You guys can play all the games you want. I know this kid is the one. I was given a complete description of this jerk. Like some other jerk has an old-fashioned White Sox uniform, gimme a break," Ernie announced condescendingly.

"Are you sure he's the one?" Antonio asked inquisitively while locking eyes with his best friend.

"Damn right! He's the one. What's he doing here dressed like that?" Ernie cited.

Astonished by this revelation, Eddie demanded, "Where have you seen this ghost who resembles me? I heard you say something about a back room. Where is this back room?" Eddie asked. He immediately looked over at Lou and remarked, "We might just be on to something here."

"You guys must think we're stupid. You want us to believe that this whole thing is some kind of coincidence. I don't understand you guys. Why don't you just fess up, and we'll call it a day? There's no need to continue this charade anymore. You two are a couple of pranksters, and the joke's been on us. It wasn't that funny, but it's over. Why don't you just come clean, and we'll forget all about this little misunderstanding and part as friends... Okay?" Antonio rationalized.

"Not so fast. We'll get the kids down here to see our ghost in person, Antonio, and then we'll let these two assholes go," Ernie unilaterally bargained.

"Mister we need to sit down and talk to you about this whole situation. It's not what you think it is. If you'll open up your mind and give me and my friend just a little time, I'm sure we'll be able to give you some insight into this matter. As your friend said before, here on the street is not the place for this little talk. Can we go inside?" Lou appealed to Ernie.

Antonio and Ernie stared over at each other and tacitly agreed to at least hear their suspect's story. Antonio walked over to the front door and held it wide open stating, "This better be good."

Eisen helped Eddie get back on to his feet and the two of them entered the restaurant with Ernie following closely behind. Eddie kept a constant leery eye on Ernie, fearing another unprovoked attack but so far without merit. The four sat down across from each other at a table covered with a cloth depicting a map of Italy. Lou looked down at the map of the country, in the shape of a boot, and thought about how he had not traveled enough during his lifetime. There was so much of the world he hadn't seen yet and time was running out. He quickly snapped out of his wanderlust to focus on the issue at hand. Before he could explain what he perceived was occurring at the restaurant, he was quickly interrupted by the waitress, who asked, "Can I get anybody a drink here?"

Antonio was quick to respond, "Forget the drinks, Jennifer. Get the kid an ice pack." He stared over at Ernie and added, "You might need some stitches, man. That cut does not look good, Earn."

"I think the bleeding has stopped, Antonio, and I wouldn't miss this explanation for the world," Ernie said condescendingly.

Jennifer glanced back at Ernie and asked, "What in hell happened to you?"

"Long story. I'll tell you later," Ernie replied adding, "Just go get the kid some ice and get me a wet cloth."

Jennifer hurried off, and Lou quickly introduced himself and Eddie. As you can imagine, the pleasantries uttered were kept to a bare minimum. Lou immediately apologized for any misunderstandings and hard feelings over the altercation outside. He explained awkwardly, "I really don't know where to start. This whole story is going to sound so far-fetched. If I were you, I would have a hard time believing it, but I swear it's the truth. First of all, I'm not a charlatan. I'm not a quack. I've spent my entire adult life as a sportswriter. I wrote for the Tribune. I'm retired. I'm seventy-eight years old. After I retired, for the most part, I gave up on sports. I had no interest anymore. Well, anyway about a week ago, I had this dream. I usually don't remember my dreams, but this one I remembered in vivid detail. There was a messenger, like an angel, who asked to use my body. He implored me to start showing interest in sports again. I promised him that I would, and I don't really recall what happened after that."

"What does implore mean, Antonio?" Ernie interrupted.

"It means he begged him to start showing an interest in sports. Now quit interrupting, Ernie," Antonio impatiently explained.

"Well, like I was saying before the interruption, the next day I'm skimming through Sunday's newspaper and I'm drawn to the sports section. I get fixated on this photo of Eddie over there dressed in that old White Sox uniform of his, but what I'm really enamored with is his glove. You see, he's wearing exactly the same glove that this missing ballplayer wore. The player's name was Billy Green, and I knew him pretty well. He played for the Double-A Memphis squad back in 1952. I realize it's a long time ago. I was a photojournalist back then, and I took a picture of him and his prized glove. He languished in the minor leagues for most of his career. I never thought he would ever go any farther, but I was wrong. Astonishingly, he got hot and made it to the big club. In fact, he played a game right here on these grounds. After that game, he was never seen again. I used to write an annual story about his disappearance."

Ernie and Antonio were fascinated by the story and stared over at Eddie's glove that was now resting on the table in front of them.

"Is that the glove you saw in the picture, Lou?" Ernie asked, utterly intrigued. "Could I look at it?"

"Yes, it is. Eddie, let him look at it," Lou demanded.

Eddie hesitantly handed over his glove. Ernie marveled at it. "Wow, this is unique. Absolutely fascinating. Look at the detail, Antonio. Somebody spent a lot of time designing this. Who decorated it for you?" Ernie asked in amazement.

"I found it like that. That's Billy's authentic glove. I found it here," Eddie revealed.

"What do you mean here?" Antonio asked worriedly.

"Bingo! So you have been here? You've lied to us. See, Antonio, I am never wrong about these things," Ernie implicated.

"Well, guess what? You've got it wrong this time. I found it here when the ballpark was torn down. That's before this place was even thought of. So can you please stop accusing me? I'm innocent and so is Lou," Eddie rebuffed.

"Can I continue?" Lou asked meekly.

"We're all ears," Antonio quipped.

"Anyway, I wondered why this kid, Eddie Romano, had Billy Green's glove and why he dressed like Billy. I figured the picture had to be tied into a story about the disappearance but I was wrong. It turns out that this kid's a stellar ballplayer who's on his way to the big leagues. So I tracked him down to get to the bottom of all of this. When I caught up with him, he was so misguided that it's hard to imagine. Believe it or not, he was on his way to kill some scoundrel, who stole his glove. You couldn't make this story up if you wanted to. He tried ditching me at first, but I'm not that easy to get rid of. I imposed my will upon him so to speak. I wouldn't let him out of my sight. I actually followed him into one of those dilapidated project buildings."

"He must have followed him over to Mrs. Muhammad's place, Antonio," Ernie joked.

Antonio did not care to hear Ernie's joke. He was more concerned about what Lou had said about Eddie wanting to kill someone. Fearfully, he looked over at Ernie, wondering what Lou and Eddie's true intentions were.

"Can I continue?" Lou asked.

With a deprecating look on his face and his senses now on red alert, Antonio said, "Yeah. Go on."

"Like I was saying before, the people in that project building were living in abject poverty. They all looked like drug dealers or some sort of criminal. I was pretty scared to say the least. The place smelled like a urinal. I've never witnessed such squalor firsthand. Well to make a long story short, Eddie used me to gain entrance to the thief's apartment," Lou verbosely rambled on.

Antonio had heard enough. He now suspected that Lou and the boy were playing some kind of game on them in order to get access to their restaurant. Anxiously he asked, "So what are you getting at? What's this got to do with us? You're starting to scare me."

"Yeah. What's this murder bullshit you were talking about earlier? We don't know you from Adam, and you're talking some crazy shit now. Maybe it's time for you to leave," Ernie announced threateningly.

"If you will just let me finish, I'll explain. You are in no danger from us. Please relax, okay?" Lou said, trying his best to appease them.

"Okay. Go on. But you better get to the point fast," Ernie forewarned.

"The point being that Eddie was about to break the most important of the Ten Commandments, but the unimaginable happened, Billy took over my body and basically told him not to," Lou did his best to articulate this story without sounding hokey.

"What he's telling you is the God's honest truth. I was about to waste this dude until Lou went into this trance and stated the exact same words that Billy had told me in one of my dreams. There's no way Lou could have known any of that. Billy was speaking through Lou," Eddie declared fervently.

"This is just a little too far-fetched for us to believe. So how is this Billy speaking through Lou? I don't get it," Antonio asked in bewilderment.

"I think Billy's dead. I think his spirit has been spending a lot of time with Eddie. I think that glove is the key to another realm of existence. I think from what you've said outside that Billy's spirit is now haunting your back room," Lou deduced frankly.

"You know, I wouldn't believe one word of this normally, but we have been having some strange occurrences in our ball playing room. The only reason Ernie attacked the kid was because he fit the description of our ghost. Our kids said the ghost was dressed in an old-fashioned White Sox uniform. Now the kids won't step foot on the premises until we do something about this. We were hoping your friend Eddie was the answer to our problem but now it seems like we really do have a ghost," Antonio dejectedly explained.

Ernie quickly interjected, "So you guys think that somebody murdered this Billy Green and buried him on our premises? I never believed in ghosts before, but I can't explain what's been going on around here. So what do you propose that we do?"

"Obviously, his soul's not at rest. What kind of disturbances are you having?" Lou inquired.

"The ghost throws baseballs at the kids with messages written on them. The ghost has been asking for help," Antonio revealed glumly.

"You see! He needs our help, Lou. We've got to find him," Eddie blurted out impulsively.

"Maybe we could use ground penetrating radar to find out if he's even here," Lou suggested.

"That's the technology they use to find dinosaur bones, right?" Ernie asked shaking his head in dismay. He added, "Antonio, how much do you think that's going to cost us?"

"A hell of a lot less than it would cost to dig up that playroom blindly. I mean, we can't be sure that the body's even there. He might be just haunting this place," Antonio declared with candor adding, "One thing is for sure and that is we can't have the police involved in this matter. If word leaks out that we've got a ghost or a dead body buried on the premises, our business could be sunk permanently. We need to be underneath the radar on this one. I think it's time to do a little research on the cost of either having somebody come in and survey our ball playing room with this ground penetrating radar or find out whether we're capable of running the equipment ourselves. If we could do it ourselves I wonder what it would cost us to rent the equipment?"

Antonio stared over at Ernie utterly confused by this dilemma. "So what do you think, Earn?"

"I don't know what to think. I just can't believe this is happening to us."

Overwhelmed by this problem, Antonio articulated, "Guys, we're going to have to get back to you on this. One thing's for certain, we have to do something, and we have to keep this on the QT. You have certainly shed new light on our problem, and because of this, we're going to keep you in the loop. I apologize for my friend's rash behavior. I hope that no criminal charges are going to be filed over this misunderstanding."

"If you're gonna help us find Billy, you can smash my head into the pavement another time if you want," Eddie said as he got up from the table. "But I'd prefer if you didn't. I know I can speak for Lou and guarantee you our confidentiality, but I must insist that we be here when this thing is going down, fair?" Eddie asked with a glimmer of hope in his eyes.

"Hey, let me answer this, Antonio. We welcome any help you could give us with our situation. I flew off the handle, and I guess I deserved to get kicked in the head. I guess I'm a bit of a hothead. I'm sorry. No, that's not good enough. People use that word too loosely these days. I just want you to know that I'm sincerely sorry, Eddie. Make sure we've got your numbers. I promise you that we won't do anything here without you. My word is my bond," Ernie virtuously pledged.

All the men shook hands and exchanged information. They all agreed to do whatever was humanly possible to solve this problem. A renaissance filled Eddie's soul as he and Lou departed to go home. There was a new glow in his eyes. He truly believed that he would aid Billy in finding his way "home."

GROUND PENETRATING RADAR

I t had taken two days for Ernie and Antonio to agree to bring in the guys with the ground penetrating radar. Although it was not cheap to do this, it seemed to them to be the best course of action. Since both were honorable men, they also kept their promise to Eddie and Lou, allowing them to be present while the search was taking place.

This costly endeavor was to begin the following day on Wednesday. The plan was for the search to take place in the "playroom" during regular business hours. No one was to know what was going on back there.

As you can imagine, the news of this upcoming search brought joy and jubilation to Eddie and Lou. Eddie couldn't remember a time when he was more excited. To him it was a chance to pay back a debt that he thought he would never get a chance to repay. Billy Green, his dream coach, for all intents and purposes was responsible for all the good times and the happiness that he had experienced so far in his young life. Thanks to him, stardom was blossoming on the horizon. Their friendship was the most important thing in his life. Their times together and the lessons he learned from Billy were priceless in his estimation. If they had built a temple in Billy's honor, Eddie would have religiously worshiped there. Eddie knew he would be lost without him, and before he closed his eyes to sleep at night, he always said a prayer for him. Billy had taught him to be a man and better than that, as far as he was concerned, a great ballplayer. His encouragement and love nurtured him through those awkward teenage years. Miraculously, he had a once-in-a-lifetime opportunity to do something to reciprocate. With these thoughts in mind and with a heavy heart, he would assist the ground penetrating radar people in locating the grave site. He wondered if he could handle the truth, the stone cold reality, of uncovering his hero's bones. How would he deal with the finality of that? He didn't know the answers to those questions, but he did know that he had to find Billy's remains since obviously he was crying out for help. Maybe by finding his remains he could somehow alleviate the pain that his other worldly friend was experiencing. All he knew for sure was that something had to be done, and he wanted to be the one to do it. So far his detective work couldn't have gone any better, and with a little luck, he just might be able to solve this mystery and hopefully be able to cope with the consequences involved.

The wait was now over for Eddie as he, Lou, and the ground penetrating radar operators entered Androlina's Restaurant at around 10:00 a.m. Antonio, trying his best to not arouse suspicion, quickly whisked them and their equipment into the "playroom." As soon as the four entered the "playroom" area, he hung a large sign over the door that led there stating, CLOSED TO THE PUBLIC DUE TO REMODELLING. KEEP OUT!

Quick introductions were made between the four men, who were now standing in the "playroom." Pete was the man in charge of the ground penetrating radar duo. He was a middle-aged man with a beer gut and a thick brown mustache. His hair was thinning badly, and he wouldn't be accused of being on top of the "fashion" game. He wore corduroys, work boots, and a not very heavy brown sweater. His looks were the epitome of average and nondescript, but his intelligence was a whole different story entirely. He knew his profession inside and out and gladly shared his insight with all who spent time with him.

He was frank, to the point, and had a good-natured rapport with his friends. To Pete, everyone was a friend, and it took about five minutes being with him to know that all were made comfortable and welcome.

Those who knew Pete knew his standard introduction of always asking whether or not someone would like to share his "Fig Newtons." Later he would always ask if he could buy someone a soda pop. You might ask, *"Why was he so fixated on sharing his Fig Newtons?"* The answer to that one was easy; his wife insisted that he snack healthy, and she literally stocked his home and work bags with the nutritious treats. He had such a plethora of them, that it made him very anxious to give a few away. This way he could convince "the little lady" that he had stuck to the diet that she had created for him.

Pete's assistant did double duty as his college-aged son. He was a skinny kid who wore an AC/DC T-shirt and a pair of jeans. It didn't seem like he had a muscle in his body. He had long, stringy dark hair and a prominent piercing through his nose with a silver ring attached there. The kid was about 5'9" and was obviously a musician. His name was Luke.

Pete looked out toward the netted portion of the "playroom", which enclosed the combination, pitching, and fielding machine and announced that the area was not that large and should not take more than a day to scan. He also reminded his son to forget any ideas he might have of playing loud music during the search, remembering the promise he made to Antonio to do this job in as stealthy a manner as humanly possible. He looked over at Eddie and Lou, who now were seated on the couch, and forewarned that this work was both tedious and time consuming. Eddie and Lou sunk deeper into the couch after hearing Pete's warning. They both were getting relaxed since they knew that it might take some time before any discoveries were made.

Pete, taking note of how each "helper" was sprawled out on each end of the couch, joked, "You guys look like card carrying members of the Loath and See More union. You loath and you see more. Get it? Luke, take a look at these two," Pete said, grinning.

Luke glanced over at Eddie and Lou, who by now had thoroughly made themselves at home and replied, "Dad, I want to get paid for what they're doing. Do you think you could you arrange for that?" Luke inquired.

"Not on your life," he replied. He then forewarned, "We'll, call you two when we're ready to teach you something,"

Eddie stared over at Lou and asked, "I wonder how long that's going to be."

There was no reply, just the sound of the old man snoring away. Eddie just smiled and thought about how lucky he was to have found a friend like Lou. He understood why Billy must have liked him so much. Then suddenly he got sad when he thought about how old his new friend was. He realized that someday he would lose him too. It dawned on him that he was developing a fatalistic view on life and that just got him more depressed, so he closed his eyes to rest. Eddie was exhibiting the classic signs of manic depressive disorder, extreme mood swings. He was happy one minute and sad the next.

Pete and Luke removed the equipment from the boxes they carried in and carefully put everything together. When assembled, the ground penetrating radar equipment resembled a wheelbarrow if you removed the container portion. Instead, the wheel elevated the radar unit so that it could scan the terrain without being dragged on the ground. There was also a video monitor attached and mounted to the handle bars, so that the operator could get a visual look at any anomalies underneath the ground being scanned.

It took the two men about fifteen minutes to complete the assembly; Pete immediately turned the ground penetrating radar unit on. He took a moment to examine the image underneath the artificial turf surface before awakening Eddie and Lou. He informed the napping duo that it was time for them to learn how the ground penetrating radar unit worked.

The power nap energized Eddie and Lou, and they anxiously got up from the couch and gathered around the unit that was now fully operational. They both stared at the video monitor and did their best at guessing what they were looking at. They both looked puzzled.

"Confusing, huh?" Pete asked while winking over at Luke.

"Yeah. It sure is. What are we looking at here?" Eddie asked dumbfounded.

"What you're looking at here is a profile of what lies beneath the surface. This unit provides us with a two-dimensional image. We are looking for disturbances in the ground. I just want you guys to know up front that we most likely won't see any bones. I've been informed that's what you're looking for," Pete announced.

"Excuse me, son, but how will we know where the body is if we don't see the bones?" Lou Eisen asked, stupefied.

"Good question, Lou. Do you see these wavy lines and the layering?" Pete asked with down home charm.

"Yes, I certainly do," Lou affirmed as he pointed to an example on the video screen.

"Good. Let me move this unit a bit so we can possibly find something we're looking for," Pete stated as he wheeled the unit across the turf to another spot. He added, "Now, see right here, the ground has been disturbed. Take a look, you can see there's some sort of pipe down there. You see how chaotic the ground looks? You can tell that somebody did work down there. Of course, we're not looking for pipes."

"If you don't mind me asking, how's the machine getting that picture we're looking at?" Eddie asked inquisitively.

"Okay. Let's get down to the meat and potatoes of this thing. This unit has an antenna that is constantly shooting radar down into the surface and that signal is what's bouncing back. What I get on the monitor is the reflections of that radar and any anomalies it might pick up. It also picks up static or concentrations of water or, of course, disturbed soil. You have to run this thing back and forth awhile to get a good reading. But it collects and records information about the subsurface. It will even map and measure physical or chemical changes in the ground. To make a long story short, the computer in the unit tells you later on where the more or less dense areas are. The less dense, the more likelihood that the ground has been disturbed and the greater the possibility of finding that body that you're looking for. Whose body are you looking for anyway?" Pete asked curiously.

Lou Eisen quickly stepped into the foreground and solemnly revealed, "A friend of mine, who disappeared many, many years ago. He was a ballplayer and a wonderful human being. Most everyone who met him fell for his charm. His disappearance has haunted me for many years now. We finally came up with a lead and that's what you're here for. Me, the boy, you, and your son are going to help Billy get a proper resting place. One with a monument inscribed with a few words to tell the world about this totally unique individual that I was so fortunate to have called my friend. He was a beautiful soul, and the world was very lucky to have him. Unfortunately he was with us for way too short a period of time."

Eddie promptly interjected, "He was an overachiever, a true underdog, and the most beautiful person I've ever met." Eddie wept as he pictured Billy, lying disillusioned on that pitcher's mound staring up into oblivion.

Startled by this revelation, Pete replied, "You knew him too? I thought this happened a long time ago. You seem way too young to be involved in this matter."

"Hey, Lou, doesn't he sound just like that lady detective? I swear she said something exactly like that in that cage that she called an office." Eddie snickered.

Lou Eisen quickly interjected, "Yeah. I remember that, Eddie." He quickly added, "Pete, I swear the kid really does know him. This is a ghost story, my friend. Something extraordinary has occurred here and now's the time for this particular ghost story to come to its logical conclusion."

"Ghost story?? Wow, you guys are really freaking me out. So what is this logical conclusion you're talking about?" Pete asked baffled.

"Well, you're going to find him and he's going to rest in peace at last," Lou announced confidently.

"You know, most people wouldn't give either one of you guys the time of day. They'd just close their minds and look at you two like you were lunatics, but I'm getting older and I think a lot more these days. I would like to, but I can't say you're crazy. When the mere fact of life makes no sense at all, then why should death? I have to admit though, it would make life a whole lot more interesting if you guys are really on to something," Pete commented nervously as he came to grips with the extraordinary search he was about to begin. He stared over at Luke and added, "Wouldn't it be great if there was an afterlife?"

Luke rolled his eyes at his dad and gave him a funny look. Luke obviously wasn't buying any of this supernatural stuff.

On the other hand, Eddie brazenly stepped forward announcing to anyone who would listen, "Believe me there is. I've seen it with my own two eyes. Now, can we start looking for our friend?"

Luke did his best to hide his laughter. He rolled his eyes again at his father in disbelief and flippantly said, "Dad, you always meet the strange ones, don't you?"

Pete looked over at his son and stared at the ring, dangling from his nose and thought that truer words had never been spoken before, but it was now time to work. As he moved the ground penetrating radar to a new spot, he was actually anxious about what he might find there.

LET THE
DIGGING BEGIN

B y late afternoon the ground penetrating radar scan was complete. The easy part of the process was officially over with but the backbreaking labor remained. The ground penetrating radar computer analyzed the data and produced a floor plan of the different "hot spots" or places of interest where further investigation would be necessary. Unfortunately for Eddie, Lou, and Luke, the further investigation entailed strenuous manual labor in the form of digging. They had to choose the highest probability "hot spots" to start their investigation. Pete decided that his "helpers" would begin digging at "hot spots" located inside the enclosed fielding area since that's where the ghost was last seen according to the accounts of Mario Androlina and Ernie's son, Craig.

They started digging at a spot near where both Mario and Craig were allegedly accosted by the ghost. This spot was in the general vicinity of the door leading to the enclosure. Lou acted as the foreman and supervised Luke and Eddie's digging. Both boys took turns shoveling. They broke the ground using pickaxes and posthole diggers after cutting away a small section of the artificial turf.

Mario and Ernie looked on in complete dismay as their "playroom" was being systematically dug up. As they helplessly watched the digging, they started getting second thoughts about this whole search that was now underway. The only prevalent thought on both of their minds was that something better come out of all this. After a while, they got so irritated watching the destruction that they just shook their heads in disbelief and wandered back into the restaurant. They made sure that Pete knew that they wanted to be informed immediately if something was found.

Unfortunately, the first two holes dug were a complete bust. In the first hole, they found some lumber and pieces of concrete that got buried during the demolition of the Old Comiskey Park and in the second hole they found some stagnant water that smelled really bad. It could have been sewage that somehow leaked into the area and created a less dense pocket that the ground penetrating radar misdiagnosed as a spot where a body might be buried. Sadly, nothing of consequence was found, which put a cloud of doubt in the minds of the searchers, who had worked hard to no avail.

The boys were tired. It had been a long day. It was agreed upon that the search would continue the next morning, bright and early. Pete handed Lou the keys to the restaurant that Antonio had given him. Pete did this so that he could sleep in. Pete didn't trust the kids though. He wanted an adult supervising the work, and he was impressed with how well Lou was handling the job. Lou was to open the place up for the kids first thing in the morning and then monitor their work. Pete stressed how important safety was. He wanted Lou to make sure they only dug at the locations of the clearly designated "hot spots." He knew that there were no underground electric lines underneath those particular spots. As Pete and Luke made their way toward the exit, they talked rather loudly about beginning tomorrow's search where the ghost's messaged baseballs had emanated from. This was the "hot spot" that was located on the right side of the pitching machine.

Eddie was eavesdropping at the time and clearly heard the conversation taking place between the two. He too thought their plan had merit and started to obsess over it. He started to get a second wind and wanted to continue searching, but for Lou's sake, he decided to call it quits. He knew Lou was way too old to handle anymore labor at least not on this day. So Eddie reluctantly followed Lou out to the street and without incident they got into Lou's Cadillac and headed home for rest and relaxation.

BILLY COMES TO VISIT

After arriving home, Eddie took a quick shower and climbed into bed. His muscles were aching from all that digging. It was truly backbreaking work, and he needed some rest. His mother knocked on his door persistently in a futile attempt at finding out how he had spent his day. He responded by shouting to her through the closed and locked door that he was too tired to talk at the moment but everything was okay. Eventually his mother was forced to accept his brief reply and gave up her efforts to gain access to his bedroom. When his mother's commotion came to an end, he quickly fell into unconsciousness.

He started to dream. This was a real dream, not some kind of altered reality like when he found his way to that dreary major league ballpark before. He had broken his deal with the Manager, so his magic glove had lost the power to send him to any other realm of existence. He thought he was dreaming, like the rest of the human race, when Billy suddenly appeared. Billy looked so happy to see him. He told him that something beautiful was going to happen soon and that both of their dreams would come true. According to Billy, Eddie would soon unlock the door to his prison and something wonderful was going to happen. Billy promised him that he would never leave him and that true love never dies. Eddie felt the warmth of Billy's embrace. Eddie squeezed him so tightly and promised him that he would never let go of him. Eddie, while still holding Billy, suddenly opened his eyes to prove to himself that this fantastic event was really taking place. As soon as his eyes opened, Billy evaporated into the air and disappeared. Eddie was sweating profusely and his heart was pounding rapidly. His hero was there for a moment but just as quickly had disappeared. Eddie cried a river of tears, wanting so badly for him to come back. He kept mulling over the question, *"Why would Billy forsake me?"* There was no answer other than love is loss. He realized that once you choose to love, you are forever vulnerable and, therefore, forever disappointed.

Eddie composed himself and then stared over at the clock on the nightstand. It read 3:00 a.m. He knew that he wouldn't sleep another wink. He realized that he had slept at least seven hours. He wanted to go back to Androlina's and start digging on the right side of that pitching machine. That was the place Pete and Luke were talking about before they left for the day. Billy coming to see him was a good omen. It was a sign that something "wonderful" was happening soon but just not soon enough as far as Eddie was concerned. Eddie compulsively picked up the phone and dialed Lou's number.

To Eddie it seemed like the phone rang forever. He patiently let it ring and then ring some more, finally Lou answered in a groggy tone of voice, "Hello."

"I'm sorry, Lou, for waking you up. I just can't sleep anymore," Eddie said apologetically.

"What's wrong?" Lou inquired as he started to come back to his senses.

"Billy came to see me. I swear to God, I felt him in my arms, and when I opened my eyes, he vanished into thin air. I literally felt him, Lou. He was here. I'm sure of it," Eddie professed.

"Well? Did he say anything?"

"Yeah. He told me that I was going to release him from his prison, and it was going to be beautiful."

"Are you sure it wasn't just a dream? You know if you want something badly enough you can delude yourself into believing that it really happened," Lou said rationally.

"I don't think so. You know, I'm not tired anymore. What do you think about us getting an early start?"

"At this hour?" Lou asked in amazement.

"You got anything better to do?" Eddie asked impatiently.

"Well, I was going to go back to sleep, but it sounds to me like your heart is set on doing this, and if that's the case, I guess this old man can tag along," Lou conceded.

"I have a strange feeling that something wonderful is going to happen, and I'd rather have just you and me there when it does," Eddie said, convinced by Billy's words. He added, "Billy did not come to see me for no reason. He must know something. Let's go and unlock his jail cell."

"That's what he said, huh?"

"Well, not word for word, but that certainly was the gist. How about I meet you at Androlina's in an hour?"

"Let's just make it 4:30, okay?"

"That's perfect, Lou. I'm not going to forget that you did this for me. I owe you big time."

"You know? You're a good boy, Eddie Romano."

"I'm kind of fond of you too. I'll see you at 4:30."

Eddie hung up the phone and raced into the shower. On his way out the front door, he said to himself, "Eddie Romano, you are a real life Don Quixote, the Man from La Mancha on a glorious quest."

SOMETHING
WONDERFUL

Lou Eisen sat in his big Cadillac staring across at
Androlina's Restaurant. The whole parking lot was absent
of activity, and every store was closed in the big strip mall
except for the cab stand. Lou looked over at it leeringly. He was
glad that he didn't have to interact with those unfriendly people
again. He customarily arrived early although he knew that Eddie
would probably be a couple minutes late since he was driving in
from Palatine. The extra time gave Lou a chance to reflect upon
the situation at hand. He was hoping that the police would not
take notice of the predawn activity that would be taking place
inside the restaurant. He went searching through his wallet and
was happy to find the alarm code. He was sure without it, a silent
alarm would go off, and he and Eddie would have to do some
explaining. He did not want to explain anything taking place
at Androlina's. He tried to come up with a plan if the miracu-
lous occurred, and they actually found something. He figured
the first call he would make would be to that woman detective,
the one who pointed an accusing finger at him. He went back
into his wallet and found her card. He decided that Detective
Dominguez would hear from him whether she wanted to or not.
Before too long, he saw a couple headlights illuminating in the

distance; soon they were beaming on the rear end of his vehicle. They went out suddenly, and momentarily, Eddie was knocking on his driver's side window. Lou pushed the button that brought down his window and was quickly greeted by Eddie.

"Hey, Lou. I hope you weren't waiting long. I got here as quick as I could."

"Don't sweat it. I was just getting mentally prepared, just in case we find something. If somehow that happens, I think the first call we'll make will be to that detective we talked to. You know? Dominguez."

"The one I was talking about yesterday. The one who wouldn't do anything for us. She was such a total bitch," Eddie said venomously.

"Well, I have her personal cell phone number. At least she knows the story. Could you imagine the looks we'd get if we just called the regular police?"

"Yeah, they'd want to know what the heck we were doing there. Imagine what they'd say about us digging up that back room. Boy, we'd have a lot of explaining to do, wouldn't we, Lou?" Eddie interjected.

"Yeah. That's a nightmare I could live my whole life without. So if we find anything, we'll call Antonio and Ernie first and then take our time calling Dominguez. Okay?"

"Sounds like a plan. I'm really excited about this. I don't believe Billy came calling for nothing. We must be close. That's why I want to start at the spot that Pete and Luke were talking about yesterday. The place where they said the baseballs with the messages were thrown from. I heard them say it was to the right side of the pitching machine," Eddie stated.

"That makes pretty good logical sense. That's as good an idea as I could come up with. Right now though, let's do ourselves a favor and go inside before someone calls the police and tells them that we're outside casing the joint," Lou said with some urgency in the tone of his voice.

Lou got out of the Cadillac and locked it up. He and Eddie went to the front door of Androlina's. Before Lou unlocked the door, he told Eddie that they had one minute to disarm the alarm system or the police would be there in minutes. As soon as the door was opened, a prealarm went off, and the two men raced as fast as Lou could go to the alarm box. Lou punched in the code and the warning noise ceased.

The two then did their best to find the lights. This was a bit of a problem since they were unfamiliar with the floor plan. They fumbled along the travel paths until they located a circuit box and flipped a few switches to the on position which to their complete surprise lit up the restaurant. Before long, they had the lights on in the playroom. Next on the agenda was finding the knife that was used to cut the artificial turf. It was of course a carpet knife, and it was lying next to the shovels. Eddie took the knife and entered the netted enclosure and marched down along the right side of the pitching machine. He saw the X drawn on the artificial turf there and began to cut a space that circumscribed it. Eddie did his best to replicate the carpet removal procedure he and Luke had performed the previous afternoon. He felt a bit uneasy cutting the carpet since he was doing this job alone at an hour that many would consider inappropriate. It was ludicrous for him to feel that way, but he couldn't overcome the feeling that he was committing some kind of crime, and he got an anxiety rush as he completed the removal. He frowned as he peered at the space that he would have to remove the dirt from. He was not looking forward to doing the digging on his own but realized that Lou would be of little help in this matter.

"I'm going to take my time doing this. We're in no hurry, and I'm not going to break my back. Okay?" Eddie shouted out to Lou who was now comfortably seated on the couch.

"This is your ball game. I'm just an observer. Call me if you find anything," Lou replied as he laid back and tried his best to fall back to sleep.

Eddie started to dig, using the pickax to loosen the ground. It took a few minutes to complete this procedure. Eddie stopped loosening the soil and wiped some sweat off his brow. He took a moment and stared over at Lou who was by now fast asleep. His mind started to wander as he started shoveling the dirt out of the "hot spot." He thought about Billy's visit and then debated as to whether it was real or not. It sure seemed real. He felt him. He thought, *How could that be a dream?* Everything about his life and dreams was bizarre. How in the world did he get here? He knew that everything that happened to him had to be real. How else could he account for his baseball prowess and his superior knowledge of the game? He had heard that certain individuals could learn things through their subconscious mind. He heard that some people could play a tape recording of a lesson and while they slept they somehow retained a great portion of its contents. That was kind of like what happened to him when Billy taught him baseball. Maybe these other people who learned things while they slept we're having similar experiences and were just too embarrassed to admit to the truth. Maybe these lessons were taught in places other than ballparks? Maybe there were other special angels like Billy, teaching in classrooms instead of ballparks. He just hoped they weren't under the duress of a Manager like poor Billy. He also secretly wished that Lou's idea, the one about the Manager being the devil, would turn out to be totally incorrect. He figured that there had to be another explanation, but he just couldn't come up with any at the moment. At this juncture, his mind was busy second-guessing every conclusion he and Lou had come to. He stopped digging again and listened to Lou snoring away. He went through the same ritual as before, wiping his brow and this time taking off his shirt. He listened for unfamiliar noises and heard none. He stared back over at Lou and wished he could go lie down and sleep too but believed that something "wonderful" was going to take place. Billy wouldn't lie to him. He picked up the pickax and began loosening the dirt. If this trench was going to get deeper, he was going to have to work his butt off. He was going to find something significant if it was the last thing he did. Nothing was going to sway him away from completing this mission. He struggled as new soil was broken. He was smart because he was wearing work gloves. There would be no blisters for him. That was the great lesson from batting practice, realizing that blisters occur to those who do not wear batting gloves. Eddie knew this correlated to digging with pick-axes and shovels. After about five minutes of constant labor, he decided to take another break.

"Lou! I'm making good progress!" Eddie shouted but immediately took notice that his friend did not stir from his slumber. *"Lucky bastard. He could sleep through a hurricane,"* he thought.

Eddie climbed out of the ditch and brushed off the dirt. He sat down on the coffee table and removed his work boots. He then got up and went into the restaurant and found the soda cooler. He quickly grabbed a liter bottle and chugged it down, then stared out the window noticing the dawn's breaking. He was enamored by the unusual orange tint on the horizon. He realized that he had not paid attention to the beautiful "little things" of life and decided to spend a little more time smelling the figurative roses. He immediately went back into the playroom and put his work boots back on. It was time to clear more dirt out of the hole. He was beginning to lose hope of finding anything. Maybe it was just wishful thinking. Maybe he did delude himself into believing a dream, like Lou said. He remembered something Billy had said to him a long time ago, *"Eddie, when you think it can't possibly happen and you've given up all hope, that's the time when something good is about to happen for you. It never happens to quitters because they won't persevere. Just give it one last try, and it will make all the difference in the world. Just believe me on this one."* Eddie pondered Billy's words and decided not to quit. He spent another ten minutes methodically clearing that trench of dirt. He stopped and wiped off his sweat. He gave the trench a cursory look and then noticed something unusual. In the furthest corner from him he saw what appeared to be some kind of plastic tarp that was barely protruding the surface. He walked over to it and pulled on it, but it didn't budge. He ran over and grabbed his pickax and began loosening the dirt that surrounded this piece of field tarp. He wondered why it was buried. *Was there something inside it? What was inside it?* These questions monopolized his thoughts as he dug around it. He painstakingly used his bare hands to remove the dirt and after a while was staring at a half-buried tarpaulin enclosure. He got a sunken feeling in his stomach as he stared sadly at what looked to be some kind of body bag. He was afraid to open it. He really didn't want to see what was inside it. A sixth sense made him aware of what he was about to find, but he was compelled to leave nothing to the imagination. He hesitantly grabbed a shovel, and using its sharp edge, he punctured the tarpaulin. He immediately started cutting it with the carpet knife. When the hole was large enough, he reached his hand inside and blindly felt around. Something inside felt familiar; he grabbed a hold of it and pulled it into the light. The first thing he saw was a bony hand, but before he could let it go in revulsion, it suddenly had skin and warmth. The most amazing transformation was taking place right before his eyes. He was suddenly giving Billy Green a helping hand out of his grave. Billy had no dirt on him and was impeccably dressed in his old-fashioned Chicago White Sox uniform. Eddie, bare-chested and sweaty, felt embarrassed to be standing like that in front of his hero. Billy smiled at him, noticing his chagrin, and pleasantly told him, "Hey, Eddie. Don't worry about it. You look great. You finally found me, huh?"

"Yeah. Somebody buried you. I have this terrible feeling in my gut that I won't be seeing much of you anymore," Eddie stated somberly, trying his best to hold back his tears.

"Don't cry, Eddie," Billy said as he reached over with his hand and wiped away the tears from Eddie's eyes. He added,

"Unfortunately, I think you're probably right. I don't think I get to stay here. I feel like the weight of the world has been lifted off my shoulders though. I'm free at last, but where do I go from here? Eddie, my wonderful little man, it is so good to see you again. I missed you. I never knew how much until now. Did you know that I wanted to be a father? I would have loved to have had you as my son. Eddie, I guess you were the only son I was ever to get. You'll always be my son, Eddie. I've got so many things to say to you, and I'm sure just not enough time. I want you to know that I never ever wanted to leave you, Eddie," Billy lamented with tears running down his face.

"How did this happen to you? Who did this to you?" Eddie eagerly asked.

"I'm convinced now that I did this to me. I just can't believe I went through with it. I used to think about it when times were bad, but I never thought I would really have the guts or better said, the lack of brains to act upon it, but obviously on one day, I was the stupidest person on the face of the earth. It is my only regret although I can't really tell you that I remember doing it. I do remember being so desperate that I asked the devil to intercede on my behalf. How was I to know that there really was one? I always thought it was like a fable, a story made up to keep people in check. You know, so you don't do the wrong thing. I had no idea the consequences of inviting such beings into your life. What a mistake that was. He gives you what you want but takes away all the fun of getting it. You, of all people, understand that dilemma," Billy mournfully recounted.

"So that happened to you too?"

"Unfortunately, the answer is yes. And I'm really sorry that I let you down and led you astray, Eddie. I'll never forgive myself for doing that," Billy regretted.

"What do you mean? You never led me astray. I had to do those terrible things in order to maintain the magic of the glove," Eddie rationalized.

"No, Eddie. I was manipulated to tell you those things. I was like a puppet on a string. The truth is, you're the magic, Eddie. You've always been the magic. You always had it in you. I taught you a few things, but you supplied the magic. I was the one who needed magic, Eddie. I was the one who couldn't accept the cards dealt to me. I was always looking for a way to cheat. I was always looking for an edge and look what it got me. I'm dead. That's the bitter truth. You, on the other hand, are going to achieve all your goals, and you didn't need a magic glove to do it. You're going to be everything that I dreamed about. I'm going to be watching you, Eddie Romano," Billy foretold as he noticed the sudden appearance of a beautiful bright light entering the playroom area.

"I think they're coming for you, Billy. I can't see you anymore. It's so bright."

"I'm scared, Eddie. I want so badly to stay here with you, but I'm sure I don't belong here anymore. They're telling me to come with them," Billy explained passionately.

"Who's in there, Billy?" Eddie urgently asked. He then begged, "Please, God, don't take him from me. I love him! I love him so much! I can't go on without him. Billy, please don't go! Billy, please don't leave me. I need you!"

"I love you too, Eddie. I'll always love you. I'm sorry I never told you that before. Everything's going to be okay, I promise. I know we'll meet again someday in a much better place than this. Please don't make this any harder than it already is. Come into the light and let me hold you and let me say good-bye."

Eddie stepped blindly into the light and felt Billy's loving embrace and tried desperately to hold on to his hand, but the light suddenly disappeared. Eddie looked down at his hand and found it firmly gripped upon the skeletal hand of Billy Green. Eddie cried but he did not let go. He screamed, "Lou! I found him! I found Billy!"

Lou, startled, jumped to his feet and stared over at Eddie, mortified by what Eddie held in his hand. "You've got to let him go, Eddie. Please put him down," Lou pleaded with tears in his eyes.

With the greatest of reverence, Eddie set Billy's remains down gently and declared, "But he was here, Lou. He was here!"

"I know he was," Lou said sullenly as he walked over and put his arm around the boy, leading him lovingly out of the playroom. Lou kept saying over and over again, "There's hope. There's always hope."

EPILOGUE

The discovery of Billy Green's remains was an interesting story for the newspapers to cover. Since it took some time for DNA testing to make a positive identification, there was a lot of speculation in Chicago as to whose body had been unearthed. Eventually the police concluded that it was not a case of foul play and since nobody from Billy's family stepped forward to claim the remains, Lou and Eddie took charge of them. Lou sprang for a funeral for his friend and he and Eddie held a memorial service that many curious Chicago White Sox fans turned out for. Some even claimed that they were in attendance at Comiskey on Billy's fateful night. Eddie and Lou had their doubts about the authenticity of their claims but gave them the attention that they obviously desired.

Eddie and Lou both spoke at the eulogy that was attended by Detective Dominguez, who just happened to have tears in her eyes throughout the ceremony. That's one of the odd quirks about people in general. The ones that want you to believe that they are heartless are usually the most sensitive. There was not a dry eye in the funeral home when Eddie spoke of his undying love for Billy. Onlookers sat in their chairs stunned by the revelations recalled by Eddie as he informed them how Billy had taken over Lou's body to prevent him from ruining his life, by killing the scoundrel from the project building. Even non-believers in attendance had a hard time trying to explain how that possibly could have happened. When Eddie told the mourners that a blinding light had magically appeared in the playroom and had taken Billy's soul to heaven, there was complete silence. Those gathered could see that Eddie was not making this up. One could look into his eyes and know that he was telling the truth. People left the gathering with hope in their hearts for their deceased loved ones. Many asked Eddie to show them Billy's prized glove, which he gladly allowed them to hold and to kiss. Many made the sign of the cross over their hearts while holding it. All realized that a miracle had taken place in their city.

Billy's body was laid to rest with a monument that featured a photograph Lou took of him back in the minor leagues, etched on the stone. It was engraved with his name and a few heartfelt words: "He gave his life to accomplish a dream and play in the Major Leagues of Baseball. He will forever be a Chicago White Sock and he will always be missed by me—his last worldly friend. I love you, Billy. May your soul finally rest in peace. Your friend forever, Eddie Romano."

As for Eddie, he would continue to play baseball at what many referred to as a professional level. It was rumored that the Chicago White Sox were very high on him and that he was going to go near the top in the upcoming Major League Baseball draft. He never played with Billy's glove again, although he kept it with him wherever he went.

Lou replaced Billy as Eddie's best friend and kept a close eye on him in the years to come. He would become Eddie's confidante and adviser and would walk alongside him as he approached the bright future that lay ahead for him.

Lastly, the Manager never got over the disappointment of failing to capture Eddie's soul. The last time I checked, he was plotting and planning a scheme to get even. Some things never change.

ABOUT THE AUTHOR

A 1992 graduate of Western Connecticut State University, Mr. Agnello, the first born son of a professional writer, took his time growing up. The former Weston (Connecticut) High School standout quarterback, from 1977–1978, started college at Western Connecticut and won varsity letters in football his freshmen and sophomore years and in the fall of 1979 had his breakout moment as he returned the opening kickoff of the homecoming game ninety yards for a touchdown against Plymouth State College.

The next year he would transfer to Southern Connecticut State University and "red shirt," meaning sit out a season in the hope of landing the starting quarterback job there. It was not to be. While attending Southern Connecticut he studied to be a coach, learning the ins and outs of the game of baseball. A game he has loved and followed all his life. During these college years he became a pioneer in the brand-new "male exotic dancing business" that was becoming a fad all over America.

The next season he went back to play for Western Connecticut but the passion was not there anymore. He quit and became a favorite with the "Chippendale style" reviews that toured throughout New York and New England. As a headliner, he co-featured with male model and future poker star Downtown Chad Brown and made appearances at the hottest clubs of the day.

In 1986 he gave the professional acting business a try. He studied at Lee Strasberg in NYC and made cameos on ABC's *Ryan's Hope* and *One Life to Live*. He also appeared on CBS's *Guiding Light*. He and his stripping monkey, Mr. Mike, appeared as guests on Regis Philbin and Kathy Lee Gifford's show and made a prime-time appearance on Margaret Colin's show, *Leg Work*.

He's had bit parts in Spike Lee's film *Crooklyn* and Nicolas Cage's *Kiss of Death* among others. He credits the Strasberg "method" for his engaging mastery of lively dialogue.

In 1992, he went back to college and finished his degree earning a bachelor's degree in English Writing. Shortly after, he officially retired from performing in the male burlesque industry and since then has appeared as a studio guest with Bill O'Reilly, Sean Hannity, and Judith Regan. He has entertained radio audiences nationally with his quick wit, glib speaking, and engaging personality.

On the evening of August 22, 2008, Mr. Agnello was accosted by two gunmen and shot twice in the leg in Sleepy Hollow, New York. The motive for that shooting was never determined. As of this date, no one has been arrested.

Agnello recovered from the shooting and currently resides in Sun City Center, Florida. This is his first novel. The author believes that his colorful past gives him greater insight into the plights of the people we meet in our daily lives. He truly hopes you enjoy the adventure.

In Loving Memory of My Father, Louis Agnello Sr.

When I was growing up in Weston, Connecticut, my father always told me that someday he was going to write the "great American novel." Unfortunately for him, someday never came. He was a talented writer who knew how to "coin an original phrase," as he put it, but was always too busy making life easy for my brother and me. He gave up upon his dreams so that we could live ours. He worked long hours and never took vacations so that we could have the better things in life.

In 2011, I was looking back at an incomplete novel I started to write back in 1992; it would later become the novel you've just read. *The Devil's Glove* was originally written as a vehicle to get me to the top of the acting game back in 1992, but the problem was I had given up on acting. I stared at the 80 percent complete manuscript and asked myself if I had the strength of character to finally finish something. Most of my life the answer to that question would have been a definitive "no." I talked to my mother, Eunice, about my dilemma, and she told me to look at my father's old news story archives from when he was a columnist and editor for *Chemical & Engineering News*. I did what she asked of me, and as I looked at my father's published work, a bell went off in my head, and I finally realized what I was meant to do. I had found my way. I was the firstborn son of a professional writer and somehow some of the man's talent had rubbed off on me. So this novel is a tribute to a man who will always be larger than life in my eyes. Although he was long gone, he had left me something. It's a gift that I'll never be able to repay, and so I humble myself to the man that I emulated. I did it for the both of us, Daddy!